RISE OF THE EXPS

BOOK 5

SACRIFICIAL SAVIOR

By: Alex McCarty

Editor: Gabriel McCarty

ISBN 978 1 943733 31 6

Published by Sphere of Compassion, Inc.
authoralexandermccarty@gmail.com
alexanderjmccarty@facebook.com
gabrielOfTheExps@instagram.com
of_the_Exps@twitter.com
oftheexps@tumbler.com
https://sphereofcompassion.com (Fun and interactive website!)

Cover design by Najeeb Shabazz

Books from ***Sphere of Compassion***

THE MAIN CHARACTER!

Hero's Epic Journey Arc

1. ***The Hero's Epic Journey Begins***:
2. ***The Hero's Epic Journey Continues***:

The Main Character: Legendary Origin Stories!

-1. ***Guardian Angel:***
-2. ***Broad Spectrum Assassin***:

The Main Character! Manga

1. **The Main Character! The Manga! Issue 1**
2. **The Main Character! The Manga! Issue 2**

OF THE EXPS

Rebellion Arc

1. ***Exp 8*: Rebellion of the Exps**

Resurrection Arc

2. ***The Hero of Sel*: Resurrection of the Exps**
3. ***Sellum***
4. ***Destruction, Creation, Absence***

Origins of The Exps

1. ***Fate's Apotheosis*: Origins of the Exps**

Rise Arc

5. ***Sacrificial Savior*:**
6. ***Pathos*:** (2021)

Manga of the Exps

1. ***Awakening* (Fall 2020)**
2. ***The Crimson Coliseum***

Escapades of the Exps

1. ***Intimate Interrogation* (18+) Read on the link below**
   https://www.patreon.com/Sphere_of_Compassion?filters[tag]=hentai%20manga

Table of Contents

Part 21: The Next in Line

Chapter 174: A Step Forward~~~~~~~~pg. 029
Chapter 175: Party Demons~~~~~~~~~pg. 034
Chapter 176: A Godless Realm~~~~~~~pg. 040
Chapter 177: Time Lost~~~~~~~~~~~~pg. 048
Chapter 178: In Memorial~~~~~~~~~~pg. 054
Chapter 179: Bittersweet Reunion~~~~~pg. 057

Part 22: Children of Destiny

Chapter 180: Homeschooled~~~~~~~~~pg. 063
Chapter 181: Nomadic~~~~~~~~~~~~~pg. 068
Chapter 182: Surrender~~~~~~~~~~~~pg. 072
Chapter 183: Shinx & Lilith~~~~~~~~~pg. 083
Chapter 184: Coaxing the Pawn~~~~~~pg. 089
Chapter 185: Family Party~~~~~~~~~~pg. 095
Chapter 186: Lum's Decree~~~~~~~~~pg. 101
Chapter 187: Dark Prophecy~~~~~~~~~pg. 107
Chapter 188: Dark Gods~~~~~~~~~~~~pg. 112
Chapter 189: Necessary Sacrifices~~~~pg. 118
Chapter 190: Corruption~~~~~~~~~~~~pg. 125

Part 23: The Hunt Begins

Chapter 191: Adorable Anomaly~~~~~~pg. 133
Chapter 192: Intimate Interrogation~~~pg. 139
Chapter 193: My Friend~~~~~~~~~~~~~pg. 149
Chapter 194: I'm Going to Save Nina~~pg. 159
Chapter 195: Ambush~~~~~~~~~~~~~~pg. 164
Chapter 196: Exp Hunters~~~~~~~~~~~pg. 168
Chapter 197: Agents of Apocalypse~~~pg. 175
Chapter 198: Blood~~~~~~~~~~~~~~~~pg. 182
Chapter 199: Exodus~~~~~~~~~~~~~~~pg. 188

Part 24: Religious Warfare

Chapter 200: Discipline~~~~~~~~~~~~~pg. 195
Chapter 201: Treason~~~~~~~~~~~~~~~pg. 199
Chapter 202: The Right Choice~~~~~~~pg. 205
Chapter 203: Pointless Sacrifice~~~~~~pg. 213
Chapter 204: Inspiration~~~~~~~~~~~~~pg. 218
Chapter 205: Exiled Spy~~~~~~~~~~~~~pg. 224
Chapter 206: The Weight of the Truth~~pg. 230
Chapter 207: Betrayal of Betrayal~~~~~pg. 238
Chapter 208: The New Death~~~~~~~~~pg. 244

Part 25: The Soldiers of Strength

Chapter 209: Inner Armory~~~~~~~~~~~pg. 251
Chapter 210: Reunion~~~~~~~~~~~~~~pg. 254
Chapter 211: Reason to Live~~~~~~~~~~pg. 262
Chapter 212: Weakness~~~~~~~~~~~~~pg. 267
Chapter 213: Teaspoon of Cinnamon~~pg. 273
Chapter 214: Gateway to Torment~~~~pg. 281
Chapter 215: For Her Sake~~~~~~~~~~~pg. 284
Chapter 216: Driven by Her Memory~~pg. 287
Chapter 217: Master of Portals~~~~~~~~pg. 293

Part 26: Murderer's Memories

Chapter 218: The Taste of Justice~~~~~pg. 300
Chapter 219: The New Assassin~~~~~~pg. 306
Chapter 220: Angel of Death~~~~~~~~~pg. 313
Chapter 221: Target or Client~~~~~~~~~pg. 323
Chapter 222: The Capsule~~~~~~~~~~~pg. 329
Chapter 223: Debt that Must be Paid~~pg. 335
Chapter 224: The Day a City Died~~~~pg. 341
Chapter 225: The Monster Within~~~~~pg. 351
Chapter 226: Forging a Family~~~~~~~~pg. 357
Chapter 227: Fear of Love~~~~~~~~~~~pg. 367

Part 27: Sacred Sacrifice

Chapter 228: Assembly of the Gods~~~pg. 372
Chapter 229: Challenge to Overcome~~pg. 375
Chapter 230: Way of the Samurai~~~~~pg. 380
Chapter 231: Duality~~~~~~~~~~~~~~~pg. 384
Chapter 232: True Test of Strength~~~~pg. 389
Chapter 233: The True Enemy~~~~~~~~pg. 396
Chapter 234: Broken Alliances~~~~~~~~pg. 403
Chapter 235: Sacrificial Savior~~~~~~~~pg. 410
Books from Sphere of Compassion~~~~pg. 420
About the Author~~~~~~~~~~~~~~~~~~pg. 430

Acknowledgments

I give reverent thanks to my brother for planning and fleshing out scenes, drawing out the characters, and brainstorming to create new characters and hone old ones. I give thanks to my loving and supportive parents. I thank my family and friends who read any part of this book either digitally or in manuscript form.

I want to express my appreciation for the new friends and fans who have supported me during this book's production. Some have helped us manage our booths at conventions and all have encouraged us with their kind words. I also want to thank the artists who've been making new fan art for the series. Be sure to check them out in the Fan Art section of sphereofcompassion.com.

Lastly, I thank you, the reader, for purchasing this book. I hope you enjoy the story/characters, reflect on the themes, and continue to support me in my future works. Keep an eye out for *Rise of the Exps: Pathos coming in 2021.*

Thank you! =(:3)* (That's a bunny, by the way.)

This book is dedicated to those who sacrifice their time to make the world a better a place for all living beings. Those who walk a path of internal sacrifice have made true efforts to improve themselves and the world by proxy. May we all look to improve and help those less fortunate than us.

Introduction

It has been a very productive but difficult year. Thankfully the worst has passed and I've learned a lot. Both ***The Main Character!*** & ***Of the Exps*** have begun their official manga series. Working with Mangagawa (***Hero of Sel*****,** ***Intimate Interrogation, The Main Character! Harem Brothel Special, Manga of the Exps)*** Kapumax Omega (***The Main Character! The Manga!)***, Aisa Ha (*Colorist for* ***The Main Character! The Manga!)***, Kenny Calderon ***(Rebellion of the Exps: Awakening)*** and Cesar Escobar ***(Guardian Angel: The Manga!)*** has truly been a dream come true.

This book went through some large changes from its original form. I swapped out Zenero's past for Koshi's, which really worked out with both the character motivations and focus as a whole. One of my favorite battles of the entire series was imported from the upcoming book into this one, putting it near the climax where it deserves to be. Almost half the original book has moved to the upcoming book, where we will explore a new faction of Exps. My absolute favorite addition to this book is the cross-over character. You'll understand after you've read. She just opens up so many opportunities with her involvement. The Rise Arc is full of characters so don't feel bad consulting the character reference sheet if you need to.

I hope you will follow us on our social media pages. We also have a website *sphereofcompassion.com* where you can sign up to get notified when a new book drops and a Patreon with exclusive content (NSFW included). Please spread the word about this series, take a moment to give the first four books a review (on Amazon or Goodreads), and enjoy the intense conclusion to the Resurrection Arc. =(:3)*

In the Last Volume:

Book 4,

Destruction, Creation, Absence: Resurrection of the Exps

The Freedom Forcers, led by their indominable Queen Hope, breached Samsara. Despite successful negotiations, Lum sent her minion to wipe out the Samsara group. The Omni God came to their rescue and convinced the wise queen to join forces with him. After reuniting with Exp 8, the Freedom Forcers successfully protected Tcetorp from Sel's forces. Successful in their endeavors, they journeyed back to Earth to gather Zenero's Exps as reinforcements against Sel's army. Despite unwarranted interference, Hope was determined to continue her goal of attaining rights for her people. She sent her people out on missions to further this goal, while negotiating with Senator John. When D.S. was fooled into attacking the law enforcement, and Hope ordered his death, her people became divided. The internal skirmish ended in D.S.'s demise and the queen was left with only her pragmatic followers. She used Pathos' attack on humanity to reopen negotiations with the Senator. The noble queen was tricked and, if not for her father coming to her rescue, her dynasty would have come to an untimely end. After escaping the tricky situation, the queen was faced with the madness of Agent Beta, whom tossed aside certain victory for the sake of planting a seed of chaos. Despite Sel's forces, the government, and dissention in her own ranks, the Queen of the Exps had seized victory for her people. Last she heard of the dissenters, they journeyed to Absence to keep Zenero Sel's grasp. The success of this mission has yet to be determined.

Hope's Political Data

QUEEN HOPE'S NATION

Consists of those who I am gleefully sworn to protect and fight for. Some have gone astray momentarily, but that shan't be a lasting problem.

Hope Kagaku: The Queen of the Exps
Personality: Regal, clever, calm, proud diplomat, the perfect leader
Loyalties: My people and my allies; all Exps are kin to me
Powers: Uses the weight of truth to turn my enemies into vassals
Goals: Equality for all my people under my queenship
Assignments: Uniting the Exps and our other allies with my leadership
Developments: Gained a new unlikely ally after nearly losing everything
Current Status: Writing by the fireplace as my feet are given a gentle massage

Deceivant Kagaku: A flawed man driven by a passion for science little girls, still he is my father
Personality: Submissive, loving, clever, intellectual, semi-reasonable, dependable
Loyalties: Mika regrettably, I fear his loyalty to Mother and I are still secondary to his thirst for that succubus
Powers: Able to make me feel warm when no one else can, it's because I've trained him so thoroughly mind you
Goals: Safety for his family is top priority, he is genuinely loyal to my cause & does his fair share
Assignments: Making a bath, once he's finished tending to my feet
Developments: Came to rescue you me when I was in danger, my chest still feels warm
Current Status: Giving me a gentle foot massage and apologizing for leaving me

Atlas: Ex-God of Hate, a loyal bodyguard who understands the importance of our cause
Personality: Dependable, reasonable, firm, strong willed, all good things
Loyalties: To Lord Sellum first, then to the Realm of Sel, lastly to his people and to me by proxy
Powers: Molds the souls of enemies he vanquishes into emotionally charged weapons
Goals: To end Sel is his ultimate goal, but he's a man of many missions
Assignments: Runs Unity, a disaster relief fund, also serving as my bodyguard
Developments: Many of his allies lost faith in him after he took my side in the skirmish
Current Status: In Absence on an important mission to prevent Zenero from escaping

Image: Atlas' wife and a psychological expert on many fields
Personality: Helpful, intelligent, odd at times
Loyalties: Atlas and my cause
Powers: Manifests her own emotions in various ways, excellent therapist
Assignments: Was helping Exp 8 with his speeches, that's clearly over now
Goals: Wants to vacation with her husband and keep her loved ones safe
Developments: Joined my side after the skirmish
Current Status: Making me some tea

Durga: A yoga instructor and therapist for prisoners
Personality: Even tempered, caring, a bit shy
Loyalties: To the prisoners she teaches, even more than her own kin
Powers: Manipulation of pain and pleasure, though to what extent is currently unknown
Assignments: Veganize Samadhi prisons on a global scale
Goals: Keeping her job, helping others,
Developments: Came out as an Exp and DXM member, not the best move in hindsight
Current Status: Image is talking with her about joining back with our side

Captain of Carnage: Courageous fluffy demon lord who follows Atlas and thus is obedient to me
Personality: Loyal as a dog, proud as peacock, and quite skilled as a technician
Loyalties: Atlas and me by default
Powers: Uses poison blades, a blunderbuss and ziplines to outmaneuver his enemies
Assignments: Sewing my clothes during his downtime, Mother used to fulfill that important task
Goals: Aiding Atlas in whatsoever he asks of him
Developments: Went to Absence with his lord
Current Status: Unknown

Muffins: An Absence god turned into the most adorable plump bunny
Personality: Loyal to the balance, level-headed, enjoys cuddles, how quaint
Loyalties: Comrades and to the balance of all the realms of Sellum, took my side in the skirmish
Powers: Able to coat herself in Absence energy and can launch paralyzing/space erasing needles from her fur
Assignments: Helping poor neighborhoods rebuild, working with Atlas
Goals: Balance in Sellum; the protection of Absence
Developments: Joined the others to defend Absence
Current Status: Unknown, likely alive though

Kelly Reyes: A reporter who has become a great ally to me, always happy to chat and serve me delectable treats. Her home is rather lovely too. I just adore the velvet drapes.

FREEDOM FORCERS (Absence)

A faction of Exps and modified humans who seek freedom like all animals. These blokes broke apart from me after a certain incident. Surely, they will come to their senses after cooling off.

Sellum: The Current Lord of the Afterlife and the legendary rebel Exp 8
Personality: Bipolar but focused on his goals
Loyalties: Balance in Sellum and for the Earth
Powers: Near infinite, yet Sel still lives
Assignments: Was supposed to rally the DXM followers, but I suppose it all worked out
Goals: Stability in the afterlife and equality on Earth
Developments: Revealed Exp 8 was an avatar after inciting global panic, then runs off to Absence
Current Status: Doing all he can to prevent Zenero's escape

Kaity: Prodigy ex-assassin, ex-leader, destined Sellum
Personality: Playful, naive, childish,
Loyalties: The ex-Viper Squad, other allies; I'm sure she will be loyal to me again after a lil chat
Powers: Love artifact which is basically magnetism, but can work on emotional levels too
Assignments: Can't even ask this girl for dirty work without incessant whining & insubordination
Goals: She's too busy trying to keep her friends alive to form a grand vision
Developments: Went to Absence to keep Zenero from falling into Sel's clutches
Current Status: Unknown, should be returning soon

Stabby: A weapon with the mannerisms of a baby; I'm well aware of the game she's playing
Personality: Naive, childish, dependent
Loyalties: Serves Sellum, calls him Daddy to try and be cute
Powers: Can fire blades from her body, nothing unique or interesting
Assignments: To stay out of trouble which she absolutely failed to comply with
Goals: Pwotect Daddy
Developments: Followed the others into Absence
Current Status: Hopefully perished in the battle, not a heroic death though, something meaningless

Opti: A joyful morale booster
Personality: Optimistic, loving, cheerful, simpleminded
Loyalties: His friends, and the people of Lum as well
Powers: Sends out positive energy to cheer on or influence others
Assignments: Working with Durga to convert hypocritical institutions into Vegan ones
Goals: Protect Lum, seems thirsty for romance as well
Developments: Joined the others on their mission in Absence
Current Status: Unknown, but is rather stubborn so most likely alive

BoneSaw: Robot assassin

Personality: Focused, silent, loyal

Loyalties: The Viper Squad, Kaity too, despite her being an ex-member

Powers: Stealth, a handy ability in combat, skilled with its many weapons

Assignments: Given targets to dispose of

Goals: The mission at hand and the safety of the Viper Squad and Kaity

Developments: Joined Kaity in Absence

Current Status: Unknown

Fusion: Exp 09

Personality: Nonexistent

Loyalties: Freedom Forcers

Powers: Merges with and controls objects

Assignments: Using her powers to help rebuild homes with Atlas

Goals: Unknown

Developments: Came along with the Absence defense team

Current Status: Unknown

Destructus Supplious: D.S; an absolute simpleton who traded brains for brawn

Personality: Naively infatuated with the concepts of heroism, friendly to a fault

Loyalties: His family, friends, and whoever he is told is a good person

Powers: Skilled with scissors, but I wouldn't trust him near my regal locks

Assignments: To be a hired bodyguard for Kanasta's targets, may to reassign to the Captain

Goals: On a mad quest to make everyone his friend

Developments: Killed by BoneSaw in a skirmish between those with sense and those bereft of it

Current Status: In Lum, possibly captured by divine brigands

FREEDOM FORCERS (Earth)

Ada: My sweet mother, tends to me & receives praise when she properly performs her duties
Personality: Optimistic, idealistic, determined, loving, motherly
Loyalties: Her husband, her children, students, and nearly any one she knows even the tiniest bit
Powers: Cooking, cleaning, washing me, snuggling, information sourcing, oh and illusions as well
Assignments: Spread Exp interest by making a children's book in schools around the nation
Goals: Keeping her friends and family safe; to be wholeheartedly loved by Father
Developments: Still recovering from the shock of taking the life of a piece of filth
Current Status: At the hidden cabin, making my favorite sweets for some undeserving miscreant!

Kanasta: Assassin Boss who puts capitalism before practicality
Personality: Stoic, bound by his own expectations
Loyalties: Kaity, Viper Squad, clients, & harbors a twisted sense of responsibility for his targets
Powers: Physically strong, agile, industrious, all wasted because of outdated philosophies
Assignments: To never get in my way or else be mentally repurposed
Goals: Becoming the ultimate assassin, how utterly naïve and childish
Developments: Released from his one useful role as my hostage
Current Status: Who cares honestly, he leaves without the slightest notice in advance

Chipko: The idol of the Furies
Personality: Unstable, dependent, caring, broken
Loyalties: To Exp 8, the Earth, and every forest on the planet apparently
Powers: Creates controlled shockwaves to blast her foes to bits
Assignments: To stay and guard the base to avoid problems
Goals: The preservation of Earth and the ascension of the Furies
Developments: Dared to try and kill me; she best hope our paths never cross again
Current Status: Went to Absence to kill Zenero

Toxic: A worthless creation

Neutral Parties (Earth)

Were once a part of something greater. Now they lead selfish, simple lives

Devlin Kagaku: My deliciously dark brother

Personality: Intelligent, needy, loving, loyal

Loyalties: Kaity and apparently being a father

Powers: Makes me tremble, that's no small feat, also a destined Sellum

Assignments: His self-assigned mission is to be a good father to his and Demonica's children

Goals: Abandoned for the sake of proving something to himself

Developments: Passed up on his chance to be with his cherished irreplaceable little sister forever

Current Status: Regretting his decision, and longing for Kaity no doubt

Demonica: The Goddess of Death, the woman who raped my brother

Personality: Violent, vengeful, sadistic, obsessive

Loyalties: Devlin primarily, then Sel and perhaps her sinful sisters

Powers: Blood manipulation, brother theft

Assignments: None that I know of

Goals: Making Devlin her soulmate and forcing him to live with her

Developments: Stole away a big brother from his most precious and remarkably intelligent little sis

Current Status: She better be treating my brother with proper respect!

The Vibrator: A delusional world-renowned masseuse

Personality: Clinically insane, narcissistic, utterly mad

Loyalties: Himself and his company

Powers: Can make any part of his body vibrate, surprisingly handy for those sore mornings

Assignments: Last I heard he was fighting Nina in Peru, perhaps he has been hired by the Senator

Goals: To be acknowledged as an all mighty deity by every being in existence

Developments: His business is on an upward slope, perhaps I should repurpose him

Current Status: Unknown

Demo: An Exp created by Father. Last sighted in Peru where it tried to kill Nina, instead of Kanasta for some reason

Damien: Head priest of the primary Seltanic Church
Personality: Friendly, benevolent, hopeful, courteous, a true gentleman
Loyalties: Regrettably to that accursed beach ball
Powers: Charisma and genuine love for what he does
Goals: To help more people heal through his churches
Developments: Was nearly killed by the Prince of Pleasure
Current Status: Considering the time, probably giving a sermon

Mika: The Matriarch of the Seltanic Church, my sworn enemy; sadly she's made a reappearance
Personality: a thief, a minx, a flirt, a liar, a siren, and a filthy succubus
Loyalties: To the floating eyeball, I hope those two wretches hook up
Powers: To steal the hearts of men, even my own father
Goals: To ruin everything I care about
Developments: Was nearly killed by the Prince; why won't this little demon just die already?
Current Status: Getting horny men to fawn over her cute façade

May: A Zenero Exp still in hiding. Couldn't hurt to bring her under my wing if discovered.

OTHER HUMANS OF NOTE:

DEUS EX MACHINA
Charles David: Branch leader for the New York DXM

FURIES
Blood Beak: Recruiter who met Devlin in Russia

HUMANS FIRST
Derrick Donovan: Deceased head of HF along with his entire family, Kanasta's doing not mine
Micheal Kormac: New leader of that detestable bigoted group of Exp haters and carnists

OTHER
Richard: Construction worker who is helping with the Unity project
Shelly, Robert, Gary: Vegan activists who frequently talk with my father
Sunshine, Kitten, Elise: Grade-schoolers who give my father advice (none as cute as me, of course)
Georgy: D.S.'s ex-gangster boss; his girlfriend will make him miserable once I've broken her

Exp Hunters

Government agents who are trained and willing to capture and kill my people to suit their master's agenda.

Senator Jo John: A handy ally or great adversary, the power he holds is very dangerous indeed

Personality: Cunning, malicious, volatile, ruthless, ambitious

Loyalties: To himself, like most politicians

Powers: Able to twist any situation to become advantageous to him

Weaknesses: His obsession with his goal can make him a bit careless

Goals: Total control of the American populace

Developments: Betrayed me and nearly had me killed

Current Status: Plotting his next move while crying into a pillow since nobody will ever love him

Death: AKA the Reaper, AKA Koshi, AKA Alpha, the lead Exp Hunter

Personality: Flirtatious, dark, obsessed with protecting his sister, I can work with this one

Loyalties: His sister is absolutely his first priority, then Kaity, then his boss

Powers: Incredibly skilled with energy manipulation, harbors three capsules

Weaknesses: Protect his sister and he's putty in your hands

Goals: Not sure if he has a grand goal, seems to just live in the moment

Developments: Helped his sister capture Exp 8

Current Status: Unknown, he often goes off and does whatever he wants

War: AKA the Tank, one of the Senator's four super soldiers,

Personality: Quiet, sensitive even, shouldn't be hard to break if I can get in range

Loyalties: He once saved my brother from being experimented on so…I don't know honestly

Powers: Takes the impact of an attack and redirects it back at his attacker, child's play for me

Weaknesses: Doubt and insecurity

Goals: I can only assume he's not totally loyal to his boss based on the data at hand

Developments: Helped Devlin escape the clutches of Agent Lambda

Current Status: Searching for Exps, but perhaps to protect them not kill them

Famine: One of the Senator's four super soldiers, Abyss is his Exp name

Personality: A miserable child filled with hate, a loving big brother

Loyalties: He will protect his little sis no matter the cost, is also the adopted child of Kioshi

Powers: Craves more of whatever he eats; I can't stop eating yummy grapes so I can relate a bit

Weaknesses: His love & desire to protect his lil sis, only a monster would exploit that sacred bond

Goals: Protecting his loved ones no matter the cost

Developments: Went to Absence in exchange for the Sellum restoring his sister's memory

Current Status: Thinking of ways to make his sister smile, such a good boy

Beta: The second in command, real name Debbie
Personality: I'm not sure, it seems to change constantly, most intriguing
Loyalties: Apparently will do anything to make things more interesting, but this could all be a very elaborate ruse
Powers: Manipulates energy into claws, like Kaity come to think of it
Weaknesses: Can be reasoned with in a very unusual sort of way
Goals: I don't know, but there's something dark about this one
Developments: Went from killing me to joining me; I didn't break her mind you
Current Status: Reporting back to her boss, but I don't know the details of the report

Pi: AKA Kioshi, AKA the Possum, a sweet girl who seeks approval, was once Agent Zeta
Personality: Sunny, dependent, friendly, clever, suicidal for reasons I respectfully won't divulge
Loyalties: Has fooled even her leader into thinking she is still loyal to him; she is mine entirely
Powers: Just learning her energy manipulation, but she's already very skilled in combat
Weaknesses: She's ticklish, eager to prove herself, she's a precious snowflake that I shall keep safe
Goals: To make love to and marry her brother and surpass him as the number one Exp Hunter
Developments: Took bullet fire to protect me; one moment, the thought brought a tear to my eye
Current Status: Training to become a great warrior, got a cute possum helmet when initiated too

Lambda: AKA the Spider, the main interrogator for the boss
Personality: Sadistic, friendly, caring, cruel, disregards personal space; the information from Kioshi is all over the place
Loyalties: Has gratitude to her boss and loves her job, but her loved ones come first
Powers: Uses energy needles to torture, my poor brother
Weaknesses: Her fondness for Kioshi and sisterly love for her brother
Goals: To have Kioshi as her girlfriend apparently
Developments: Lost sight of her prisoner Devlin
Current Status: Either making one of her lovers feel Heaven or one of her enemies feel Hell

Gamma: AKA the Owl, the mainframe of the organization, figuratively speaking of course
Sigma: AKA the Priest, Leader of the Hunter heavies and a zealot who believes Exps are demons
Kappa: AKA the Turtle, the buff reporter; he hired Kanasta to kill the head of Human's First
Iota: The head of public relations for the organization, worked with Durga at her prisons
Epsilon: If a building needs to destroyed or a forest burned down, she does it without question
Pilot: Met with D.S. and Crisis, apparently he's an inventor too

Allies of the Hunters

The Prince of Pleasure: Kioshi's boyfriend and a demon lord of lust
Personality: Sadistic, alluring, intoxicating, malicious
Loyalties: Only to himself
Powers: Uses poisons to paralyze and intoxicate
Weaknesses: Too eager to fight those far beyond him, arrogant as well
Goals: To rule over the Realm of Sel, utterly absurd
Developments: Built a following among Seltanists & tried to kill the Matriarch
Current Status: Struck a deal with the Senator so they are indeed allies

Absorb: A worthless sponge who joined the organization to kill my father

Prisoners of the Hunters

Wringer: Marxist vigilante
Personality: Acts with no regrets, kills without weighing the consequences
Loyalties: To the impoverished people
Powers: I…don't want to talk about it
Weaknesses: Wears insecurities as armor, I'll delight in taking his mind apart
Assignments: Joined us only to get the list of new targets
Goals: The fall of the capitalist empire
Developments: He tried to kill me!
Current Status: Regretting the worst decision of his life!

Crisis: Real name James
Personality: Loves Nature and unpredictability
Loyalties: Was a proud follower of our cause, it's dreadful what happened
Powers: Creates forces of nature, which of course leads to mass destruction
Goals: Freedom from his current predicament
Developments: Once an Exp with a purpose, now a prisoner cursing his fate
Current Status: Is of no use to them without his power, so quite possibly dead

Nina: A selfless warrior or a selfish narcissist, depends on who's at the wheel
Personality: One is devout, focused, obsessive and lonely;
the other is fickle, pompous, careful and needy
Loyalties: One is wholly devoted to Devlin, his family and is fond of Kaity;
the other loves only herself and her fans, not including Kaity
Powers: Speed, cunning, weaponry
Goals: Both personalities seek the other's destruction
Developments: Tortured by Agent Lambda
Current Status: I pray she's dead for her sake

LUM GODS

Followers of a manipulative idealist

Lum: Followers call her Great Goddess, a leader with an empire built of lies and broken promises

Personality: Thickheaded, obsessed, seductress, enslaved by her own twisted sense of justice,

Loyalties: Loyal to only her realm

Strengths: Possesses all the powers of creation, an utter waste

Weaknesses: None come to mind, unless of course she was lying about hating Kaity

Goals: To protect her realm and wipe out all she deems wicked

Developments: Made Kaity want to personally kill her after revealing her backlog of lies

Current Status: Bracing for Lord Sel's next move

Efil: Goddess of Life, ally to my people

Personality: Loyal to a fault, friendly, insecure, humble, benevolent and even ruthless at times

Loyalties: The Great Goddess, the realm of Lum and its denizens, including my Exps

Strengths: Time manipulation, healing, some creation abilities as well

Weaknesses: Thirsts for appreciation and praise, shouldn't be too difficult to crack

Goals: To be acknowledged by her Great Goddess and to protect the Realm of Lum

Developments: Recently vexed that Violet was chosen as the second in command

Current Status: Likely moping about

Etaf: Goddess of Fate, diviner for Lum

Personality: Ruthless, cold, manipulative; miserable

Loyalties: I can tell she's fond of Efil, but beyond that her loyalties are shrouded

Powers: Takes the future and brings it into the present, can also carve out new possibilities

Weaknesses: Broken beyond repair, which makes repurposing a rather tedious chore

Goals: Seeks to be free from the cursed existence she believes plagues her

Developments: Sliced Sel in half to protect Lum

Current Status: Quite likely she's in a trance trying to predict Lord Sel's next move

Napkin: A fearful kitten

Personality: Frightened by the smallest thing, enjoys being pet under the chin

Loyalties: Is fond of Kaity, but is loyal only to Etaf it seems

Powers: Not only can this kitten paralyze its foes with fear, it can create lasting phobias

Weaknesses: Incredibly insecure

Goals: To help Etaf with whatever she wishes

Developments: Was revealed as a spy for Etaf

Current Status: With Etaf, likely getting a guilty massage for a job well done

Tcetorp: A Lum goddess who is trapped in Absence no more, guards the Elysium Asylum

Violet Gold: My niece and a religious zealot

Personality: Dutiful, fanatical, supportive, fickle

Loyalties: Devlin, her friends, gods both mythic and material

Powers: Manipulates and wields her aura, skillful with various weapons

Weaknesses: Doubt riddles her body like bullet holes

Goals: Not certain exactly, protecting Lum & her friends, yes; but there may be something more

Developments: From broken slave to Lum's brainwashed god, bit of a downgrade honestly

Current Status: In Lum, preparing for the coming battle I assume

Ecnedurp: Manager for Samsara, leader of the Virtues

Personality: An obsessive planner who sees seconds wasted as lives lost

Loyalties: The Realm of Lum, balance in Sellum

Powers: Strong as a comet, fast as a bullet, stubborn as a rock

Weaknesses: Can be reasoned with through simple logic

Goals: Defending Samsara; keeping everyone and everything on schedule

Developments: Nearly killed me and some of my people before Sellum showed up

Current Status: In Samsara doing her duty

Ytitsahc: A giant knight of the Virtues

Personality: Simple-minded, has a fixation obsessed with virtuous action, ruthless to her enemies

Loyalties: The Realm of Lum, balance in Sellum, virtuous beings

Powers: Equally strong as she is stubborn

Weaknesses: Lewd or perverse things throw her off guard

Goals: The protection of Samsara

Developments: None to speak of

Current Status: Guarding Samsara as always

Fatima: Lum's newest angel

Personality: A young girl who wants to help others but is in a situation far beyond her understanding

Loyalties: Lotus and Lum as a whole

Powers: Mild light bending abilities, same as other angels

Weaknesses: Her mother was killed by Lum, I don't imagine she's too fond of the Great Goddess

Goals: Keeping Lotus and its people safe

Developments: Has been turned into the idol for future Mawali

Current Status: Likely assuring others of their choice to be Mawali, while having doubts herself

Rambir: A religious leader who seeks peace with the angels but also freedom for his people.

ABSENCE GODS

Protectors of a realm that harbors no treasures except dangerous prisoners

Absence: The realm god of Absence who is wholly devout to Pathos

Void: First Guardian; a self-aware stone who is also a teacher

Occupy: First Guard; a warrior monk whose humble sacrifice was to become a god

Plagiarism: Second Guardian; a chameleon skull obsessed with sensation and pleasure

Crystal: Second Guard; a lay-about mineral warrior who has a very interesting romantic past

Loyal: Third Guardian; a massive dragon and ex-angel

Limit: Third Guard; a heroic knight who will face any foe to defend his cherished realm

Separate: Fourth Guardian; an amoeba that has grown fond of Absence

Spin: Fourth Guard; a bunch of tops pretending to be a cute girl

Htols: Goddess of Sloth; a Sin gone rogue, now dutifully defends Absence

Führer of Fortune: Ex-demon lord and ex-leader of the Hero's Militia, very happy he's a god

Baroness of Blades: Ex-demon lord of pride; and ex-warrior of the Hero's Militia, now a goddess

Zenero: A fellow leader& tactician, if set free he will no doubt change the course of this struggle
Personality: His incarceration has dulled his resolve, but a true visionary can rise up from anything
Loyalties: Loyal to his ideal world and will do whatsoever he must to obtain it
Powers: Once had the power of teleportation, now Stabby has it
Weaknesses: Paranoia and being too meticulous
Goals: Freedom from his imprisonment
Developments: Is now the focus of a battle in Absence
Current Status: Trapped in the prison of Absence

SEL'S PAWNS
THE SINFUL SORORITY

An entire squad of goddesses who follow Sel and support each other

Lord Sel: The cruel, deceptive, sarcastic and cunning ruler of Sel

Personality: Obsessed with the title of Sellum, relishes deception, easily bored

Loyalties: A being that relishes betrayal has few loyalties

Powers: Death is merely a phase for this entity; soul possession & absorption are just a few tricks

Weaknesses: Emotionally unstable, but deconstructing his psyche would be quite challenging

Goals: Seizing the title of Sellum

Developments: Went off to Absence to free Zenero

Current Status: Hopefully crying over a failed plan, but it is unlikely

Tsul: The Goddess of Lust

Personality: Independent, level-headed, rivals with Demonica

Loyalties: The Realm of Sel and Lord Sel

Powers: Instilling seduction and madness in others, self-control in herself

Weaknesses: More than you'd expect

Goals: To become Lord Sel's most trusted ally, mission accomplished now that Demonica quit

Developments: Nearly broken by me but I had a play to go to

Current Status: Surely she's fighting in Absence

Edirp: The Goddess of Pride

Personality: Arrogant, insecure, weak-willed

Loyalties: Herself and her sisters

Powers: Cripples foes with no finesse, like an angry child throwing sand about, not like mine

Weaknesses: Emotionally fragile

Goals: For everyone to respect and worship her

Developments: Lost a battle against Exp 8 and Atlas

Current Status: Fighting in Absence

Yvne: The Goddess of Envy

Personality: Depressed, needy, covets both possessions and the experiences of others

Loyalties: The Realm of Sel and her sisters

Powers: Transformation

Weaknesses: Her covetous nature is easy to exploit

Goals: Protection of her family

Developments: Defeated by my big brother

Current Status: Fighting in Absence

Regna: The Goddess of Anger

Personality: Hot-headed, volatile, needy, justice obsessed

Loyalties: The Realm of Sel and her sisters, passionately hates angels

Powers: Trigger her body to burst, can also ignite rage and violence in others

Weaknesses: Longs to be loved, would be too easy to destroy

Goals: Overtake Lum and kill the angels

Developments: Defeated by my big brother

Current Status: Enjoying the thrill of a fight in Absence most likely

Deerg: The Goddess of Greed who was decapitated by Kanasta and thus unable to function

SEL'S PAWNS (OTHER)

Gimpy: A powerful demon who relishes pain and servitude

Personality: Needy, clingy, loyal, but surprisingly strong-willed

Loyalties: Demonica is the slave's true master, but Lord Sel can issue non-conflicting commands

Powers: Can transport itself and others between realms

Weaknesses: Masochists are highly resistant; I'd need time to figure this one out

Goals: To serve dutifully and be appreciated

Developments: Captured Flash Girl for Sel

Current Status: Gleefully taking attacks for their allies

Riufen: The Immortal Samurai

Personality: Stoic, yearns for battle, fights for honor

Loyalties: Devlin and his own insipid code of honor

Powers: Immortal, skilled, and determined to surpass every foe he's faced

Weaknesses: His obsession with honor can be twisted; he harbors doubts about serving Lord Sel

Goals: Growing stronger through honorable battles and dying honorably

Developments: Was defeated by my father, I do not joke

Current Status: Likely searching for a sword-wielder to test his mettle

Gladius: A living god sword that resembles a crocodile

Personality: Confident, deceptive, cunning, fickle

Loyalties: Not sure if he has any

Powers: Can slice any armor, cover any object, magnetize all weapons

Weaknesses: I haven't had an opportunity to examine them yet

Goals: To feed off the perfect host

Developments: None I recall, which is concerning

Current Status: Likely working alongside Riufen to fight my people

Pesi: A simpleton fueled by hate

Personality: Violently arrogant, full of rage

Loyalties: Likes to kill things

Powers: Spreads negativity and depression

Weaknesses: He's a ticking timebomb of insecurities

Goals: Survival, as always

Developments: I don't keep track of the activities of imbeciles

Current Status: Running away from a battle he's unqualified for

Duke of Deception: Demon lord of Envy and a tactician

Personality: Devout, cunning, likes to wear the skin of women

Loyalties: Lord Sel

Powers: Uses strings to trap and eviscerate enemies

Weaknesses: Only mortal, not a god

Goals: To be useful to Lord Sel

Developments: Helped capture Flash Girl

Current Status: Losing a battle in Absence

August: Bounty hunter of bounty hunters; some boys never grow up

Personality: Confrontational, single-minded, bitter about losing his crush

Loyalties: To his secret crush

Powers: Surface manipulation

Goals: Free Zenero to kill him

Developments: Joined Sel's forces

Current Status: No doubt fighting to free Zenero in Absence

Casey: Zenero's loving and loyal wife

Personality: Desperate to bring back her husband and take back her children

Loyalties: Zenero is her everything, loves her children too

Powers: Can create boxes to encase and crush her foes

Weaknesses: You can grab her attention merely by saying "Zenero"

Goals: Freeing Zenero, haven't we been over this?

Developments: Aided Demonica in converting August to Lord Sel's side

Current Status: Running through Absence and calling out to her beloved

Part 21
The Next in Line

Chapter 174: A Step Forward

The world felt empty.

Mother's white robe was reddened. And it was my fault.

I was the one who...

When I reach my hand out to her, the floor beneath me sinks. My fingers stretch to their brink as someone carries me away from my mother. I strain with all my will to touch her one last time.

Through my tears I see her blow me one final kiss.

Her body then turns into dust and is whisked away by the wind.

Light is all around me...why does everything looks so dark?

My head aches like rocks are dancing inside it, scratching the edges of my sanity.

My captor leaps.

A bright light pillar erupts behind as I freefall from the Observatory to the ground below.

We hit the ground.

My captor and I become a single heap of flesh.

Our bodies instantly regenerate.

There's no escape from a world without her. I won't ever be free.

My captor rushes on ahead.

I should stop him. But I don't care about anything. Sefiwah is really gone.

My captor sets me on the ground, looks down at me and nods.

The immortal samurai Riufen has never looked so exhausted. His stonelike features can't hide that look of doubt and guilt either. I feel the same way.

Did he get back from a battle with one of my friends? Who did he kill?

Dad...Mom...Sefiwah...who else have I lost now?

Riufen looks at the clouds above. "Still muddled." He closes his eyes and draws a circle in the air. The circle expands and becomes a portal to Absence. He picks me up and walks through it.

Since when can he do that? And why not bring me to Sel?

Occupy immediately appears and confronts the samurai. "No...why are you here and not...? Where is the Lord of this realm?"

Riufen taps his chin. "Hmm. I suppose the one bearing that honored title is me now."

"What?" Occupy's spiritual calm was no more. All his training and meditation couldn't stop his eyes from shaking.

"He fought with all his strength. It was a glorious death for a glorious warrior."

"And what is to become of this realm?" asks Occupy with a quivering lip.

"I shall defend it with all my power. But ruling it…I'm a warrior. Such things are beyond me."

"I will speak with the others." Occupy walks off.

I notice a few familiar faces rushing toward me. It's my friends. They're smiling at me. Looking at me as a hero who won the battle.

I'm not a hero! I'm a murderer! I killed her and dad too!

"Stop!" I yell, my tears rushing down my cheeks.

Opti lifts me up into an empty hug.

No matter the situation, he manages to pull through and put on a smile. His skin is so pale…like Mom's.

He holds my head to his shoulder. "No matter what happened, it's going to be okay, friend."

"She loved me! She loved me more than anything! She always loved me! I…should have known." I find myself smiling through my tears.

Her love still lingers in me. But it won't last. Everything will be taken from me.

I push off and start wailing. I slam my hands to the ground.

Why did you tell me? Why not let me believe you hated me? If you lied, I wouldn't be suffering.

Riufen steps in front of Opti when he tries to approach me.

I find myself smiling again with a single jolt of Mother's love. Her warmth envelopes me.

You did love me. Thank you. Thank you for telling me the truth.

The love vanishes and fear seizes me!

No! It was a lie. This is just another way to torture me. She only pretended to love me! She made me murder my dad!

I wipe my sides, trying to get their blood off me.

Riufen shakes his head. "There's nothing there anymore. Lum energy cleanses all."

I claw at the ground and then scream at the sky. "Damn you! Damn you! You murdered my father! I hate you!"

The comfort of anger abandons me. Leaving me again with only sadness.

I grab onto BoneSaw and stare at him. "This is my fault! I should have known it was a lie! Sellum told me a lie. He said she hated me! It's my fault, right?"

BoneSaw looks away in silence.

What's it like to not feel pain; not feel remorse? Not feel? You kill without purpose as your purpose. I used to enjoy killing too. It must have made Sefiwah suffer. She became a killer to protect me. She made love to me just to keep me away from love.

I turn away. "Mom said he knew the truth. Sellum tricked me into…I'll kill him! I'll kill Bob too and all his minions! It's all their fault!" I jump at Riufen with my claws engaged.

"I was following orders," says Riufen calmly, knocking my hands aside after being slashed open. He grabs my arms and turns me around as I thrash about screaming.

Stabby comes out from behind Opti. "Daddy wouldn't lie unless he had to."

I glare daggers at Riufen, hoping my rage will manifest. "Where has your honor gotten you? You helped Bob kill her! Was that honorable?"

Riufen closes his eyes but says nothing.

A cloud of light and darkness suddenly enters my body.

My skin feels aflame, yet it doesn't hurt.

Nothing hurts anymore.

Divine adrenaline spreads throughout my entire body.

Riufen bows his head to me. Muffins hops out from Opti's arms and lowers her head too.

"The transfer is complete," says Riufen.

"Twansfer? Wait!? Where's Daddy?" asks Stabby, her face going pale.

That's right. She's like a daughter to him? If I'm Sellum…then he is gone. We've both lost our parents.

"Sellum was killed by Bob," says Riufen bluntly.

"No." Stabby holds herself. "That's a wie! Daddy is invincible!"

Abyss picks her up and cradles her as she cries. "You're alive. That's what matters."

Riufen gazes into a wet puddle. "Invincibility is only an obstacle to Sel."

Wait. That pillar of light from before. That was when he died. Did he reach out to me in his last moments? Did him and Mom really entrust the future to me?

The weight of my responsibility brings me to my knees.

"Absence also fell to my blade in an honorable bout." Riufen nods firmly, most likely to respect the person he murdered.

Stabby looks at Riufen and cries. "Why kill nice people?"

How does he do it without regrets? I can hardly breathe.

"I no longer follow the Dishonorable One's orders." Riufen turns to me and bows. "I would like to join you."

I turn away in tears. "Well we don't want you."

"Yeah! You're a bad guy." Stabby hides behind Opti and stares intensely at the bad man.

Atlas speaks up. "I was once an enemy as well."

I didn't even notice he was there. It's true. He killed so many of our comrades...so many friends. But now he's a part of the team. Could Riufen really become like that? One of us?

Atlas grabs my hand. "We should return with the others."

Why is his hand shaking?

I look up and see he is trying to hold back his tears as they rush out from his eyes.

He wipes his eyes. "Kaity. Please, make a portal to Earth. They need to know what has been lost...who we've lost."

The Captain of Carnage raises his sword. "Death is a part of any war. We must not lose faith!"

I put my hands out but nothing happens. "I don't know how."

Stabby holds my hands. "Daddy told me. You gotta close your eyes. See the place you wanna go. When you open your eyes. Whoa! You're there," says Stabby with a teary giggle.

"Okay, I'll try it."

"I'll help!" Stabby runs to me and holds out her hands.

Abyss watches with teary eyes of pride.

BoneSaw and Muffins nuzzle my legs.

Everyone is counting on me to pull it together...but I can't. I can't picture anything in my mind right now.

Riufen opens a portal to Earth. "As simple as taking a step forward, is it not?" he asks, looking at me curiously.

Stabby looks at the portal and shakes her head. She dries her eyes and then pours her energy out into a Lum portal.

I look at her fondly, admiring her bravery. "Are you really going there, all alone?"

Stabby pushes out her chest. "Umff!"

Abyss shakes his head. "No you're not! I finally got you back! Sellum has to give you back your memories and..." his voice dies "he's gone!" He turns to his little sister with hope clinging to his eyes. "Do you remember me?"

"Umm...I remember the warmth."

"Anything else?" he asks with a weak voice.

Stabby nods and smiles. "Yeah! You're super nice. You fought that bad sword guy." She glares at Riufen. "Saved me when I was caught! And you hugged me when I cried." She grabs his hand and smiles. "We share lotsa memories! You're my big brother."

Abyss loses his grip on her hand and sobs.

Stabby musters up her courage and grabs his hand. "Big Bro."

"Yeah," he says with a choked-up voice.

Stabby pats his head. "Your Sis has a weally important mission for you." She grabs his cheeks and smiles at him. "Don't make your parents worry."

"They'll be okay without me! You need me!" he yells, gripping onto her tightly.

Stabby cuts his hand, licks the blood off and then heals it. "I'll be okay."

Abyss covers his mouth as he sobs.

Riufen lifts him up. "Your orders have been given. Be dutiful." He tosses the reluctant warrior into the portal.

Stabby walks towards the Lum portal.

Opti beams at her. "I'll come with you! We'll meet you at Earth when we make sure D.S. is okay. Muffins, do you want to join us?"

That's right! D.S. is here because he died. I hope he's safe.

Muffins looks down in thought. She then pops her head up and nods.

"What about you, Nibbles?"

The small pink bunny with a black tail approaches Muffins.

Muffins nuzzles him affectionately.

Nibbles walks up to Kaity and squeaks.

"Okay, I'll bring your love bun back as soon as I can!" cheers Opti.

Stabby, Opti and Muffins enter the Lum portal.

Riufen tosses Gladius into the Earth portal and offers me his hand. "Shall we?"

Riufen, Atlas, the Captain of Carnage, BoneSaw and I walk into the Earth portal.

Taking a step forward right now...takes everything I've got.

Chapter 175: Party Demons

While the Freedom Forcers come to grips with their loss, Lord Sel's followers gather in the Core to celebrate his victory.

The lava flowing around the hidden realm illuminates the otherwise dark surroundings.

Regna glares at Pesi. The fiery demon goddess' sharp teeth gnash together. "What the Lum are you doing! I told you not to put up party streamers!"

"But they bring me some semblance of…joy?" Pesi puts his hand to his mouth in confusion. The depressed Exp with long spiky hair sits down on the heated floor of the Core.

Edirp lowers the ground and starts filling it with rubber balls. "This isn't about you! This is about Lord Sel's triumph!"

"Who's to say he even won?" Pesi puts out the surrounding candles with his negativity.

"Stop ruining everything!" yelled Regna, jumping and attacking Pesi.

Tsul wraps her whip around her sister and pulls her into a hug. "We're all excited about the party, but there's no need to lose control of ourselves." The leader of the Sinful Sorority's hair tenderly caresses her sister. "Duke, how is the mural coming along?"

The Duke holds his feminine cheeks with glee. "It's absolutely wicked!" He lifts up her masterpiece.

Lord Sel is portrayed in the center of the cosmos, his spectral tendrils stretching out to the planets.

Regna looks at the mural with shimmering eyes. "Utterly diabolical!"

Etaf, the somber Goddess of Fate, is pacing around nervously.

Gimpy approaches her and wags his or her tail in excitement. The fully bound servant of Demonica was feeling lonely now that Mistress had moved on.

"I'm not going to punish you. Go away," said Etaf, her voice a bit shaky.

A Lum portal appears and everyone rushed around it.

As soon as Lord Sel emerges he is assaulted by party poppers. The beach ball sized eyeball took a moment to reorient himself.

His dark energy devours the confetti and he smiles at them. "I told you no point in celebrating until I'm Sellum."

Etaf turns to him. "What happened? I was worried." She fiddles in place.

"Aww, worry not, darling. The old Sellum, Lum and Absence have all met their intended doom!"

Regna turns to Sel with a blank stare, she drops the pinata she's holding. "Darling?"

Lord Sel grabs Etaf's hand. "Yes, Etaf and I agreed to reveal our bond after Lum was killed. We're platonically betrothed! Lum and Sel hand in hand." He pats her cheek.

Etaf turns away. "I…didn't get the powers."

"What?!" Sel blinks and then looks at her. "Did she give it to Violet?"

"Perhaps Efil. Is she alright?" asks Etaf, worry weighing her voice.

"Alive, but no doubt miserable. She was very useful indeed!" Lord Sel's eye bent into a grin.

Etaf let out a sigh of relief. "I know she is…we're fated to kill each other. I just…got worried."

"We don't have time to worry and we certainly…" Lord Sel sinks into the ground and pops up in the ball pit, lifting Edirp out with a massive hand "don't have time to play."

"But I wrote different nice things on them see," said Edirp, pushing a ball with the words 'champion' on it.

"Fools party while geniuses study. Now, let's review the next little box on our agenda. I still have two more souls to destroy before I become Sellum!" Lord Sel stops and then bounces around with glee. "I did it! I killed him! Sent his soul to oblivion! I killed that unappreciative fool Pathos. Now who isn't fit to be Sellum?" Bob points at the dark sky and growls.

Stabby went up to him and popped a party popper. "Banzai!"

Lord Sel rolls his eye. "Yvne, what are you doing?"

Stabby blushes. "Huh? I'm Stabby. I uhh…love my daddy?"

Bob slices her head off with a bladed tendril. "If you're going to try and deceive me, put some effort into it!"

Stabby's body transforms into a blob with deerlike horns. "Sorry. I lost her. I failed you."

"I only needed her momentarily. We're not to harm either her or Abyss. It's a promise I made and if any of you break it…" darkness flows out from Lord Sel as wicked shapes that encircle his allies "I will consume every bit of prana in your husk."

"You're not mad?" asks Yvne curiously.

"It's impossible to be mad right now!" Lord Sel created a spectral trampoline and bounced on it. "I defeated you, Pathos! I will rule over all the destinations of the universe and you will only be a forgotten pile of ash. Your precious Kaity must die and it's all your fault. Then Devlin goes poof, and that's it! Once they're dead I've won!"

The Duke of Deception lifted up the mural. "Your future is already writ!"

Lord Sel fired a dark beam that consumes the Duke's masterwork. "We mustn't get cocky! It's so easy to fall into a pit of arrogance when we're so high!" Bob grabs Regna with his tendril and smashes the massive Kaity pinata open. Red candy spills out over his followers. "Have your fun and then let's assess our options."

Yvne eats multiple candies but then looks up at Pesi. "Gimme."

"You have your own." He snarls.

Etaf approaches her dark lord. "I'm going to go check up on Efil." She places a gentle hand on the top of him. "Have some fun. It will be good for all of them. Don't they deserve it?"

Bob beamed at her. "Wise as a forest, beautiful as an eclipse and powerful as a volcano. I'll heed your words."

Etaf bowed and created a portal to Lum. "I'll see if she's the new Lum. If she is…I'll kill her."

"Ruthless as time itself! I knew I forget something." Lord Sel pats her head before she leaves. "Pesi, get over here! Your recent efforts deserve some recognition!"

Upon arriving in Lum, Etaf sprouted wings of light and shot into the sky. She flies to the steps leading to the Observatory, the place where the Great Goddess watches over all her visitors. Several angels were huddled together, pooling in their energy.

The moment she lands, Etaf rushed to the gathering. "Move."

The angels disperse.

Etaf places her hand on her friend's mossy skin. She then turns to the angels. "Go find the other Goddesses and tell them to meet me here. Now."

The angels nod and fly off.

The Goddess of Fate caresses Efil's cheek. "Will you ever forgive me?" She focuses her aura and brings the destiny of her friend's awakening into the present moment.

Efil wipes her eyes. She notices Etaf and embraces her. "I had a horrible dream!"

Etaf grips Efil tightly. "You're alright now."

Efil's eyes widen and she stands up. "Lum is in danger! We have to help!"

"Do you feel any different?" asks Etaf, examining her friend's aura.

"I feel tired. Like a tree on its last days." She leans forward and Etaf catches her.

"Let's relocate." Etaf divebombs into the Sel portal she formed to the Core.

"Oh, didn't expect you'd bring her here," says Lord Sel with a curious look.

"What is going on!" Efil tries to focus her aura but nothing comes out. She creates small light daggers and wobbles as she stands up. "I won't let you kill me without a fight."

Lord Sel looks at Etaf who shakes her head. "We aren't going to kill you. But torture isn't off the menu." Drills take shape from his dark aura and closes in on her. "Who is the new Lum?"

"What do you mean? And why is he talking to you? It…wasn't a nightmare." Efil's eyes shrank. She drops like a puppet without its strings.

Etaf crouches down and holds her friend who pushes off.

Lord Sel sniffles before breaking out into sobs. "I missed the grand betrayal! How could you!" He turns to Etaf with a wounded face.

"Silence!" Etaf glares at him. "She's suffering enough already."

Efil looks up at the Dark One. "What lies did you feed her?"

"Oh geez, that was a long time ago. But it wasn't lies. We have mutual goals. She came to me. And after you reveal who the next Lum is–"

Efil turns to Etaf. "If you don't join back, I'll have to tell Lum. But if you do, my lips will be sealed," she says, pantomiming a zipper with teary eyes.

Lord Sel couldn't hold back his laughter. "Lum is dead!"

"Stop saying that! Lum can't die! She's too powerful! You're trying to scare me! It won't work." She covers her ears.

"Denying the truth because it hurts." Lord Sel combs her hair and makes a pouty sound. "You think that will make your dearly departed Goddess happy?"

Efil falls to her knees and removes her hands. "How could she be dead? She can't die. I love her more than anything. She's my goddess."

"You are purer than she could ever be. Your tears are wasted on her," says Etaf, looking away.

"Blasphemy. I couldn't… How could she have died?" asks Efil, holding her head and crying.

"Oh, Kaity killed her," says Lord Sel bluntly.

"It wasn't supposed to be this way. Kaity was supposed to die." Efil glares at The Dark One. "You were supposed to die!"

"Ha! Now you're just being silly. You're trapped in a living nightmare. Ask yourself the only question that matters. What are you going to do about it?"

Efil clenches her fist till they bled. "I'll avenge her!"

"Huh?" Lord Sel blinks.

"I'm joining up with you until she is dead," says Efil intensely.

"What?" Lord Sel pulls Etaf aside. "Has your friend completely lost it? Not that I'm complaining."

Efil stands tall. "You will not attack Lum until Kaity is dead. Withdraw your forces and I'll help you end her!"

Etaf smiles. "Seems perfectly sane to me. Fighting for Lum, even now."

Bob grins. "This is amusing but childish. Once she's dead, your deal will no longer stand. What is your plan then?"

"To help Devlin kill you." Efil takes a step toward the God of Destruction.

"You're serious? A flower-child like you wanting vengeance, I'm impressed. Very well! You will be a unique addition to the team." Lord Sel places a party hat on her and shoves some candy in her mouth.

Etaf turns to Efil. "*Mataki*, this is no joke. If you join us, you will have to do some truly wicked acts."

"Kaity will die just as my Goddess desired. I will use this pursuit of fairness to justify my actions. Lum was my life. She was my soul," cries Efil, gripping her chest.

Etaf embraces her fellow fallen goddess. "She never truly appreciated you."

Efil looks at her friend with tear-filled eyes. "How can you not care that she died? She was your God too."

"She never respected you, so she means nothing to me."

"Are you really so empty inside?"

Gimpy approaches Efil with some cake.

"Oh, thank you." Efil pats him. "Looks like I'm not the only angel here."

Gimpy beams at her and rolls around.

Lord Sel glares. “Do not spoil the slave. Ignore it, but do so passively. Otherwise it will feast on the isolation.”

Efil turns to Etaf. “So, this is your real family. I’ve only met them on the battlefield.”

Efil looks out at the party demons. Edirp is lowering the platform Regna is on. The fiery goddess is throwing her finger daggers blindfolded at the balloons. Tsul is tossing candy to Yvne. The Duke is burning himself for angering his dark lord. Pesi is beating the broken pinata with mad fury.

Efil smiles. “They seem so different.”

Etaf holds Efil’s hand. “You’re my family. Only you.”

Bob suddenly pops out of the ground. “Family! I forgot! I have to visit my daughter Demonica and tell her the great news!”

Efil scratches her cheek. “Even Sel seems different.”

Etaf taps her friend’s nose. “Hey, you’re smiling.”

“Tears only slow down a warrior. Kaity won’t be easy to kill. I will need all my strength.”

Etaf places her friend’s head in her lap. “Then lie down and rest.”

Chapter 176: A Godless Realm

Stabby arrives in a lush Lum forest with Opti and Muffins.

"Lead the way!" exclaims Opti with great charisma, pointing to the horizon.

Muffins turns around and gazes up at an eagle.

"Oh! Great idea!" Opti waves at the eagle angel to come down.

The eagle lands on a nearby tree branch. "I am on an urgent mission to find Efil and Etaf. The Elysium Asylum is under attack by a horde of demons. Do you have any idea where they might be, Exp?"

"We don't but we're super happy to help you protect the prison from those mean demons!" He shakes the eagle angel's wing.

She pulls her wing away and looks them over. "I suppose it couldn't hurt to have your help. Follow me!"

Stabby is crouching and muttering to a tick on a log.

"Made a new friend?" asks Opti with a smile, patting her back.

Stabby beams. "Yeah! I can speak bug now! Ticky and me both wike bwood a whole lot!"

"I'm so jealous happy! Can you speak fluffy animal too?"

Stabby bounces up and turns to Muffins, who twitches her nose. "The big bun says we should get moving."

"Oh, good idea. The bird angel is expecting us to follow."

Stabby creates a portal and then opened her eyes. "I…I did it!" She hops with a chipper expression.

"Great job! How did you know where the prison was?" asks Opti.

Stabby points to her head and grins. "Daddy taught me lotsa stuff!"

The four of them enter the portal.

The sound of metal, cannons and screams greet them the moment they exit the portal. Angels, many of which are human, are battling against hordes of demons from all seven regions of Sel.

Muffins fires needles out to knock out the demons as she makes her way to the Goddess guarding the entrance.

Stabby follows along, shooting daggers at the demons.

Opti fires bullets of positive morale and self-worth at the angels who are fighting.

Tcetorp looks down at Muffins. The Goddess of Protection's own aura coat her body in reflective armor.

Tcetorp smashes a group of demons with a barrier and then has the barrier split apart and slice through several other groups. “Always appreciate the help of another Goddess. Efil and Etaf have gone missing. Ytitsahc and I are the only ones holding the fort.” She gestures to the fully armored giant warrior that is using a pillar to smash through waves of demons. “I’m not sure how long we can hold out.”

Opti gives Tcetorp a big hug, sending his aura into her.

“I…feel great!” She pools her energy into a massive barrier, stretches it out and then sends it raging forward, pushing the demon hordes back.

A Lum portal appears and Evol peacefully steps out.

The blue-skinned devotee turned god, sings a song that makes the demon hordes dance with religious glee.

Etaf’s personal kill squad, the Sassanians, exit through the portal, immediately cutting through the untrained demons.

“I’m riding a shark!” D.S. cheers, using his dual scissor blades to slice enemies as he zooms by. The bandaged face child in a man’s body looked as vital as ever.

In the distance an elephant demon lord with a horn in his or her tusk plays a loud note.

Demons all over the battlefield suddenly ambush their fellow sinners.

Stabby looks at the conflict with wide eyes. “Daddy’s group! The Hewo’s Miwitia! It’s still alive! Daddy’s spirit is saving the day!”

Rambir flies through and cuts down a horde of demons. “My people, did they make it back home to Earth?”

Opti lowers his head. “I don’t know how to answer without making you sad.”

Rambir decapitates three demons with a single slash and nods. “It’s my burden to carry. You must press on. I’ll hold this position.”

Opti makes his way to D.S., hugging both friend and foe along the way. A Samba line of angels and demons gathers behind him.

D.S. notices him and jumps off the shark. “Hey uhh…I’m on the good guys side, right?” He shifts his foot embarrassedly. “I know I messed up last time really bad.”

Opti gives his dear friend a hug brimming with affection. “Yeah! We’re protecting Heaven! Doesn’t get more good than that!”

D.S. grins.

Efil and Etaf emerge out of a Lum portal in front of the Exps.

Opti smiles at Efil who lowers her head.

The Goddess of Life focuses her energy into a time sword and cuts down a squad of golden greed demon warriors. "Why are they attacking the prison?"

Etaf turns to her and cuts the air, killing both angels and demons. "It's not about the prison. Our mission is to kill Tcetorp. Her death means the entire prison collapses."

Efil holds out her blade to Etaf. "There is absolutely no way I am allowing that. We had a deal!"

"Bob never agreed and I'm not asking you to. Our job is to keep up appearances as loyal Lum Goddesses. Lord Sel's forces will handle the rest."

Efil points at the broken army of darkness as it attacks itself. "It doesn't take clairvoyance to see that Lum is going to win this fight."

Etaf signals her Sassanians to come to her.

"What are your orders?" asks the gorilla angel.

"Focus on the demon lords. Pincer attack."

They nod and rush off.

Etaf turns to Efil. "Lord Sel wants the demon lords wiped out anyway. I just want this conflict to end." She cuts through demons as she slides across the battlefield.

A Sel portal materializes at the center of the battlefield.

Tsul, Yvne, Regna, Edirp, Gimpy, The Duke of Deception and Pesi, rush out along with their dark lord.

Etaf nods. "And now we win." She carves an image into the sky. The blurry image comes into focus, showing the Great Goddess' death at the hands of Kaity. When the image fades, the sky is painted with the words "LUM IS DEAD."

Efil falls to her knees and shivers, being protected from incoming demons by Etaf.

The angels lose all morale. Fear surges through the battlefield.

Opti fires hefty optimistic balls from his aura cannons, but they do little to alleviate the grief.

Etaf turns to Efil and smirks. "It's done! I've altered the course of this battle! It's so invigorating!"

Pesi lands in front of Opti. "You're always getting in the way! But I'm stronger than you are!"

"Then why do you keep losing?" asks Opti, genuinely confused.

"Shut up!" Pesi's black aura goes red and melts the area around him. "I'm no longer just an Exp!" He fires a blast of red energy at Opti who is blasted off his feet. "I'm a god!" He cackles as he sends beams of destructive energy at the nearby angels. Their bodies explode as he crosses his arms making devil horns with his fingers and sticks out his tongue. "I'm the new God of Hate!"

Stabby sends Lum energy into Opti, stopping the violent aura from consuming him.

Pesi continues firing at the angels with his finger pistols.

Opti clenches his fist and takes a stand. "Pesi!"

His nemesis turns around. "What, you're still alive?"

Pesi fires a shot.

Muffins leaps into it and goes Absence form, erasing the projectile.

"Damn rabbit! I'll tear off your fluffy ears and choke you with them!" Pesi fires a red beam of explosive energy.

Opti grabs Muffins and takes flight to dodge the attack. He closes his eyes and tears up as he hears the angels screaming as they die." He clenches his teeth. "I don't have a choice anymore and so I've made my decision! I will break my vow! If I must end your life to save these angels, then I absolutely will!" He gallantly charges through the air.

"Ha! You're just an Exp. Bring it," says Pesi, sticking out his tongue and coating himself in a hateful aura.

"My love of life shall become my blade and it shall vanquish you!" yells Opti, his aura erupting. His valor manifests itself into a bright pink blade of light that coils around his arm like a cuddly serpent.

"I don't need god powers to beat you! My hatred of all life sets my soul ablaze!" yells Pesi, releasing his aura and focusing it in his hand. The new god's hand catches fire.

The black flames shoot up, creating a sword of darkness.

"The Pink Sword of Optimism will cleave through your hatred," say Opti, thrusting his sword at Pesi.

"The Black Blade of Pessimism shall consume your flesh!" yells Pesi as he vigorously deflected the pansy's swipes.

They take to the air and slash furiously.

Pesi kicks Opti and then flies behind him, grabbing his prissy nemesis' arms. "I'll kill you with your own sword!" He pulls his foe's arms back to make Opti stab himself with the pink sword.

The love-driven pacifist glows with newfound determination. He tears the black sword out of Pesi's hand and thrust it into him.

"No…my will…it's fading," wails Pesi in tears.

Opti repeatedly strikes Pesi with his own sword.

“I hate you!” yells Pesi, blasting Opti off with a sudden explosion of hateful energy.

“Even if you’re a god, you’re on the wrong side. Victory is assured for me!” exclaims Opti, as Muffins nuzzles away the fiery energy on her friend.

Pesi pools his hatred into a red sword and then sends it forth. The sword ignites the earth as it drags across the ground but Opti takes flight again to dodge it.

Pesi screams out in frustration, making the sword zoom across the battlefield, killing demons and angels.

“You know what you need? A song,” says Opti, sending beams of optimism from his fingertips to various angels.

“What? Don’t you dare!” Pesi condenses hate energy. “I’m a god now! You hear me! I’m no longer Pesi! I am Loathe!”

Bob starts laughing. Then yells with serious intensity. “No you’re not! Pick another name.”

“What?” asks Pesi, turning to Bob.

“It’s taken! Choose something else!” yells Bob, using his tendrils to beat back Ytitsahc with her own angelic guard.

“I am Hatred!” The new god sends his powerful condensed hate forward. The ball of hate pulses, sending out destructive waves.

“Muffins, you are the guiding light that can pierce through any storm!” Opti flings his bunny buddy into the ball and obliterates it.

“No! That’s not fair! How?” asks Hatred, stomping his foot.

“That’s easy! It’s because.” Opti breathes in.

“♪ Bunnies are the best.
Better than the rest.
Bunnies I love them all.
With population not to fall.
Just takes two.
And boom they rise.
Up to the skies. ♪”

“Stop singing! I hate music!” Pesi sends multiple beams at Opti’s location that converge when he dodges and then fire off from behind as an even more powerful beam.

Muffins squeaks, creating a barrier that disintegrates the attack.

Opti pats her head lovingly.

“♪ Bunnies are the best.
They never rest.
With ears that flop.

And love that's nonstop. ♪"

"Bunnies are just cotton candy that bleeds when you take a bite!" Hatred takes to the skies and turns himself into a living mortar by coating his body in rage.

"I'm so sorry Muffins, it won't hurt I promise." Opti plunges the Pink Sword of Optimism into Muffins, filling the bunny with positive morale.

Muffins sends Absence-coated needles at the new Sel God as Opti takes evasive maneuvers.

Opti looks at his sworn enemy with overflowing kindness. "Come on Pesi, sing it!
♪ Bunnies are the best.
You don't need a test.
They're so fluffy and cute. ♪"

"Screaming under my boot!" yells Hatred, firing his aura out as bullets.

Muffins destroys each shot with a needle and is held out as Opti charges into his nefarious nemesis.

Opti smiles as the bunny makes a hole in his rival's chest.
"♪ Because bunnies are the very best!"

Pesi crashes, coughing and crying. "I'm dying."

Bob pins Ytitsahc down with a horde of black tendrils. He then flies to Pesi. "Bunnies are truly remarkable creatures. You tried your best but you were still holding back. You need to lose control of your emotions." He plunges the Atma Blade into Pesi.

"Are you eating my soul?" asks Pesi, his face dark with existential dread.

"Yes, and you should be thanking me! I can reform your body this way. Duke, guard me while I'm busy."

"It is my honor to," says the Duke, pulling a string that coils around an angel. He flicks his fingers, causing another string to slice the legs off the angel. The Duke then turns his back to Lord Sel as he fends off incoming angels with his string whip.

Further up the battlefield, Regna fires a concentrated blast of her rage energy into Etaf.

The intoxicated Goddess goes into a frenzy, slicing both friend and foe.

"Why must we continue this charade?" asks the Duke of Deception before shielding his eyes.

An angel human with a beard and a sword comes to the injured angel's aid. "For the sake of my people, I will stop you." Rambir, now fully an angel, coats his sword in light and severs the string.

"Your people were slaughtered by the Virtue of Chastity when they breached Samsara if I'm not mistaken," says the Duke, slicing the hand off the new angel. He coils a thread around the angel's legs and spins him around. "You should be fighting them, no?" He pulls the angel in close. "Why not come with us, become a demon lord?"

"I don't fight for the angels. I fight to protect the realm. Even if I was the last of my people, my sword would stay righteous." He unsheathes his blade and cuts off the Duke's head.

"Demons cannot die!" The Duke traps Rambir in a web of threads.

Fatima swoops down from above, grabs Rambir's sword and cuts off the Duke's arms. "Then we'll just have to keep cutting until you're no longer a threat."

"Finished!" Lord Sel unsummons his weapon and sends a pool of dark energy into the angels, making them writhe in agony as they are devoured. "We only want Lum! One of you Goddesses is the new Lum, and until I find out who, my forces will swarm this realm and kill everyone!"

Violet speeds by, slashing away the darkness and forming an escape route from Sel's dark beam by using his army as cover.

Efil cuts through a horde of lust driven demons and approaches the Goddess of Lust. "Return to your realm!"

"Are you acting or did you actually forget you joined us?" asked Tsul, flailing her whips at the Goddess.

D.S. is using both scissors to fend off the attack of Yvne, who has taken the form of a giant bunny. "Why are we fighting?" he asks in tears.

"I'm not important enough to ponder such questions," says the bunny before whacking his arm and making him drop a scissor.

Muffins climbs up Edirp's pillar, shooting needles to deflect the incoming insults.

Gimpy moves Stabby away each time she is about to be attacked, following his orders from Lord Sel to protect her absolutely.

Stabby looks out at the battlefield, at both strangers and friends killing each other. She ignites her blades and starts stabbing herself.

Gimpy looks at her curiously.

Stabby's Lum aura suddenly juts out as massive swords that crash down. The four-meter swords radiate healing energy to both the demons and the angels. Light then pierces her like blades and juts out like wings.

She raises her hands to the sky and creates words of light, along with a giant arrow pointing to her. “I AM WUM!”

“Whaaaaaaaat?!” Lord Sel stares blankly. “Damn!” His dark energy erupts out as a pillar. He then molds all the darkness in the area to creates multiple Sel portals. “Retreat. Disobey and be abandoned to die.”

Stabby points at Bob with Lum energy bursting out of her. “I will beat you, Bad Ball!”

The Lum army pushes back the demons but Efil stands in their way. “They are leaving. We’ve won this battle.”

Once all of Sel’s forces fled, the Goddesses gather around Stabby.

Efil looks at her with a blank stare. “You’re Lum?”

Stabby looks at the glowing white energy in her hands. “Spose so.” She shrugs.

Tcetorp paces around. “Why would she choose an Exp to take over? Let alone a child.”

Fate turns away, biting her thumb.

Efil pulls her aside. “Tell me. Why did she do it? What did I do wrong?” The Goddess of Life let her tears flow freely.

“There’s no way she knew about Pathos’ deal with Sel, unless they planned this from the start. Either way Sel’s hands are tied. I could kill her but he’d hate me for it.”

“I won’t let you. Lum must have chosen her for a reason.” Efil looks at Stabby who is distracted by a butterfly and runs off. “Just a very umm unique ummm…the Great Goddess works in mysterious ways.”

Etaf lowers her head. “Lum lied to me. She said I’d be her heir. Did she know I was working for Lord Sel the whole time?”

“She kept so many secrets from us, but I know that she must have had her reasons. This is just another test.”

Tcetorp bows to Stabby. “What are your orders, Great Goddess?”

Stabby tilts her head. “I dunno yet, but I’m gonna protect this place for Daddy!”

Chapter 177: Time Lost

Once we arrived on Earth, I focused my thoughts and created a portal directly to the cabin in Melbourne.

Atlas lowers his head. "My comrades, I bring with me grave news."

I tap his back. "Nobody is here."

Abyss rushes at Riufen. "Why did you do that!? I was supposed to go with my sister!"

"Your loyalty is fickle," says Riufen.

Abyss turns to me. "Send me to Lum! Now, Kaity!"

I close my eyes but don't feel any energy flow. "I don't know how."

"Damn it!" Abyss kicks a chair and walks off.

"We must find the others," says Atlas.

We search the whole cabin but it's abandoned.

Could they have all been captured? We were only gone a few hours. But that could mean weeks have passed.

The Captain of Carnage scoured the place for clues.

BoneSaw followed along, awkwardly opening up drawers with its saw blades.

Wait. He must know.

I turn to Riufen. "Where are they? Did Lord Sel attack them while we were away?"

"I know nothing of the sort."

Gladius opens the fridge and gorges himself. "That would have been a clever plan."

I turn to Abyss. "You work for the Senator. Did he know our location?"

"He doesn't share that information with me. Just uses me to create hatred and fear. But you're going about this all wrong." Abyss turns on the T.V. "Well there's your problem." He points at the screen. "Time really flies in that place, doesn't it?"

2115? No way. How did five years pass? What is going on!?

Abyss tosses a chair in a sudden fit of rage. "I finally meet my sister and her memories are gone! Now we're split up and it could be years before I see her again!"

Atlas grabs Abyss' shoulders and presses him down onto the sofa. "The past is dead. Regrets only serve to narrow your field of vision. Ask yourself what future you desire. Then go forth and claim it!"

Abyss blushes. "I…what's with the pep talk?"

Atlas scratches his head. "It's a message from my comrade Atatasuki. He knows what it's like being a brother struggling for his sister's affection."

Abyss lowers his head. "I don't know what to do."

Riufen stands in front of the melancholy warrior. "You have a commander to report to, do you not?"

Abyss' eyes flicker. "My parents! They haven't seen me in five years! I have to call them!"

The Captain climbs up my body to my shoulder. "Should we allow him to do that? Shouldn't we capture him?"

He's right. Especially if the Senator has captured my allies…my friends.

I grab my pistol and look at my target.

He's crying.

I shake myself to my senses.

Mother wanted me to be strong. I'll make her proud!

I signal the Captain to get into position and pull out my pistol. "Drop the phone!"

Abyss turns to me with a look of confusion.

The Captain zooms by and takes the phone from the enemy's hand.

BoneSaw pops out from behind the couch and places a sawblade to the back of Abyss' neck.

Gladius swallows a watermelon and licks his lips. "I guess this team won't be boring after all."

Atlas turns his gaze at me. "Why are you intimidating our ally?"

Riufen knocks my gun aside and slams me to the ground. "I left Bob to follow an honorable leader. Should I be looking elsewhere?"

He's right. But what choice do I have?

Abyss notices my tears. "Let's calm down. I can't fight my way out of this." He raises his hands. "I can help you."

"Why should I trust you?" I ask, moving so he can see the gun pointed at his head.

"I don't hate Exps. The one I hated…he's gone. I'm not going to betray my parents, but that doesn't mean I can't find out where your team is. Got it? Good. Now hand me my phone."

I nod and the Captain returns the phone to him.

Atlas turns to the Captain. "You took her side over mine?"

"I made my decision on behalf of all of us. I am wholly loyal to you." The Captain raises his sword in respect.

I lower my gun, fall to my knees and sob.

Why am I so weak? They need my help and I...just don't know what to do.

Abyss closes his phone. "Five years. Of course the phone number changed. I'm going to have to head back to base to find out what happened."

I wipe my tears and raise my gun. "We're just supposed to let you go?"

Abyss stands up and walks toward the door. "That sums it up. Next time we meet, I doubt it will be anything pleasant."

I don't do anything as he walks out.

A gun probably wouldn't work anyway. Why can't I think straight anymore?

Atlas salutes Abyss and then turns to me. "We need to find Hope."

"Yeah! Good thinking." I nod.

Atlas uses the TV to search the web. "Well, well. We may have just found everyone."

The trip to Hope's new base took several days. Atlas drove us to the dock. We took a large boat with four rooms inside the cabin- apparently it was meant to be a getaway vehicle for Deceivant.

It's odd. I'm aware of things even when I sleep. Must be because I'm Sellum now. I'll have to figure out my powers on my own since Pathos is gone.

Atlas lifts up the covers. "Time to get up. We've arrived. I'll get the supplies." He heads out to the back of the cabin.

I stretch as I yawn. I hop in place to get myself fully alert.

Chains suddenly tear open the door.

A snake rushes in with her fangs bared.

Wait, I recognize her! It's Toxic.

The metallic plated snake loses all intimidation once she notices it's me. She sends herself flying into a hug. "You're alive! It's really you, right? Not that shapeshifter demon?"

I pet her and smile. "I didn't know you were so fond of me."

"Of course I am! The way you stood up to Hope! I could never forget it!" Toxic stretches tall on my shoulder and then nuzzles my neck. "I can't wait to share all my awesome upgrades with you!"

"Hope, is she with you?" I ask her.

"Oh? Yeah, of course you don't know what happened." Toxic scratches her head with her tail.

Wringer still guards the door, his chains ready to strike.

BoneSaw stacks boxes and then climbs atop them, matching Wringer's height and taking a confrontational stance.

Toxic notices and signals him.

Atlas approaches Wringer from behind. "My old companion! I hope you're in good spirits!"

Something seems off about Wringer. Then again, he's always been hard to read.

My eyes flash.

Broken. His mind...it's in pieces. How do I know this? Why...is it hurting me?

The Captain whispers in my ear. "It's alright. I've got my eye on him. If he tries to attack, I'll counterattack."

Something heavy lands on the boat from outside and it shakes.

"Yes! Let us do battle!" exclaims Riufen at the front of the boat.

He didn't even bother to try and stop the Wringer from attacking me? Then again, what can he even do to me? I'm a god now. It's crazy, but it's true.

I shake myself to my senses and push past Wringer.

Riufen slices off the arm of a twelve-foot robot.

The robot slides back and sends it's fist out at the samurai. "If you weren't on my boat, I'd use my ion cannon and erase your cells!" yells the pilot.

"Stop fighting! We're allies!" I yell.

"Disintegration is not enough to kill me. Don't waste our time with it. If you have no sword, I shall beat you bear handed!" The stoic samurai grabs the fist and then rushes up and smashes the robot's legs with it. He then pummels the cockpit until it spits the driver out.

Even with that visor on there's no mistaking that goatee.

"I'll sooner die than let you into the Queendom!" Deceivant points his Gravity Gun at Riufen and fires.

The bullet hits the samurai's chest and then creates a vacuum.

Riufen's body is pulled into the single point, breaking apart into a bloody mess. He then reassembles instantly. "I shall give you an honorable death." The samurai tosses Gladius aside and unsheathes his spinal cord from his back.

"Amy, looks like we won." Deceivant fires the bayonet off his gun.

The blade buries itself in the samurai's chest and lifts him in the air, creating a zero-gravity field.

Riufen's chest starts to gather Absence energy. "No! I refuse to win like this! Stop!"

"Ummm…that's new," says Deceivant with wide eyes.

"I command you to cease!" yells Riufen.

The clear energy consumes the blade and the samurai lands.

Deceivant raises his arms. "Okay, I surrender!"

Riufen grits his teeth. "Do not mock me. I am the one who lost the battle."

"Good, you two are done." I shoot a bullet near the scientist.

Deceivant removes the visor and looks at me with tearful eyes. He fumbles a bit as he gets up.

I grab him just as he trips.

"Sorry you have to see me like this. I think he broke one of my legs."

My energy follows my will and pools into him, healing every injury on the exhausted scientist.

"Looks like nothing is broken to me." I give him a peace sign and grin.

A surge of worry furrows his otherwise smooth facial features. "Where have you been? Are the others with you? Is Stabby okay?"

I hug him so tightly. "She's gone. Sefiwah." I do all I can to hold back from crying on his shoulder.

"She always held back her tears. Kept her guilt to herself, right? Was afraid to cry in front of others?"

I gulp my sadness and nod.

He grabs my cheeks. "Well then it looks like she's not gone to me."

I want to punch him but instead I just hug him tighter and sob.

I kept it all in during the ride here, trying to steel myself for the big reunion, but he always knows how to get under my skin.

I hear my other allies…my friends gather around as I sob in Deceivant's arms. I feel their concern for me and it warms me up a little.

I dry my eyes and look intently at Deceivant. "Bring me to Hope. I have to tell her what happened."

"So then, you've forgiven her for what she made you do?" he asks softly.

I shake my head resolutely. "I'm willing to put it aside to help out."

"Duty before emotions. I'm the same. It wasn't easy building a country for Exps, but I stood by Hope's side every step of the way." He wipes his eyes. "Every time after I read her a bedtime story, she says 'I love you, Daddy' in the sweetest voice imaginable. It makes it all worth it. Well, I'll lead the way."

I grab his arm as he turns away. "Who else is with you? Please tell me nobody else was sacrificed on our side."

"Wouldn't you rather see them yourself? We were just having a meeting when a familiar boat invaded our borders. If this wasn't my boat, it would have been blasted to bits."

"Wow. So, she really did it? She got her goal. A nation for Exps."

Deceivant chuckles. "The smallest country in the world is not fit for a queen." He scratches his chin. "She says that when I try to congratulate her. This nation, the Queendom is only the beginning. You'll see more at the war table."

War table?

"Wait, when did a war happen?"

Deceivant looks down and clenches his fist. "It's been so hard."

What has Hope done?

Chapter 178: In Memorial

The Queendom wasn't at all what I expected it to be. It was a humble nation, no bigger than a city with buildings of modest size. Trees were throughout the whole area. There were no roads. Moss clung to the buildings and life was everywhere. The only large building was the main castle, and it was currently undergoing construction for a right wing. The entire nation was on a massive floating barge, keeping it isolated from the world. There was absolutely no way Hope would ever be complacent with such a place.

I felt such warmth from this place. It was so lively and the air was so clean. It was as if a piece of Lum had been broken off and turned into a getaway island.

I find myself smiling when I see Nibbles lying belly up on the grass.

Deceivant notices my smile and raises out his arms. "It's a true Vegan paradise. We even make soy milk, agave and other food to export to people in need."

"Where is the training ground?" asks Riufen.

Deceivant looks away. "I'm not telling you anything. I don't trust you for a second." He motions me to stop when we arrive at a large wall of foliage. "Headquarters is just past here." The scientist meticulously pulls a single leaf and the barrier parts.

The massive Gothic castle at the top of a large hill isn't what catches my attention first. There are statues lined up in the front. Statues of people I know well.

I walk up to them solemnly.

Deceivant and the others follow behind.

"Look, it's you," says Atlas, showing his Searing Sword to the memorial statue of Atatasuki.

They're all here. Everyone we've ever lost is lined up in the order we lost them.

Tempo's statue seemed to look down at me. The inscription on it read "Always strive for the top."

He never did like me, but at least he respected me.

I feel a little guilty when I approach Ego's statue. "Experience is what turns novices into pros" is inscribed on it. My old friend is grinning and standing proudly.

It hasn't even been that long since he died. Why don't I miss him that much? We were close. He was like a big brother, but I just feel empty.

Pharma's statue was holding out a bag of cocaine powder. "Friendship is something that should be shared with everyone" is the phrase that was chosen for him.

To think he died a hero. He was our enemy for so long but it was actually the noble Karson who betrayed us.

I was a bit surprised to see the gunman's statue. "Don't let fear poison your well of honor", the phrase wasn't something he ever said, but was rather a lesson from his mistakes that we could learn from.

That was it for the first row of memorial statues. The next set was everyone who was killed by Atlas, who is now one of our greatest allies.

How did things turn out this way? Why do I get to live when they don't?

Atatasuki's statue says "cherish your glitches" and he's posing proudly, holding a muffin.

He really was one of a kind.

Kawai's statue says "it's alright to love anyone" and she's sending a love beam.

I wish we had a chance to get along better.

Matteria and Anthrax's statue share a podium. They are holding each other in a loving embrace. "Use your gifts to bring light into the world."

Gifts. My only gifts are killing people. The only light I bring is from snuffing out darkness.

NoOne was the last one in the row. "There is great power in solitude."

It's true he was so powerful. All he ever really wanted was to be loved. To think he died so unfulfilled.

The next row is mostly of people I know are alive.

D.S. is in Lum, so he should be alright. I hope.

His statue is in a battle pose with Snippy 2. "A childlike mind is a gift" is the heartwarming message that was chosen.

Opti's statue has its arms out to give out his loving energy. "Kindness is a gift that costs nothing and heals everything."

I wipe my eyes from the sweetness of the message, knowing that he's still alive means there's still some light in this world.

Muffins' statue was definitely not life size. It was big enough to wrap your arms around. "Always be willing to do what is best for the balance".

Muffins is with Opti and Stabby. She'll definitely keep them safe. Hey, why doesn't Stabby have a monument?

BoneSaw tilts as it examines its own statue.

I pat my robo pal on the top. “It says ‘Always be willing to make the choices that others are too afraid to’.” I pick up and nuzzle my little friend.

Atlas stands next to his statue and copies the pose. “It’s so heroic. I would have preferred something a bit more relatable,” he says, hopping off the stand.

“Companions are our greatest weapons,” I read aloud.

My stomach turns as I remember just how many of our companions are gone because of him.

The Captain of Carnage gazes up at his statue, which depicts the demon lord with blades ready to strike. “Wonderful! ‘Loyalty is the fuel behind a true warrior!’ Now that’s inspiring! I hope me being alive doesn’t mean they’ll have to take this down.” He wipes his teary eyes. “I want to inspire warriors till the sun gives out!”

I turn to the next one and my vision blurs.

Flashes of her death, Nina’s death attack me.

I grab my sides and start shaking.

Mom said she’s alive but what if that was a lie? I saw her die. I felt it.

Deceivant grabs my hand. “We never found her so she could still be alive.”

I shake my head. “Then she’s gone.” I wipe my eyes to see the inscription.

“Love isn’t a choice we make.”

My head goes dizzy and my heart aches.

I’ll never see her again.

I wobble forward, taking a stop at my own statue.

“We must rise to the destiny chosen for us.”

Reading the inscription just made me feel queasier.

Deceivant has me lean against him. “You’ll feel better once we meet with the others.”

Who else has been lost? I’m so afraid. I’ll never be fit to be Sellum. I’ll be killed off and the only thing left of me will be that statue, reminding everyone how I failed.

Chapter 179: Bittersweet Reunion

Deceivant takes me up the grassy steps and opens the castle doors.

The inside of the building is nothing like the outside. There's not a plant in sight. Everything is spotless, there are famous paintings along the brick and mortar walls. An expensive carpet runs down the hallways and the chandeliers reflect various colors beneath them.

"A place fit for a queen!" cheers Deceivant as he brings me down the hall to the War Room. He does a special knock. A few seconds later, the door opens.

Hope stops speaking mid-sentence and just stares at me with a blank face.

"Tada!" exclaims Deceivant with jazz hands.

Hope closes her mouth and composes herself. The little blonde queen at first appears taller than before, but its only because of her Gothic Lolita boots. "How do we know it's really Kitty."

Riufen enters, with Gladius hoisted over his shoulders. "I can vouch for her."

Hope glares at Deceivant with her golden eyes. "You brought an enemy into our country? Are you completely mad?"

Riufen shakes his head. "I'm done following Bob's dishonorable missions."

"Well then everything is just fine and dandy now, isn't it?" asks Hope, rolling her eyes. She then turns to me. "Well go on then, explain where you've been for half a decade. Who was killed?"

My vision goes blurry.

Who have they lost?

I look at the people there through the tears in my eyes. They all look like misty silhouettes.

Ada is shaking Riufen's hand, her long flowing green hair defying gravity like always.

Why couldn't I trust her? She told me the truth. I thought I knew Sefiwah. I am so stupid! I should have sensed that there was only love in her heart. I should have known that the tears from her eyes were tears of lament not joy. She could never enjoy killing. And I did. I'm the one who should have died.

I fall to the floor, crying in front of everyone.

Ada rushes to me and lifts me up from the floor.

I look at Ada, hoping that she's really my mother. I embrace her tightly, tears pouring out of my eyes as I remember when my momma would hold me.

"You're going to be Sellum one day. You must pull yourself together," says Hope.

"She is Sellum," says Atlas and Riufen.

I let go of Ada and give her a thankful smile.

Hope's cheeks un-puff when she sees Atlas. "Thank goodness the sensible one survived. Report!"

Atlas stands at attention. "Zenero was freed and fled with Chipko, Casey and August."

The Captain pops out from behind Atlas' shoulder. "Have you seen Zenero?"

Hope shakes her head. "I have not, but I wasn't told I should be looking for him. Continue."

Atlas nods. "Riufen killed October and has now taken his place as Absence."

"You did what!" An Exp in a skintight suit stood up.

Flash Girl, but her outfit is so different. I didn't even recognize her at first.

Her once white suit was now green and had windy patterns along it.

Flash Girl approaches Riufen with fiery eyes. "You killed my brother?"

"In an honorable battle! The greatest I've been blessed with." Riufen smiles fondly at the memory.

Flash Girl turns to her leader. "Queen Hope, I humbly ask permission to beat down and subdue this villain."

"Permission denied. If Riufen is indeed Absence, then engaging combat with him will only bring casualties. Continue your report, Atlas."

I steel myself and turn to Hope. "I…killed Sefiwah."

Flash Girl's face goes pale.

Hope smiles with pride. "Very well done."

I want to say more but my guilt chokes me up.

Ada raises her hand and waves.

Hope chuckles. "Speak, Mother."

"When is Exp 8 coming? I miss him dearly." She bounces in excitement.

Atlas lowers his head. "Pathos, my brother, is no more."

"That's not possible," says Hope in horror.

"It is. He was killed by Bob. Efil's time powers created an opening in his defenses," says Riufen emotionlessly.

"How could he have died?" asks Ada, her hands over her mouth and her eyes watering.

"I don't know the specifics," says Riufen.

Flash Girl grits her teeth and cries. "Three of my siblings are dead and we're not going to do anything about this!"

Atlas looks at her intently. "We've lost much but we must move forward with what we have!"

"Screw that!" She coats her hands in wind and sends it flying into Riufen.

He stands his ground.

Hope hops out of her chair and looks up at Flash Girl. "I was the one who gave you that artifact, Whirlwind! Disobey me again and I'll have it removed." She points to a vase in the back. "You nearly destroyed a priceless antique."

Durga taps the table, the prison therapist has cut her hair short. "Let's think about this. If Pathos was killed, how can we hope to win?"

Hope swats the idea of failure away. "Bob cannot win as long he doesn't know where Devlin is, the most he can do is kill Kaity. Considering he was unable to for five years, or more likely five days, there must be something he is lacking to accomplish his goal."

Deceivant places his hand on my shoulder. "I was wondering the same thing. He must want Kaity to lead him to Devlin."

I wipe my eyes. "We weren't up there for more than a few hours. Something happened when we passed through the portal."

"So, am I to assume the others are dead as well?" asks Hope.

Riufen shakes his head. "Opti and Muffins went to help Stabby protect Lum. Also, Stabby is Lum."

Wait, that's why she could make a Lum portal? Why would she be chosen to be Lum? What was Mom thinking?

Deceivant and Ada beam. "Cutest god ever! Jinx!" They giggle and poke one another.

Hope puffs her cheeks and looks at me curiously. "You left them behind to stall for time. How very cold of you."

Atlas steps up. "It was Stabby's decision. Queen Hope, I am reticent to ask but…where is my wife?"

"War talk doesn't sit well with her conscience. She's in her study, it's the tall building to the right of this one. Has her own personal library now."

"May I be excused to see her?"

"Very well but you are to report to me immediately after. No exceptions or excuses."

"As you command." Atlas bows.

I look back at Hope. "After we got back, Abyss left and then we took Deceivant's boat here. I'm so happy you're all okay." I go to them one by one and give them warm hugs.

Just like Exp 8 used to do. He's really gone. But he always manages to come back, right? He can't just leave me alone.

Hope raises her hand to stop me from snuggling her. "It's my turn to inform you on the developments." She clears her throat. "After you left, I was put in a rather compromising position. Were it not for Deceivant, I would have been killed and framed for nearly causing humanity's extinction. However, I turned the tables in my favor, becoming their savior instead. After that, getting laws passed for us to become citizens was merely a matter of paperwork. Exps can also legally run for office, though fear of our power has made claiming any governmental positions quite trying indeed. This is especially true considering it was our followers, the Dues Ex Machina, that released the Zika virus in the first place. That organization was shut down, and anyone wearing the associated tattoo is brought to prison. I'll spare you the minor details, but we are currently working with the Furies to help them create a sovereign nation. Despite my actions being entirely benevolent, no other nation will join us. Warfare is hardly my preferred means of advancement, but I will do what must be done."

I frown. "You're just as you were five years ago. You don't need to make sacrifices to progress. You already reached your goal."

"I will decide what my goal is." Hope silences me with an intense look. "If you don't want to contribute, then leave."

That's the same as running away. I'm not going to run.

Hope's phone rings in her pocket. She takes it out and answers. "Who is this?" Her face goes pale. "Devlin?"

Devlin is calling. I hope he's okay.

"Yeah, it's me. Bob is on his way to me. Gimpy says it's only a matter of time till I'm found. Please, I need your help. My family is in danger."

"I'll have a squad there immediately. Find a way to stall him. Stroke his pathetic ego."

"Yeah, good thinking."

"Oh, and one more thing. It's…" Hope wipes her watery eyes "It's good to hear from you." She hangs up and holds her chest.

Ada goes to comfort her. "Are you alright, Sweetie?"

"Not now, Mother. We must leave at once. We'll need everyone we have to stop Bob."

I smile at Hope. "I'm glad that part of you is the same too."

"Yes, yes. You can fawn over me later. Go find Atlas and Image, I'll have our jet prepared." Hope turns to Deceivant. "Go! Start up the jet!"

I'm Sellum so I should be strong enough to stop Bob. But what if I'm not. What if Devlin gets hurt because of me?

I stomp my foot. "I should stay. We can't give Bob what he wants."

Unless you lost your claws, you're coming along, Kitty. You're no damsel, you're a warrior. Act like one."

She's right. I can do this. I will protect Devlin!

Part 22
Children of Destiny

Chapter 180: Homeschooled

"Lilith, I know you're a good girl and this brat is lying. But no phones, okay?" He smiles at me.

My mind wanders to him picking me up and kissing me.

Geez. I really do have the libido of a demon.

After class, I go to the locker room. P.E. is my final subject of the day so I'm excited to go home and see Daddy.

The girls gather around me.

"They shouldn't let Exps be with us normal kids."

"She's not even an Exp. She has no powers. She's weak."

At first some of the kids thought it was cool I was an Exp. But when they realized that I couldn't do anything special, it just made me seem extra bland.

"What were you looking at, creepy girl?"

Not all the girls bully me, but the ones who don't just stay out of it.

One of the girls presses me to the wall. "I saw you looking at Jamal. Better watch yourself."

I rush out, still in my gym clothes and run to the bathroom to cry.

Today is Valentine's Day. I was hoping for something good to happen, but things just keep getting worse. I hate Middle School. I'm learning slower and there's so much drama. I wanna just stay at home, reading Theoretical Physics in Daddy's lap.

I enter the bathroom.

Thankfully, no one is here.

I rush into the stall and drop my gym shorts.

My ugly worm pops right out and pulses.

I grab it and glare. "Do you have any idea what would happen to me if they found out? What if they told Daddy? If he thinks I'm a freak, then I'll be all alone. I give you what you want but you keep coming back. Stop being so stubborn or I'll castrate you."

The threats I make just have it pulse more.

Why can't I just be a normal girl?

I jerk myself in tears, hating every second of it.

There's a knock at the stall.

"Occupied!" I yell, wiping my tears.

"Umm, Lilith. Is that you?" asks a boy.

What is a boy doing here? Wait, I recognize him. It's the shy kid. Ugh. I can't remember his name.

The boy knocks again. "I got you something. Umm…I thought it would be private here. Can I come in? I don't want to be caught."

I tuck my demon snake between my legs and pull up my shorts. I slowly open the door and he slides inside.

Cute!

Freckles, messy hair and glasses.

He's holding a letter. It's Valentine's Day. No way. This can't be real! Am I going to get a boyfriend?

He looks at me, wet with sweat and gulps. "There's a Vegan rally near my house tomorrow…umm do you want to go with me?" He puts his hand out. "Wait! That's not it! I mean it is, but it isn't."

"Give it to me!" I grab his hand and make him press me against the wall, my member throbbing.

Damn it! Control yourself, Lil.

I grab the letter and open it. I try to read it but my face is leaking with tears. I hug him tightly. "Of course I'll be your Valentine!"

It pulses…pressed against him.

Please…don't let him notice.

He pulls away. "You're a boy?"

"No! Don't leave, please. I like you too." I lean and kiss him.

He pulls away. "I don't want to get kissed by a boy! I can't believe you tricked me! Why did I like you?"

I grab him as he tries to open the door. "Please don't tell anyone. I'll be your sex pet! Please! Anything."

"Get away freak!" He pushes me off my feet and runs out of the bathroom. He yells "Lilith has a dick!" all throughout the hallway.

My life…is over.

I huddle myself in tears and my damn dick is still aching for attention.

I've always felt like a fake. Posting for gay rights, racial equality, when I'm a hetero white girl. I get teased about doing it because of white guilt, but I really just wanna make the world a better place. I have trans friends online. I don't tell any of them my secret. I'm a coward.

A bunch of boys and girls rush into the bathroom.

"Show it to us Lilith."

"Are all Exps freaks."

"Does it bite?"

A female teacher, with security guards makes the kids leave the restroom.

Mrs. Rodriguez. Thank goodness, someone who doesn't hate me.

"Your father is coming to pick you up. Don't worry. I won't let the other students bother you."

"Thanks so much. I don't think I'm coming back though. I…I hate it here."

"Aww, but all your teachers will miss you."

"There's no going back after what happened."

I sit in silence, waiting for Daddy.

When I'm told he's here, I rush out of the bathroom.

Golden eyes, slicked back hair, strong arms and a loving embrace greet me.

I rub my face against his chest. "I don't wanna go to school anymore. Please, Dad."

He combs my hair, instantly calming me. "Let's go home and watch a movie together. Your pick tonight."

I beam at him and he carries me to the car.

The other kids glare at me from the hallway but they don't dare to confront my daddy. A single look in their direction is enough to scatter the bullies.

I begin chatting with him the moment he closes the car door. "I really did try to fit in."

"You're not to blame. I was foolish to think Hope's progress would end discrimination against Exps. I…was being selfish. I'm deeply sorry." He looks at me with great remorse.

My capsule's circulation speeds up and my body heat rises. "You're always looking out for me."

"Lilith, I…I thought that you should socialize more with kids your own age. Well, at least physically your own age. But that's not the whole truth. I wanted everyone to see just how smart, friendly and loving my daughter is." He holds my hand, putting the electric car on auto. "How about we stop by the toy store and get you something special."

"My room is already full of plushies. I hardly fit in my bed." I lean forward and kiss his cheeks. "You've given me everything I've ever wanted…almost."

"Almost?"

My cheeks go red. "Hey, I'll try school again! Just not at that school, please."

Dad shakes his head. "Human society isn't ready for you yet. You're too pure for it."

If he knew about all those online sex role play groups I am a part of, he'd never see me the same way.

The car screen shows an image of the woman I hate more than anyone - Demonica.

"Is everything alright?" he asks.

"I was just informed that Bob's begun his search for you. I'll meet up with you as soon as I can."

"Bob? Grandpa is coming?"

I never got to meet Grandpa Bob, though Dad barely talks about him, so maybe that's a good thing.

"I'll inform the others. No way am I letting him see my children," says Devlin, burning with passion.

I grab onto his arm. "I'm scared. Is everything going to be okay?"

"I was a fool to think I could just run away from this. Call up Hope!"

The car system obeys.

I look up at to see worry has sunken my papa's face.

I have a feeling that my happy days with Dad are coming to an end.

Chapter 181: Nomadic

I stare up at the dangerous beast before me. With claws like steel and the rage of a protective mother, the beast charges me.

I can see exactly what you're going to do.

I duck under the first swipe and then punch her belly.

The territorial momma swipes again, but I slide behind a tree, having her cut the bark instead.

Get the enemy to come to you.

I climb up the tree and she follows.

Bad move, bear.

I throw a rock at the branch supporting her and it snaps.

She falls flat on her back.

I chose this tree for a reason.

I kick a beehive off the tree and have it land right on her.

She flails about, swiping at the incensed insects.

And that is how you win a fight.

I kick off the tree and stab the mother bear with a large stick.

She wails and opens her mouth.

I shove my hand in her open maw until she gags, ignoring the irritating bees stinging me.

Once she passes out, I pat her head.

"I could have killed you. Grow stronger so that you can protect your cubs."

I emerge from the bushes without a scratch. "I did it, Mommy!"

I run to her, but something peculiar happens. The bloodstains on the ground form a cage around me.

"You let your guard down, Sweetie. You're better than that." She paces around the cage, giving me a great view of her plump booty.

One day that ass will be my prize.

I grab the blood bars and pull with all my strength.

But to claim a woman, you must first conquer her!

The bars spread and then the cage collapses into blood around me.

The blood hardens into chains that bind me tightly.

I'm still so weak!

Demonica sits on me.

That sweet demon booty is on my back. Damn it! Why couldn't I have lost my shirt in that fight?

"Sweetie, if you're going to fight Exps, you can't get defeated so easily."

Oh right. I should be trying to break these chains. Strength isn't merely muscles. True strength is experience.

"I'm going to kill Devlin and take you as my bride!" I exclaim.

My mother blushes deep red, losing focus.

A little ripple in the mind causes a disturbance in the power.

I break out of the chains and then hold my hands out. "Wait! Calm down. I just said that so I could break free!"

Momma leans down, her cleavage in full view. "If you want something, then grow strong enough to seize it. Don't take back your words like a weakling. If I hadn't raped your father, you wouldn't be here." She kisses my cheek with her serpent tongue.

My stomach churns.

I don't want to rape her. She's everything to me. I want to conquer her body, mind and soul. I want her to love me. Only then will I complete my journey by returning back to her warm womb! Forcing my way back home would be cheating. I'm far better than that.

Momma picks me up and hugs me. "You did very good today. I'll go get us some food." She flies off, leaving me alone with my boner.

"Pathetic! You aren't even rock hard. And you're so short too. Grow stronger! We're supposed to be a team!"

I flick my erection while glaring at it.

A bear drops in front of me, causing me the slightest surprise.

Mommy catches me before I fall over backward. "So, you gonna prepare it?"

"She…helped me. I'm stronger now, even if it was just a bit."

"Strength? You could have choked the life out of her but you didn't. That's mercy, not strength. Here I thought Lilith was the Pollyanna. Sehuhuhu!"

I growl and blush. "Just what do you expect me to do?"

"Kill it with your hands and let's share it's flesh."

But she's a mommy too.

I put my hands to the bear's throat.

She's breathing. And she's warm.

"Sweet boys are a bore. You can sleep alone tonight." Mommy takes to the air.

"Wait! I'll do it!" I start to choke the bear.

She wakes up and flails around, clawing at me, clinging for life.

No. This isn't strength. Mommy doesn't want a pet. She wants a man.

I release my grip and stare at her. "I'm an Exp. I don't need to eat. I won't kill needlessly. I've made my decision."

Mommy lands and picks me up. "Well, well, you think you can defy me so easily? Defiance without strength leads only to death, Boy." Her fingernails cut into my back and the blood hardens into spikes.

I scream in pain and writhe around.

"The pain won't stop until you're done whining!" She stomps on me.

Aha! Now my flesh sword is harder! Perhaps I misjudged you.

Mommy suddenly stops stomping me. She glares at a person wrapped in bondage gear. "You're interrupting my bonding time with my son, you filth." She spits and hisses at the intruder.

"I'll take care of this creep!" I rush at the gimp but he or she, or whatever the hell, just teleports away. The moment my fist is about to hit, we swap places and I miss.

So humiliating!

"Lord Sel…" the gimp speaks in a very scared feminine voice "he's begun his search."

Mommy's face goes dark. "G-G-Get out of here! Before he notices you're gone."

The gimp nods and vanishes.

"Mommy, you okay?" I ask.

"Just fine." She smiles at me but fear fills her eyes. "It's time."

That's not fear. It's dread.

"Mommy, what's going on?" I ask in a voice of great courage to calm her.

"We have to head back home."

"But we haven't explored the whole world! We've only done a few dozen countries. We're nomads. Devlin doesn't even want us there! He doesn't love you!"

I do.

It takes all my strength to hold back my tears, my weakness.

Demonica holds her chest and trembles. She summons up power from within, and silences me with an intense look. "I'm calling your father."

I cross my arms. "He's not my father."

She looks at the hate in my eyes and she becomes more relaxed.

Lord Sel zooms through the clouds, searching the lights below for a special soul. "Come on Devlin, you can't hide from me. I just want to see my grandchildren. There's no need to hide."

He tears through the sky as fast as a jet, cities whizzing by as he scans the mortal's souls.

"My ascension is inevitable. There's no way to overpower me. And any delays I encounter are only allowed for my own amusement. Ugh. Am I talking to myself? Global soul-searching is quite the bore."

Lord Sel notices that a bright light on the horizon. Or rather that the horizon is itself a vast illuminating light. "Well, well, looks like I found the kitty. Where could she be heading, I wonder?"

Lord Sel follows along, several thousand feet above the new Sellum.

Chapter 182: Surrender!

The Freedom Forcers land the jet onto a wide open plain.

Hope gets out of her seat. “My royal buttocks will need a thorough massage tonight, Mother. Eight hours of sitting in a chair is not my idea of a good time.”

Ada smiles. “Just added to my schedule.”

Image suddenly leans over and kisses Atlas.

“That was a pleasant surprise.” He holds her hands with gentle passion.

“Just as I promised. You brought me back home. So…I forgive you.” She leans in and kisses him deeply.

Hope looks over her team. “Welcome to Canada, everyone. Our priority is bringing Devlin and his children back to base with us. Do not engage unless you absolutely must. His home is just a few miles walk from here. We must not fail! Also, I’ll need someone to carry me.”

Deceivant lifts her up into his arms. “It will be my honor! Everyone, give yourselves a hand. You’re all warriors fighting for a just cause! My son is counting on us and we’re all going to return home safely!”

Hope pats his head as the others applause. “Nicely done.”

The plane hatch lowers.

Lord Sel is just outside, staring up at them with a big smile. “Why did everyone stop clapping? Go ahead; finish up your final moments of joy. I didn’t come to ruin your triumphant moment. After you’re done clapping…” he looks at Riufen with a sinister grin “then I can wipe you out.”

“Kaity, get my daughter to safety,” says Deceivant, tossing Hope.

Kaity catches the little queen.

Hope glares at her. “You will do no such thing. We expected a confrontation. We shall stand together and face him.”

Bob looks up at Gladius. “Why are you with that quitter still? Return to me!”

The sword growls at Riufen and then scurries to Lord Sel.

“Very well. Step out, quitter.” Bob glares at the samurai.

Riufen walks past the others and approaches his old master. “I will not let you bring harm to Devlin-sama’s family.”

“Oh, come now. Can’t a grandfather just want to visit his family?” Bob makes a pouty face.

“Then why are you standing in our way?” asks Riufen.

"You're the one I want. I can't let a quitter just run free. You should have betrayed me."

"The joy it would bring you would dishonor me!" yells Riufen, tearing out his spine.

Bob holds the samurai in place with telekinesis.

Riufen holds up his hand. "Wait. I made a promise with the ruler of Absence. Since I cut him down, you are not allowed to attack his realm."

"Ehehaha! Why would I have to keep your promise for you? If you just obey me, then maybe we could work out some sort of protection plan." Bob smirks as he circles the foolish samurai.

"I will defend that realm with my life. Enter it and you must fight me."

"Oh no! Wait, what was your win to lose ratio again? Oh, that's right, you've lost every fight we've had."

"It wasn't a threat but a declaration."

Hope steps out of the plane and approaches Bob fearlessly. "If you don't stand in our way, then we have no quarrel with you. The moment you come after Kitty or my brother, I shall destroy you."

"My word your cheeks are cute." Bob pokes her puffy face.

"I will not be mocked!" yells Hope with a deep blush.

Kaity and the others come out of the plane, making a circle around Lord Sel. She walks directly to her sworn enemy. "My own mother made me kill my father…she made me kill her…so that I…I wouldn't ever be swayed by your demands. I'm not going to throw my life away and make everything she did meaningless."

"Oh, this is an interesting development," says Bob. "So you don't care if I kill the honor-bound fool?"

"I won't surrender, but I will fight. I'm giving you a chance. Let him go. Riufen is with us now. We're not going to see Devlin without him."

"You expect me to face Devlin with the shame of losing my best warrior!? Absurd! Fine, be difficult." Dark energy pools from Sel.

Kaity fires a Lum beam at the portal, dispelling it.

"Oh, not bad. I suppose I'll improvise." Bob smirks.

Gimpy appears and groans.

Regna, Yvne, Pesi, and Etaf appear from nowhere.

Kaity's eyes widen. "You knew about Lum's plan, didn't you?"

"What do you mean?" asks Etaf with a curious look.

Atlas looks at Etaf and shakes his head. "To think you would side with the Dark One."

Lord Sel looks at Kaity. "Tsul and Edirp are attacking Lum as we speak. Maybe you should try and stop them."

"I'd rather kill you." The new god's claws jut out.

"Now we could just go for an all-out brawl like savages, or we can be more civilized. Kaity, if you only fight me, I'll only attack you and Riufen. It's a deal that works in your favor, I assure you."

"I'm tired of standing around!" Regna fires a rage wave forth that shoots into Toxic.

The snake Exp suddenly lashes out at Deceivant.

Ada moves to help but is blocked by Gladius.

"Stop!" yells Hope. "I'll turn over Riufen to you. Now call off your minions! I will not allow any harm to come to my family!"

Bob grins. "Surrendering so quickly? I expected better from you."

Hope falls over. She looks up to see Wringer, bringing her in. "You're on our side, you buffoon!"

"Now my pawns, I want you to fight as unfair as you wish. The less of them that escape, the better. Have fun," says Bob joyously.

Hope glares at Wringer as the chains pulls her in. "Were you really waiting all this time to kill me? I broke you before and I'll do it again. Or perhaps you're attacking me to spare the swordsman. I'm doing this for the greater good. You of all people shouldn't fear doing what must be done."

"Innocent. Innocent," says Wringer through a prerecorded voice box.

The chains wrap around Hope's arms and legs.

"My priority is protecting my brother. The true poor are those that lack the will to strive for more. Your morals keep you in the poverty of your miserable situation."

"Murderer. Murderer," says Wringer.

"It seems I must show another serf his place," said Hope as the chains stretch her arms to the brink.

Wringer approaches her and watches as she squirms.

"Your primitive mind will be as easy to crush as a soft grape. MENTAL CRUSH!" exclaims Hope.

Chains burst from below and squeeze her throat and belly.

Hope chokes and writhes.

A stray gravity bullet zooms by, knocking Wringer off his feet.

Hope glares at him.

"The chains of a slave trying to bound a queen, how ironic," says Hope with a confident smile. "You have no idea how meaningless this is.

Exps needs no oxygen to circulate their capsules. Your ability is completely harmless to me. I am a queen. Royalty outlives poverty. Even after death royalty is remembered and worshipped. Kings are imprinted in history through text. Pharaohs live eternally through scriptures. Your weak people believe they should choose their rulers. Rebel cowards like you will rot and be forgotten by history."

Wringer snaps Hope's legs with a harsh tug.

Hope glares at him. "Got me all tied up like a marionette. You want to make the queen your puppet. This is amusing, the chains of poverty seek to shackle a monarch. Your whole purpose in life is tied to your weakness. You know you can't beat the system, but you can't help but try. It's cute."

The chains move suddenly, snapping her arms.

Hope screams out in pain but bites her lip. "You no longer have a drive. Your only purpose is to serve me to heal your broken chains. I shall help you reconstruct your shackled mind."

Wringer shook its head fiercely and then collapses.

Hope coughs and sobs. "Why am I so weak?"

Deceivant looks at Hope in the distance. "I should have been there to protect her!" He turns around and glares at Toxic. "You're nothing to me! You hear that!? Just a failed experiment! Same with Absorb! I let him get captured! But you can't hear a damn thing I'm saying because you're mad with rage!"

"Despicable!" yells Toxic before shooting at Deceivant. The living metal projectile slices his leg.

"I have antibodies to all sorts of poisons in me. That includes yours," says Deceivant, firing a gravity bullet her way.

The blade pushes one snake back, but three more slither along the grass nearby him.

Toxic's scales start revolving as she lunges at her enemy.

Deceivant fires a gravity bullet to his side, causing her to swerve out of the way. "I haven't just been inventing these past five years. I've been training to protect Hope!" He tosses a Gravity Grenade at the ground.

Toxic smashes into the ground over and over. Once the assault ends, she digs to conceal herself.

"Toxic, because of you the queen is hurt. As her knight it is my duty to smite you," says Deceivant, pulling out a beam katana.

Riufen hollers in the distance. "We must do battle later, scientist!"

Toxic shot out of the ground, slicing Deceivant's arm before digging again. "You think you're the only one who upgraded me? You must be delusional! Succumb to my **TOXIC HALLUCINATION**!"

Hundreds of Toxics shot out of the ground at Deceivant. He fires frantically, but it has no effect on them.

"Do you remember the day you made me?"

"Yeah. I…know you didn't mean to hurt Hope."

"She cut her hand petting me the wrong way! She always does things wrong. And you! You made me one minute, and the next, threw me away," yells Toxic in tears.

Deceivant lowers his gun and closes his eyes, ending the hallucinatory assault. "You have every reason to be angry at me. But you must understand that Hope is more than my queen, she is my daughter. As a father I cannot allow any harm to come to her. Whether intentional or unintentional," says Deceivant, standing proud.

"Your daughter?" Toxic pops out and looks up at him with sad eyes. "But…she's not the only one. You have many children, not just Hope. You're my father. You have an obligation to raise me with love just as you did Hope. And you have an obligation to save Absorb too! He's lost in the fires of revenge. But Daddy, I can forgive you. Please, just take care of me like a father, even if I'm not as cute as Hope," says Toxic in a super girly mumbly tone.

Deceivant was quiet for a while. "With my eyes closed, I can truly hear your cute voice." He opens his eyes and crouches down. "I've been a terrible father to you. I've been so selfish and stupid. I've failed you, Absorb, Devlin…and Hope." With tears in his eyes he removes his shirt and exposes his chest. "If you really want to kill me, then do it! It's what I deserve for failing all my children."

Toxic disengages her scales and climbs up to his shoulders. "I deserve much more than revenge! If you think I'm just going to let you die and be free, you are wrong. I ask of you much more than that," says Toxic with a big smile.

"Just please protect Hope in my stead," says Deceivant in tears.

Toxic wraps around his neck and gives him a soft kiss on the cheek. "Silly daddy, if you died, who would take care of your children? You will earn my forgiveness. You will take me up as your adorable daughter. Atonement through parenthood. It's only fair," says Toxic, nuzzling his cheek.

Deceivant nuzzles her back. "That is more than I deserve. Thank you…sweetie. Thanks for forgiving me," says Deceivant as he embraces his serpentine daughter. "Now, let's get your sister to safety." He pats her head as he rushes to Hope. "You'll be okay. I'll get you out of here." The smitten scientist reaches for his injured daughter.

"No!" Hope glares at Deceivant. "This pain I can handle, but I won't permit you coddling that piece of trash. Why didn't you kill her when she attacked you?"

"Because I'm her father," says Deceivant as he embraced Hope.

Hope glares at him. "I would smack you if my arms weren't broken! I forbid you from touching me, failed knight," says Hope, spitting on his face.

Deceivant leans forward and kisses her forehead. "I'm tending to you as your father."

"I suppose I don't have much of a choice at the moment." Hope puffs out her cheeks and then then looks at the snake. "Don't expect me to call you sister."

"Oh, so I shouldn't you call you…Sister!" Toxic's eyes shimmer as she snuggles Hope.

"No! Stop! I order you to cease this at once!"

Deceivant smiles as he watches Toxic snuggle Hope. "I have two adorable daughters. I'm a truly fortunate father." He then carries them away from the conflict.

Regna glares at her enemy and fires a wave of rage forth.

"Whirlwind leaps off a gust of air and divebombs the fiery demon!" narrates the superhero girl.

"How did that little snake overcome my ability! I'm a god!"

"Do not underestimate the power of love!" Whirlwind coats her legs in swirling gusts and speeds by, knocking Regna off her feet. She scratches her head. "Okay, that was too corny. Sorry. Oh, I got it! The heroine leaps in the air and dive kicks the Sinisister! Their bonds are stronger than your evil!" She lands and grins. "Oh yeah! Totally nailed it that time."

Regna stabs her fingers into the annoying pest. "I will tear you to pieces!"

"The villain believes she has won–"

"I have won!" yells Regna, digging her claws in deeper.

"Eeesh! Hurts like a…as I was saying. She is unaware that our heroine has the full arsenal of mother Earth at her command. ***STATIC STOMP!***"

Electricity bursts out from her legs and fries the demon god.

"Get blown away!" The heroine smirks. "Whirlwind spins in place, creating a tornado and riding it up, along with the Sinisister!"

"Don't think you can just run away!" yells Gladius, launching himself and grabbing the cowardly woman in his maw. His teeth go right through her. "What the!? What's going on!?"

"I hear that you're very sharp but ohh…I misunderstood. My apologies." Thirty Adas bow to the scary reptile.

"Mocking me is foolish!" He glares at the Adas. "Aha! None of you cast a shadow! You're all fakes! Now who's dumb?"

All the Adas rush him at once. "We will overcome you with Exp 8's strategy. Never show fear."

"Are you sure you shouldn't help your wife?" asks Atlas, shielding Deceivant from Etaf's attacks.

The Goddess of Fate points her sword. "If I wanted to, I would cut right past him and slice you in twine."

"Hey, I just want to talk," says Deceivant, coming out with his hands up.

"Speak."

"Why are you working with Sel? Aren't you a Lum Goddess?"

"I'm going to be his queen. The next Lum is me."

"Wait, are you in love with Bob?"

"What we have is eternal."

"Oh okay. I was just wondering how you two copulate," says Deceivant with a nervous chuckle.

"What Bob is capable of doing with his spectral drills is something only I know," says Etaf with a slight smile.

Deceivant whispers to Atlas. "Once I fire the first shot, just run for it, okay?" He then turns to Etaf. "If Amy is the next Lum, then I'll protect her from you! If you want her dead, you will have to kill me first," says Deceivant, lifting his Gravity Gun and firing.

The bullet shot forward, creating a gravity field that causes Etaf to stumble and lose grip on her sword.

"Seems gravity defies fate," says the scientist with a grin.

The goddess shakes her head. "You cannot avoid destiny."

The blade shot right back into her hands.

Deceivant fires another spray of bullets her way.

She snaps her fingers, redirecting the bullets back at him.

Deceivant is flung off his feet and Atlas slams the Suffer Sword against Etaf's blade.

Pesi looks at the sight and grins. "To think I was once the weak link of my team! Now I am a god!"

Image looks at him and shakes her head. "Overcompensation, for sure. What is your suggestion?"

Durga shrugs. "Meditation is always good. Maybe some asanas."

"I don't need your help!" Pesi fires a giant beam of red energy that crashes into Image. When the beam clears, not even dust remains of her.

"Your pain shall be your prison!" yells Durga, using her fumes on Pesi.

The violent god thrashes around.

Atlas, clashing swords with Etaf, looks over. "What just happened?"

"She met her fate. I'll gladly send you off to go see her."

Atlas summons up the Misery Mace and shoves it into his chest. He falls to his knees in misery, expelling all his sadness before removing the weapon. "I'm needed here. I'll search all of Lum if I have to. But I will do so after Hope has accomplished Zenero's dream."

Etaf slices the air, cutting Atlas as he shield's himself. "This isn't about Hope. You're only with her to find Zenero. He left you behind and took everyone else. You want to know why."

Atlas rushes at Etaf and braces the cuts of the Destiny Sword. "Zenero didn't know I was there! He hasn't abandoned me!" He rams into her and twists her arm until she drops the Destiny Sword.

"Everything you love is going to end. The Kali Yuga is upon us. Best to accept it now." She slid into a Lum portal.

"Excellent work!" yells the Captain of Carnage, ziplining up a giant demon of flesh and metal.

BoneSaw rides up the arm, slicing it along the way.

Deceivant fires at the behemoth from on the ground. "Yvne is too big. I can hardly make her budge!"

"Heads up!" yells Whirlwind, sending her explosive foe into the shapeshifter's head.

Atlas looks up at the giant. "We're only agitating her. We need Absence power. We need Riufen."

"I'm the one you want," says Kaity, firing multiple Lum arrows at Bob while using a vine to pull Riufen around to dodge Sel bullets.

Bob's Atma Blade glows brightly and shoots multiple spectral blasts at the annoying kitty.

Kaity jumps out of the way of the first, running on all fours up to Bob.

"Stay still, damn it!" yells Bob as his tendrils chase the new Sellum.

Kaity fires a Sel beam at the giant, but Lord Sel pulls it in and absorbs it.

"It's incredibly rude to ignore your playmate." He grabs her with a Sel tendril and slams her to the ground.

Kaity creates a tree on impact, rising up and firing Lum blasts at Bob. "Riufen, we're going to have to work together to take him down!"

"I will only draw my sword when you stand down." He sits defiantly and glares at Kaity.

"Why don't you just join me? I'll let you fight her all on your own! Come now, there's no need to be upset with me," says Bob, firing a massive Sel beam at Kaity who counteracts with a Lum beam of equal size.

"I harbor no hate, only disgust," says Riufen, approaching the Dishonorable One during the power struggle.

"You could have been so much more," says Bob, having his tendrils sneak behind Kaity.

The tendrils hold her down and Bob approaches Riufen.

The samurai slashes with his Absence-coated spine.

The attack phases through Bob. He summons up the Atma Blade and readies the killing blow. "Now prepare to…oh, I can't kill you." He pats Riufen's head. "You're too valuable and just so fun to manipulate."

Riufen glares at him. "You shall regret this moment when next we cross paths."

"Fall back! Return to Sel!" yells Bob, loud enough so that all of his pawns can hear. He creates a Sel portal and uses spectral tendrils to pull his allies in. He then turns to Kaity. "How about we call a truce?"

Kaity stares blankly. "What?"

"I want a truce, what is so surprising about that?" asks Bob with an annoyed tone.

"Just a few moments ago you told your minions to kill us," says Kaity, collecting Lum energy in her palms.

"Well now I've decided that I can't wait to see my grandchildren any longer," says Bob.

Hope is carried to the Dark One. "You should be asking me. To which I will absolutely refuse."

A pillar of dark energy erupts from Lord Sel and creates massive black swords that hover above the Freedom Forcers.

"Are you sure?" asks Bob, poking Hope's cheeks with her hands.

Hope gulps. "Please elaborate on this truce."

"Well, now that I no longer want to kill Riufen, this is all pointless. I…should be enjoying myself…but I really just want to see my grandkids!"

"Wait, kids? There's more than one? How do you know that?" asks Ada curiously.

"Found out just recently actually. Twins."

Deceivant rushes up. "Are they both girls?"

Bob puts an arm around him. "Wouldn't you rather find out yourself?"

"I'm a grandfather all over again." Deceivant cries.

"I'm even more grandmother than before! Oh, Devlin has grown up so fast," says Ada proudly.

Bob and Ada hug. "We're grandparents!"

"Don't touch her!" yells Deceivant.

Ada shakes her finger at her hubby. "Now, now, he's being nice so we can be nice too."

Bob turns to Kaity. "Come on, let's go see the kids together. Aren't you tired of fighting all the time?"

Toxic glares at Bob. "How can we trust anything you say? You're the Befriender of Betrayal!"

"I kept my promise not to hurt Sellum's children. When I learned that Stabby is Lum, I told my forces to retreat. Well, Kaity. Will you agree to my truce? I think it's better than me just murdering all of you."

Hope glares. "It isn't her choice. It's mine! And I say we agree to avoid getting slaughtered," she says, looking up at the dark weapons hovering above.

Ada smiles at Kaity. "Think about it, having a treaty with Bob is a glorious opportunity. We can all become friends and accomplish so much! Maybe Sel and Lum can be united too!"

Bob scratches the top of his eye. "Let's dial it down a bit."

"How temporary is the treaty?" asks Kaity sternly.

"Until we all leave Devlin's house. I think that is fair, don't you?" asks Bob with a big smile.

"I don't trust him to keep his promise, but we're at a disadvantage here." Hope puffs out her cheeks.

"No. I can blast the pillar," says Kaity, focusing Lum energy. She fires a blast but it's too small to harm the massive Sel pillar.

Bob hops in the air. "Drained already. You need to conserve your energy better."

Kaity fires another shot and then nothing. "It's not working. I have to…I have to save them."

Hope looks to Kaity, signaling her to stand down. "We agree to the terms of the treaty. Kitty, bring us there."

Kaity nods but can't create a portal. "I'm sorry. I can't do it."

"We mustn't allow Bob to be alone at any moment." Hope looks to Lord Sel. "None of your minions are allowed inside. Understood?"

"Minions? I only have friends," says Bob, cuddling Gimpy.

"No friends either then," says Kaity.

He tosses Gimpy aside. "That's fine. They're all just pawns."

"Nobody on your side is allowed to enter his house!" yells Kaity.

"Let's agree to disagree. Bring us there, Slave," says Bob, firing a laser at Gimpy.

The gimp screams in delightful pain and then teleports everyone.

Chapter 183: Shinx & Lilith

Devlin's house is a two-story log cabin, situated between tall trees and a cliffside overhead, keeping it in the shade. The front yard was home to many home-grown veggies and there was a playground in the backyard. Bob was nowhere in sight.

"Kitty, heal me," requests Hope.

Kaity pours Lum energy into her small frame, fixing the broken limbs. "It's working now."

"Good." Hope hops off Wringer and knocks on the door. She straightens her skirt and fixes her hair. "Devlin, it's your sister. I've arrived."

"We don't have time for this." Kaity kicks down the door.

Devlin, his hair now cut so it's out of his golden eyes, pulls her in with a net of wires. "Kaity!?" He untangles her and blushes. "Sorry, I thought you were Bob."

"Bob is already here! We have to find him!" yells Kaity, gripping Devlin.

Kaity and Devlin are lifted off the ground by spectral tentacles and brought into a hug.

"Aww, there's no need to worry. We're all friends now. It will be quite some time before I must end you both."

Devlin glares at Bob. "I won't let you hurt my family."

"Come now. I'm just here to visit. I promise I won't try anything devious." He bows and releases them.

Devlin suddenly grips Kaity and cries with her. "It's been five years. I thought about you every single day."

Hope tugs on Devlin's shirt. "You had better have been thinking about me." She puffs out her cheeks.

Devlin smiles at her and looks up at everyone. "I was thinking about all of you." His eyes quiver. "Is this everyone?"

Hope pinches his arm. "I'll answer your questions after I receive a proper greeting."

Devlin picks her up and hugs her tenderly. "Are they all dead?"

Demonica lands in front of him. The demoness' purple skin and long red nails glisten in the sunlight. "Where's Bob?"

Bob hugs her from behind. "Aww, I missed you too."

Devlin looks at Kaity and his eyes water up. "You're suffering. What happened?"

Kaity wipes her eyes. "No…I'm fine. Nothing happened." She chokes on her words and holds her shivering body.

"Lies!" yells Lord Sel. "I killed Sellum! Riufen killed Absence and Kaity killed Lum! The whole afterlife is under new management!" Bob bounces around with glee.

Demonica bites her lip and turns to her Dark Lord with tearful eyes. "You really did it!? We should celebrate!"

"That's what I'm here for! To celebrate with my grandkids."

Deceivant approaches Devlin. "Level with me son. You have how many kids? Any girls?"

Devlin glares at his father. "You're not allowed anywhere near my daughter."

"Daughter! We have a new granddaughter!" exclaims Deceivant, picking up Ada and spinning around with her.

"Why did you bring him?" asks Devlin, looking over at Hope.

"I'm beginning to question my decision in hindsight," says Hope, brushing the dirt off her skirt.

Ada pulls Devlin into a squishy hug. "Come on, Sweetie. Let's get along for the children!"

"Do anything to my daughter and I'll sever those lecherous hands," says Devlin, lifting his father by his shirt collar.

"Just because I'm a pedophile doesn't mean I'm incestuous," says Deceivant with a pained expression.

"Ada is your daughter, isn't she?" asks Devlin, rolling his eyes.

"In a manner of speaking perhaps. Though merely fiction, the sculptor Pygmalion was not incestuous for loving his creation. Neither were you for loving Nina."

"Where is Nina? Is she dead?" asks Devlin softly.

"Most likely," says Hope bluntly.

Devlin turns to Kaity and grabs her hand. "I know you must have done everything to protect her."

Kaity hugs him and sobs. The two of them cry together.

"This is what Devlin loves instead of my Mom. Pathetic," says the voice of a bratty kid.

Deceivant lifts up the kid and snuggles him. "My granddaughter is an adorable little tomboy!"

The kid blushes and punches Deceivant in the face. "I'm a man!"

Ada looks at him sternly and then lifts him up and snuggles him. "You're soooo cute!"

The boy nuzzles her breasts and grins. "Soft and bouncy, not bad."

Devlin pulls the boy off. "Ada is your grandmother, you little cretin!"

The boy kicks Devlin and lands. "My name is Shinx!"

Shinx is a muscular ten-year old boy. Pitch black hair covers one of his golden eyes. He was wearing a comfy sweater with tigers on it that his Mommy knitted for him.

Hope looks at him and blushes. "It's like a tiny Devlin."

"I'm nothing like him!" Shinx spits on the floor. He then scans the Freedom Forcers. "Who are these freaks?"

"It's not nice to judge people by their looks," says Demonica sweetly.

"Yes Mommy. I'm sorry, please pardon my rudeness," says Shinx in a tender voice while bowing.

Bob looks at him, shimmering.

Shinx turns around and jumps back. "What the hell is that thing?"

Bob lowers his pupil, deeply depressed.

"I knew Devlin's side of the family had to be weird, but this…is bizarre," says Shinx.

Demonica crouches down and pats the depressed eyeball. "He is your grandfather. He was the one who gave me my rebirth!"

Shinx reverently bows. "I cannot take back my cruel words. I deeply apologize for my blasphemy. Thank you from the core of my being for creating Mommy."

Riufen looks at Shinx and nods. "Devlin-sama's loyal spirit rings true in you."

Shinx gags. "Yuck. Are all of you Devlin's relatives?"

Atlas smiles. "Yes. We are all family. I'm your great-grandfather."

"Hmm." Shinx shrugs. "At least you look strong."

Bob pulls Demonica aside. "I would appreciate your help killing Kaity. Can I count on you when the time comes?"

"I've been traveling the world with my little hell spawn but I can't say no to that. Her death would bring Devlin closer to me."

"Aww, that's my girl." Bob pats her. "Soon enough, you'll be the only one for him."

"Thanks, for everything." Demonica hugs him and gives him a good squeeze. "If it weren't for you, I wouldn't even have kids."

"Never mention that again please," says Bob with a queasy look.

A girl with long red hair, golden eyes and glasses comes out the front door, wearing her owl pattern pajamas.

Devlin runs in front of her and glares at Bob. "Lilith, I told you to stay inside. It isn't safe."

"You also said that running and hiding won't work." She looks up at Ada and Deceivant who are beaming at her. "No way, are you–?"

"Cutie!" exclaims Ada and Deceivant, picking her up and snuggling her.

"I never thought I'd get to meet you! I've heard so much about you!" She nuzzles Ada back. Lilith then turns to Deceivant with an awkward, embarrassed look. "Is it umm true what he says about you?"

Deceivant pinches her tummy and beams. "What a darling little angel?"

"I'm gonna go uhh, greet the others," says Lilith, sliding out of his embrace.

Deceivant folds his hands in prayer. "Thank you, oh great Big Bang, for bringing me such a beautiful granddaughter." He wipes his eyes in tears.

Lilith looks up at Kaity. "You're even more adorable than Father said! Can I pet you?"

Kaity wipes her eyes and crouches down. "Of course you can."

Lilith turns to her Father. "Kaity's my real mom, right? You just wanted to keep it a secret from me because she was traveling," she says with a grin.

"I wish with all my soul that was the truth," says Devlin with an exhausted look.

Shinx glares at the cat-girl. "You're the flat pussy whore that Devlin has been cheating on Mommy with."

Devlin lifts Shinx off the ground and glares at him. "Insult Kaity again and Lilith is going to be an only child."

"Get your hands off me, you're not real my father! He is," says Shinx, pointing to Bob.

"I finally have a son!" cries Bob with radiant joy. He stops. "Oh wait, am I the father?" Bob throws up spectral energy.

Demonica approaches Devlin with heavy breaths. "I missed that dark side of you." She runs her hands down his back. "It's been years since we've seen each other. Get down on the ground! Let's do it right now!"

Devlin turns to face her, looking very uncomfortable. "Do you not care that our daughter is right in front of us?"

"Yeah! Why not show her how she was made firsthand right now?" Demonica turns to Lilith. "My lil' succubus, don't you want another sibling?"

"Yeah but from Kaity, not you! Keep your hands off my dad!" yells Lilith.

Shinx looks at Devlin with disgust. "Why go for a weak man like him?"

"Because she's a wicked monster!" yells Lilith.

Shinx punches his sister in the face and pulls her by her hair. "If your tongue can only spit poison, perhaps it should be removed." He pulls out a sharpened knife of wood and puts it in her mouth.

Wires come out from Devlin and coil around Shinx. "Don't test me."

Kaity grabs Devlin's hand and cries. "Can we please just stop fighting?"

Devlin's rage leaves and he holds Kaity.

"Awww! They're so cute together!" Lilith wobbles in excitement.

Shinx rolls around while giving Devlin a dark glare. "Why would you rather pursue an impossible love with that weakling than be with Mommy?"

"Father never gives up on true love. He's a real romantic," says Lilith, nuzzling her cheeks.

"He only wants Kaity because she denies him. He's a fool who can never be content with what he has," says Shinx angrily.

Lilith crosses her arms and pushes out her bottom lip. "If he's so bad, then why does your great Mommy love him?"

"Mommy sees something in nothing, it truly is inspiring." Shinx holds his chest and beams.

"You're still a jerk! She raped our father!"

"Father? Devlin is a pathetic fool that doesn't know when to give up on a hopeless love with an underage lesbian. As for the rape, well if he was strong enough, he could have prevented it. Her love overpowered his indifference. That's all."

"If you love someone you should put their happiness before your own!" yells Lilith.

"You read too many fairytales. If they don't love you, then force your love. If you accept the hopelessness, or even worse, deny it, then you do not know love. Rape was the only choice he gave her," says Shinx with a smug look.

"Don't you get it? We're…we're both mistakes," says Lilith in tears.

Bob nods to himself. "Devlin spoils his daughter and Demonica over-disciplines her son. Despite this, the daughter came out insecure and the son is a brat! Ah, the wonders of soul memory!"

Deceivant approaches to cheer her up, but is pushed aside by Demonica. "Don't you ever say that, my pet. I raped your father on purpose. I wanted his children more than anything," said Demonica.

"You should be in prison," says Lilith, staring down the monstrous demon.

Shinx put his hands behind his head in a lax manner. "You're really whining about crimes? So basic. Laws are only put in place to control the weak. In the natural world, the real world, there is no crime. The strong and resourceful thrive while the weak-willed perish. Maybe you'd know about that if you didn't spend your whole life inside your room. All your knowledge is pointless. Wisdom is what truly matters."

"I hate you!" yells Lilith before running off.

"The whining of someone without a proper comeback. Pathetic."

Devlin looks to Demonica. "I thought you were going to train him to be more respectful."

"Says the man who won't even share the same bed with me. I left with him to get away from you. Being under the same roof as you…it was so lonely."

Bob nods and puts a spectral arm around Shinx. "Respect is very important. Let's have a little chat." He looks to Gimpy.

Gimpy nods and then both Lord Sel and Shinx vanish.

Devlin grabs Gimpy. "Where is he?"

Gimpy mumbles a response.

Devlin turns to Demonica. "Make him tell you where our son is!"

"You don't know him like I do. He wouldn't hurt Shinx. I trust him," she says with quivering eyes.

Devlin rushes to Kaity. "Can you use your powers to find out where he went?"

Kaity looks at him nervously. "I'll try. I just…I don't know how to use all my powers yet."

"Please."

Kaity nods and closes her eyes.

Chapter 184: Coaxing the Pawn

Shinx arrives at the edge of a cliff, overlooking a several thousand-foot drop.

"Careful. One false step and I'll be having pancakes for breakfast." Bob pops out beneath him, snickering.

"Are you really the God of Destruction?" asks Shinx, mustering up his courage to stare down the entity.

"More importantly I'm your grandfather." Bob lifts up Shinx and nuzzles him over certain doom.

"I'll listen to what you have to say. But speak quickly. I plan to one up Lilith and cook Mother a delicious meal."

"So assertive. It's just adorable." Bob drops Shinx.

He starts to scream but then stops and braces himself.

Bob then pulls him all the way back up.

"I've already had that test. Mommy has trained me well." Shinx smiles fondly.

"You're a true child prodigy. How handy are you with your powers?"

Shinx looks away with rosy cheeks. "I…don't have any."

"None that you're aware of. I assure you there is an ability within you just waiting to be discovered. But you'll have to miss out on cooking breakfast."

"Teach me! I want to grow stronger! I will grow stronger!"

"You're already a child prodigy. What about your sister? Does she have her powers yet?"

"Nope. She's a waste of time. Lilith was home-schooled by Devlin. He hasn't taught her how to fight. He's just filled her head with weak idealism."

"Idealism can be a powerful fuel…for simpletons."

"Yeah, she's definitely a simpleton. She believes in altruistic love. It sickens me," says Shinx with a grimace. "Now spit it out. What do you want?"

"We have plenty of time. For now, let's get that power awakened."

"Do you think one day I'll be stronger than Mommy?"

"I can see your soul. Once we unlock your potential, you'll become a force of destruction!"

"Alright, how do I unlock it?"

Bob grins. He lifts the boy up with telekinesis and slams him against the cliffside. “A near death experience should do the trick. Or would you prefer a slower method.”

“Give me everything you’ve got! If I die here, then I’m not worthy of being her son!”

“Truly inspiring words! Let’s hear them again when your bones are broken and your choking on your blood.” Bob smiles before smashing Shinx against the cliff repeatedly.

Kaity opens her eyes. “I…don’t know what I’m doing. I’m sorry, Devlin.”

Demonica smirks and runs her fingers up Devlin’s arm like a spider. “Looks like your little pedo crush can’t give you what you want, after all.”

“Gimpy, I demand you tell me where my son is!” yells Devlin, shaking the black clad minion.

“Loyal to me and me alone. Now, how about we relax a bit.” Demonica slices off his shirt. “Make love to me, take me out on a romantic date. Appease me and I’ll help you find our son.”

Ada smiles. “I’m sure Bob just wants to teach Shinx some manners!”

Hope rolls her eyes and then glares at Demonica. “Shall I crush her for you?”

Devlin gives her a gesture to calm down. “I’ll handle this.”

Deceivant points the Gravity Gun at the wicked mother. “A child is in danger and you don’t even care. You don’t deserve to be a parent.”

Demonica slashes Deceivant, cutting his body with her blood red nails. “You don’t know what I deserve!”

Kaity stands in front of her. “Stop it! Devlin, go be with your wife!”

“She’s not my wife!”

“I don’t care! Just make her happy. It’s not a big deal. You aren’t betraying your love for me! I’m done with love. I’m done.” Kaity sobs and Ada pulls her in to comfort her.

Devlin bites his lip and turns to Demonica. “Fine. I’ll go with you on a date after I make sure Shinx is safe.”

Demonica grabs Devlin’s arm and twists it. “The only thing you’ve given me is children. You can’t make demands when I have had no affection from you. You will obey me now.”

“Let him go!” yells Lilith, trying to yank the demon off her father.

Devlin pulls Demonica into a deep kiss. He bites her tongue and then pulls away. "Name the place. Let's get moving."

Hope signals Wringer to clang his chains together. "Before you leave, I have a request." She turns to Gimpy. "Send my forces and Lilith back to the Queendom."

"My daughter is staying here," says Devlin, grabbing Lilith's hand.

Hope shakes her head. "Bob already knows where this place is. There's no reason to hide anymore. My country has actual defense systems. She's safer there. There is no debate."

Devlin gulps and then crouches down to Hope. "You'll do everything in your power to keep her safe?"

"I'll make her feel welcomed and cherished. And I'll have Kaity at her side like a shadow to shield your dear daughter from harm."

Devlin smiles. He leans in and kisses Hope's lips.

She flares up and falls off her living stand. Muttering and holding her cheeks.

Demonica lifts up the embarrassed child. "You can't order my slave to do what you want."

Hope clears her throat. "My plan keeps your daughter safe. If you object, then I cannot allow you to be with Devlin and will have you killed."

"Whatever. Send them away, Slave!" Demonica kicks Gimpy.

The Freedom Forcers instantly arrive at the Queendom.

"How did the Gimp know exactly where we live? It's a moving island," says Deceivant.

"It is rather concerning," says Hope.

Atlas approaches Kaity. "Please send me to Lum. I must find my wife and make sure she is safe."

Hope approaches him and shakes her head. "I do not grant you permission to leave. A day in Lum is a year on Earth. Now more than ever, I am in need of your strength."

Kaity fires a Sel beam at the ground and then extinguishes it with a blast of Lum energy. "I'll take on whatever obligations he had."

"He knows more about Sel than any of us. He stays." Hope nods.

The Captain of Carnage stands upright and salutes Hope. "Will you allow me to search for her and our other dead allies?"

Hope closes her eyes and thinks. "Very well. Send him to Lum. BoneSaw, you will join him as well."

Kaity crouches down and lifts up BoneSaw. “Don’t you dare do anything reckless. Got it?”

BoneSaw salutes.

“Okay.” Kaity pools her energy into a Lum portal. “It worked! I don’t know if I can do it again.”

“We will return with reinforcements!” The Captain then rushes into the portal and BoneSaw follows along.

Whirlwind whispers to Durga.

Hope gazes their way. “Speak up. We can’t hear you.”

Whirlwind stands proud. “My sister is just going to get killed if she stays here. She’s not strong enough to fight the Evil Eye. I want her out of this place.”

Hope signals Wringer to crawl to Durga. “And what do you want?”

“I don’t want to die. Being with you…on your side…it’s dangerous.”

“You’ve contributed so much to our cause. Are you really going to back out now?”

“My apologies, but yes.”

“We don’t have Image.”

“I know…I should have protected her. I was with her. It was my responsibility.”

“You know that blame accomplishes nothing. Besides any casualties are my responsibility. I’m your leader.”

“You didn’t want to fight.”

“Silence.” Hope closes her eyes. “Image kept us together. She kept…me together. I need you to tend to everyone’s emotional well-being in her stead. Use that toxic guilt inside you to push you to help others.”

“You’re right. I just need some time alone.”

“There’s a boat by the docks. It’s yours. Whirlwind, are you leaving as well?”

The super hero shakes her head. “No. I’m going to stay and fight!”

Lilith looks up at Ada. “I don’t understand what’s going on? Is someone after us?”

Deceivant crouches down to look into Lilith’s golden eyes. “He didn’t tell you anything, did he? So sure that he could keep you safe. I didn’t raise my son to be so foolish.” He pats Lilith’s head. “Your grandfather on Demonica’s side is a dark god. He seeks Kaity’s death and will kill any of us to attain that goal.”

"That's crazy. I mean, I believe you of course! We have to stop him!" says Lilith firmly.

Deceivant pokes her belly. "Right now we need to get something yummy in that wittle tummy."

Lilith blushes. "Hey, I don't need to eat. I'm an Exp. Devlin says that—"

"He's not here right now. Come with me to the kitchen, sugar plum!" Deceivant offers his hand and heads inside the castle.

"Wait!" Lilith pulls away and runs off. "Why is there a super cute kitty girl statue? She's the one from 'Exps are so Cool!' I wanna hear all about her!"

Deceivant chuckles and smiles. "That's Kawai. She was one of my creations."

Lilith squeals in excitement. "Sooo adorable! And you made her! Who else did you make?"

"Well I made your grandmother and your father." He crouches down and tickles Lilith.

"You made Daddy!" She beams at him and wiggles.

Toxic looks at them from a distance.

Deceivant points at her. "Hey! Stop spying on us! Get over here!"

Toxic's eyes light up and she joins him in tickling and snuggling Lilith.

"I want to meet the kitty!" Lilith says with excitement bouncing in her eyes.

"You…can't."

Hope kicks Wringer. "Slave…get me out of here. Now!" She breaks down in tears.

Deceivant rushes to her side.

Hope stops him with her intense gaze. "You lied to me. Speak and I will break your mind and so you can never lie again!"

Kaity approaches her. "Calm down. We need to stay focused."

Hope yells through her tears. "No! You need to learn how to use your powers! Atlas, you're in charge of training the novice god."

"I'll join you," says Riufen with a firm nod.

"You will stay with Lilith and protect her."

Riufen turns away from Hope. "I won't dull my blade. I've made my decision."

"Insubordinate fool! Damn! Wringer, bring me to my room now!" yells Hope, repeatedly kicking her living chariot.

Ada picks up Hope in her arms. "He lies but he doesn't do it to hurt. Let's go, Sweetie. I'll make you some tea."

Lilith looks up at her grandpa. "I'm so sorry. I messed things up, didn't I?" She grabs his shaky hands.

"No. You simply brought out a truth that I foolishly tried to bury. Thank you, dear." He pats her head.

Lilith wiggles in excitement and then turns back to the statue. "Hey, grandpa." She wipes her eyes. "Do you…believe in what this says?"

Deceivant crouches down. "It's alright to love anyone." He blushes. "I believe in this more than anyone."

Lilith embraces him and cries against his shoulder.

"You can tell me anything, dear."

"Dad told me…about you and little girls." Lilith grabs his cheeks and kisses him. "Will you love me?" She grabs his hand and holds it to her chest.

Chapter 185: Family Party

Deceivant pulls his granddaughter into his embrace. “I already love you. I’d die for you, Lil-chan.” He grabs her cheeks and stares into her eyes. “That’s not a statement. It’s a declaration. If someone came after you, I would die to protect you!”

Toxic bites his ear. “No! No dying! We talked about this.”

Lilith pats Toxic. “Hey, I don’t know your name.”

“I’m Toxic!” The snake Exp shakes the girl’s hand with her tail.

“Can I have some alone time with grandpa?”

“Oh! Yeah, of course.” Toxic lowers her head and slithers off him.

“It’s just for a bit!” hollers Lilith. “Afterwards we can all watch a movie together!”

“Really!” Toxic beams.

Deceivant ruffles his granddaughter’s hair. “I’ve got a better plan! You go pick out a movie while I prepare dinner! We can chat alone afterwards. Right now, you need to unwind. We all do.”

Lilith stares into his golden eyes. Her eyes widen. She grabs Toxic and rushes into the castle.

Toxic nuzzles her ear once they’re inside. “You’re in love with him, aren’t you?”

Lilith turns bright red and walks awkwardly to the couch.

Toxic gives her niece a big hug. “You are! Auntie Toxic is here to help!”

“Wait, you’re reading into things wrong. It’s not like that. He’s my grandpa,” says Lilith, waving dismissively.

“Aww, you’re so cute! I think you two make a great couple!” Toxic nuzzles her niece’s cheeks. “It’s alright to love anyone, after all.”

Lilith blushes. “Hey, that girl. The kitty girl. Who did she love?”

“Oh, I don’t know. I never met her. But anyways, it’s movie time! So get off the couch!” She tugs on the girl’s arm.

“Hey. There’s a TV here. Pick something out. I’m not picky.”

Toxic shakes her head. “Wouldn’t you rather watch at a theatre!”

“Yeah! But we have to stay inside where it’s safe. Demon gods are after me, right? Also, aren’t theatres kinda extinct?”

Toxic slithers off the girl’s lap. “Just follow your Auntie.”

They arrive at two sliding doors.

"Welcome to the Regal Theatre!" Toxic smacks the doors open with her tail.

Lilith enters. "Wow!"

The seats are all facing the massive screen in the back and there are tables in front of them.

"Movie, food!" Toxic hops in one of the chairs and presses a button on the arm. "And a massage!"

"This place is amazing!" Lilith scoots next to Toxic. "You're amazing."

Toxic lowers her head. "I'm not. I can't protect you. I'm just a snake with sharp scales and toxins. I'd die if I fought someone strong."

Lilith taps Toxic's head. "You're so nice to me, even though we just met."

"Nah! I'm just trying to catch up on lost time." Toxic nuzzles her niece's arm. "Time is precious. With the way things are, we don't know who will be gone the next day. My brother…he was captured. I don't even know if he's alive."

"No way would he die when he has such a cute little sister waiting for him." Lilith tickles Toxic, but the snake Exp is unaffected.

"Thanks. But it's been five years. It's hard to have hope for that long."

"Well, I've been in love with someone since as long as I can remember. And still no luck."

"Wait, so it's not Deceivant?"

"Oh! Movie! Umm, let's pick a movie."

Toxic slides to the front and lifts the remote. "Every movie throughout time is in this database. Okay, not every film, but over a million!"

"That's…a lot of choices."

"Well then let's start with genre. What do you like?"

"Something lighthearted, animated…umm…a feel-good movie."

"A family film!"

"Yeah!"

"I love family films!"

"Me too!"

"Me three!" exclaims Deceivant, bringing in a cart of food.

"Daddy!" Toxic rushes up and snuggles his leg.

"Hey there, my sweet serpent. Now, who wants candy?" he asks, pulling lollipops out from his sleeves.

"Umm, I only eat at school to keep up appearances. Daddy says eating is wasteful."

"It's also fun!" He pops a loli in her mouth.

Lilith melts with joy. "Sooo tasty!"

"You want one?" asks Deceivant, offering to Toxic.

"Nah." The snake climbs up to Lilith's shoulder. "We can share." She licks the candy.

Deceivant smiles. "So, what are we watching?"

Lilith scratches her head. "Oh, we haven't decided yet."

"Well then I'll get you some pasta," he says, searching the cart.

"Pasta! Like with Vegan meatballs?" asks Lilith with wide eyes.

"Thank goodness my son raised a lil' Vegan." Deceivant looks fondly at his granddaughter.

"I'm not a very good Vegan. I love the taste of meat…of Vegan meat, but still."

"Ha! Come on. We're not going to judge for liking a flavor. I'll make Vegan bacon, steak whatever. Sweetie pie, all that matters is that you aren't hurting anyone. Vegan meat is all plants."

"Yeah…thanks."

"Your dinner, madame," says Deceivant, giving her a plate of noodles with veggie balls.

After the movie the three of them are chatting and laughing together.

"…the whole time she glared at me with puffy cheeks." Deceivant puffs out his cheeks and Toxic pokes them.

"Oh wow! Hope sounds super adorable!" exclaims Lilith.

The room suddenly shakes. Metal plates come down along the doors.

The speakers blare. "You lied to me. And now you mock me. Thought I wouldn't notice your family bonding. Even after all these years you still resent me for what happened to those children. Since you love Lilith so much, you can stay locked in with her." Hope shuts off the speaker.

"Umm, what just happened?" asks Lilith.

"We're locked in," says Deceivant.

"Sleepover!" cheers Toxic, launching into a hug with Lilith.

"She's testing me. We have to find a way out of here. I have to prove how much I want to see her." Deceivant looks intently at Toxic.

"Forget about her." She nuzzles Deceivant. "You have two cuties who wanna spend the whole night with you."

Deceivant grabs Toxic's tail. "Please. She's hurting. You can go through the vents. Tell someone that we're locked in here."

Toxic salutes and rushes off.

Lilith slurps her soda and licks her lips. "So, it's just us now." She pulls up her shirt. "Wanna touch my tummy?"

Deceivant's eyes shimmer and beam. "Absolutely!" He bends her over on his lap and tickles her little tum-tum.

Lilith moans and wiggles. She grabs Deceivant's arm. "Grope me! Squeeze hard!"

Deceivant's eyes light up with bliss. He pinches her tummy and her sides.

"My boobies! Grope my boobies!" Demands Lilith, crying from anticipation while holding her erection down.

Deceivant turns away in tears. "You're my grandchild. I…don't feel comfortable."

"I need it!" She pulls him into a kiss and sucks on his tongue.

Deceivant pulls her off and stands up. "Lilith, you need to stop. You're acting strange. Maybe the juice was spiked or something."

"Pin me down now!" She chases after him, driven by a crazed lust.

"Get up!" yells Bob, splashing Shinx with his own puddle of blood.

"I…can't move," says Shinx weakly, covered in wounds.

"Wonderful! Then now the real test begins." He lifts up Shinx and dangles him over the cliff. "Awaken your power or become a meaningless mess of flesh and regret."

"Still talking? Drop me already." Shinx grins with a bloody smile.

"You will be the most courageous splat ever to exist!" Bob releases his grandson to certain doom. He listens intently but there's no sound. Grandpa Bob looks over the cliffside. "How interesting."

Lilith is in a jacket and shivering. She looks up at Deceivant nervously.

"Are you feeling better now?" he asks.

She nods.

"What happened?"

"Can you please leave?" She cries in her hands.

Toxic arrives. "What did you do to her!?"

Lilith stands up. "He didn't do anything. Nothing happened. I'm okay." She stumbles as she tries to sit and falls over.

Deceivant turns his gaze to Toxic. "She needs someone to care for her. Someone other than me."

Ada appears and brings Lilith some tea.

Lilith looks up at Deceivant. "Just…stay away from me. Please. I'm so sorry."

Ada escorts Deceivant out of the meditation room. They walk down the hall. "Are you alright, honey?" she asks, gripping his hand tightly.

"Me, I'm fine. I'm worried about her. I think I broke her heart. If she hates me–"

Ada pokes his tummy and smiles. "Don't be silly. I'm sure she loves her grandpa. I see you and Toxic getting along." She leans in and kisses his cheek. "You kept your promise to rescue her."

Deceivant shakes his head. "The promise had nothing to do with it. I just finally realized that she's my adorable daughter. I'm not going to abandon my responsibilities to her."

Ada holds his hand tenderly. "That's the man my capsule purrs for." She giggles and kisses his lips.

Deceivant returns the kiss. "So, love muffin, how is Hope doing?"

"Oh." Ada looks down.

Deceivant grabs her shoulders. "She hates me too, doesn't she?"

"She's taken every pillow in the room and made a fort. Nobody is allowed in her futon fortress."

"Oh, geez it's that bad. I have to make this right."

"Are you sure that's a good idea?"

"Every second I don't, she suffers." He rushes down the hall and enters Hope's room.

Deceivant squints as the jeweled chandelier shines in his eyes. The room sparkles and shimmers. He walks behind the Queen's royal bed to see a seven-foot tall pillow castle.

"Breach my walls and your life is forfeit! I don't care who you are!" Hope yells from inside.

Deceivant kicks a single pillow, causing the whole cushy castle to topple down. He pulls his daughter out from under a heavy pillow. "I already gave my life to you."

"Why…why were you with her instead of me? Is it the glasses or something else? What does she have that I don't? Wait! Don't say it. It's her personality. I've become a sour grape, haven't I?"

Deceivant plops a grape in her mouth. "You'll always be my favorite. You know that, don't you?"

"There's only so much time in a day. Toxic and now Lilith. That means you'll have less time to be with me. And if Kawai was alive…would you even care about me?"

Deceivant pulls her into a hug.

Hope clenches him and sobs into his shoulder. "I'm a coward."

"You're brave and wise."

"Shut up!" Hope slaps him. "Of course I'm upset about you lying to me about promising to never make a little girl again, but that's not what this is about. I used that as an excuse to run away."

"What are you afraid of?"

"Losing more of my people. We've already lost so many. There's only a handful of us left. I don't have the strength to fight Bob. And Wringer…I put him in the prison. My hold over his mind broke. I'm useless. I'm going to end up with nobody. I don't ever want to lose you." Hope hugs him and sobs into her father's chest. "Kaity is our only chance at stopping Bob. She isn't ready. She won't magically become ready. We're going to lose and everything will be my fault."

Deceivant turns her over on his knee and unzips her blouse.

"Unhand me, you wretch!" yells Hope, flailing about.

"You need a bath, my little angel. A nice relaxing bath to clear your mind."

Hope puffs out her cheeks and glares at him. "I can bathe myself."

"No you can't. You always get ticklish so you can't scrub yourself." He picks her up and brings her to the massive bathroom with the indoor hot spring. "And hey, if you're really worried about missing out on father daughter bonding time, then join us!"

"I won't be anywhere near that worthless serpent!"

Deceivant tosses Hope in the bath.

"What in my glorious name do you think you're doing?"

"How long before Toxic dies? Do you really want her to never have felt sisterly love from you?"

"I honestly don't care." Hope crosses her arms.

"Then you can bathe yourself." Deceivant starts to walk off.

A rubber ducky hits the back of his head.

"I'll try! Fine! Just don't leave me alone. I'm scared when I'm alone." Hope reaches for the ducky.

Deceivant strips down and hands her the ducky. "One is never alone with a rubber duck." He pokes her cheek with the duck's bill as he makes it squeak.

Chapter 186: Lum's Decree

Tcetorp leads a line of prisoners out of Elysium. Fate walks at her side.

Tcetorp whispers to Etaf as they walk out. "I'm not so sure if I'm making the right choice. We need Mawali now more than ever."

"You don't trust the new Lum, do you?" asks Etaf.

"I don't know why she was chosen. She's so small and childish. We're lucky Sel's forces retreated."

"Yes, and I'll inform you as soon as I learn when next they will strike."

"Confiding in me that you're a spy for Lum was a great risk. Thank you for trusting me, Etaf."

"Trust is what will keep Lum alive in these trying times."

Tcetorp's eyes widen. "A demon lord is closing in on the Great Goddess!"

"Keep formation. I'll handle it," says Etaf, summoning her sword.

The Captain of Carnage rushes to Lum.

Lum raises her hand to signal Etaf to stop. "Hiya friend!" She hugs the armored ferret.

"Umm hiya. We need your help. Image was killed and we don't know where she is. Can you send some angels to track her down?"

Lum taps her cheek. "Oh! You!" She points to Etaf. "Go do what he said."

Etaf sighs and bows. "As you command."

BoneSaw pops out from its hiding spot and salutes Lum. It then does a bunch of gestures with its saws.

"What my metal brother is trying to say is that Lord Sel is on Earth. We will need everyone should he attack."

Lum nods. She points to Efil.

Efil approaches and smiles. "Yes, my goddess."

"I gotta go help on Earth. Come get me if you need me."

Efil crouches and holds her hands. "I think you freeing these people…giving them a choice to become Mawali is a noble act. I'm starting to see why Lum chose you, after all. I'll get you if you're needed. But time flows differently here, so you should have plenty of time on Earth."

Stabby pats Efil. "Good goddess. You're in charge while I'm away."

"I…I am?" Efil blushes.

"Mhhmm." Lum creates a portal to Earth.

Opti lifts up Muffins. "Should any of us stay to defend this place?"

Stabby shakes her head. "Gotta help our friends. Must pwotect Kaity!"

Efil looks away in tears. "Why does she believe in me?" she mutters to herself.

Stabby, Opti, Muffins, BoneSaw, the Captain of Carnage and D.S. all enter the portal.

After arriving at the docks, Lilith climbs off the boat. Her hair now has a purple clip to keep it in place.

"Thanks for the ride!"

Ada pats her head. "You don't have to thank me every time. It's a joy to bring you to college orientation."

"Yeah. I'm just gonna keep focusing on my studies and not worry about friends."

Ada leans down and kisses her forehead. "You do whatever you want, sweetie."

Lilith turns to Ada. "Thanks Mom!" She blushes deeply. "Sorry. I just…I'm sorry."

Ada lifts up Lilith into a big warm hug and spins around with her.

Lilith smiles at her with teary eyes. "So, it's okay…to call you mom?"

"Absolutely wonderful. dear." Ada nuzzles her little one.

They enter the castle and are greeted by Hope.

"I called Devlin up. Still searching for his son with Demonica. Lilith, go get Kitty for breakfast."

Lilith nods and exits the castle and follows the path to the training grounds.

Riufen and Kaity are engaged in combat.

Kaity coats her plasma claws in Sel energy and drags them across the ground. The dark energy disperses and circles Riufen before shifting into spikes and piercing him.

Riufen coats a single finger in Absence energy and erases the spikes, breaking free.

Kaity puts her hands together, activating seeds she had buried. They grow into trees and catch the samurai.

The new Sellum runs up the trees and places her Sel-coated claws to Riufen's throat.

"Hmm, still no Absence," he says, shaking his head.

Atlas approaches them. "Sel energy takes rage and violent emotions to conjure up. Lum takes loving and benevolent emotions to manifest. Absence can only be utilized by a calm mind."

"I tried." Kaity hops off the tree. "I'll keep trying."

Lilith rushes behind Kaity and gropes her breasts from behind. "Got ya! That was for yesterday." She sticks out her tongue and giggles.

Kaity tickles Lilith. "Since when did you get so good at sneaking around? You little ninja."

Stabby suddenly joins in the tickling.

"Stop!" giggles Lilith, wiggling about on the grass.

Kaity looks up and her eyes widen. She pounces on Stabby, snuggling her. "You're back!"

Stabby smiles.

Lilith looks at the new girl. "Nice to meet you. I'm Lilith."

"Stabby," says the girl with a sharp grin.

"Are the others with you?" asks Kaity.

Opti waves at her, holding Muffins. "We sure are!"

D.S. is behind him, keeping his distance from BoneSaw. "Do you guys still want me?"

Kaity hops up and approaches him. "Of course we do!" She turns to BoneSaw. "You owe him an apology."

BoneSaw shakes its frame.

"Wait…did you hear that?" Kaity turns to Opti.

"Hear what?"

Kaity grabs Muffins. "You spoke too! Am I the only one hearing that?"

Atlas chuckles. "Sellum can understand all beings. You're becoming more connected with your abilities."

Kaity beams. "Muffins you have the cutest voice ever! No, thank you." She rubs the bunny's chin.

Nibbles comes out from the bushes and Muffins approaches him with a snuggle.

"I wanna hear too!" whines Opti.

Kaity crouches to BoneSaw. "So, why did you kill D.S.? Were you trying to end the fighting?" She gulps.

D.S. steps up. "What did the robot say?"

"He killed you because you got in the way of the Viper Squad." Kaity turns to D.S. "I'm so sorry."

"Phew. So it was just a misunderstanding. Kanasta is my brother! I was trying to help him!" exclaims D.S. with a big smile.

BoneSaw drives off.

Hope, being carried by Ada, approaches the group. "Well, at least I know why you were late for breakfast."

Opti rushes to her. "Did you make that statue of me? It's so sweet!"

"It was my idea, but manual labor is beneath me," she raises her head.

Ada chimes in. "Deceivant made them! Hope had to approve the designs and quotes."

"Why doesn't Stabby have a memorial statue?"

"Why waste my time with filth?" asks Hope, staring daggers at the new Lum. She exhales sharply. "Though considering her new abilities, we might need her after all." The Queen of the Exps turns to Sellum. "Kitty, bring Whirlwind to the breakfast table. She's probably jogging at this time."

"Hey, Hope!" Kaity lifts her up and nuzzles her chest.

"What are you doing?" asks Hope, pushing the girl's head away.

"I like your boobies much more without the pads."

Hope blushes and crosses her arms. "I only wore those to spite Deceivant. Now, get a move on!"

Kaity salutes and walks off into the thick forest. "June, you there?"

A figure drops onto Kaity's shoulders and then flings her to the ground. "You gotta be more aware of your surroundings."

"I wasn't expecting to get ambushed." Kaity spanks June's booty.

"Hey! Keep it PG." She slugs Kaity.

"You coming to breakfast."

"Yeah, but umm, there's something I have to tell you. We're friends, right? And you know what it's like to…well…like girls."

Kaity looks frightened and steps back.

"You okay, Kit Kat?"

"I'm not ready for a relationship. I don't want one ever again."

June takes off her mask and blushes. "That's not what I meant. I just meant you get me. Whirlwind, the beautiful super heroine, she is married to her job. But me, June, I like girls." She puts on her hat and turns away.

Kaity smiles and flicks her friend's hat. "No need to be so shy about it."

"I'm no good at flirting though. Can you please help me?"

"Just pounce her and cop a feel. That's my strategy." Kaity grins.

"Yeah, that's a bit too direct. She's really sensitive and I just don't want to hurt her."

Kaity puts her hand over June's mouth. "Did you hear that?"

June puts on her mask. "Who goes there?" she asks in a heroic girly voice.

The leaves die as they flow through the wind. The grass crinkles and goes brown as the figure steps forward.

"I am carrying out Lum's decree by putting an end to your life." Efil points her time sword at Kaity.

Kaity turns to June. "She can't kill me. Go make sure Stabby is safe."

June shakes her head and turns to Efil. "I was in the middle of a really important conversation. Can you just wait a moment before you fight her?"

"You have ten seconds," says Efil, pooling her aura into a second sword.

June pulls Kaity aside. "It's Lilith. I'm in love with Lilith! Can you help me find a good way to let her know how I feel?"

Kaity smiles. "Yeah, sure thing. I'll be just a little late for breakfast. Get me a plate!"

June grins and rushes off.

"I will make your end swift," says Efil, calming her hands.

"Lum wanted to die!" Kaity yells as Efil approaches.

Her eyes widen before she swipes her blade at me.

Kaity dodges frantically and whip out my side arm. After Kaity unloads all her bullets into the Goddess' legs, she infuses it with Sel energy and keep up the assault.

Efil pours Lum energy into her legs, giving Kaity time to place plasma claws to her throat.

Efil pierces Kaity's chest with time blades, but it doesn't do any damage.

Chains pull Efil back and assault her from behind.

"Get out of here!" Kaity yells to Wringer.

The chains rust upon hitting the goddess' back. She approaches Wringer.

Kaity fires Sel blasts at the goddess but she creates a shield.

Efil buries the one who killed her goddess under a battalion of vines.

Wringer wraps his chains around Efil in an instant.

"Rust," says Efil calmly.

The chains around her body became wrought with age.

He shoots his chains into the ground. They emerge, entrapping Efil in a chain cage.

"I cannot lose to you. I must avenge my God and you are in my way," says Efil as she placed her hands on the chains.

They instantly rust.

Efil places her hand on Wringer. "If I am to pass judgment on Kaity, I must be able to kill. You will not get in my path. TIME LAPSE."

The Wringer's body fades into dust.

Efil blew the remains away. "Anyone who stands in my path shall be dust."

Kaity cleaves through the vines and sees her comrade's end.

Efil turn to Kaity, creating vines to ensnare her legs.

The new Sellum forms an arm of Sel energy that grabs Efil and brings her up to her.

"Are you really going to kill her daughter without hearing her out first? You killed my comrade. Is that who you are now?" asks Kaity with an intense look.

Efil, shaking with misery, looks up at Kaity and sobs. "Why did you do it?"

Kaity shivers and tries to speak.

Efil dispels her swords. "I don't know what to do."

Kaity holds her tightly. "I don't either."

Chapter 187: Dark Prophecy

Bob shakes Shinx to his senses.

"My apologies, Father. I drifted off there."

"You slept for a day and a half, so get up!" He pulls Shinx to his feet.

"What is the next step of my training?"

"You're done for now."

"Then you're finally going to tell me what your request is." Shinx smiles.

"Indeed, it is time. I need your help to get Demonica a new husband."

"That's not specific. What exactly do you want? I won't even consider making a promise to a dark god until I know all the details."

"Straight to the point, I see."

"Two simple questions. What do you want me to do and what's in it for me?"

"Fair enough. To put things bluntly. I want you to assist me in killing Devlin. Is that specific enough?"

"And what do I get in return?"

"Well, your training has merely begun. I can make you so much stronger! You will have the power to defend your mother and strike down your father."

"There's something you're not telling me. Why would a dark god need my help to kill an Exp? I refuse to help you," says Shinx, crossing his arms.

"Well then, let's test just how strong you've become. Let's see if you can break free of my telekinesis. It only works on the weak-willed."

Shinx pulls Bob up to him with some invisible force and punches. "I'm done training with you. Bring me back to Mommy!"

"So strong now…are you?" Bob summons up the Atma Blade and stabs Shinx.

The blade swirls as it sips the child's soul.

"Wait, why didn't my powers work? What did you do to me?" the boy asks as he writhes around.

"I'm just showing you how weak you still are. The choice is yours though. Come back to me when you want the power to kill a god."

"Devlin isn't a god!"

"Oh, so she's been keeping secrets from you too." Bob turns to Gimpy. "Send him to the others and bring Demonica to me!"

Gimpy groans and vanishes with Shinx.

"Are we going to change the plan, Bob?" asks Sel.

"Oh no, I foresaw this obstacle and our initial plan will be enough to get rid of it," says Bob, talking to his other self.

"Is that why you allowed that boy to refuse us?"

"He's a clever one and so willful! He will make a perfect apprentice and unlike Devlin, we don't even have to kill him later," says Bob with a smile.

"He may be a great ally, but that means he will be a worthy enemy. Once he has true power, he may turn against us."

"His weakness is easy to exploit. Shinx will serve us. Now, shall we begin?"

"The pieces are in place?"

"Every last one." Bob smiles.

"Then let operation Dark Prophecy begin." Sel smiles.

Demonica and Devlin are at the canyon, searching for Bob.

The demoness rolls her eyes. "I told you, Bob will let me know when he's done training Shinx."

"That's not good enough for me. We have to find him now! If you had just brought me to him first then he'd be safe right now!" yells Devlin.

Demonica grabs Devlin and sobs. "I just wanted some happy memories with you."

"A whole week before you'd tell me where Bob went. Now he's gone. Bring me to Lilith."

Demonica turns to Gimpy. "Go on, send him away."

Devlin arrives at the Queendom. "Please let her be safe." He rushes inside the castle. "Lilith, are you in here?"

Opti notices Devlin and rushes into a warm hug. "You're back!"

"Same to you, my friend. Where is Lilith?"

"She's in her room. I'll lead the way."

Whirlwind suddenly rushes into the building.

"Everything fine and dandy?" asks Opti.

"A Lum goddess is attacking Kaity," says Whirlwind.

The speakers suddenly blare. Hope clears her throat. "Gladius is trying to sneak in from the back entrance. I want a small group to engage and the rest to stay on guard. Those who are not particularly adept at fighting need to accompany me to the safe house."

The speakers throughout the Queendom send a message. “All citizens are to stay indoors. This is not a drill. Remain calm. I repeat this is not a drill.”

Devlin grimaces. “Bob’s already begun his assault. Lead me to Lilith and then join the others in the safe house.”

Muffins looks up at Opti.

Opti shakes his head. “Oh no, you’re a preggy bun now. You gotta keep those baby buns safe.”

Muffins nods and hops off.

Opti leads Devlin out of the castle to Lilith’s room. “Apparently this was Image’s place, but now Lilith stays here. I just got here this afternoon, but Ada gave me the grand tour so I know a whole lot.”

When they arrive at the separate building, Devlin swings open the doors. The library spans twelve stories and has a spiral staircase at each corner. “Start from the top! I’ll search the bottom for her.”

Atlas enters the bathhouse.

Lilith covers up. “Where were you? I’m supposed to stay here until things calm down, right?”

Atlas tosses her clothes to her. “There’s an intruder. We have to move to the safe house.”

Kaity rushes in. “You deal with the intruder; I’ll bring her there.”

Atlas nods.

“Wait, where is the safe house?”

“Outside near the fountain there is a hidden door.” Atlas rushes out the back door.

Kaity grabs Lilith’s hand and rushes off.

Kaity takes Lilith to the large fountain and feels around for the hidden door. She snaps her fingers and Edirp appears.

“What the? Where am I?” asks the Sin of Pride. She glares at Kaity. “What do you want?”

“The enemy is hiding underneath here. Bury them.” Kaity’s body instantly transforms into Gimpy.

Edirp’s eyes widen. “Sure thing!”

The fountain and everything around it start sinking.

Lilith throws a flash bomb to the ground and runs off. “Save me!” she yells into her phone.

Devlin, Opti and Lilith are all in the library together.

Devlin opens the book Lilith hands him. "So, this is really it?"

The book's title is 'Exps are so Cool!" and has a picture of a chibi Kawai on the cover.

"Yeah. I was thinking maybe I could help write the next one," says Lilith, playing with her hair.

"Oooh! I wanna help too!" cheers Opti.

Devlin looks at Lilith. "I've been trying to shelter you for so long. I'm sorry."

Lilith giggles and kisses his lips. "It's okay, Daddy."

Devlin's eyes widen. "So, what do you think of the book?"

"Oh, I uhm, haven't read it yet."

"You haven't read your favorite book?" asks Devlin as his wires slowly sneak along the ground.

"Oh, I mean not this copy! Yeah, of course." She flips through it nervously.

"You're not charming enough to be my daughter." Devlin constricts the fake.

Lilith turns into goop and then looks up at him. "I wish I had a Daddy."

"Opti, go find her! I'll take care of Yvne." Devlin drops two bookshelves on the blob.

The bookshelves are pushed aside as Yvne expands. "You wouldn't hurt your darling Kaity, right?" she asks, taking the cat-girl's form.

Devlin stabs wires into the fake's neck and rips off her head. He then rushes for the door.

Yvne whisks him off his feet with her fan. "You're not allowed to leave!"

Gladius feasts on the remains of one of the human residents he had caught. He gazes up when his adversaries arrive.

"No baddies allowed!" yells D.S., pointing his scissors at the big reptile.

Atlas steps in front of him. "Careful, a single slash means death."

Pesi notices Kaity and Efil talking to each other in the forest. "Well, well, looks like the Goddess went traitor! You were supposed to kill her!"

Efil stands up. "Kaity is Lum's legacy. I understand that now. I only stayed with Sel so I could discover his plot. He compartmentalizes information which means we're both in the dark."

"Wait." Kaity steps in front of Efil. "You have a war to stop in Lum, right?"

"The war is at a standstill at the moment."

"And for how long? Mobilize the angels. I can handle Pesi."

Efil nods and creates a Lum portal.

Gimpy teleports after Lilith as Stabby creates light fog to cloud the area.

"Mmrph!" The gimp summons up a sword and slashes the air to displace the fog.

Riufen hops off the balcony and lands. "To think you were a swordsman all along." He points his spinal cord at his foe. "Let us fight."

Stabby and Lilith emerge from the mist cloud.

The new Lum forms a white portal. "Gotta go."

"Yes you do!" Bob pops out and tosses her into the portal before blasting it with a dark beam. "Now, what to do with you?" He summons up the Atma Blade.

"Stay away from her!" Demonica slices Bob to bits with her crimson claws. She then sprouts wings and grabs Lilith.

"You saved me?" asks Lilith, looking up at Demonica.

"I know what Bob is planning. We have to tell Devlin." She swoops down toward the library.

Lilith hugs Demonica and cries. "You saved me! I was so scared!"

"I had hoped Pathos would have killed Bob, so we could all live in peace. Kaity isn't the only destined Sellum. D-Devlin is too. The dark prophecy can't be avoided. We're going to have to learn to get along." She kisses her daughter's forehead.

Chapter 188: Dark Gods

Pesi blasts Efil before she can enter the portal. "You can't ignore the murderous killer grip of death itself!"

Efil heals herself and then sends light arrows at the dark god. The goddess' arrows turn into flames that scorch Pesi's face.

"You're just giving more burning fuel to my flaming fire!" Pesi is lifted off the ground by his powerful aura.

Kaity turns to Efil. "Will Sel energy work?"

"Only Absence can cleave through that aura." Efil creates trees around her to conceal her from Pesi's rapid assault.

The dark god readies a powerful beam with one hand while spraying hatred bullets with the other! "Ending lives is the greatest thrill! And you're the Goddess of Life. If I kill you and take your powers, then I'll make sure all living things slowly decay until they die! I'll make the process as slow as possible! A death that lasts centuries! Can you imagine!?" He fires the massive beam. It bursts through the trees and explodes a building in the distance.

Efil flies behind him. "That's called aging. It's all part of being alive. Your hatred has blinded you to simple truths."

Kaity closes her eyes to focus enough to summon up Absence energy.

A vine pulls her out of the way of a red blast.

Sellum looks up at Efil. "It's fine. I can't die from him."

"You're not immune to pain. I won't let this demon harm you," says Efil, dodging another massive beam. She was then blasted by a black aura. It clung to her but didn't devour her like Sel energy.

Pesi's fist pulses before he opens his black palm.

"PESSIMISM CORRUPTION"

The aura crawls into her mind and plagues her thoughts.

Kaity flinches as she hears her friend screaming. She opens her eyes. "Leave her alone!" She fires a Sel blast at Pesi.

The God of Hate grabs the energy and then smashes it into Kaity.

Efil holds herself in tears. "It's pointless. She's gone. My goddess is dead and I'm not strong enough to protect her daughter."

Gladius is wrapped in the Chaos Chain and is being zapped by Whirlwind.

The heroine scratches her head. "Guys, I don't think WW is gonna cut it anymore. Any chance you have an idea for a cool name?"

D.S. waves his hands excitedly. “Woosh! Zappy! Disastra! Calamitous! ThunderQuake! Destructia!”

“I’m a hero, bro. What’s with the villain names?” she asks with a chuckle.

Gladius glares at her while he’s being electrocuted. “How about lunch?”

D.S. bounces and waves his hands. “Oh, Green Girl! Natura! Uhm Earthia!”

“Natura is so pretty!”

“Okay, I’m Natura now! Gonna have a big comic for my new name.”

D.S. beams at her. “Can I be in it?”

“Sure thing, kid,” she grins.

Gladius screams and then buries himself.

“Crocodastardly tries to flee from the hero, but her new powers are in full force!” exclaims Natura as she floods the area where Gladius buried himself.

D.S. suddenly screams.

Gladius’ teeth burst out of the ground and bite down on him.

D.S. stabs the violent animal with his scissors. “Bad reptile! No biting!”

Atlas brings down the Agony Axe on Gladius, but the weapon is repelled by the crocodile’s now bladed tail.

Gladius digs as he chews D.S.

Natura jumps on the croc and tries to pry his teeth open. “Release that child!”

“You truly are an ancient god, aren’t you?” asks Atlas.

Gladius spits out D.S. and raises his snout proudly. “Indeed I am!”

Natura sends a gust of wind beneath the gator, launching him into the air. “Belly is exposed! Let’s end this! Our heroine sends Arsenal up with a valiant gust.”

Atlas summons up the Searing Sword and then plunges the blade into the crocodile.

Natura juggles a lighting ball in her hand. She hops through the air, and then tosses it on the sword, frying the rowdy reptile.

Gladius collapses, his fully red eyes vacant. “I’m unkillable. This wouldn’t be possible before. Let’s try. **REVERSE SWORD STYLE**.”

Natura and Atlas check D.S.’s wounds as Gladius transforms.

Gladius laughs maniacally as his mouth is pulled back. His bones break as his body is forcibly turned inside out. The flesh inside was now fully exposed.

Natura smacks her face with her palm. “Worst transformation ever. You’re all soft inside. Seriously dude, what were you thinking?” she asks, losing her heroic accent.

Gladius buries into the ground.

Natura sighs. “Different form, same strategy. Arsenal, get Destuctur…Schoolboy, get Schoolboy out of here. I can keep Knife Croc busy. Natura says, beaming with confidence!”

Fleshy spikes shoot out from the ground and slice Atlas.

The ex-god rides one of the spikes to get above his opponent and then fires Appalling Arrows at the source of the attack. He sends the Chaos Chain into the ground. “Found him.” Atlas summons the Misery Mace, attaches it to the Chaos Chain and sends it smashing through the ground.

The area caves into a pit. Gladius holds the Misery Mace between multiple fleshy spikes.

More elastic spikes come out from the inverted reptile and chase after Atlas.

The ex-god counters with the Grief Gauntlets. “Damn. I’m still tired from all that training with Kaity. I shouldn’t have summoned Unity.”

Gladius attaches multiple spikes to the ground before he’s blasted into the air by a horizontal tornado.

Natura turns to Atlas and grins. “He’s one with the clouds now.”

Once Gladius’ spines stretch to their limit, he skyrockets downwards, guided by the recoil of his spikes.

“Retreat!” yells Atlas, firing Appalling Arrows to offset the trajectory.

Natura grabs D.S. and speeds into the right wing of the fortress, which was still undergoing construction.

Ada materializes in front of Atlas. “Edirp buried the others. I was the only one able to escape. They’re by the fountain. Please save them.”

Atlas nods and rushes off.

Ada leaps into the air and focuses on the attacker speeding toward her. “My loving husband has given me the strength to fight if I have to! DE-CONSTRUCT!”

Gladius’ body falls apart like data and vanishes completely before he can hit the talking blueberry. When he rematerializes, he crashes against the ground and creates a crater.

Ada looks back in horror as he immediately shot backwards, slamming right into her.

Her body was pierced with holes all over.

They tear through the sky until reaching the extent of the stretch.

"Once I land, you'll burst like a watermelon!"

D.S. smashes through the window of the castle and rushes to the rubbery spines. He tries to cut them with Snippy 2, but they are way too sharp. "I'm sorry, Mom!" D.S. ran out of the way as Gladius began his descent.

Gladius crashes into the ground, creating a cloud of smoke.

Once the dust cleared, the only trace of Ada was the blood on his spikes.

"What? She wasn't an illusion! I had the real target!" he yells.

Ada reappears just above him. "That's right! Don't worry. It's not your fault. I just deconstructed myself."

"Fine! I'll just destroy the castle and scatter your friends!" Gladius shoots back into the sky.

"Oh! I know!" Ada goes to the spikes implanted in the ground and deconstructs them one by one.

She waves at Gladius as he vanishes over the horizon.

Inside the safe house, the remaining Freedom Forcers wait impatiently.

Deceivant paces around in the cramped metal box of a room. "I should be out there protecting Ada."

Hope flicks a grape at him. "You're were you belong. Mother can handle herself."

Regna suddenly appears. "Time to die!" she yells firing her fingers into Hope.

The Captain swoops by and slices her arm as BoneSaw speeds along the ground to cut her legs.

Muffins rushes to Hope and nuzzles the explosives in the queen's legs into oblivion.

Toxic stands in front of Hope, ready to deflect any attack.

Durga showers the demon goddess with her mist.

"That won't work on me!" yells Regna, firing her head off at the Exp.

The head freezes in place and Regna's body shivers. "C-C-Cat."

Napkin stands on Durga's shoulder and meows at Regna, trapping the goddess in a mental cage of fear.

The moment the samurai knocks his opponent's sword aside, the bound swordsman vanishes.

Bob looks over while swinging Stabby around with spectral tentacles. "You're allowed to fight back. You can't kill him anyways. He's bound to Gladius. Just beat him into submission and we'll take him with us!"

"Fight me! Why won't you fight me?" yells Stabby, sending a barrage of daggers at Sel.

The Dark One exhales a smoke cloud that eats the blades. "Because I was cornered into making a promise with your Daddy. Had I known you would have been chosen Lum, I'd not have made that mistake." He jerks her to the right, causing her Lum blast to misfire.

"But you hate Daddy! Don't undewestimate me!"

"Nobody is undewestimating anyone! If I didn't keep my promises, then my betrayal would be meaningless. Promises are the core of trust. Without trust, betrayal loses its sting." He forms another Sel portal but Stabby dispels it with Lum energy.

"Well done! You've got quite the quick draw! If only you were at my side. You did an excellent job keeping those demon lords organized. You'd make an exceptional ally!"

Stabby looks at the Bad Ball with teary eyes. "Why do you hate Daddy?"

"Let's stop talking about him. Oh, I know what to do!" Bob blasts away her Lum beam and then pulls her to the side to dodge the blast. He then reels her into a hug. "I can be your new daddy!"

"You killed Daddy!" yells Stabby, slicing him in a mad rage.

"Precisely. He basically killed Zenero and became your father. So, since I killed him, call me Daddy!"

Stabby cries and buries her face under her hands.

"Take some time off to think about it." He flings her into a Sel portal. "Hopefully she's too weak to teleport back." He turns to Gimpy. "Need any help?"

Gimpy flings Sel energy at Riufen, corrupting the surrounding foliage to transform and attack the samurai.

"Is this some twisted form of my Life Artifact?" asks Riufen, slicing the possessed plants.

Gimpy teleports above the samurai and blasts him with black energy.

Riufen's cleaves through the aura and cleaves the Gimp in two.

The two halves of the dark slave teleport around, slicing the samurai from all angles.

Bob snickers. “You’re holding back, Riufen. That may not be wise when your Devlin-sama is in danger.”

Riufen’s eyes widen. He coats his spine in Absence energy and slices through the gimp’s weapon.

The gimp comes back together and creates another sword.

Bob suddenly falls to the ground. “What happened? It can’t be!” he speeds off with terror in his pupil and then stops.

Chapter 189: Necessary Sacrifices

Previously: Demonica went to the library with Lilith.

Lilith is brought into the library by her mother. "Why is Devlin fighting Kaity?"

"Sister, help me," says Yvne, appearing as Kaity while being overwhelmed by Devlin's wires.

"Leave or I'll end you," says Demonica with a deathly glare.

Yvne collapses into a puddle and runs off.

Devlin runs past Demonica and picks up Lilith. "Thank goodness you're safe."

"Why are there so many fake Kaitys?" asks Lilith in tears, gripping him tightly.

"Did you find Shinx?" asks Demonica.

"I don't know where he is. Bob probably has him captive. I hope you realize this is your fault."

Demonica lowers her head. "Yes…it is. Devlin, I need to talk to you about something."

"Is it about Shinx?"

She shakes her head.

"Then it can wait."

"It's about Lilith." Demonica's eyes water up.

"What about her?" asks Devlin, holding his daughter tightly.

"She's destined to kill Bob."

"What?"

"I don't believe it either, but Bob does. She's in danger."

"Don't worry. I'll protect you from that lunatic," says Devlin, petting Lilith lovingly.

Lilith looks over at Demonica. "I don't like fighting. I think Bob is lying to you about the whole thing."

Demonica paces around nervously. "Your powers haven't awakened. Maybe when they do, it will make more sense."

"Are you seriously buying this nonsense? This is just another of Bob's schemes to get power. He must really be getting desperate to come up with something so lame. You had me worried." Devlin chuckles and smiles.

Lilith notices something in the corner and walks off.

Demonica clenches her teeth. "How can you be relieved? I've seen Sel and Lum torn apart by a prophecy. But in the end the prophecy was fulfilled. I don't want to lose Bob. He's my father."

"Lilith isn't capable of hurting anyone. Look at this destined killer," says Devlin, gesturing to Lilith letting a spider out the window to freedom. He approaches Demonica. "Okay, let's say it's true. Who cares? You wanted me to become the ruler of Sel before, didn't you? I couldn't do that with Bob alive."

Demonica holds her head and groans.

"Are you okay?"

"The only way she'll be safe is if she dies." Demonica grabs Devlin by the arms.

"Have you completely lost it?"

"Please trust me. He'll devour her soul. She won't go to Sellum. She'll become lost forever if we don't act before him."

"You're saying you have to kill her to keep her safe?"

"If Bob thinks she's dead, then he won't come after her. I'm not crazy. And I can make it painless. I'm the Goddess of Death."

"If he comes for her, then why don't you fight him? We can fight him together."

"I have the arrangements made. Efil will find her and keep her safe in Lum when she arrives."

"She's not safe until Bob is dead. He's powerful but not unbeatable. Kaity will kill him, not Lilith."

"I'll do it myself if you won't. He'll be here any moment. He's keeping Kaity busy elsewhere."

"You're insane!" yells Devlin, slapping her across the face.

"It's true about the arrangements in Lum. She'll be protected."

"Why can't Gimpy just send her then? Why should she have to die? What aren't you telling me?" Devlin shakes her.

"It's all my fault he's in danger. Devlin, it's her or Shinx. Either I kill her or Shinx's soul will be consumed. I'm not losing him!" she yells, summoning up the Death Scythe.

Lilith looks up from the book she's reading. "Why are you two arguing again? Can't we just get along?"

"Run away!" yells Devlin, coiling his wires around Demonica.

The floor shakes and book shelves fall over as the tower is torn from the ground by a giant Yvne.

"I've got you," says Devlin, pulling Lilith into his arms while pressing Demonica against the wall with his wires.

"If I close my eyes, then the scary stuff can't hurt me, right?"

"That's right, my treasure."

The building shakes and tilts, but he stays in place with his metal web.

Lilith holds on tightly. "I should be scared, but I can't be around you." She kisses his cheek.

Devlin flings bookshelves at Demonica who slices them with her fingernails.

Demonica's body turns crimson. "Nothing will stop me!" Blood erupts from her. The crimson liquid solidifies into multiple scythes that overlap, creating a spinning wall of death. "Kaity is going to die too! Accept it!"

Devlin's wires shoot out but are cut to bits.

Devlin could faintly see Demonica's smile, gleaming maliciously through the small spaces of the bloody wall.

"Is Demonica trying to hurt you?" asks Lilith, still keeping her eyes closed.

"We're going to make it through this," says Devlin, holding Lilith close to him.

A single wire sneaks through a tiny hole in the wall. It latches onto Demonica's head.

"You never loved me," says Demonica, a tear falling from her eye. The wire reels Demonica into her own wall of death. She wails in agony as she is sliced to pieces. She then cackles with glee. "You can't kill me like that." The Goddess of Death sprouts wings and flies toward them.

"Don't freak out. This is the real me!" Devlin's wires slice his skin and reveal his Exp form. He layers his wires, creating a wall to protect his daughter.

Lilith looks up at the metal creature in tears. "You look so scary…but I know it's you. Dad, she was so sweet to me just before she brought me here. I don't know why this is happening."

A puddle of blood comes out from the wall and then solidifies into the dark goddess.

Devlin's chest opens up and he pulls out Bravery.

The sword clings to his arms with its golden strands.

"If you don't stand down, I will kill you," he says, pointing the weapon at Demonica. His tail detaches and creates a wire cocoon around his daughter.

"You forgot who gave you that weapon," says Demonica.

Bravery's golden strands burst out and wrap around Devlin.

Demonica watches as her beloved struggles. "You were so foolish. I was tasked with watching over you. Your days were numbered as soon as

Pathos chose you as a destined Sellum." Htaed steps toward him as she summons up the Death Scythe.

"You never loved me," says Devlin with hateful eyes. His stomach opens up, shooting out wire grenades that are quickly liquidated by Demonica.

"Of course I do! But why cling on to someone who is destined to die? Pathos is gone. The only one who stood a chance died against Bob. He died protecting his children. Will you make the same sacrifice? Will you die for her sake?" asks Demonica, holding the Death Scythe over his head.

"Do it then! The Death Scythe only works if you strike with killing intent. If you love me, then it won't work," says Devlin with an intense glare.

"No! Nobody is killing anyone!" yells Lilith in tears, pulling at the wire wall separating her from them.

Demonica glares. "Don't pretend you care! Every night you slept on the floor rather than with me in bed. You never kissed my lips. You lie to calm Shinx down, saying that you love me." She sobs as she grips the scythe tighter.

"I'm not the one for you. But I thank you for bringing Lilith into my life," says Devlin, caressing her cheek with a wire. "Now stop this madness."

"Kaity will never love you!" yells Demonica, slashing his face with her crimson claws.

"You don't have it in you. Put the weapon down and let's all save Shinx as a family," says Devlin, shaping a hand from some wires and offering it to Demonica.

"I love you, Devlin." The demoness wipes her tears and brings the scythe down on her enemy.

The Scythe pierces his head.

"Daddy!" wails Lilith.

Devlin turns and smiles at his daughter. "Everything is okay. See?"

"I can't kill you." She walks past Devlin and places her hand on the protective mesh of wires around Lilith. It liquidates, leaving the girl defenseless.

Lilith screams and cries as she pees herself in terror.

"Don't you dare! Stop! I'll never forgive you! I'll hate you! You can't live with that!"

Demonica holds Lilith in place with bloody chains as her dark energy pulses in the scythe. “You already hate me!” She brings the Death Scythe down on her daughter.

The scythe pierces flesh.

Demonica’s eyes widen.

Her weapon is lodged in her chest, redirected by Devlin’s wires.

She falls backward with vacant eyes.

Devlin breaks free from Bravery’s hold and flings the weapon out the window. He walks to Lilith. “Are you okay?”

“Is…she…dead?” Lilith looks at Demonica’s vacant eyes with horror.

“She can’t hurt you now,” he hugs her tightly.

Lilith faints, going limp in his arms.

Shinx hops in from the window. He freezes when he sees Demonica’s lifeless body. “Mommy?” He stumbles toward her.

Devlin looks up at his son. “She was trying to kill Lilith. I’d have done the same for you. I know I look different, but it’s me, your father.”

Shinx grabs Demonica’s hand and holds it to his face. Tears erupt in an uncontrollable torrent.

Devlin approaches him in a daze. “It’s over now. You’re safe.”

“How am I safe if the killer that murdered my mommy is still alive?” asks Shinx with a crazed grin.

“I had no choice, she was going to kill Lilith,” says Devlin in tears.

“I would rather have killed that weakling myself!” wails Shinx as he tries to pull the Death Scythe out from Mommy’s body. He falls over and then grabs her face. “Mommy, please wake up. I need you! Come back, Mommy!”

Devlin put his hand on Shinx’s shoulder.

“Don’t touch me! You…killed her!” yells Shinx, lashing out at Devlin.

“I’m sorry but I had to do it,” cries Devlin.

A red dot appears on Shinx’s hand.

The Death Scythe shakes, unlodging itself from her body. Shinx catches the weapon.

“I won’t kill you alone. I have Mommy with me,” cries Shinx.

“I won’t fight you and you can’t kill me.”

Lilith is pulled from Devlin’s arm by an unseen force.

Devlin’s wires shoot out to protect her, but all converge on a meaningless dot on the ground.

Shinx holds the Death Scythe over his unconscious sister. "Fight me or she dies."

Devlin pulls in his wires. "Let her go. I won't ask again."

Shinx points to the ceiling, creating another red dot.

Devlin rushes at him so Shinx gravitates himself and Lilith up to the new roof of the inverted building.

"Let her go and I'll fight you! Just don't hurt her," says Devlin, holding out his arms to catch his daughter.

"Too late." Shinx brings down the Death Scythe on Lilith.

"No!" cries Devlin in vain.

The scythe unexpectedly swoops past her and chases after Devlin.

Noticing the dot, Devlin tears off a part of his body, having the scythe hit it instead. He then lifts up a bookshelf and hides behind it.

"You can't hide from me, murderer!" Shinx makes multiple dots on and around the book shelves and then opens his bag. He flings four grenades that each move to a different target.

Devlin rushes out from cover and throws shredded paper in the air.

Shinx creates multiple dots, but each one misses Devlin and instead hits the torn pages.

A wire suddenly rushes up Shinx's pantleg and wraps around his throat.

Shinx loses hold of his sister and Devlin rushes to catch her.

As Shinx falls, Devlin sends multiple wires to attack, but they unexpectedly veer toward Lilith.

Shinx places a dot on his wrist and another on a support beam, grabbing it. He lifts himself up while Devlin catches Lilith. "I choose where your attacks hit and how frequently they hit that target. I now control both accuracy and precision. That means not only can you not hit me, but I can make you kill your own daughter," says Shinx with eyes swirling with rage.

Devlin removes Lilith's shirt and thus the targets on her, but her bare chest is red with the dots.

"Checkmate!" Shinx swings the Death Scythe around, giving it power with his killer intent.

Devlin falls to his knees. "It's over. I give up. Please, spare Lilith." He looks at his son with a pitiful face.

"Did you give Mommy mercy when she begged you to love her? You already destroyed her heart. All you've done now is desecrate her body. I will kill Lilith in one quick, decisive blow. But not because of you!" Shinx yells at Devlin, eyes burning with hate. "I see some of

Mommy in her smile so I refuse to mutilate that!" He drops the Death Scythe.

Devlin opens up his body and puts his daughter inside. He grabs The Death Scythe as it pierces into him and tries to keep it from its target while fading in and out of life and death.

Shinx lands and watches with great wonder. "You really are invincible." He claps his hands together and then brings the scythe back to him. "Devlin, I swear upon my Mommy's soul, I will grow strong enough to kill you," says Shinx, stoic with dark resolve.

"Shinx, please…."

The lost child hops out the window.

The building is suddenly thrown through the air.

Devlin creates another web of wires, keeping Lilith steady even as the building bursts upon impact with the castle.

Books litter the ground.

He places his hands to his chest. "Shinx is lost but I will not lose you. I will never lose you," cries Devlin with resolute eyes of misery.

Chapter 190: Corruption

The collision against the castle is witnessed by all the Freedom Forcers. Gimpy notices and vanishes.

“I will not accept a draw!” yells Riufen, running off.

Kaity is fighting off Pesi when she hears the crash.

“Mission accomplished! Dumb idiot kitty cat didn’t even realize her friends were being attacked!” Pesi sticks out his tongue as he throws a ball of red energy at the cat-girl.

Kaity creates a tree in the orbs path, having it get blasted in her stead. “I knew they were being attacked, but I wasn’t just going to abandon Efil. I’m going to defeat you and make you take that energy out of her.”

“You’re God, right? You should be able to do it! But you’re a weak pathetic god! You’re letting them all down because you’re pitifully worthless!” Pesi pools his energy into a massive orb.

A figure suddenly drops from the trees and lands in front of Kaity.

Kaity looks up with shaky eyes. “N-Nina?”

Nina erotically runs her hands through her long dark purple hair. “The Goddess of Sexiness has arrived.”

Pesi points at her. “One chance, be my girlfriend and I won’t kill you.”

“Beauty is unbound and free.” Nina turns to him.

“And burning and screaming!” yells Pesi, flinging the massive Hatred Orb at Nina.

Kaity shakes herself to her senses. “No!”

A giant shield manifests in front of Nina and protects her from the blast.

Kaity then shoots a dark beam from her mouth that pierces through the shield and the God of Hatred.

Pesi screams and creates a portal to flee into.

Kaity looks up at Nina. “It’s really you?”

“Of course. I’m one of a kind.”

“But you were kidnapped and…I thought you were dead.”

“I couldn’t possibly allow this sexy body to stay imprisoned. My sexiness is my gift to the world! But the world wasn’t ready. So, after I escaped, I lived in the shadows.”

“But you came to save me?”

“I’m here to save Ada. The attack is all over the news.”

Kaity hugs her and sobs. “I was so scared I had lost you forever.”

Nina pets her. "Relax, just gaze at my healing beauty and everything will be just dandy," she says with a smirk.

Kaity shakes herself to her senses. She looks around the area.

"What are you doing?" asks Nina curiously.

"Efil must have left but the others are still in danger. We have to go!" She grabs her dear friend and rushes off.

"Hold on I wasn't finished yet," whines Nina.

The castle is in shambles, the library spire had burst the foundations of the roof, causing the whole thing to cave in.

Hope is on a remnant of her torn flag, being healed by Stabby. "I'd rather never recover than owe you a favor. And why is this taking so long?"

"Tired," says Stabby with drowsy eyes.

Deceivant is holding his unconscious granddaughter in a blanket. "You'll be okay."

Hope grimaces. "Atlas can protect Lilith. Stop looming over her and go assist your wife in checking under the rubble. That fool Devlin ran off to find Kaity and the brat; that doesn't mean you get to coddle Lilith while there's important work to be done. And how dare he hide his true form from his cherished little sister." She crosses her arms and puffs out her cheeks.

A group of citizens gather around the Queen.

Hope sits up. "You are all to remain indoors as instructed. I do not know if the threat has left."

Atlas stands in front of Hope, ready to guard her from a potential imposter. "Stand back or be detained. I will not allow any harm to come to the queen."

Toxic is rushing around the broken castle, calling out to those who may be trapped.

Ada dematerializes the rubble and checks if anyone is underneath before it rematerializes.

Natura checks another section of the building by lifting up the broken bits with her wind powers.

Durga is with some of the frightened civilians, trying to calm them down and assure them they will be alright.

The Captain of Carnage, D.S., and BoneSaw split up to search for Devlin, Shinx and Kaity.

Opti is searching the skies, holding Muffins close to him. “Complain all you want, but I’m not letting you out of my sight.”

Muffins stops squeaking and nuzzles him.

Devlin, still in his Exp form, waves at Kaity and then beams when he sees Nina. “You’re alive!” He rushes in and hugs them. “The others are gathered by the castle; we should hurry back.”

Nina pushes him off. “No touching!”

Kaity grabs Devlin’s arm. “Are the others okay?”

Devlin gulps. “Come on, let’s go.”

Kaity stomps her feet. “Don’t treat me like a child. Who did we lose?”

Devlin cries and looks directly at her. “D-Demon….” He sobs.

“What did she do? Where’s Lilith?” asks Kaity, horror clouding her jade eyes.

Nina’s eyes sank in. “Demonica?”

Kaity turns to Nina. “She’s the mother of Devlin’s kids now, not our enemy.” She whispers to Devlin. “Are you saying she’s dead or did she kill someone?”

Nina fell to her knees and starts muttering to herself.

Devlin sobs in his hands.

Kaity crouches to Nina “Are you alright? I didn’t know you were so close.”

Devlin’s eyes open wide. He pins Nina to the ground with wires. “Another spy. Well, Kaity’s here now so there’s no escaping your death.”

“What are you talking about?” asks Kaity, yanking on Devlin’s arm.

Nina glares at Devlin with all her rage unleashed. “She loved you! You killed her! It was you! Admit it!”

Dark energy spreads on the wires.

“It’s one of Bob’s demons! Kill it now!” yells Devlin.

Kaity slices the wires with her plasma claws. “Devlin, whoever it is, they’re suffering. Is it true? Did you kill her?”

“I did what I had to do.” He glares at the demon. “Yvne, is that you? You were a part of it too, don’t try to remain blameless!”

Kaity forms a prison of light around the demon, but the fake vanishes.

The fake Nina appears and shoves her katana deep into the murderer.

Devlin notices the tears in her eyes and starts to cry himself. "Kaity, go see if the others are okay."

"But you're–"

"I'm not in danger."

Kaity runs off, looking back nervously.

Devlin looks into the fake Nina's eyes. "She tried to kill Lilith…I had no other choice." He embraces the demon.

"Lies. She wanted children more than anything. She's always wanted to raise a family with you!" The fake Nina plunges the blade in deeper.

"Your boss Bob told her to decide between her two children. He's the one who did this. You love her, so join us! I promise you, once Bob has been killed, Kaity will use her powers as Sellum to bring her back," says Devlin.

The fake Nina releases the weapon and holds her shivering body. "Lord Sel…promised he wouldn't kill Shinx. He promised her. Never breaks promises. Never."

Devlin grabs the demon's hands. "Thank you. My son…Demonica's son…he attacked me and ran off. I need your help. I need you to find out where he went, so I can bring him home."

Nina fiddles with her fingers. "Can't betray Master. Not possible."

"Gimpy, I know it's you. You've helped us out so many times. Thank you. There's no need to hide you face, okay? I'm not your enemy."

The fake Nina's head is instantly replaced by a new one. "My name isn't Gimpy. I…." The slave raises their head, revealing long locks and an androgynous face. "I am Noitpurroc, the Deity of Corruption."

Nina's body was swapped with the Deity's true form.

The deity's long hair is bright yellow, draping over their shoulders and covering their chest. A metal plate covers everything under the deity's nose. In their mouth was a dark black choker. The demon's irises were white, reflecting innocence as tears pour out of them.

"That's a bit of a mouthful. Just gonna keep calling you Gimpy if that's okay. That's some outfit," he says with a nervous smile.

Tightly around the demon's neck is a collar with chains that connect to the slave's nipples. Around their crotch is a black chastity belt.

Noitpurroc holds themself in a tight embrace and removes the choker. "These are the clothes Mistress bestowed upon me. My voice is grating on her ears so she ordered me to snuff it in her presence. But I…I'm going to need to speak to find out the truth from Master," says the deity in a gentle, reverent and whispery voice.

"What was your mission exactly?"

"First to deactivate the Queendom's defense system; had some help with that. Main mission was to take Lilith to the library, but Stabby got in the way. Then I was told to fight Riufen and bring Shinx to the library when given the signal. Once the library crashed into the building, I was supposed to become Nina and stall Kaity till Master came to kidnap her. But he never came." Noitpurroc looks at Devlin. "You meant what you said about bringing her back?"

"Absolutely. If it's possible, then I know Kaity can do it."

Noitpurroc clenches their chest and cries. "Order me."

"What?" asks Devlin.

"Order me to find her son."

Devlin shakes his head. "No orders here. That's not who I am." He holds Gimpy's hand. "I request that you find out where he is and what Bob is planning for him. That's all I can do."

Noitpurroc looks at Devlin in tears. "You killed her, but I don't...hate you?" Noitpurroc claws at their miserable face.

"You're welcome to join us if that's what you decide upon."

Noitpurroc snaps their fingers and vanishes.

Noitpurroc arrives at the meeting spot, the rocky mountains where Bob had trained Shinx.

Bob is on the rocky floor, getting dusty and fiddling with some rocks. He turns to see his minion and wipes the liquid misery off him. "The mission was a success."

Noitpurroc approaches Master and opens their mouth to speak.

"Yes, you're allowed. Go on."

"Mistress...." Noitpurroc's voice gives out and they to their knees.

Bob rolls over to his most loyal minion. "She's gone. My little girl is gone."

Noitpurroc turns to Master and tries to scream but ends up speaking in a hushed voice. "What...happened?"

"The plan was simple. Demonica was supposed to kill Lilith, causing Shinx to either join her side...our side...or creating a darkness in him that we could use to turn him. It was perfect. Devlin ruined it! He ruined everything!" Bob fires a massive dark beam into the sky. He then turns to the dark deity. "She wasn't supposed to die."

Noitpurroc holds their head and cries. "Orders! Please Master."

"Anything to distract from the pain. I understand. Your orders are to find Shinx and bring him here. We can't let her death be in vain."

"Revive?"

"Only Sellum can swap souls and only an experienced Sellum. I assure you the first thing I will do when I become Sellum is go to Absence, kill that traitor Htols and exchange her soul for Demonica." He draws a heart in the sand. "My little girl isn't gone. She's just going a way for a bit."

Noitpurroc snaps their fingers but nothing happens. "Broken."

Bob turns to his loyal follower. "You're not broken, just shaken up. Demonica's son is out there right now. We have to find him before someone else does. I'll join you."

"And the others?"

"Lum's death caused a resurgence in those accursed demon rebels. The Sins are dealing with them. Regna was captured by the enemy but don't fetch her. I gave her a new mission. All my children are connected to me. I can send them orders or offer them comfort, but I feel so alone now."

Noitpurroc puts a hand on Master. "Search together?"

"You're really taking initiative! I'm so proud! Wallowing about what we can't change only limits our capabilities to alter what we can! Let's bring the boy home!"

Noitpurroc smiles and then vanishes.

Devlin returns to the other Freedom Forcers.

Deceivant looks up at him. "She won't stop crying. Please, tend to your daughter."

Devlin claps his hands together and addresses the crowd. "Bob's plan was to keep everyone separated so that Demonica could bring Lilith to me. He threatened to kill Shinx if she didn't kill Lilith. Demonica was corrupted by fear. And to protect Lilith…I…I took her life." Tears drip down his cheeks.

D.S. looks up in tears. "She had to become a bad mommy to be a good mommy?"

Lilith rushes up to Devlin and hugs him, sobbing against him.

Deceivant looks up at Devlin with a firm expression. "You did what you had to do. Regret won't change anything."

Devlin gulps down his misery. "Shinx saw me kill her. He attacked me and then ran off. It's only a matter of time before he gets corrupted by Bob. Who will help me find him?"

Hope stands up. "You're not going anywhere. You have a responsibility as a father to help your daughter put her life back together. I won't allow you to ruin us with another brash decision."

Lilith clings onto him. Her mouth opens but no words come out.

Devlin turns away and then approaches Hope. "My son is out there! Bob plans to corrupt him! That was the reason for all of this!"

Ada chimes in. "What if he gets abducted by Lambda?"

Devlin shivers. "Yeah, we have to find him."

"We will." Hope stands up. "Even in the safe house we were attacked. Regna wounded me but a little helper came to our rescue." She points to Napkin who is snuggling up to Regna. "We have one of the demon god's captive."

Devlin clenches his fist. "Bob only told them what they needed to know. None of them knew the whole plan. She's a worthless hostage."

"I will decide that on my own after a thorough interrogation!" yells Hope.

Kaity approaches Hope. "When Sefiwah…when Mom attacked me…Napkin took away my fears. Back then I thought it was because he cared about me…but he was just following Lum's orders. We can't trust him. I'm almost positive he works with the traitor, Etaf."

Napkin looks at Kaity's dark gaze and runs off. He creates a Lum portal and rushes inside it.

Hope stands tall. "Atlas, you are to guard the prisoner. Opti, you will search the Queendom and the nearby waters for Shinx. Deceivant will join you once we clear the path to the armory. Our defenses were deactivated from within, so be extra vigilant even among allies. Devlin, if you leave your daughter behind when she needs you most, then you will be barred from the Queendom."

Devlin pries Lilith off of him and gives her to Ada. "So be it." He sprouts wire wings and flies off.

Hope stomps her foot. "Insubordinate fool."

"Should I go after him?" asks Opti.

"Don't bother." Hope wipes her eyes.

Lilith looks up, silently screaming for her daddy to come home.

Shinx is on the waters, shivering under a towel as he points to the horizon, using his powers to carry himself far away from the place where Mommy was murdered.

Part 23
The Hunt Begins

Chapter 191: Adorable Anomaly

The DXM call it Hope's Salvation. It's the five-year anniversary of the day that Hope saved humanity from extinction. The event would usually take center stage in the news, but the Assault on the Queendom was only three days ago. People were beginning to fear Exps again. The Senator was currently deciding what his response should be. One of the Furies was spotted in the area, and I was sent to bring the eco-terrorist in.

I drive my taxi at a leisurely pace and then park when I spot him.

"Target located," I say, my earpiece sending the message to the Senator.

"Excellent work, Agent Lambda. Tail him until he leads us to the base," says the Senator through my earpiece.

"Roger Sir."

The screen at the dashboard of the car turns on and projects the image of a young boy.

"Agent Lambda, urgent report," says the young boy hologram.

"What is it, bro?" I ask, fixing my hair for my date while I follow the target.

"I'm getting crazy readings near your location!"

"Exp…or something supernatural?" I ask, scanning the area.

Just snow and trees. Such a lovely view.

"I don't know. Wait…they're gone. See anything?"

"Nope. I'll keep my eyes peeled for anything suspicious."

A girl walks out from the trees on side of the road.

She certainly looks suspicious. Could she be connected to the readings Gamma was getting?

I smile and lick my lips. "This requires further investigation."

"What does? I'm sending some drones to check out the area. Did you find anything?" asks my little brother.

"A girl." I put on my special spy shades, which are both fashionable and practical.

"Oh, I see her now. I'll cross-reference her facial structure to search for a match."

"Send someone to tail the Fury in my place. I'm going to find out more about this cutie."

"You're not gonna believe this. I don't believe this. I found a match."

"Aww, of course I believe it. You're always so helpful," I say, pinching the computer screen's cheeks.

"She's deceased. We may be dealing with a shapeshifter Exp or maybe some demon."

I tap my shades and zoom in to see her face. "She looks worried to me and she has just the cutest freckles."

"Can you please focus? This girl is an anomaly."

"An adorable anomaly."

"I think you should get out of there. I will track her to see if she does anything suspicious."

"Sorry, but there's just no way I can leave a girl alone and scared. I'm picking her up."

"She's been dead for one-hundred years."

"Are you sure?"

"Her death was shrouded in superstition too."

"She's talking to the Fury guy, but she doesn't look suspicious. She's admiring his tattoo. Hmm…he gave her some cash and his business card. I'll be sure to swipe that."

"We don't know what she is!"

"Just give me her name."

She sure does look delicious though.

"Racheal Summers."

Cute name for a cute girl.

"Oh, gotta go, little bro."

"Don't engage!" he yells before I turn off the hologram.

I smile at Racheal and she opens the door.

"No leather. That's nice. Just a few years ago, it was a pain just to find a car without cowhide," she says with a smile.

That's not true. It's been nearly half a century since leather was banned.

I look at her from the mirror.

The girl is in her early 20s and is wearing a black zip up robe with a red interior hood. Her hands are kept snug under black gloves with golden puzzle pieces on top. She has two more large puzzle pieces as shoulder guards. Her hair is short and a lovely shade of red. It's almost as beautiful as her amber eyes. She has a pink tattoo of a heart and the numbers "58" on her cheek. More numbers are just above her cleavage.

Now I recognize her. Racheal Summers, the creator of The Missing Piece indie horror comic series. Her series took off after her fans made her death into a supernatural legend.

Why is she dressed like her character? And how is she alive? Best to just keep my cool.

"A little early for Halloween, isn't it?" I ask with a disarming smile.

She shifts in place.

"Cute tattoo though," I say with a chipper voice.

"Thanks. I think?"

"Where to?"

She looks around, noticing my maple leaf trinket dangling on the front mirror. "Just take me to the nearest train station. Wow, is this an electric car? It's great that you're driving green."

She really is from the past. This is bizarre.

"Aww, you're too cute. Most cars these days are electric. Leather free as you noticed. Part of the big ecological movement."

"Wow, that's great to hear. I guess a lot can change in seven years."

More like a hundred.

"But you're still just as cute as ever."

The girl looks nervous and grabs the door handle. "Actually, just let me off here. I'm fine."

"Now. Now. Behave."

Racheal fails to open the locked door. "I'm calling the police if you don't let me out of this car."

I lower the tinted window between the front and back seat and show her my ID. "Agent Lambda."

"FBI? But I didn't do anything. I'm just a cosplayer. A cosplayer who is really scared right now." Her gorgeous eyes water up.

"I was following that man you talked to but you're much more interesting. Now, I'm not going to hurt you. Just want to ask you a few questions and you can be on your merry way."

"Okay, but if I play along, then you have to help me find my mom. Oh, and some other people too!"

"What?"

Is she making demands?

"You're FBI, then you can do a little search, right?"

"Making a deal with an agent. You're really something."

Racheal zips her lips, crosses her arms and leans back.

"You have my word," I say, placing my hand atop hers.

"Okay. So, what do you want to know?"

"Not here. There's a procedure to these things." I press a button that tints the back windows.

"Are we close?" she asks, shifting in her seat.

"Very close."

"I'm…I'm scared." She holds her shivering body. "You won't hurt me, right?"

"You're in no danger, but then again you always loved the thrill of fear." I poke her with a hidden needle and she falls asleep in seconds.

I call up my little brother. "Agent Gamma, I've apprehended the girl. I'm bringing her to the base for questioning."

"I heard everything. It really does sound like she's been away for one-hundred years."

"Yep. I'll need some plane tickets."

"No need, I'll just get a private jet sent to your location."

"You're a dear."

"Keep an eye on her, okay?"

"Oh absolutely," I say, looking at her from the mirror.

Once I arrive at the base, I bring the unconscious girl directly to my room without being stalled by anyone. I lie her down on my pink love bed.

"Do you need anything?" asks Nina from behind me.

I turn around. "Geez you startled me. Print out every comic written by Racheal Summers and stack my shelves with them. Oh, and use the body printer to create a replica of her."

"It will be my pleasure. Happy Salvation Day," she says, giving me a hug and a deep kiss before leaving the room.

Such a good pet. I've really groomed her well. Time to groom this little ginger pie.

The Senator enters my room.

"Sir, what seems to be the problem."

"We must have a meeting immediately."

I point at the little ginger treat on my bed. "Can't it wait just a bit?"

"It concerns her and ISEKAI!" he exclaims.

Oh no. Another of his ridiculous conspiracy theories. Nothing to do but placate him.

I shrug. "I would, Boss. But we can't leave her unattended."

Koshi squeezes inside. "Not a problem. I'll keep her warm."

"Good, then it's settled," says the Senator, pulling me out of my room.

I'm brought to the meeting room. A silver place with tons of glare and barely any personality.

I sit down and sigh. "Alright, let's just get this over with."

He starts up the slide show, showing various cases of missing children.

"The organization primarily targets children from ages twelve to seventeen. All of these supposedly unrelated cases are all connected. And that girl is the key to it all! They were all killed by a man in a black cloak. But what if that man was actually not a man?"

"I'm tired from the flight. Is this your Exp speech, your demon speech or your alien speech?"

"What if that man was an alien!?" He flips the slide dramatically, showing a zoom in of the starry faced cloaked killer.

"Why are important pictures like these always blurry?"

"That's a conspiracy for another time," he says with a nod.

Of course it is.

He slams the table. "Did you not see her file? Racheal Summers died one-hundred and seven years ago! And she reappeared now! Do you know why that is?"

"I would be getting close to finding it out if you didn't interrupt my girl time with your theories."

He clicks to reveal the next slideshow. "A portal between worlds!"

"So not aliens?"

"Interdimensional aliens killed her and made her immortal in another world! It's the only logical explanation."

"So logically, by dying she becomes immortal."

"She was skinned alive in front of hundreds of witnesses."

"Otaku witnesses in a dangerous situation could easily hallucinate. Look, a bunch of Exps just show up out of nowhere after disappearing. And according to Kioshi, the Prince of Pleasure came from a place where time flows differently. A hundred days there would be a hundred years here. And get this, you travel to that special place by dying. There you go, no aliens involved. Can I go now?"

"Hmm, perhaps she was killed and her killer is simply wearing her skin. We've been infiltrated by the alien you brought here!" The Senator hits his watch and it projects an image of my little brother.

"Sir, I'm in the shower right now," he says, covering his cheeks with embarrassment.

"Did the results of her analysis come in?"

"I sent them to your inbox already. Racheal is one-hundred percent human. I'm sure my sister can figure out more about her after an interrogation."

I stand up and lick my lips. “An intimate interrogation.”

The Senator clicks to the next slide. It’s a picture of a blonde boy with spiky hair. “There was only one other case of a person coming back from the dead after being attacked by these shadow creatures. This boy left the world in 2019 and returned a year later during the Covid-19 pandemic. He then vanished again that same year.”

“I don’t care. I’m leaving.” I walk off.

The Senator blocks my path. “Agent Lambda, there is some organization out there kidnapping our youth. I don’t think those kids were sent back here. I think they came back here through some portal. The boy declared on his independent channel “The Main Character!” that he was going to return to take down ISEKAI before he vanished from the Earth! See if that girl knows anything about it.”

I salute the boss. “Roger, Sir.”

We have enough to worry about between Exps and demons. Don’t need to add shape-shifting assassins into the mix. Time to get suited up and begin the intimate interrogation.

Chapter 192: Intimate Interrogation

I enter my room dressed in my white skin tight suit.

Racheal's eyes drift to my thighs and her lips quiver.

Koshi looks at me. "So Lambda, who gets to interrogate the freckled cutie?"

"We're not interrogating. Just want to chat." I turn to Koshi. "Well, go on. Get out of here."

"Fine but if you fail to get the information, I go next," says Koshi, walking out.

"You better not turn her into one of you," says Kioshi, glaring at me with those adorable eyes.

"Love you too, sweetie," I say, blowing the girl a kiss.

Kioshi shivers and then scurries off.

I place my hand on Racheal's leg. "You're shaking," I say tenderly.

"Just a bit nervous?"

"Who would have guessed the writer of The Missing Piece, one of the most controversial Indie Horror comics, would be such a scaredy cat." I paw at her leg playfully.

"Can't have courage without overcoming fear!" Racheal exclaims with tomboy charisma. "Hey uh, you read my comics? Is this your room?"

"It is and I have."

Skimmed them while taking the flight here but I had read a bit of them in the past. Bet she has no idea her stories are a cult classic.

"Okay, so what are your questions? Are they about my book? Please, I just want to get this done with and go home. I don't want my mom to worry a second longer about me."

Such a sweet girl.

"I already looked it up." I place my hand on her glove. "Do you want to find out for yourself? Or are you ready to hear the truth?"

Racheal takes a deep breath and musters up her courage. "Where is she?"

"Your mother is no longer with us. She's passed on." I look up at the poor girl with great compassion. "I'm so sorry, Racheal."

Racheal wipes her eyes. "It's okay. I'm a grown up now. I won't cry."

Telling her that her mother died seventy years ago would just cause problems. I'll let her know what year it is once I've got her in my web. My codename isn't the Spider for nothing, after all.

The girl hugs herself and shivers.

I hold her in my arms. "It's fine to cry, sweetie."

She sobs in my embrace.

There we go. Relax. Poor girl. She doesn't deserve all this grief.

"Hey." Racheal pulls away. "Sorry the government is an enemy in my comics. I'm not unpatriotic. I love Canada and our prime minister. I just wrote it that way to make the story interesting." She smiles through her tears.

Cute, Charismatic and Canadian. Kindred spirits we are. Time to begin the questioning.

I look her over. "So how are you alive? I saw the whole video, many, many, times." My finger glides up her arm.

She shuffles a bit but seems to enjoy it.

My nails dance down her thighs. "Skinned alive, just like Amanda Panda's girlfriend in the comic you never published. You look good for a dead person. Impossibly good. And yet, it's definitely you." My finger runs up her neck to her bottom lip before stopping.

Racheal mimes shooting herself in the head and then mouths words.

Okay, she's a bit loopy apparently.

"I can read lips, you know. What do you mean 'is this working'? Is what working?" I ask.

The girl pulls the invisible bullet out of her head. "Nothing. Just being silly. Sorry."

"You sure look happy. So, are you going to tell me how you survived?" I ask, my eyes sharpening into daggers that cut away her fear.

"You must have me mistaken with someone else," she says, looking away.

"Come on, little lamb. You should know you can't lie to me." I run my finger directly under her eyes. "I can see the truth absolutely."

"If I did…if I told you the truth, you'd lock me up in a crazy house!"

The girl wobbles a bit as she daydreams.

Nina knocks at my door.

Time to dazzle her.

I walk out of the room and meet with Nina. My special surprise for Racheal is under a black curtain. I wheel it in.

Racheal smacks her cheeks and comes out of her fantasy.

"Tadaa!" I remove the curtain, revealing the large glass container and the body inside it. An exact replica of Racheal's body.

The body printer always has its uses.

Racheal stammers, opening and closing her mouth like a cute little fishy.

"I sewed the skin back on myself. I'm quite the seamstress. My my, you look like you haven't aged a day," I say, looking back and forth between her eyes and the eyes of her corpse.

"That's a wax figure. It's gotta be!" She finally says with a forced chuckle.

"It's you. I preserved…" I place my finger on her lips and lean in close "you."

"Why would you preserve the body of a random murder spree?" Racheal points accusatorily.

Oh, she thinks she's some kind of detective. Little miss detective just gave this spy a clue.

"I didn't say it was a murder spree." My finger touches my bottom lip and my eyes slant like a predator's.

Interrogation is a mix of friendliness and fear.

"Your body was different than the other ones that were slaughtered that day. You were targeted. We want to know why."

"Because I write hero comics. I know how dumb that sounds, but that's the truth. Those things, they take people who have passion and they force them into becoming heroes."

Those things. Oh no. Please don't let them be aliens. The boss will never stop bragging if they're aliens.

"You know what those things are? Despite our best efforts, we've never been able to catch one."

Racheal leans in and smiles.

Oh, she thinks has the upper hand now.

Racheal straightens her back. "Okay, so if I tell you about everything, then you have to promise me you will believe me. Fair?"

"Aww, but you want me to torture you." I press my sharp nail into the back of her neck. "At least a little bit."

I pay attention to your breath, your eyes and every tingle in your body, my pet.

"I died and was brought to another world!" exclaims Racheal.

Another world. Alright, I'm interested.

My eyes slant with intrigue. "Any proof?"

"You're an agent of the government, right? So, it's your job to help people in need."

"Aww, your idealism is just adorable," I say, pinching her cheek.

"There are lots of people in danger and I want to save them! They're kids, most of them and they just want to go home."

The Senator's theory might be true after all. So many secrets to uncover! Can't wait to tell my little brother!

"The more you tell us, the more we can help." I lower her hood behind her head and smile. "But for now, just relax." I gently push her onto my comfy bed.

"I want to go home and see my…."

"I never knew my mother. I can't imagine what you're going through. But I do know that she'd be proud of you. Single mothers are heroes. Looks like you followed in her footsteps in your own way."

Racheal sits up. "Then you believe me?"

"I told you, you can't lie to me. I can tell that you're absolutely telling the truth. But there will be time to get all the details later." My hands move in a flash and roll her onto that cute belly. "How about a nice relaxing massage?"

"I dunno. The nicest people are sometimes the serial killer." Racheal gulps down her fear and excitement. "Koshi's sister said he was a serial killer. Is that true?"

Why did she have to bring him up? Talk about a mood killer.

I sit on her squishy butt and starts rubbing her shoulders. "You're safe with me."

"Please don't avoid my question," she says between bated breaths.

"The same rules don't apply to us. I can't say anymore."

"Because you're agents. Wait, I know your identity. That's why you're being so nice." The cute redhead tries to wiggle free, but my thighs hold her in place.

"Come now. I couldn't bear to harm such a sweet girl. I've had my eye on you for a while now."

"But the rules don't apply to you? Isn't that right?"

"Since you're so interested in me, I suppose I should explain." I gesture to the fake corpse.

Racheal looks at the body and zones out. She blushes and starts breathing heavily.

I bring her back by gently tapping her head. "You're quite the daydreamer."

"I'm very focused unless there's something scary or if there's a cute guy talking to me. Then I'm…well, a bit scatterbrained."

"And it makes you all the cuter."

"You'd think so, right? I know I'm cute, but I was always too weird to get a boyfriend at school. I was too pastel for the Goths and too macabre for the jocks. And the nerds fear me like I'm a diclonius. Legit run in terror if they're alone in a room with me. You ever felt like you're cursed before?"

"Hard to feel cursed when such a cutie pie is in my web." My hands run up her back like a spider, sending chills of terror up the girl's spine, which then subsequently sent erotic pangs throughout her body.

"Oooh. I felt those shivers. You know, you don't need a boyfriend."

"Yeah. Heard it before. And I know getting a boyfriend makes me statistically more likely to get cornered by a serial killer. But maybe I want that!"

This girl is really one of a kind. Actually, she reminds me of Kioshi. So morbid yet cute. Let's see just how much they have in common.

"So, then every inch of you is…" I brought my hands up her back all the way to her ears "virgin?"

Racheal shifts and I allow her the space to turn over to face me. "Look Lamby."

"Lamby. You gave me a little nickname. I'm honored."

"I give everything that terrifies me cute nicknames. Anyways. I think there's a big misunderstanding. Amanda Panda is gay, she ends up with her best friend, and yes, I wrote her. But that's not me. I wrote her like that because I wanted to. It felt right for the story and…I didn't want to get jealous of my OC." She puffs out her cheeks.

Too cute. I'm losing my breath. She's just too darling.

Once I can move again, I lean into her until my lips were inches away from her lips. "You're too darling. And don't worry. I never do anything without permission. I'll wait for you to ask me."

It won't take long.

"Umm, not into girls. Sorry. What Annie and I did was a one-time thing and I need to stop talking."

"Annie. What a cute name."

"Her full name is Annolette. And she's still there. I might never see her again."

So, she has a friend in the other world? This is truly a historic day. But things are already so complicated here.

"You two have a special bond, don't you?"

"Yeah, she's like a little sister to me."

"And that one-time thing?" I smile so calmingly that it puts the ginger tomboy on high alert.

"Th-That is something just between the two of us. There were circumstances. The damn planets were in alignment. And I was under the influence of her demonic pheromones!"

"Demonic?"

Alien demons from another world. I can never let the Senator know.

"I'm being dramatic. The point is I don't like girls."

"Then why were you looking at her lips?" I ask, gesturing to the girl's corpse.

"I have every right to check out my own dead body!" She crosses her arms.

The things this girl says are truly one of a kind! She's so fun!

"You asked before what I meant when I said the rules don't apply to me." I gesture to the corpse. "I sewed every patch of skin back onto your body." My smile became as gentle as a cloud. "I've also done the opposite."

Usually I'd keep these sorts of things to myself, but perhaps this will excite her.

"You've really skinned someone alive?"

I lean in and whisper. "Many times. I keep them alive through it all. If someone dies under my watch, that means I made a mistake. I don't make mistakes."

"And you skinned them…because they didn't answer your questions?" She asks, scooting back against the bed.

I place my hand on her chest and seizes her other arm, holding the girl in place. "They were an enemy. A hostage. As agents we can do what we want though. No crime is beyond us."

Racheal's cheeks flare up with embarrassment as she pees herself.

"Still a bed wetter? How deliciously adorable."

"I uhh…did that on purpose. So um, what other forms of torture do you like?" She asks, fiddling with her fingers.

"Acidic manicures for my female clients," I say with a tender tone. I lean into her and whisper. "You aren't the only one who is into the macabre. You said you had a little sister. Well, you can think of me as your big sister." I lightly blow into her ear.

The cutie squeaks and then composes herself. "Big sister?"

"That's right. My adorable little sister," I tap her nose and her thighs convulse with a sudden jolt of pleasure.

"Have you ever killed anyone?" Her eyes sparkle as her hips wiggle.

"Only when they became expendable."

"What was it like?" she asks her voice chirpy like a small bird.

"There are some prisoners that are no longer of use. Would you like to pick one out? I'm not all that interested in killing, but I love bonding with cute girls." I lean in so she can feel my heated breath.

Racheal's lips press against my supple purple lips.

Interrogation successful.

Racheal pulls away once she realizes she's kissing me. She seizes the nearest pillow and hides under it. When she lowers it, she starts stammering. "I'm sorry. I-I-I don't mean to put you on. Or turn you on. I…that was an accident. I didn't mean anything by it. I had to kiss you. You were just too. Rrrgh!" She hides under the pillow again.

Too cute. I've really found myself a gem.

I lift up the pillow and smile.

"I've never murdered anyone before. Self-defense is another story. Not that you were offering to let me try. Were you? Doesn't matter. I'm a hero, so that stuff is off limits. I only kissed you to get it out of my system so I wouldn't do something bad!"

A hero. Hmm. That must mean she can fight.

I put my hand behind her head and gently caress her hair. "Want another one?"

The darling ginger closes her eyes and nods.

"Sorry. Speak up."

"Just…one last one. To, uh, get it out of my system."

I lean in and kiss her neck.

She's so fun to play with.

Racheal grabs my hand. "On the lips…please."

"As you wish." I lean in ever so slowly. I barely touch her lips with my own.

She pulls away just enough to speak. "Can you…touch me?"

I keep one hand behind her head but the other I place on her breast.

Oh my. She's really heated up.

Racheal wiggles her legs and slides her hands down to her garden. Her other hand the slides up my thighs toward mine.

My suit is so thin it's like she's touching me directly. I didn't expect her to take initiative so soon.

Her hand gently rubs the area around my garden.

Racheal slowly slides her fingers in me. My suit doesn't put up any resistance and instead just coats her fingers like a glove.

I moan ever so softly.

Racheal breaks the kiss. A trail of saliva connects our lips.

Racheal blushes. "Can you get off me for a second?"

"Mmm. I don't think I can." I nibble her ear.

"I just want to get my fingers in deeper. The fabric is blocking my spoooooky cave," she says, sticking out her tongue.

This girl is squeezing my capsule with her adorable personality.

I sit up and lean over her as my suit dissolves around my juicy bits. I pull my black lace spiderweb bra and take my butterfly panties off. I then look at her and my fingers glow. My eyes turn dark.

Time to take this to the next level.

I place my energy blade above her belly and cut, dragging the dagger down her suit as the girl looks at me with confusion.

The bottom half fabric of her clothes is sliced into squares in a matter of moments. I toss the clothes aside, leaving Racheal in her strawberry underwear.

The same underwear as Kawai. That's an odd coincidence.

I look at her fruity panties and smirk.

Racheal covers her undies. "There's a reason for these, okay? They're from my middle-school days!"

"Huh?"

She fiddles with her fingers. "Well, no guy ever wanted me, so nobody was going to see them…so I never bothered to get new ones."

I flick her nipples, bringing her back into thrill mode.

Racheal blushes and mumbles. "Wow. You're like really good at that. Did you practice? I mean, of course you practice but like wow you're good. And pretty. Like anime femme fatale levels of sexy!" She fingers herself at a quickened pace as her excitement rises.

I spread her legs leisurely and looks at her wet strawberries.

"Nobody is supposed to see these! Only Annie has."

I smile before leaning in and kissing her deeply. My tongue makes circles inside her yummy mouth.

Racheal moans and wiggles, fervently fingering herself with her now soaking wet gloves.

I break the kiss with intensity. Several trails of drool connect our mouths and our breaths overlap.

"I love cute girls," I say with an enchanting lustful gaze.

"I like…boys?" she says, more like a question than an affirmation.

I've made love countless times to girls who said that exact thing.

Racheal moves her strawberry panties aside as my suit creates more openings.

Our lips and flowers both kiss in a gentle passionate motion.

I suck on her tongue as I rub my body against hers.

Racheal screams like a banshee before gushing.

"Still want a boyfriend?" I ask, nuzzling her nose against mine.

Racheal giggles like a drunk. "I dunno," she says with a wobbly smile. She suddenly hugs me, rubbing our cheeks together. "Will you be my girlfriend?"

"As long as you don't mind me dating other girls."

Lots of other girls.

The girls smile drops and she looks away with disappointment.

"I only select the cutest girls for my harem," I say sweetly.

"Lambda. I know how to fight." She tightens her fist, which is wet with her own ginger juices.

"And you have powers," I say, nibbling on her finger.

I noticed the slight vibrations when she was touching herself. I wonder what she's capable of.

Racheal blushes. "Yeah. And I can fight really well with my powers. I want to join you guys. I want to be an agent."

"You'll have to start at the bottom. Of course, I'll make sure it's under my tutelage in my all girls division." I smile sweetly. "Is that okay with you?"

"Yeah! That's fine. You know, in movies the torturer usually uses lots of awesome tools and sadistic techniques to get the information they want. But you've opened my lips with kindness," she says with watery eyes.

"I sure have." I slide my hand up her leg, grazing her flower garden.

Racheal squeaks. "So then, I can help lead the rescue mission?"

What rescue mission? This may become a problem.

My suit reforms around me. "You'll have to talk with the boss. But I'll certainly vouch for you. We've been busy dealing with the near extinction of humanity."

"Wow. That sounds pretty crazy." She looks up at me in embarrassment. "Do I have to wear one of those lewd suits?"

"I'll make you one you'll like."

Racheal hugs me. "You're the best."

"I know," I say, sewing the bits of fabric of her clothes.

Things are going to get a lot more complicated, but it's worth it for her.

Koshi swings open the door.

I glare at him. "What is it? You frightened this little darling."

"Suit up, we've got a mission." He smiles at Racheal. "Looks like you had fun."

Racheal blushes and hides under the covers.

"What's the mission?" I ask, getting up from the bed.

"Don't have a damn clue yet, but he's sending a full squad of us. That includes your little brother."

"Out in the field?"

"Yeah, my sister too. And the other Agents of the Apocalypse. Things are about to get crazy."

Chapter 193: My Friend

Shinx's boat is lifted up by the waves before slamming down. He looks at the massive storm above and points in the distance to make sure lighting doesn't strike.

His eyes widen when he sees a red droplet land on the boat.

A lightning bolt hits the spot and burst the boats to pieces, frying the boy along with it.

An invisible force raises Shinx out of the water.

A green pupil beams at the dark child.

"You...."

"Saved you, yes. You can thank me later."

"Help me," says Shinx weakly, flesh missing from his face.

"Well yes, that's the plan."

"Grow stronger. Help me become strong."

Bob's eye sparkles and he creates a portal. "Your wish is my command."

Back at the Queendom, the Freedom Forcers take a break from the reconstruction to avoid the thunderstorm. They find refuge in the living room of one of the human residents.

Natura looks out at the black sky. "Do you think Opti will be okay?"

Hope scoffs. "You should be able to end this storm."

"Sorry, I'm not Crisis," says Natura.

"It's been five years. You should have figured out your artifact by now."

Natura wipes her tears. "This artifact doesn't belong to me. The Flash Artifact and I, we were meant to be together. My whole persona was designed by Zenero with my artifact in mind."

Hope sighs. "That's just an excuse. You're holding back. Afraid of the deadly power of the Calamity Artifact, aren't you? No, it's deeper than that, you've been broken since your sister defeated you. I tried to piece you back together, but you're still clinging onto darkness. Absence sent you to me because he had faith in you."

"If I hadn't lost my powers, if I fought Chipko with all I had, maybe he'd still be alive."

"Can't turn back the cogs of time. But you can end this dreadful storm."

"I'll try," says Natura, getting up and walking outside.

Kaity sits next to Hope. "That was nice of you."

"Getting rid of a storm should be as simple as taking a breath for you. Your powers are waning. It's about Nina, isn't it? She's dead, which means she's somewhere in Lum. We can locate her when Sel has been stopped. So, if you want to save her, then get stronger."

The phone in Kaity's pocket buzzes.

"Sorry, gotta take this." Kaity walks off as Hope calls after her.

"Is it really you?" asks the voice on the phone.

"Koshi? What do you want? How did you get this number?" asks Kaity.

"I saw you fight that demon god. You fought well. How did you vanish for five years?"

"I don't have to answer you. Where is Nina? What did your people do to her?"

"She's here with us."

"Wait, she's alive? Is she alright?"

"Shit, I gotta go. I'll text you the coordinates to the base."

"Koshi! Don't you dare hang up!" yells Kaity, she then growls and puts away her phone.

"Koshi?" asks Deceivant, coming out from behind Kaity.

"That was a private conversation," says Kaity, pinning him to the wall. "I'm going and nobody here is going to stop me."

"If you're not here, Bob can just come back and take Lilith. We need you."

"So does she."

"Why would you even believe him? He's leading you into a trap."

"Doesn't matter. He doesn't know what I'm capable of. None of them can stop me." She cleaves a portal and pushes Deceivant away before closing it.

Deceivant rushes back to the living room, spotting his little queen on the sofa, getting a foot rub from his wife.

"Why are you here and not with…." Hope's eyes widen. "She left, didn't she?"

"Never even got a chance to stop her."

"Didn't even consult me." Hope dries her eyes. "Am I a failure as a leader?"

Deceivant and Ada both embrace their dear daughter. "Never, sweetie. We will rebuild."

"Wringer and Image died on my watch. Durga left us just yesterday. As for my citizenry, we've only retained a tenth of our human population which was only several hundred to begin with. We don't have a steady income anymore. I had to resign our forces from the war for the Furies independence. And despite all my powers I still can't get that girl to speak a word."

Ada kisses her daughter's forehead. "We believe in you, Sweetie."

Deceivant holds Hope's hand. "Lilith will speak when she's ready."

Hope sighs. "Now that Kaity is gone, Stabby is our best bet at defending Lilith. Atlas can guard the prisoner until Kaity returns."

Atlas looks over from the doorway. "But then who will protect you?"

Hope points to the fluffy brown bunny, staying warm by the fireplace. "Muffins, of course."

Atlas nods and follows Deceivant out into the storm.

"These winds are intense," says Deceivant.

Atlas lowers his head. "Son, there's something that's been on my mind."

"What is it? You haven't called me son in years? Is it about Image?"

"Are we on the right path?"

"What do you mean?"

"I thought I could help Hope bring about Zenero's vision. I saw his ambition in her. But I'm not strong enough to shoulder that ambition."

"We're all going through rough times now. It will pass, just like this storm."

"If I died, would it even matter?"

"This isn't you."

"You're right. I'll keep silent."

Atlas and Deceivant lift up the secret hatch in the dining hall and traverse the basement until they find Regna's prison.

Stabby is watching the prisoner with intense eyes.

Regna is behind a four-way barrier of Lum energy, making it impossible for her to create a portal to escape.

"Kaity left. Atlas is going to guard her while you keep Lilith safe," says Deceivant.

Stabby looks up at him and grins. "Smile!"

Deceivant smiles back at her. "Thanks, Amy."

Stabby scratches her cheek. "Did I know you before?"

"Yeah, without you, Exp 8 never could have been created."

"I cweated Daddy?" asks Stabby.

"Well, you helped recweate him. You bwought his soul to a new home. He helped me become a better person, a leader."

Stabby hugs his leg and then rushes off ahead.

Deceivant looks back at Atlas. "I know you've tried to bring them back, but some things just can't be undone. Let their strength be yours. I heard you fought Bob in Absence. You're incredibly powerful and you're like a father to everyone here."

Atlas smiles at him. "My worries are cut to shreds by your kind words."

Deceivant smiles and then rushes off to catch up with Stabby.

Atlas looks at Regna. "The Sins are supposed to protect the Balance. All the gods are."

"I want every angel in Lum destroyed!"

"Do you know where Shinx is?"

"Why would I tell you even if I did?"

Atlas lowers his head. "I thought you still considered me a friend."

"You divided the people! The Sinner's Fury was created because they knew you were a false god. They knew they didn't stand a chance against the true God of Destruction!"

Atlas turns to the approaching figure. "This is an odd place to spar. You know you're not allowed down here."

"Rules are chains that bind a warrior. I am free." Riufen points his spine at Atlas. "No tricks. I'm here to break her out. I'm resigning from the Freedom Forcers."

Atlas turns to him and summons up the Torture Trident. "I'm not going to just let my friend abandon his responsibilities."

"We were never friends."

"We sparred together every day since you joined!"

"I did so without attachment," says Riufen, coating his spinal sword in Absence energy.

"Once you're locked up like her, we'll have plenty of bonding time. We'll become as close as brothers," says Atlas, taking a step forward.

Riufen slices the Lum wall, freeing Regna.

Atlas coils her in the Chaos Chain and whips her around at the samurai.

Riufen knocks her aside and rushes in.

He's suddenly lifted off his feet.

"Now, I get to fight him, right?" asks Natura.

Atlas nods. "Proceed."

Natura slams into the brother killer and punches him with electric fists of fury. Her arms shoot powerful gusts at the warrior, smashing him against the ceiling until it bursts open.

She follows up the attack in mid-air.

"Why does rage drive one so noble?" asks Riufen, slicing through her wind at point blank range.

His bones suddenly jut out and press her into the ground.

A mecha samurai speeds by, slicing the blade.

Riufen lands. "Deceivant, did you make this for me?" he asks, gazing at the mechanical swordsman with wonderment.

Hope looks at the confrontation and orders her forces to get into position. "Mother, go with Stabby."

Ada shakes her head. "No. We're not losing anyone else. I'm staying to protect you."

Riufen unsheathes a second spine from his back. "It is dishonorable to battle multiple opponents at once. However, if I am to grow stronger, I must swallow my pride. This is a grand opportunity for me. Hope, I formally resign from the Freedom Forcers. If you can stop me here, I will swear undying loyalty to you and your cause."

"If you kill any of my people, I will destroy your mind," says Hope, gazing at him with all her strength.

Riufen nods. "Fighting without killing, a new challenge that I gladly accept."

Natura, who is holding her hands up to create a powerful twister, sends it forth at the murderer.

Riufen's blades move in a flash, cutting the tornado apart.

D.S. flings a scissor and then connects the other scissor to it and holds Riufen's swords between it. "Are you going back to Bob? Why not stay a good guy?"

"My decision and my path are my own." Riufen trips the bodyguard and slices his arm off. He then kicks him aside. "Ten against one! Don't hesitate! Come at me all at once!"

Deceivant's samurai mecha fires a spray of bullets at the samurai who deflects them.

"I was mistaken. You were thinking only of yourself." Riufen slices the air with a second spinal sword to cut through Natura's lightning storm.

Deceivant's mecha raises its shoulder turrets and fires a gravity bullet storm at the samurai.

Riufen plants his feet in the ground to keep his footing.

Natura punches bursts of lightning at the sibling killer. "How is he still deflecting me?"

Ten Toxics close in on the enemy from the tall grass.

Riufen's leg bones splinter and he kicks the snakes aside. The true Toxic shoots through his chest.

His intestines wrap around her and use her to deflect her other copies.

Riufen contemplates as he keeps up the barrage. "I wonder is it honorable or dishonorable to fight oneself and be used as a sword. This is a most unusual situation."

"Damn it!" Natura stops her lighting strikes and instead decides to bury the samurai under a torrent of snow.

"Everyone, get down!" yells Deceivant, his mecha docked and gathering energy in its cannon.

Natura creates gusts that launch all her allies in the air.

Deceivant fires a powerful purple anti-matter beam at the small hill of snow.

The beam splits and shoots off into the distance, obliterating a good section of the forest.

"I did not authorize that!" yells Hope.

Riufen exhales sharply, sending the snow flying in all directions. He pierces the Toxics one by one as they land, kabobbing them before stabbing the weapon into the ground. "Nine."

Muffins fires Absence needles at the warrior who bursts his own body to pieces to dodge them.

Riufen reassembles, instantly locked in combat with BoneSaw. He deflects the multi saw barrage and redirects it at Hope.

Ada stands guard, dematerializing the incoming projectiles.

Hope looks up at her. "I need to get in close. Swap for the illusion artifact." She hands Ada the artifact.

Ada nods and swaps the artifacts as Riufen slices the Captain of Carnage's zipline with BoneSaw's saw.

Atlas' chain wraps around Riufen. "Your mind shall be lost in the chaos."

Riufen coats his sword in Absence energy and slices the chain. "I've honestly never felt more focused."

Ada multiples their forces by a factor of ten by creating illusionary clones of all the fighters.

"Thank you. I was relying too much on my eyes." Riufen tears out his eyes and only focuses on the enemies he can feel, moving more fluidly as he deflects the assaults.

D.S. rushes at him and then quickly ducks.

Riufen notices the Agony Axe swirling over the bodyguard's head and coming toward him. He speeds behind D.S. and pushes him into the weapon from behind. "Eight."

Ada rushes in to help her son as Deceivant charges at the samurai.

"Keep your distance!" yells Hope.

Riufen's sword clashes against the mecha's blade before it overpowers it and sends it tumbling. He then rushes toward Ada.

Natura coats her feet and carries Hope to him.

Hope glares at Riufen as Natura keeps her just out of range of the samurai's strikes. "MENTAL CRUSH!"

Riufen silences all sound and then pierces Hope and Natura with his extending ribcage.

"Do not harm the queen!" yells the Captain of Carnage, zooming by and slicing Riufen's hand off.

The hand chases down the furry warrior and slams him against the ground repeatedly.

The immortal samurai grows a new hand and readies to strike Ada.

"DE-CONSTRUCT!" Ada holds out her hands.

The samurai is deconstructed digitally.

Ada grabs Hope and runs off to bring her to safety.

Riufen reconstructs two seconds later, right into Muffin's Absence Needle barrage. His body instinctively coats itself in a thin layer of Absence, just enough to deflect the attack. "Wait, if I'm Absence, then…." The samurai's fingers shoot out needles at the bunny.

Deceivant's mecha takes flight. "Damn it, we can't pierce that Absence aura. Why did Kaity leave!?"

Riufen grabs BoneSaw when the robot layers multiple saws and leaps up. "Let's see."

Crystals come out from the samurai's hand, trapping the robot within.

"Four." Riufen nods.

Muffins rides a massive needle at the samurai who allows her to slam her Absence form into his.

Both layers shatter.

Riufen smiles at the bunny. "Thank you. I have not yet discovered how to deactivate my god powers." He grabs her with his veins and sends her flying in the air. "Your life is not merely your own. You mustn't put it in harm's way when motherhood is closing in."

"It's over now!" Deceivant fires the antimatter beam from above.

Riufen is fully obliterated by the blast.

"I…did it!" exclaims Deceivant.

Riufen reforms inside a zero-gravity field.

Natura focuses her power and sends an extra powerful burst of condensed lightning at the warrior.

Deceivant waves at her from his mecha. "There's no need. He has lost."

Riufen lowers his head. "I deeply apologize. I didn't fight you all fairly." He focuses his mind and summons up Gladius. "Now if your beam hits, I will surely perish."

"And me along with you! I was relaxing in a flowerbed! Why did you bring me here?!" yells Gladius, glaring at the selfish soul he is bound to.

"Why not just surrender since you lost?" asks Deceivant, powering up his cannon.

Riufen shakes his head. "Gravity is no longer an obstacle. Htols' betrayal gives me full control over my movement." He hardens his aura coated body, increasing his weight so he crashes to the floor. The ground bursts and he escapes the gravity field.

The anti-matter beam fires directly in the ground.

"Stay vigilant! I'm not sure if I got him!" yells Deceivant, readying another blast.

The air sings before the mecha's cannon is sliced in two.

Deceivant falls out of the burning hunk of metal, he grips the Gravity Gun.

Riufen approaches, deflecting Natura's snow storm by redirecting the wind with a single slice from Gladius. He approaches Deceivant with heavy steps, bypassing the gravity fields sent his way.

Ada materializes in front of the samurai and holds out her arms.

Riufen slices them off. "You rescued Hope. As expected." He slams his head into her, dispelling the hard-light hologram. He then grabs her core and rams it into Deceivant's head. "Two."

Riufen jumps along the air up to Natura.

The terrified girl blasts him with a tornado and then flees the area.

"I expected better from her. Shame." He turns to Atlas and points Gladius. "One."

"No, old friend. You face all of us," says Atlas.

Unity emerges out from the snow hill and stands in the rain.

Riufen grips Gladius tightly. “The weight of all their hopes lies on your shoulders now. Don’t fail them.”

“We will not,” says Atlas, rushing at Riufen.

Gladius whines. “Let me cleave him in two. It will be so easy.”

Unity disperses and assaults the samurai from all angles.

Riufen deflects the mad assault, sinking deeper into the ground.

June is on the ground, smiling with her mask off. “Apparently mud is one of my powers. Thought I’d give it a shot.”

Riufen slips and is assaulted by all the weapons at once. He collapses with weapons of all kinds piercing him. “No….” Riufen stands tall and goes unconscious.

Atlas unsummons Unity. “He won.”

June slugs his arm. “What are you talking about? He’s unconscious. We won!”

“His resolve is unlike anything I’ve seen.”

“Not to sound like a gritty dark hero, but we can’t let him live.” June focuses her energy and creates lava from her hands.

“Stop. A warrior like him belongs in my arsenal.” Atlas summons up Unity.

June growls. “You want that brother killer in your head? No way. He’s going to mess you up!”

Atlas coils the Chaos Chain around June and she wails around. He flips her over and hits the back of her head hard, knocking her out.

The soulful warrior looks at Riufen and at Unity. “No. These souls…my friends, they are powerful with me as their master. But they were stronger before. In the process of melding them, I chip away a bit of their spark. I won’t do it again.” He looks up at the proud samurai. “If he joins me, it will be as a comrade not as a weapon.”

Riufen’s eyes open weakly. “I…lost?”

“No. You won. Took down June with my own weapon after I fell unconscious.”

“Is that what happened?” asks Riufen softly.

“It doesn’t really matter does it. The outcome of this battle would not deter you from your path. You must answer that calling. You must go.”

Riufen smiles. “I do.” He grabs Atlas’ hand. “Thank you, my friend.”

Atlas cries and embraces him. “I hope one day we can fight side by side.”

"I'd prefer to fight you again at your full potential. But that's entirely up to the boy." Riufen beams at Atlas.

"Ah, everything makes sense now." Atlas smiles.

"Farewell, my friend." Riufen leaves and walks down into the prison. "Regna, are you here?"

Bob rises up from the ground. "She returned to me after you freed her."

"If I defeat you, will you tell me where the boy is?"

"Sheesh, so confrontational." Bob wraps a tendril around the warrior's shoulder. "We're best buddies. You can just ask me."

"Where is Shinx?"

"He's with me, where he belongs."

Riufen stares at Bob. "Then that's where I'm going."

"You aren't going to apologize for leaving me? I don't have to let you join back if you're going to be rude, you know."

"Opti helped me follow my own path. I'm coming with you, but I'm not your warrior."

"I suppose simpletons inspire simpletons." Bob turns to Noitpurroc. "Bring us to the boy."

Riufen looks at the Gimp. "I see you've revealed your true self as well. There's no need for you to follow him."

Gimpy lowers their head and they all vanish from the prison.

Chapter 194: I'm Going to Save Nina

I arrive at the government base where Nina is being held.

This is it. I wasn't sure I'd be able to teleport with just a picture, but it worked.

The building is a massive fortress with no windows. A tall wire fence bars any trespassers from entering.

Nothing can stop me. I'm going to save Nina.

I slice through the gates and approach the compound.

No alarms go off as I approach the massive metal doors.

Nothing will stand in my way.

I fire a Sel beam that devours the doors.

Koshi, standing on the metal floor, looks at me. "That's new."

"Are you here to help me? Or stop me?" I ask, pooling dark energy into my claws.

"Orders are orders." He sighs.

I shift my thoughts and convert the darkness into light. The ray of light creates vines that hold him in place.

"That's different too. Where did you get these artifacts? I guess I'll test your new limits." Energy erupts out from Agent Alpha, tearing the vines to shreds. He shapes it into a sword and rushes at Kaity.

Sellum slams her claws against his sword, pushing him back with her added strength.

"Geez, you must be on one hell of a healthy diet to get this strong."

My claws turn black with dark energy.

The Sel energy feasts on his.

"Shit! This is not good!" He rubs his hands together to strengthen and focus his energy field.

I form a massive hand of light, that becomes hard as bark.

It grabs him, lifts him up and slams him into the wall. The bark envelopes his body, merging him with the metal.

"Kaity, wait. Talk to me. You're my rival. I can't fall behind like this."

I turn to him. "Where is she?"

"If I tell you, I'm going to get fired."

"If you don't, then I'll destroy this entire place looking for her."

"Geez, why do you gotta be so difficult?"

"She's been here five years and you never helped her escape. I want to kill you right now. But you told me where this place is, so I won't. Break free and it's over for you." I rush off.

"I'm sorry, Kaity!" hollers Koshi.

The alarm blares and the building's defenses activate.

The ceiling tiles flip to reveal gatling gun turrets that immediately open fire on me.

I create a shield with my aura.

Tcetorp's power. Maybe I can use the other god's powers too.

I close my eyes and calm my mind.

A map of the area appears in my thoughts. I sense only three souls, myself, Koshi and one more at the medical bay.

It has to be Nina. There's nobody else here though. They underestimated me.

I focus Sel energy and blast a beam into the ground.

My Lum powers create a mist upon me landing, causing the turrets to lose sight of me.

I cut through wall after wall until I find her.

Nina's hair is cut short and she's wearing an Exp hunter uniform. Her eyes are the same color but they feel empty.

"Nina, I'm here to rescue you." I hold out my hand.

Her sword slides through the air, chopping off my arm.

What?

Nina kicks me off my feet and rushes at me.

She pierces my capsule but her blade becomes stuck.

My vines hold it and her in place.

I look up at her in tears. "Don't you recognize me?"

"Kaity of the Viper Squad assassins, by entering here you are an intruder and must be terminated." Her voice is as cold as a glacier.

"I love you! We were getting close. You have to remember."

"I remember. But that's irrelevant. I have a new master now." Nina glares at me, weighing me down with the strength of her Gravity Artifact.

I reach out to her but she's so far away.

I've lost her. I've lost everything.

My vision fades and everything becomes meaningless.

Hope awakens in a white medical bed with Stabby above her, asleep but still expending energy. She smiles and then covers her mouth. "That's twice she's helped me now. I should be grateful, but I still feel bitter. So petty." She looks down.

Deceivant rushes to her bedside. "Nobody died. Everything is okay."

Hope looks up at him and stiffens her face. "Did we defeat Riufen?"

"Atlas fought him to the very end, but he lost."

"All of us together and we still couldn't stop him. Pathetic. Has everyone else recovered?"

"Yeah, but June's gone. I think she went after him on her own."

"Can't put a leash on that one. We mustn't waste time. What about Opti and Devlin?"

"Both returned after seeing what happened here on the news. My antimatter cannon may have been a bit too showy. We've lost even more human residents after the battle. It's all my fault."

Hope reaches to him weakly and grabs his hand. "You've acted brashly and there were consequences. Regrets are a comfort we cannot afford. Has Kaity come back?"

"No word from her yet."

"At least we aren't entirely defenseless." Hope gets up and holds her chest in pain.

"You shouldn't be walking."

"True, but sometimes a queen must step into mud to lift up her people. We haven't lost yet. Bring Devlin here. I wish to speak with him alone."

"He's with Lilith," says Ada, coming in and handing Hope some warm tea.

Hope burns her lips and puffs her cheeks. "You should have put more ice in…no. I should have been more patient. I've been too brash lately. It's unbecoming." She blows on the tea.

"It's only because you love Devlin."

"That love is going to be the death of us, if I don't do something about it." Hope turns to Deceivant. "Well, go on then. Bring him here. Actually, I'll go to him." She wobbles a bit and falls over. "My royal legs have been too active as of late. Carry me."

Deceivant smiles and lifts her into his arms.

Hope hugs him tightly. "Thanks for staying with me."

"I'll never leave you again." He kisses her forehead.

Deceivant brings Hope to the bathhouse.

The walls are still damaged from the fighting, but the area has been cleared of debris.

Hope hops out of his arms and opens the door.

Lilith is in Devlin's lap, who is halfway submerged in the hot-spring water and sitting on the granite steps.

"Glad to see you're awake," says Devlin.

"We needed you."

"I can't stop Riufen. I'm not the fighter I used to be. I couldn't even save my own son."

Hope removes her clothes and enters the bath in her frilly underwear. "Why did you return?"

"I saw your injury on the news."

"Where did they get that footage? Does the Senator have little cameras in my kingdom?"

Devlin hugs Hope. "I've been ignoring my responsibilities as your brother."

Hope looks down with watery eyes. "I'm not a child anymore. I'm old enough to look after myself. I…need to let go of my feelings for you."

"Hope, I'm sorry."

"No apologies. You're a father now, so you should spend every moment you can with your daughter."

Lilith looks up at Hope but says nothing.

"Still won't talk."

Devlin turns to his daughter and holds her hand. "Not yet, but I'm going to help her." He pats Hope's head. "Thanks for keeping her safe."

Hope wiggles and blushes, puffing her cheeks. "I didn't come here for head pats. I came with a proposition."

"I searched the entire Queendom and the waters around it. Shinx isn't here. I can't find him. I'm staying and I'll fight to protect your land."

Hope flicks his forehead. "Don't assume you know what I'm going to speak of. I may have a way of locating Shinx, but it is risky."

Devlin's eyes light up. "Please, tell me." He grabs her hands.

Hope looks away with flushed cheeks. "St-Stop staring at me like that. I'm trying to harden my heart. And let go of my hands." She pulls away. "I can ask my contact in the Senator's employment."

"You mean Kioshi? Yeah, that's a great idea!"

"I already tried that and she doesn't know. If she asks Gamma to search, then there's a high chance that Exp Hunters will be sent after your son."

"Then what is your plan?"

"I've kept it to myself, but I've made an ally with Agent Beta."

"You befriended the second in command."

"Not a friend and perhaps ally is a bit of a strong word as well. I may be able to reason with her. No doubt there will be a cost to the information on Shinx's whereabouts."

"Every second counts. Just be careful."

Lilith smiles at Hope. "Thanks," she mouths.

Hope nods and gets out of the bath. She points at Devlin. "This is the last time I'll assist. From now on, protecting you children is not my primary goal. I'll admit I was moved, albeit incensed, that you abandoned us for your fatherly duties. That said…!" She steels herself and glares at him with puffy cheeks. "I hereby disavow any romantic feelings I have towards you." She walks off, holding back her tears and fetches her phone from her dress.

After getting dressed, she leaves the bath house. The Queen of the Exps walks down the hallway as she makes the call. "Agent Beta, this is Queen Hope."

"Ohoho! Things are about to get fun! I hope you're ready," says the agent.

"What are you talking about?" asks Hope, stopping in place.

"Hmm, let me see your face. I'll send you the link."

Hope puts on the camera and clicks the video.

The video is a live news report of military soldiers entering the Queendom and rounding up the Exps, including Hope.

"You truly can fabricate anything these days," says Hope, swallowing her fear.

"Such a lovely look for you."

"I need you to locate Shinx for me."

"Already have him found. We've been tracking all of you."

"Then where is he?"

"You don't have time to worry about that. I'll see you very soon."

Hope hangs up the phone and runs to the surveillance room.

There's a boy sitting in her chair. "That's it. Now strike on my signal," he says, speaking through his earpiece.

Hope pokes his neck from behind. "PHYSICAL CRUSH!"

The boy turns around and looks at her. "How did you know I was here?"

Chapter 195: Ambush

Devlin holds Lilith closely. "We'll get your brother back and then this whole mess will get sorted out."

Lilith hugs him tightly and cries.

"I'm not going to leave your side, ever again." He pokes her tummy. "You're too old to be bathing with your dad, but there's no chance I'm letting you out of my sight."

Lilith holds his hand to her. She mouths to him with a shaky smile.

"I love you too. You're too fragile for this dark world."

The back door opens without a sound.

Lambda tosses a full set of energy daggers into Devlin's back.

Devlin's wires come out and create a cocoon around Lilith. "How did I not hear you coming? You're lucky you didn't hurt my little angel." He turns to see Lambda and the menace in his eyes turns to fear.

Racheal bounces when she sees him. "Mega hottie!"

"Stay focused," says Lambda.

Devlin's wires jut out, but are deflected when Racheal yells.

"Yes! I did it!" exclaims the Exp Hunter in training.

"Don't expect it to be that easy," says Lambda.

Devlin's wires fling the door at them.

Lambda grabs Racheal and leaps out of the way.

Devlin lifts the wire cocoon up and flees the bathhouse.

Deceivant is with Toxic out in the grassy fields. "Go long!" He throws a fast ball that she jumps up to catch with the mitt on her tail. "You sure this is what you've always wanted to do?"

"There's no better family bonding than playing catch with your papa," says Toxic, sending the ball back his way.

Deceivant jumps to catch the ball but misses. "I'm still winded from the fight with Riufen. Shouldn't we be resting?"

"You promised you'd do whatever I want now that Hope's back on her feet, right?"

"Yeah, just didn't know you were such a tomboy." He grins.

"Go get the ball. Or should I send one of me to do it?"

"I'll get it," says Deceivant.

The ball shoots past him, followed by an onslaught of thirty more.

"Ow! Who's doing that?" asks Deceivant, turning around.

"Forgot about me already," says a dark voice.

Atlas is in the workout room, lifting up the weight machines with his feet while doing thumb presses. “Balance and strength must grow together. This isn’t the same without Durga. Feels like every day I lose someone.”

There’s a knock at the door.

Atlas slowly lowers the weight machines to the ground and then rolls out from his pose. He approaches the door.

The door suddenly breaks off from its hinges and slams into Atlas.

The ex-god of Hate throws it aside and looks up at the intruder. “There must be some confusion, we aren’t enemies. The Queendom has not broken any laws.”

War looks at the Exp. “There’s nothing to negotiate. I’m bringing you in.” He grabs Atlas’ sides and uses his powers in short bursts, dragging the target back until he hits the back wall. “Sigma, now!”

The priestly Exp Hunter raises his bazooka and fires it at the back of his own ally.

Opti and D.S. are at the playground behind the castle.

Muffins is resting on a mat by the bench.

D.S. slides down and lands in the sand. “June and I were racing down this slide just the other day. Why is everyone leaving?”

“I don’t like to think about sad stuff. Hey, how many little bunnies do you think momma Muffins is going to poof into our lives?” asks Opti, swinging on the monkey bars.

“A whole bunny bundle.” D.S. grins.

“Hey, I…can’t move,” says Opti.

D.S. looks up, his friend’s hands are frozen to the monkey bars and the sand is quickly becoming glass. He runs back and forth on the seesaw to keep elevated from the incoming attack. “No more bad guys! We deserve a break!”

“Five years is a very long time,” says a voice in the cold mist behind the playground.

“Tempo, is that you?” asks D.S. with wide eyes. “Why are you a bad guy now? Oh wait, you were always a bad guy.”

“You don’t recognize my voice. I suppose I should expect as much. It’s been five years.” A man walks out, partially coated in ice.

“I’m here too,” says Kioshi, waving at them from the other side.

Stabby is in the kitchen, cutting veggies with BoneSaw and the Captain.

Ada looks at their hard work and smiles. “Very good! It’s so wonderful to have you all helping in the kitchen.”

The Captain of Carnage de-skins a mango. “I remember when I thought this would be humiliating labor.”

BoneSaw stops cutting to look outside the window.

Stabby pats the little bot. “Don’t worry. Kaity will come home soon!”

Codename Famine sits at the table.

“Oh, I didn’t know we had guests,” says Ada.

BoneSaw readies his weapons and the Captain rushes to grab his gear from the other room.

Stabby beams when she sees him. “Bwother!”

Abyss smiles back. “I was worried we’d never see each other again.”

Stabby hops on the table and opens her arms for a hug.

“My people are here to capture every Exp and kill the non-Exps. The Senator is throwing away all the trust that has been built between Exps and humans. He wants to end the Freedom Forcers in a single attack. I’m here to bring you back with me, sister. It won’t be the best life, but we will be safe.” He hugs her.

Stabby’s Lum aura radiates and ties Abyss to the chair with vines as strong as steel. She turns to the others. “Wun!”

The Captain looks at Ada and she reluctantly agrees. The two of them flee the kitchen and BoneSaw follows soon after.

“Stay,” says Stabby, offering her little hand to her brother.

“You don’t know what the Senator is planning. There’s a helicopter just outside, waiting for you.”

Stabby slices the vines. “You want me, then fight!”

Abyss looks up at her in tears. “Is that really what you want?”

Stabby nods.

“Even if it means killing me?” he asks with a wounded voice.

“My big brother won’t die easy.” She sticks out her tongue and smiles.

Koshi enters the room where Nina defeated Kaity. He crouches down and looks into her blank eyes. “Did you…kill her?”

Nina shook her head. “Doing that would go against my mission. Have I ever failed you?”

“No, of course not, babe. I’m just–”

“Concerned about her.” Nina smiles and grabs his hand. “I love that side of you.” She kisses his lips.

Koshi bites her lip till it bleeds. "Don't get me all riled up. We've got a mission."

Nina grabs his ass with an iron grip. "Promise to pound me really good when it's over?"

Koshi squeezes her breasts. "All night long, babe."

Noitpurroc suddenly appears in the room.

Koshi jumps. "Geez, you scared the crap out of me! What kinda kinky shit are you wearing anyway?"

"This is the real me," says Noitpurroc with a smile.

"So, are you a girl then?"

Noitpurroc looks at him blankly and then smiles. "I am now."

Nina sharpens her katana. "I take it you're here to help."

Koshi pats the demon's back. "Yeah, we helped your boss attack their base by disabling their defenses remotely, so now you're going to bring us to the Queendom like you did the others."

Noitpurroc looks at Kaity. "You…beat her?"

Nina steps on the blade, digging it deeper into the girl. "Yeah, it was easy. She's a shell of her former self."

Noitpurroc snaps her fingers.

Bob appears. "I was training my grandson, this had better be good."

Noitpurroc points at Kaity. "Sellum."

Bob's eyes widened. "Go on, send them off."

Noitpurroc sends Nina and Koshi away.

Bob looms over his minion. "You go with them, bring me Lum. If all goes well, we can wipe Kaity out before lunch."

"What about you?" asks Noitpurroc.

"I promised Shinx more training and thus I am bound. You're more than capable of capturing her. You are my strongest warrior, after all."

Noitpurroc wiggles with glee at the compliment.

"Oh, and leave Demon…Yvne. Have Yvne stand watch over Kaity. Not that she's going to do much of anything."

Gimpy nods, snaps her fingers and swaps places with Yvne.

"Stand guard. Don't let anyone in this room. I'll return soon."

Yvne turns into Kaity and salutes.

"No, too obvious."

"Oh." She transforms into Koshi.

"Yeah, that works." Bob stares at Kaity. "Your soul will be mine soon enough."

Chapter 196: Exp Hunters

Previously: Hope used Physical Crush on Gamma, but it had no effect.

Hope takes a step back. “How dare you deny my powers.”

Gamma spins around in the chair. “I was really worried at first when they assigned me to capture you. I mean you’re the leader, right? Shouldn’t Koshi be the one to go after you. But he’s busy fighting Kaity right now. Still, you think Sigma or War would go after the leader.” He stands up in the chair. “But you don’t look strong at all. And as long as I don’t let you talk, you can’t do anything to me.”

Hope grabs the lamp and throws it at him.

Gamma whacks it aside. “I may not be a field operative, but I still know the basics of fighting.” He hops off the chair and lands behind Hope. “Wow! Did you see that? I’ve never jumped that high! It must be the thrill of the battle or something.”

Hope rushes to the control panel and slams the alarm.

Gamma shakes his head. “No luck, sorry. I disabled everything the moment I got here.”

Hope whips out a gun from her dress and fires with a shaky hand.

The bullet grazes his cheek, making him bleed.

Gamma rushes to her and knocks the gun aside. “Hey, you almost killed me! I didn’t hurt you, but you actually tried to kill me!”

“I’ll make you end your own life as punishment for infiltrating my Queendom.” Hope takes in a deep breath.

Gamma swipes her feet, knocking her over. He blushes and covers his eyes. “I’m sorry. I didn’t mean to stare at your cute frilly panties.”

Hope pushes her skirt down and puffs her cheek. “You cur!”

Gamma grabs her hand. “Let me help you back up so we can continue our fight.”

Hope pulls her hand away in disgust. “Do not touch me, peasant!” she says, pulling her hand away angrily.

“I’m definitely not a peasant. Hey, I’m serious. I want to thank you for the eye candy. I mean, uhh, apologize for peeking.”

Hope huffs but is too flustered to say anything.

Gamma grabs her dress and tears it off.

Hope screams and covers her chest.

“You’re really fragile for a queen.”

Hope cries from embarrassment and then wipes her eyes. “You’ve infiltrated my kingdom, brought shame to the Queen and tore my favorite dress. You shall be executed! MENTAL CRUSH!”

Gamma covers his ears and mutters to himself. He looks at Hope and tilts his head. “You’re not saying anything.”

“Im-Impossible,” says Hope with eyes of horror.

“Hey, is it true that Exps are demons? I find that kinda hard to believe. I mean supposedly the Prince of Pleasure is a demon too, but that seems pretty crazy also.” He turns to her. “You okay?”

Hope backs up to the door and grabs the handle.

Gamma grabs her by the back and tosses her to the ground. “No leaving! I can’t mess this up.”

Hope glares at him. “Leave now and…I won’t destroy your mind.”

“You were the one trying to run away. Look, I just have a few questions before you pass out.”

Hope reaches for the energy suppressor on her back.

“Don’t bother. You can’t remove them without causing serious damage. Hey look, we’re both not fighters so maybe we can just talk a bit.”

Hope reaches for the gun.

Gamma twists her arm. “I won’t let you kill me!” He throws her against the door and knocks her out. “I got her. Yeah, it was easy actually. As long as she’s embarrassed, she can’t use her powers. I’ll head to the rendezvous point now.”

Devlin ran down the halls with Lilith, his wires throwing pottery and furniture at the agents chasing him down.

“What did you do to get that hunk so afraid of you?” asks Racheal, clapping her hands to blast away the incoming wires.

“Maybe he’s just shy,” says Lambda with a sadistic smile.

Wires burst from the floorboards and wrap around the agent’s legs.

Devlin slams the enemies against the walls.

Lambda creates blades that slice the wires. “Time to hunt!” She rushes at Devlin.

A wall of wires erupts from the floor.

Lambda slashes the wall, but it’s too thick. “Damn it, we have to go around. Get outside the building, let me know if he flees.”

“Are you sure that we’re the good guys? I think he’s just protecting that little angel.”

“That girl is a demon just like him. Now go!” Lambda enters a nearby room and starts clawing through the walls.

“Yeah, but demons can be really sweet,” says Racheal to herself. She pats her cheeks. “Get it together! So many people are counting on you!” She smiles and rushes to the nearest exit to the building.

"Welcome back, Kioshi!" cheers Opti, waving at her.

"Wow, that's really sweet. But I'm here to capture you. The Senator wants more Exps. But don't worry we will be best friends after Lambda works her magic. Nina and I really get along now, and at first she didn't like me at all!"

"Nina's alive! That's fantastic news!" cheers Opti, his pink resolve causing his fingers to slowly tear themselves from the monkey bars.

The man in the cold mist signals her. "We're here to capture them. Stop gossiping."

D.S. leaps off the seesaw as it freezes. "Crisis! I never thought I'd ever see you again. Why are you with the bad guys?"

"I'm not. Last I checked it was your side that turned me over as a sacrifice." He flings a wave of cold at D.S. as the Exp grabs his weapons.

Snippy Two freezes onto the bodyguard's hands.

"I don't want to fight you!" yells D.S. while shivering.

"Then just surrender." He flings a heat wave that melts the slide D.S. is taking cover behind.

"Hey, I never really understood. Are you guys from the army?" asks D.S.

"No, we're special ops from the government. I'm a super spy!" hollers Kioshi.

"A super spy! That is so cool!" exclaims D.S.

"Tag!" yells Kioshi, suddenly lunging at Opti.

He takes flight and dodges her energy suppressor palm attack.

"We're all friends here, we shouldn't be fighting!" yells Opti, sending a beam to D.S.

"That's right! I'm going to wake you up out of this hypno stuff!" D.S. runs out from behind cover and rushes at Crisis.

"You'll melt before you reach me!" yells Crisis as his body ignites.

Kioshi whips out an Uzi and fires at Opti. "I know we were friends but it's my dream to become the best spy ever! I can only progress if I get results! So, you're going down!"

D.S.'s skin boils as he charges at Crisis. He pierces him with his scissors but they freeze before going too deep.

"Wow, how sharp are those scissors?" asks Kioshi with sparkly eyes.

"One down," says Crisis while flinging heat waves at Opti.

"Aww, you aren't going to show them your super attack?" asks Kioshi.

"Not going to risk killing you," he says.

Kioshi puffs out her cheeks and crosses her arms. "Meanie."

Opti spots Hope being brought toward a helicopter. "They're taking Hope away!" He's hit by a heat wave but doesn't flinch. "She believed in you Kioshi, when nobody else did! Are you really just going to let her get captured?"

"I…uh."

"Hope only sees us as tools to use to reach her goal. The Senator cares deeply for every Exp Hunter, you included," says Crisis, sending a barrage of heat waves at Opti.

"Why can't I just help everyone?" cries Kioshi.

"Take this energy and do what you know is right," says Opti, sending a powerful beam of optimism into Kioshi before flying off to save Hope.

Kioshi waits for Crisis to pass her up and then drags her hand down his back, covering him with energy suppressors. "I'm sorry."

"Predictable," says Crisis, super heating his back to melt the devices while freezing Kioshi's feet. "I'll be back to fetch you later."

Deceivant looks at Absorb. "Did they hurt you?"

"Don't act like you care!" yells Absorb, turning red with rage.

Toxic rushes toward him, but is pushed back by a powerful wind that bursts from his pores. "Brother, it's me. I missed you."

"You've been reprogrammed to help this despicable bastard! That's the only way my sister would ever be playing games while her brother was captured by the enemy."

Deceivant threw a ball at Absorb. "We didn't know where you were."

"You let me get captured!"

"I'm not the same man I once was," says Deceivant, signaling to Toxic.

"That's right. You're a dead man now!" Absorb rushes at Deceivant who throws a smoke bomb at the ground. "Ha! You can only delay the inevitable. Been waiting for this day for five years!" He pulls in the smoke. "What the…I feel kinda funny."

"You haven't seen your sister in five years, but you practically ignore her the moment you see me," says Deceivant.

"Oh, we'll have a big ole' hug once your corpse lies at my feet," says Absorb, having swords emerge from his pores.

"Why not ask her what she wants?"

"Because revenge is best when it's in a blaze of fiery hatred!" He rushes at Deceivant.

The scientist sprints away but, the sponge is too fast.

"Stop! He's a good father now!" yells Toxic.

"Well if you can forgive him after all he's done to us, then I'm sure you'll forgive me after I kill him!" Absorb pushes air from behind, propelling him forward. He pierces Deceivant with his swords.

Toxic screams.

"Five years and still the same tricks," says Deceivant, seething in pain.

"Why change a strategy that already works." Flames shoot out from his pores and start melting the scientist.

Deceivant aims the Gravity Gun down and fires rapidly, sending them zooming up through the sky.

"Want a view of the moon before you die?"

Deceivant fires the gun toward Absorb, having him push free of the blades. He clenches his teeth and fires down, sending himself above the sponge.

"You look like a corpse already!" yells Absorb.

Deceivant lands on top of Absorb, having his feet get pierced by the swords. He then fires the Gravity Gun upward in rapid succession.

They are sent crashing to the ground.

Absorb makes a crater upon impact.

Deceivant tears his feet out from the blades and falls to the grass. "Absorb, I owe you an apology. I treated like a tool, not a person, for as long as I've known you. But I'm done with that."

Absorb gets up, disoriented.

"I'm going to kill you and then Hope! So please die, imagining her calling out to a father that will never come!"

"Please, I want to try and make amends. I know I don't deserve it, but please let me try."

Toxic jumps out from the grass and slithers around Absorb, slicing him up.

"Stop!" Absorb pushes her off with a sudden puff off air.

"I'm only trying to calm you down. It's not fatal," she says.

"You're defending him! He threw you away just because Hope pricked her finger on you. That dumb child was petting you the wrong direction!"

Deceivant looks up weakly. "That's not the whole story. After the cut…Hope was poisoned. She nearly died and I blamed Toxic for it. I'm not making excuses for throwing you both in the garbage chute, but that's what happened. I didn't want her to get hurt by my creations."

Absorb turns to Toxic. "Please, sister, let's kill him together."

"No! He has too much to make up for! Killing him won't accomplish anything. It will just put him in Lum."

"Lum! No way! A man like him would go straight to Sel. It's time for you to die for abandoning your children!" yells Absorb.

"You're right, I don't deserve to live," says Deceivant in tears.

"I'm not going to give you mercy no matter…wait, what did you say?" asks Absorb with a curious look.

"If anyone has the right to kill me, it's you. I killed you and your sister. You were then captured and placed in Elysium, knowing only darkness. I don't deserve the gift of life."

"Wait, so then, you're just going to let me kill you?" asks Absorb.

Deceivant stood up on his bloody feet, using the Gravity Gun for support. "In the end, your vengeance doesn't matter. I have responsibilities to Toxic and Hope to be a proper father. By attacking me, you're threatening those responsibilities. If I have to kill you to continue being their father, then I absolutely will. So let go of your revenge…for Toxic's sake," says Deceivant with a disarming smile.

"You do not have the right to say her name!" Knives shot out from his pores.

Deceivant flies up with the Gravity Gun and then fires downward at Absorb.

The field slams Absorb into the crater.

Deceivant shoots continuously to keep Absorb pinned.

"You really forgot everything about me, didn't you! ***ABSORB***!"

The gravity bullets are sucked into the sponge's pores.

Gravity bullets then relentlessly shoot out of Absorb.

"There's a little switch here that projects an anti-gravity barrier, you on the other hand…" says Deceivant.

Absorb is pulled up to Deceivant by the bullets he shot out.

Deceivant fires a gravity grenade into one of Absorb's pores, before sending his opponent back down to the crater.

"I am sorry," says Deceivant, waiting for the grenade to blow up.

"You idiot, I absorbed your grenade." Gravity grenades shoot out at Deceivant, exploding as they hit him.

Absorb is pushed away and pulled back, thrown in the air and slammed to the ground while Deceivant watches.

"I made these modifications with you in mind. Unlike you, I've been preparing for this day." Deceivant lands and engages the Gravity Blade.

"I will color this field with your blood," says Absorb, still dizzy from the gravity grenades and Toxic's calming poisons.

The moment Deceivant stabs the gravity blade into the ground, another one ejects.

All the gravity in the area was gone, leaving Absorb floating helplessly in the air. "You're just a human, how can you be defeating me?"

"I've outsmarted you because I have a clear head," says Deceivant. "Please son, just give up now."

"I will give up when I am dead!" yells Absorb.

"I'm sorry to hear that," says Deceivant softly. He propels himself onto Absorb and shoves the gravity blade into the vengeful sponge. He then fires the gun rapidly. "***SOFTENING PULL!***"

They shoot into the sky.

Deceivant holds the gun tightly, keeping his ground. The gun unloads grenades as they soar through the sky. "This is your last chance; give up!"

"You'll die from my toxins!" yells Absorb, spraying purple smoke.

"I'm sorry for everything. ***HARDENING PULL!***"

The gravity increased, sending them skyrocketing downward. The descent sped up as the gravity grenades exploded.

"Wait, I surrender this time, but I will be back. Don't kill me!"

They were now zooming closer and closer to the gravity blade that was lodged in the ground.

"I'm sorry son, but it's too late, goodbye," says Deceivant with a teary smile.

The Gravity Blade pieces straight through Absorb, shattering his capsule.

Toxic looks up in tears. "You…."

Deceivant falls to the floor. "I talked big but really…I was afraid to die." He reaches out to Toxic in tears. "Please, find Stabby. I need her help."

Toxic backs away with a horrified look and speeds off.

Chapter 197: Agents of the Apocalypse

Previously: Sigma fired his rocket launcher at his ally's back.

War absorbs the impact of the explosion and then presses his hands to Atlas's chest. "**IMPACT RELEASE**!"

The impact sent Atlas smashing through the wall and tumbling into the next room.

The moment Atlas gets back on his feet, he rushes at War. The proud Exp summons up the Agony Axe and brings it down on War's shoulder.

The Agent of War screams in overwhelming pain.

Sigma fires a rocket at Atlas, who grabs onto it and throws it back. He rolls out of the way. "Stay strong my comrade, his dark sorcery is nothing compared to our gifts of light." He throws a grenade that bursts into a sudden flash.

"The Agony Axe is a part of my soul. It is not demonic," says Atlas, tossing a treadmill at the Exp hunter.

Sigma's energy bursts out in an instant and grips the heavy projectile. "Meditation has awakened abilities within us that you demons could never obtain. You will suffer greatly. Only when you are fully broken can you be accepted into the arms of the Lord."

"When you take up arms against me, you fight every soul in my body!" Atlas summons up the Torture Trident and charges at Sigma.

The Priest rushes in and punches the weapon with an energy laden fist, knocking it from Atlas' hands.

"Your demonic artillery shall never be permitted to touch me." He reaches for Atlas who grabs his hands.

War slowly rises to his feet.

"Be careful, the Devil fuels this demon's black heart," says Sigma as he engages in a power-struggle with Atlas.

"My comrades fuel me! The Captain of Carnage is the most loyal warrior I have ever met! He is a proud demon! I won't let you speak ill of his kin!" Atlas lifts Sigma off his feet and tosses him, sending him crashing into the dumbbells.

"Your Dark Lord has made you powerful," says Sigma, standing up slowly.

"No!" Atlas' shout freezes the other warriors. "My quest for power is to dethrone the Devil. The unity of souls within me has made me into what I am now. Do not speak of the Devil, if you have yet to fight him!"

Sigma signals War to stand his ground. "The Devil is your enemy?"

"Yes, my true master is a man. Zenero. All I do is to carry on his will."

Sigma's eyes soften. "Zenero was a good man."

"Yes, but he's gone now. My guide is Unity now. My own soul."

"A demon's soul is merely a vessel for the Devil! This Unity is using you for his own selfish ambitions!" Sigma runs in and grabs onto Atlas' sides in a futile attempt to lift him.

Atlas lifts Sigma by his throat as War closes in on him. "Move another step and I break his neck."

"We've already won," says Sigma.

Atlas wobbles and his grip loosens. "What?"

"It took many darkness suppressors to fell you," says Sigma, breaking free of the chokehold.

"I will protect my comrades." Atlas flings the Chaos Chain.

It wraps around Sigma and War, keeping them both bound.

The soulful warrior then closes his eyes.

Abyss flips the table and Stabby leaps off. He whips out a machine gun, but doesn't fire.

Stabby pierces the gun with a blade. "You're not weady to shed bwood. You won't win!" She gulps a bottle of blood on her belt. "MODE FOUR!" Blades sprout out like a fan along her back.

Abyss lowers his head. "The gun fires energy suppressors. But I still couldn't pull the trigger. I am the Agent of Famine. I've killed so many innocent people…but I could never hurt you." He sobs into his hands. "But I have to! It's the only way to protect you!"

Stabby creates floating Lum blades that deflect his energy knife swipes. Her chest opens up and her skin sharpens before being sent into him.

"This pain is nothing!" yells Abyss, pushing through and picking her up. He freezes when he sees tears in her eyes. "Did I…hurt you?"

Stabby shoots a light knife into Abyss that turns into flowers and heals his wounds. She smiles.

Abyss lowers his head. "If hurting me hurts you, then I can't allow that either. Please, let me explain. I'll tell you everything. Then…come with me."

Stabby nods. "I'll listen!"

The Agent of Death arrives in the house in an instant.

"Yeah, I hear ya, boss. I was only late because you had them start without me. Yep, heading there now."

Koshi flips open the hatch and walks down the stairs to the prison. He smirks when he sees Ada. "Heya."

"Oh, hi! Wait, aren't you here to capture me?"

"Nah, I'm more of a killer," he says, rushing toward her.

"I don't want to fight!" yells Ada, reconstructing a landmine on the wall.

"Oh shit!" Koshi steps on the mine and is blasted. "Was not expecting that."

The Captain of Carnage zooms by and tosses a grenade. "Stopping by the armory was the proper choice after all!"

Koshi's energy takes the forms of hands and throws the grenade at Ada.

BoneSaw zooms out from one of the prison cells and whacks the grenade at Agent Alpha.

The agent creates a shield with his energy that protects him from the blast.

"I only want her. The rest of you are worthless!" He creates energy swords on his hands and eviscerates the Captain of Carnage.

"No!" yells Ada, rushing at him.

Koshi grabs her and flips her around. He squeezes her breasts. "I love having fun on the job."

BoneSaw looks away and then flees down the hallway.

"Why did you kill him?" asks Ada in tears.

"Wow, never felt a pair this squishy. You're always walking around naked so this is kinda your fault, you know."

"You're terrible," says Ada in tears.

"Come on, we're old friends. I could have killed you and your husband years ago. In fact, I'm the one who reasoned with the boss not to kill him. Are you going to give me a reward? Or am I going to have to take it?" He drags his fingers down her side, cutting her.

"I'm not afraid of you." Ada vanishes in his grip.

"You say that, but then you run away. That's odd, I can't track you."

Ada reconstructs herself above him and dive kicks him in the face.

Koshi grabs her leg and slams her to the ground. He then steps on her back. "Force it is. Let's see if you're more willing when you're dead."

Ada vanishes under his foot and then reappears behind him. "DECONSTRUCT!"

Koshi turns around and slaps a spiderlike device on her. His skin partially deconstructs but then the process stops. He hooks Ada's leg and trips her.

After combining both energy blades into one, he thrusts it through her back.

"Now release!"

Ada shoots off the blade like a bullet, sending her tumbling down the hallway. "What did you do to me?"

Koshi rushes after her and slices her back open with an energy scythe. "Maybe it was a fluke. Tell you what, I'll give you one last try," he says with a grin. He pulls his energy in, giving Ada a clear opening.

Ada floats back up and prepares herself. "DE-CONSTRUCT!"

Koshi bursts into laughter when nothing happens. He slams his hand into her chest, covering the area with energy suppressors. He then lifts her up by her chin, still laughing. "You Exps are nothing without your artifacts."

"You can stop artifacts?" asks Ada with eyes of terror.

"I'll get undressed too, seeing as you're already ahead of me." Koshi took off his vest and pants revealing that underneath he had a skintight suit. Its colors morphed, causing it to camouflage with the floor. "So, do you like?" he asks, flexing as he stretches.

"Am I going to die?" asks Ada.

Koshi removes his gasmask. He brushes back his short blond hair gracefully, revealing blue eyes as relaxing like the ocean. "We know about the afterlife now. Better to capture you."

Ada drowsily got back to her feet. "That suit…gives you energy?"

"Nope, it's designed to filter the energy. See it's made of nano-leeches that are constantly sucking out my energy. When you have three capsules, you need to put the energy somewhere. Now, enough chit chat. It's time to release some of that energy," says Koshi, leaning toward her and grabbing her thighs.

Toxic spots Lambda chasing after Devlin outside the castle. She sneaks behind her and then shoots herself at the enemy like a cannon.

Lambda snatches her out of the air with a web of energy.

"Nice catch," says Racheal with a thumbs up.

"Don't let Devlin escape," says Lambda, stomping on another Toxic with her energy laden foot.

"Let me go!" yells Toxic, squirming around.

"You have an adorable voice," says Lambda with a smirk.

Three Toxics simultaneously shot at Lambda, throwing her off guard.

Racheal knocks Lambda over and falls right on top of her. "Are you okay?"

"Never better," says Lambda, looking into Racheal's eyes with fondness.

"I'll capture the dark hunk! You just keep the snake busy." Racheal gets back on her feet and runs off.

A different Toxic rushes into the kitchen. "Deceivant is dying! Stabby please come with me!"

Noitpurroc enters the kitchen and looks at Stabby.

Abyss slams into the demon. "Go with her and get out of here! No way am I letting this thing touch you."

Stabby rushes off.

Noitpurroc looks at him. "The bad thoughts won't go away. I'll only stay to play if you really hurt me."

"What do you want with my little angel?" asks Abyss with a dark gaze.

"Nothing…I just have to capture her. Not allowed to hurt her."

"I'm the one who's supposed to capture her!"

Noitpurroc's eyes widen. "That's not something a big brother should say. Do you desire her?" The demon tilts her head.

"Keep your twisted thoughts to yourself. I seek only to protect her from monsters like you!" yells Abyss, throwing the demon into the cabinet and having it fall on top of her. He throws a grenade on the cabinet and jumps back.

When the smoke clears, Noitpurroc emerges scorched and bloody. A single snap and her body and clothing reforms.

"That hurt tons!" she says with wide eyes before vanishing. The gimp lands on Abyss' back and kicks off, sending him into the bloody puddle. She turns into Pathos and presses Abyss' face in. "Good doggy, drink up so you can be big and strong."

Abyss pushes off, his eyes quivering. "Blood." He says softly.

Noitpurroc returns to normal and pricks their finger. "Look doggy, I'm full of blood. Come here, boy."

"Yes blood! I need more blood! STAGE ONE!" yells Abyss fanatically. He screams out in agony as his fingertips split open, revealing their sharp teeth.

"Aww, doggy has big chompers." teases Noitpurroc.

Abyss lunges at the demon with an open mouth.

"That artifact makes you into a slave. Very unique," says Noitpurroc, teleporting away each time Abyss lunges.

"Stop running! STAGE SEVEN!" Abyss tears a hole in his stomach before he explodes into fleshy bits.

"Was that the attack?" asks the slave demon with a tilt of her head.

Each chunk of flesh and organ grew a mouth. They all shift their focus to the demon.

"More!" they all yell simultaneously, launching at the demon.

The organs and flesh tear and devour.

"I have to defeat you without violence to honor Master's pact with Pathos. Maybe Stabby will come to the Core to rescue you." Noitpurroc sends the fleshy bits away one by one.

"STAGE ZERO!" yells one of the mouths.

Abyss' body parts came back together, reverting him back to his original form. His suit rides up his legs and reassembles around him.

"You can't grow back the parts I sent away," says Noitpurroc.

"Don't pretend to understand my curse!" Abyss bites into his arm. "STAGE 8!" Codename Famine's fingers devour his hands. His arms consume his hands. His shoulders then proceeded to devouring his arms. The shoulders then fell to the floor.

"Oh wow! First you explode and now your body is eating itself? Are you sure you're not a fellow demon?" asks Noitpurroc.

The shoulders dig into the kitchen floor with their sharp teeth.

Noitpurroc vanishes to dodge the shoulder when it bursts out from below her.

The shoulder upchucks the arm that then threw up the hand, which bit into the demon's leg.

"STAGE THREE!"

A huge mouth appears on Abyss' stomach with row after row of sharpened teeth.

"All your attacks are kinda slow. Not sure if you'll be able to protect your sister like this." Noitpurroc sighs.

The mouth lungs at the demon in an instant, biting off her arm.

“The pain!” wails the demon, writhing in joy and drooling. “So fast I couldn’t react. Or maybe my body just wanted it.” She rubs her breasts with her only arm. “You just lost. Replace!”

The arm in Abyss’ stomach mouth is replaced by the dark goddess’ special sword.

“”

The sword was spit out along with all the blood and flesh the Exp had consumed. The sword pierces through Noitpurroc’s forehead.

The demon goddess wiggles as Abyss grabs onto the sword and twists it.

Abyss smiles as the demon gushes and moans. “We’re not honestly that different. We both serve a Master who uses us to do his dirty work. And we both do it to protect someone we love deeply.” He slams his foot on the demon’s crotch. “Looks like we’re both a slave to our cravings too. Come after Stabby again and I’ll devour you whole and then we won’t just be alike…we’ll be the same.”

Chapter 198: Blood

I awake in an unfamiliar place. Everything feels empty. My body won't move.

Nina was my last hope. If she was okay, then maybe everything else would fall into place. I tried to push beyond my grief, but it overtook me every night. I tried to keep it from the others, but it's become me.

My finger twitches.

Where am I?

My body is in one of those black suits that those Exp Hunters wear. It's sapping away my energy. I was captured, but what does it matter?

Nothing matters.

I look beyond the glass. Two figures are fighting. One of them keeps shifting, but the other holds its ground.

The shifter becomes a raging wave that crashes the other figure against my prison.

That face…so familiar. Why can't I remember?

The figure smashes the glass.

The acidic liquid around me pours out.

My eyes heal and I see him…my dad.

Kanasta turns and smiles. "You're strong enough to escape yourself. An assassin's training never leaves them. We are connected through something deeper than blood. I have faith in you, my daughter."

He doesn't even know I'm a god now. He believes in me…and I'm letting him down.

Yvne's watery form becomes bladed and strikes Kanasta.

He closes his eyes and lowers his arms, allowing himself to be attacked.

I have to fight! I have to save him! No…I'm not strong enough for either right now. I…have to let go. I have to surrender.

"Not…afraid," I say with burnt lips.

I'm not afraid of dying. I'm not afraid of losing him even. I'm ready for whatever comes my way.

My skin loses all sensation. I fall from my restraints. The tubes in my back disappear. I fall to the floor weakly and it starts to disappear beneath me.

"Kaity, create an opening. Just a small one. As small as a bullet. Focus."

I do want to protect him. He came for me. We're getting out of here.

My Absence aura parts the slightest bit on my forehead.

Kanasta flings a dagger on a thread into the spot. It pierces into my skull. "That will hold." He pulls me back up and thrashes me around like a whip.

Only he would come up with such a clever strategy.

Yvne screeches and cries. "Stop! My power is infinite!"

Kanasta opens up his suit case, showing the dark god. "Do you want to join your sister in my collection?" He holds up Deerg's head.

Yvne shrieks, falls into her true form and flees into a black portal.

I can't turn off my Absence form. And I still…can't move.

Kanasta fastens the string attached to my head to a bar on the ceiling, keeping me from falling through the floor.

The sound of multiple hands clapping fills the room.

Kanasta stands at attention.

The Freedom Forcers are in danger. I have to get us out of here.

Devlin is suddenly blasted off his feet. He catches Lilith with his wires and pulls her in close. "If you had hurt her, I'd cut off your arms and legs. You'd bleed out wiggling on the floor as a helpless torso," he says with a dark gaze at his attacker.

Racheal screams in terror which transitions into a high-pitched squeal of delight. "That would be amazing! Wait, but I wouldn't hurt her. She's just a kid. I'm going to bring you in for your crimes."

"You stole Kawai's power and you're using it to attack my comrades. I'd rather not kill you in front of my daughter…" his wires jut out and shape themselves into swords "so don't test me."

"Maybe you can just explain to me. I wasn't actually told what you did either. I'm an Exp Hunter in training. I legit got recruited yesterday."

"I have no need to explain anything to you." Devlin's wires coil around her legs and slam her into the trees.

Several trees suddenly burst around him and his wires are sliced.

A blur speeds by and leaps over his sudden wire barrage.

She lands behind him.

"How dare you take Nina's form!" yells Devlin, his wires spreading out and attacking from multiple directions.

"I am Nina. And that girl…is Demonica's!" The ninja leaps through the barrage and slices only the wires she needs to in order to close in on her target. "Exps are only safe with the Senator."

The helicopter pilot looks over at Crisis, telling him to hurry it up.

"We can't take off until I've cut his wings," says Crisis, focusing his heat waves into blades that slice through the air.

Opti tries to dodge, but his mobility is limited by the encroaching cold wave around him. The heat wave burns his arm. "There's no way I can win. When all hope seems lost, he'd always take over and figure something out. Can't believe I actually miss Pesi." Another heat wave comes and burns his legs. "Okay! I'm going to take one final gamble!"

"Who are you even talking to?" asks Crisis, readying dual heat waves while keeping an eye on the knocked-out Queen on the grass.

"Hit me with everything you've got. If you're really not my friend anymore, then prove it!"

"Fine! You really want to die!" Crisis raises the temperature, igniting the grass around him. "Or do you really have something planned?! Bring it!"

"Thanks for clearing the path!" Opti dives directly into the heat wave. He boosts his morale, keeping steady even as his body ignites into flames. He flies down directly to Crisis and hugs him.

"You're not winning me over. I'm not possessed, you know," says Crisis as his body cooks Opti.

"They're going to take away Hope! I know you're Exp Hunters! But one of you has to care! You have to stop this!" he yells into Crisis' earpiece.

The heat stops and instead Crisis freezes Opti's body.

"That was really something. I didn't expect you to try something so ridiculous."

Boom!

The helicopter bursts and sends Crisis, Hope and Opti off their feet.

Crisis looks around in a daze. "Boss, I'll need another helicopter pronto. The one you sent just blew up. And I think I know who did it." He nods. "Understood."

Kioshi finally breaks free of the ice by heating her body with energy. "Phew. Now I just gotta convince Crisis not to tell my brother I got beat so easily." She looks up to see a massive ball of ice rolling towards her. "He's coming for me! Brother, save me!"

The ice melts when Crisis arrives. "I was nearby the helicopter. I could easily have made it explode."

"Huh? What are you talking about?" asks Kioshi.

"I know you're the one who did it! You let that Exp get into your head! But we lost one of our own because of you! A hunter is dead!"

"I was frozen here! I didn't do anything!"

Crisis freezes her legs with a cold wave and then super heats his hands. "You're going to admit it was you! And then the Boss will decide your punishment." He grabs her shoulder.

Kioshi screams and claws at his face with her hands.

Crisis freezes her arms. "Damn traitor! Just admit it and I won't have to hurt you."

Koshi approaches, his energy bursting out. "Hands off my sister!" The energy shoots out as a sword at Crisis.

The Exp lets go of Kioshi and falls to dodge the attack. "You don't understand. She betrayed us!"

Koshi rushes up and looks down at him. "Oh really. Any proof?"

"I know she did?"

"And you're the only one who knows?" he asks, his hand moving toward Crisis' face.

"Yeah, for now."

Koshi smiles and uses a small energy blade to cut out Crisis' earpiece. "Great, then I just need to kill you and she's safe." His energy forms into a scythe and his suit turns white like bleached bones. "I was worried I'd have to slaughter the whole team."

After healing Deceivant, Stabby ran off to help others. The explosion of the helicopter got her attention. She crouches down to heal Opti.

"You're gonna be just fine," she says with a sweet smile.

The helicopter rusts and turns into dust.

Efil steps out of the dust, despair in her eyes. "Why did she choose you over me?" Her Lum energy branches out as vines of flame.

Stabby creates a water barrier but is grabbed by a powerful vine and pulled away from Opti.

Efil glares at the child. "I did everything for her! Everything!" She slams Stabby against the ground who creates a flowerbed on impact. "You don't even know her."

Stabby sends a beam of Life at Efil but the Goddess slides out of the way.

"I'm not here for revenge. No, that's not it at all. None of this is your fault. And she must have had a reason, right?" Efil creates time blades as she approaches Stabby. "I remembered something Lum told me about soul exchange." More vines come out and press Stabby into the ground.

Stabby slices at the vines. "Talk later. Gotta help Opti."

"No! You have to listen." Efil cries as she drags her sword along the vine. "I need you to understand. If you die, I can bring her back. Only a realm god's soul can be exchanged for that of another realm god. I could never defeat the current Sel or Absence, but you're just coming into your powers. I'm more skilled with my Lum powers than you are." Efil emits a beam of light that becomes minerals to bind the girl when she runs. "If you die, then Lum will come back to me. Kaity will be happy too! Don't you want to make us happy?"

Stabby looks at Efil curiously. "Do you bweed?"

"You'll never know," says Efil, standing over Stabby with the time blade. "I hope you understand that none of this is personal. It's just better for everyone."

Stabby's fingers split open, revealing knives that cut Efil's leg.

The Goddess takes a step back. "Please, can't you just surrender your life peacefully."

Stabby licks the special blood off her blade. "Bwood! MODE 5!" Her eyes sharpen and her skin is sliced open by blades.

Efil stands tall and raises her blade. "You're more of a demon than I thought. This bloodlust, Lum would be ashamed! She abhors bloodshed! It makes her sick," says the Goddess of Life with teary eyes.

Stabby's body launches blades at Efil, who counters with her time blade.

To her surprise, the time blade does nothing. The blades pass through and slice her.

"Not possible," says Efil, using Lum energy to heal the wounds.

Stabby opens her mouth in pulls in the blood with an unseen force. "More!" She runs at Efil.

"If you are immune to time, then I shall break you with your own power!" Efil's vines grab the dagger and parry Stabby, while more vines sneak behind the Exp. The vines latch onto the blades in her back and tear them out.

"Bwood!" Stabby's back knives spin, slicing the vines, she lunges at Efil and cuts her repeatedly. After each cut, she accidentally heals the wounds with Lum energy. The new Lum licks her sharp fingers in disappointment. "Why is there no bwood?" she asks with watery eyes.

Efil sobs. "Violence is a solution that only spawns more problems."

Stabby's knives shoot from her back and then reign down on Efil.

The Goddess turns a blast of light into a powerful wind pillar that scatters the blades. "Stabby, if you're still able to listen, then I'm going to make you a promise. Once the true Lum is revived, all the realm gods will join forces! Once Riufen has been struck down, I will bring you back! Then we will unite the gods against Bob. We can exchange his soul for that of Pathos! Your death will give him a second chance."

Stabby leaps onto her back and slices her repeatedly. "Why won't you bweed for me?" She whines and pouts.

Efil lowers her head. "I'm not strong enough to end you. Forgive me, Great Goddess, for being so useless." Efil sees Opti and gasps. "I didn't even notice." She walks to Opti as she's being sliced up. "You fought to protect Lum. I hope you will keep doing so." She heals him with Lum energy and then grows a tree from her back.

The tree pushes Stabby off her.

Opti smiles at Efil. "Thanks for saving me. If you're having doubts, then I can help," he says, coating his hands with his aura.

"No. I don't want that. I just don't know what to do anymore," says Efil, entering a Lum portal.

Chapter 199: Exodus

The figure approaches Kanasta in the abandoned government base. She throws off her helmet. Dramatic streaks of red decorate the agent's short white hair. The black pupiled agent's face was scarred and rough. Crimson shades concealed the malice in her eyes and her suit turns bluer as she takes each step.

I dangle from above, watching things play out passively.

"That was such a cruel way to use your friend! You are tons of fun!" she says with a childish giggle.

Kanasta steps up to the enemy. "What do you want, Agent Beta?"

"You've been a great help to us these five years, but this is absolutely betrayal! That little kitten is ours! Got sooo many experiments to run on her! Kshkshksh!"

"Kaity, make an exit," says Kanasta as the enemy approaches.

I can barely move.

"Can't," I say softly.

"Fine, then I will stand by and let her kill me."

No! I have to save him! I want to save him with my whole being.

The Absence barrier fades.

Beta dances around as she slices Kanasta, who hardens his muscles to survive her assault.

If I'm not dead, then I have to fight.

Pain explodes in my head as I tear out the chain blade in my skull. I fall like a rag doll to the ground.

Kanasta grabs Beta's arms and crushes them. "They're after my brother! Only you can bring us there!" He tosses me my suit.

Devlin is there! And so is Lilith! And...Nina. Everyone's there! He's right! I have to save us!

The Exp Hunter kicks him in the face and then slices his chest with her energy talons.

I must return to the Queendom.

I close my eyes and when I open them, we've arrived at the Queendom.

Devlin's wraps his wires around Nina's arms and legs to keep her plasma blades from cutting him. "It really does feel like you."

Nina gives him a deadly stare. "You abandoned me for Demonica." She reaches for a grenade and tosses it at Devlin.

"Providing support!" hollers Rachel before blasting Devlin off his feet with a sound blast.

Nina vanishes into a smoke cloud when Devlin's wires shoot out once more.

Kunai shoot out of the cloud and explode soon after.

Devlin creates a wire shield to deflect the impact from the explosives. "Damn it, Nina. What the hell did they do to you!?"

A windmill shuriken zooms by Devin, sending explosive tags flying in all directions.

Devlin's wires grab Racheal and pull her in. "You trigger them, then she blows up too."

Racheal gulps. "Hey, maybe we can work something out? You two used to be friends, right?"

The windmill shuriken came back like a boomerang.

"He was my everything," says Nina, emerging from the smoke cloud with her katana poised.

Devlin catches the windmill shuriken with a single wire.

Nina rushes by and slices the wires that are holding Lilith. "Release my ally, or the girl dies."

Devlin tosses Racheal to the ground and sends a wire toward Nina's throat, ready to kill her.

Kanasta suddenly rams into Nina and pins her down.

"She's not the Nina we know! She's trying to kill my daughter!" yells Devlin to Kanasta.

Kaity approaches Devlin. "Gimpy is in the kitchen. You talked to them before, right? Maybe you can get them to stop all this."

Devlin shakes his head. "And if we aren't friends, then I'd be bringing Lilith into danger."

"Leave her with me," says Kaity firmly, her legs wobbling. "Kanasta, go see if anyone needs help. I have to face Nina."

"Promise me you'll keep her safe," says Devlin in tears.

Kaity grabs him and hugs him tightly. "I swear on my mother's soul."

Devlin nods and rushes off.

"Go, Kanasta!" yells Kaity.

"You've become a fine leader," says Kanasta before running off.

Nina slowly stood up. "I defeated you. You were broken and lost. How are you back?"

The way she looks at me. It's so cold. I have to reach her!

"I came back…because I want to save you," I say, radiating light.

Racheal sneaks off while Nina isn't looking.

Nina rushes in, her plasma sword being parried by my plasma claws. "You couldn't save me before. Even though I felt something for you, it wasn't love. Lambda is the one who put an end to my suffering. She made it so I no longer love Devlin. I've found someone else now. Someone who loves only me." Smoke comes out from Nina and she uses the cover to slice me. "You mean nothing to me."

"The Nina I know is stronger than this. She wouldn't let the enemy brainwash her. She was proud and loyal."

Nina kicks me into a tree and then cleaves my stomach, taking down the tree in the process. "I am loyal. And Koshi loves me dearly. You don't know what we have!" She drops a device on the ground that repeatedly shoots out grenades. The warrior ninja kicks grenade after grenade at me.

Meaningless.

I take on every hit and heal. "Nothing hurts without you. Nothing feels like anything."

Nina rushes in and pierces my capsule. "Just die." Tears fall from Nina's eye as she repeatedly kills me.

She's suffering. A part of her still cares about me.

Lum energy envelopes me, taking the form of a long dress of light.

Just like mother had.

I reach out to Nina.

The ninja warrior releases the weapon and retreats. "Don't touch me." She throws a shuriken into my forehead.

The wound heals immediately, pushing the weapon out.

Nina threw shurikens at me, but they just graze my skin as my healing powers push them off. She rushes in and slices me continuously with her metal katana.

I will save you, Nina.

I smile, sending love her way as her attacks become more desperate.

Everything seems so slow.

I grab Nina's sword.

Flowers bloom on the blade, causing Nina to drop it in surprise.

I embrace you with all of my being.

Wings of light shot out of from my back and wrap around Nina.

Time to bring back my beloved.

"I love you." My wings become hands that all pull Nina closer to me while filling her with light. I gaze into her eyes and then lock lips with her. Lum energy flows from me into her.

Nina cries and breaks the kiss. "I'm scared, Kaity. I'm scared of coming back. I'm scared of falling in love with Devlin again. And I'm scared of…hurting you. I don't know what to do." She holds me tightly.

Nina...she's not lost. She's right here in my arms.

"You're back, you're finally back," I cry as I hug her even tighter.

"It's not like I don't remember what happened. The torture went on for so long. It wasn't about information…it was just a way to break me. Lambda was the only one I was in contact with for months. She would hurt me, but she'd also care for me. She nurtured me into becoming dependent on her. She'd convince me of the nobility of their mission. I still believe in it, but I know what you're trying to do is right too."

She's suffered so much.

Nina wipes her eyes. "Koshi and I have done so many missions together. We shared joy and our sorrows too. He took care of me and eventually we fell in love. My heart bleeds for him, Kaity. I need to be with him." She clenches her teeth.

"Why did you try to kill me?"

"It had been so long. And…Lambda, she trained my mind. I see you as an enemy, all of you. I can't help it. I can't control my thoughts, Kaity."

"Whatever is going on, we'll figure a way around it. Hope can save you."

"Kaity, I'm not worth saving." Nina lets go of me and cries. "You should go."

"I'm never leaving you!"

Nina smiles at me through her tears. "Racheal has Lilith. I…distracted you so she could get away. You didn't hear anything because, well that's just how she is."

Devlin trusted me with her and I…

"Kaity, you should go. I'm not your friend. I've betrayed you. I'm sorry." Nina creates a smoke cloud and vanishes.

I clench my sides and sob.

Everything was supposed to be okay now. I thought that she would stay.

I slam my fists to the ground.

What's the point of being Sellum!? I can't help anyone! I've never felt weaker and more helpless! All I do is lose the people I care about.

Koshi breaks out from the ice prison by releasing massive energy.

Crisis points at the sky. "You see that? Because of your sister we lost our only way off this rock. This whole country is going to be razed to cinders!"

"Great! Then I don't even need to bother killing you!" Koshi's energy takes shape as a scythe and slices Crisis' legs off. "Everyone, find any cover you can. The Boss just called in an air strike!" He grabs Kioshi and flees to the prison where he fought Ada.

Devlin arrives in the kitchen.

Noitpurroc is on the floor, in a puddle of her own love juices.

Abyss is still twisting the sword in her skull.

"I need to talk to the demon. I'll kill you if I must."

"Fine." Abyss lets go of the sword. "I'm getting out of here before things get really bad!"

"What are you saying!?" hollers Devlin as Abyss flees. He bites his lip. "Damn it. Hey, wake up." He shakes Noitpurroc to her senses.

"I was having the most wonderful dream," says Noitpurroc in a daze.

"Did you get the truth from Bob?"

The demon nods. "Master was devastated by her death."

"And did you find Shinx?"

Noitpurroc nods.

"Bring me to him. Please, I have to talk to him!"

"Devlin, I…can't betray my master."

"I'm not asking you to. I'm not asking at all." His wires piece the demon's chest. "Bring me to him."

Noitpurroc's eyes sparkle. She wiggles and then snaps her fingers.

Devlin vanishes.

The demon deity slowly gets up. "Mission, what was it again?"

Koshi is in the prison with Kioshi and Ada.

"Our son is still out there! We have to go help him!" yells Kioshi, shaking Koshi's arm.

"Is something the matter?" Ada turns to Kioshi. "You saved me from your brother. Thank you. He loves you dearly."

"The whole chain of command is gone. How the hell did Crisis know about an air strike that I didn't? Ugh, the connection here is terrible. I need a direct line to Gamma."

Kioshi hands her brother her phone.

"Gamma, are you there? You have to bring back the Queendom's defenses. You deactivated them, right? Reactivate them now before were all blown to bits by anti-matter bombs!"

"Is that what's going on? Why would Diablo order an Exodus Strike when we are still here!?"

"We don't really have time to ask that, now do we? Can you get them back online?"

"Rebooting will take at least five minutes."

"Shit! Hey, kid. If you don't survive, just want you to know, that…" Koshi wipes his tears "it's all your fault for deactivating the Queendom's defenses!"

"You're such a jerk!" yells Gamma before hanging up.

Ada heads to the exit.

"Not a good idea," says Koshi, grabbing her arm.

"My husband is out there. My children and my friends are all in danger. I'm going to take down as many of those jets as I can."

Abyss lights up when he finds Stabby. "Sister, I told you they were coming. They're here now."

Stabby stands tall. "Will protect everyone." She creates a giant pillar of light.

"Those jets are faster than your powers. Make a Lum portal and save who you can!" He looks up. "It's too late."

The Death Jets drop their payload, thirty anti-matter bombs. Exps and Exp Hunters look up as their doom approaches. A massive portal appears that covers the kingdom.

Racheal, on a motorboat with Lilith, looks back at the island. "They're saved!"

A single small portal appears and releases one of the bombs. It hits a jet and bursts in the sky, obliterating all the jets down to their atoms.

Zenero stands on a portal and has another portal with a camera tripod in front of him. "My fellow Earthlings, I have returned from the afterlife! Heaven is real!" He extends his arms out from the long curtain robe concealing them. "From now on, all the Exps are under my protection!"

Part 24
Religious Warfare

Chapter 200: Discipline

Previously: Shinx was training with Bob.

The ethereal manipulator sends boulders at his grandson.

Shinx creates a dot on the center boulder, having the others smash into it. He then creates multiple dots in rapid succession.

The large rocks crash into each other until they are only pebbles.

Bob appears from the ground and lunges the Atma Blade at Shinx.

The boy brings the stone bits toward himself, which causes his teacher to retreat.

Shinx then immediately points to the ground, forcing the stones to follow suit.

Bob pops up behind him and pats his head. "Very good! As long as you keep up that speed, it won't matter that you can only summon one target at a time."

"I've decided upon a name for this ability." He points at Bob with a finger gun. "***BULLET POINT!***"

All the stones shoot through Bob and tear up Shinx.

"Did I mention I can go incorporeal? Your powers aren't all that handy against me. Good thing we're on the same side," he says, looming over the child with dark energy.

"Step away from him." Riufen arrives and unsheathes his spine.

Bob sinks and pops out from inside Riufen. "Oh, so you finally found us."

Riufen nods. "No samurai would allow a winding path to obstruct his goal."

Shinx looks up at him. "I'm training with him. You can fight him when I'm done."

Riufen shakes his head. "I'm not here for him." He gets down on his knees. "I'm here for you." The immortal samurai bows to the boy, pressing his forehead into the dirt. "I humbly beseech that you accept me as your teacher. I shall carve bushido into your being!"

Shinx blushes and scratches his head. "I won't just accept anyone as my teacher. You have to earn it."

"Of course." Riufen stands up. "My apologies."

"Geez, why are you apologizing so much? You look strong. Don't talk like a weakling."

Riufen rushes at his desired disciple.

Shinx waits for the samurai to strike and redirects the sword into the swordsman's leg. He then kicks it in deeper.

Riufen slams his leg into the boy's chin, disorienting him.

Shinx creates dots in a daze as he nearly falls over.

Riufen picks him up and places his face against the dirt. "A warrior mustn't rely on magic and sorcery. Fight me without your powers. I have decided that training you is my destiny. There is no going back. Either you will accept me as your teacher or you will die denying me." He flings Shinx toward a boulder.

The young warrior kicks off and knees Riufen in the face. He cringes is pain. "What the hell is your skin made of?"

"Determination and dedication." He grabs Shinx and slams him to the ground.

A wire pulls the boy off the ground and through the bushes.

Bob glares at Riufen. "Don't just stand there! He's stealing your childish destiny!"

Riufen nods and rushes off.

Shinx crosses his arms and waits to be pulled in. He is brought through a waterfall and into a cave. "Well, well. Not a bad hiding place. But how did you find me?"

"By never giving up." Devlin steps out of the shadows.

Shinx brushes off the dirt and blood on his face and holds out his hand. The Death Scythe flies into his grip. "I can't kill you yet, but that doesn't mean I'm just going to surrender either."

"Please, just come home. Lilith misses you. She needs her brother."

"She doesn't need me anymore than I need her." Shinx grabs a snail off the cave wall. "I was just like this creature. I carried my home with me everywhere I went. My Mommy was my home and you killed her." He places the snail back on the wall. "I'm going to get strong enough to kill you. But until then, stay out of my way!"

"You kill me and then what? It won't accomplish anything. I've been there before…wanting to kill my parents. But I was just being manipulated by Bob. You're letting him control you too."

"I'm not an idiot like you were. I'm following Bob to become strong! He's already taught me so much."

"He's the one who sent Demonica to kill Lilith. He's the one who had you held hostage."

"I was never a hostage. Stop lying."

"Demonica would want me to protect you. To take care of you."

Shinx glares at Devlin darkly. "So now you care about what Mommy wants, how convenient." He tosses the Death Scythe into the air.

It shot right into Devlin's chest. "I'm sorry, Shinx. But we can bring her back. If Kaity kills one of Bob's dark gods, then we can make an exchange for her soul."

Shinx makes a gun shape with his fingers. He fires the imaginary gun at the ground.

The scythe drags down to the dot, slicing Devlin's chest open to reach its target.

"Come on, Son. You're too smart to base your life on revenge," says Devlin with a pained smile.

"It's all I have now. Everyone responsible will die. You're first, then Lilith, then Kaity and finally me," says Shinx.

"You want me. That's fine. But leave them out of this," says Devlin with a dark glare.

"You killed Mommy to protect Lilith. If that worthless sister of mine was never born, then Mommy would still be alive. As for Kaity, she is the reason Mommy suffered. And I…I was too weak to protect her. All of us shall pay," says Shinx justly, standing tall.

"I promise you, I will bring her back," says Devlin, stepping up to him.

Shinx is suddenly lifted up by wires.

The wires cover his fingertips, stopping the boy from using his ability.

"I'm taking you home," says Devlin softly as Shinx struggles and screams at him. He takes his son past the waterfall.

Riufen spots them.

"Hey, where is this place? I have to find a way out of this jungle," says Devlin.

Riufen shakes his head. "You're not taking the boy. He's free to walk his own path."

"I'm not going to allow Bob to turn him against his family."

Riufen unsheathes his spine. "Release him now. You are no longer my master. I am a ronin who has decided training that boy is my life's mission."

"I'm his father!" Devlin's wires shoot out at the samurai.

Riufen slices a few of them. His veins shoot out and wrestle the rest.

Wire swords come out from Devlin's back and assault the ronin from multiple angles.

Riufen spins his body in a swift controlled motion, creating a small gust that throws off the weapons' trajectories. He then rushes past his old shogun.

Devlin's arms fall to the floor and Riufen's veins grab hold of Shinx.

The two tug the boy back and forth.

Riufen calls Gladius to him and then cleaves the air.

Devlin falls to bits and loses hold of Shinx.

Riufen pulls his destiny in. He then rushes off while Devlin regenerates. He sets Shinx down when they are far enough away.

Shinx looks up at him with starry eyes. "That was incredible."

Riufen nods and turns away.

"Wait." Shinx lowers his head. "I need to become strong. I need your help. Please, teach me sensei."

Riufen turns to Shinx and smiles at him warmly. He places his spine above the boy's head. "It's official now. Our training begins immediately."

Chapter 201: Treason

I step into the training room and sure enough, she's there.

Racheal, my sworn nemesis.

"Hey, Kioshi. What up?" asks Racheal, giving me a toothy boyish smile.

Stupid tomboy and her friendly smile and her dumb freckles.

"My name is Agent Pi! Don't get so formal with me." I approach her and take a fighting stance. "I know what you're planning."

"Huh? What are you talking about?" asks Racheal.

"You're a spy trying to take my place! You're so cute, determined and you love macabre stuff too! You're trying replace me as the little sister of the team! I saw you eyeing my brother. Don't you deny it."

Racheal grins and wiggles. "Yeah, he's such a hunk."

"You're trying to take everything from me." I glare at her.

No way am I losing him to this wannabee!

Racheal's expression softens. "Hey, I just wanna be friends. I'm sorry for upsetting you." She grabs my hands.

I pull away and I am absolutely not blushing. "Stop being so sweet! I'm going to beat you right here and now! Then everyone will realize you're useless and I'm awesome!" I stand proud and push out my chest.

"Alright, but after I win, I was hoping you could help explain some things to me." Racheal speaks softly.

It's not fair! Nobody is going to want a brat like me around when Racheal is so friendly and adorable.

I rush at her and grab her arms.

She swipes my feet but I just grab her with my legs and bring her to the ground.

She rolls on top of me and grab my arms.

I notice sweat dripping down her freckled cheeks.

Rrrgh! Why is she do damn cute?

I knee her in the crotch and throw her over me. "Ha! Thought you had me."

Oh yeah. I've been training like super crazy! I can counter any attack now!

Racheal somersaults around me.

I spot my opening and swipe with my right leg.

She pushes off the ground and grabs my head between her legs.

Girl thighs...in my face.

She flings me to the ground and pins me down. "Kioshi, you okay?"

Damn it. My lezbo-phobia is acting up. Can't focus. I'm going to lose.

Koshi pushes Racheal aside and grabs my hands. "Are you okay?"

Brother's here. He always comes to rescue me.

I hug him and cry against his chest. "Do you still love me?"

He pats me and smiles. "More than every living being on the Earth. I'd burn everything to ashes to keep you safe."

I pull him into a kiss and then push him off. "So you don't like Racheal more than me?"

He chuckles a bit and pats me. "Aww, you're jealous. Racheal's fun for sure, but nobody could ever replace you."

"I'm a whiny brat."

"Yep." He grins and pokes my nose.

"Hey!" I slug him and we laugh.

Racheal waves at me. "I really don't mean to upset you. I just wanted to make some friends. I uhh, actually have a husband. We were supposed to meet up already."

She's married?

"Well that's news to me." Koshi smiles at Racheal. "I hope he treats you right."

Racheal smiles back. "He does. We really love one another."

Koshi pats my cheeks. "You good now?"

"Yeah. No way am I going to die because I got scissored by a tomboy's thighs."

"Okay? Anyways, the Boss has called a meeting. Racheal, you can keep training here if you want."

Racheal approaches Koshi. "Hey uh, Captain. I uhhh…sorry about losing the girl."

Koshi shakes his head. "Not your fault. You explained what happened as soon as you got back. You were ambushed by Zenero. None of us retrieved any targets. We were lucky that Gimp Exp got us all out of there when she did."

She!? I thought Naughtypurroc was a boy!

Koshi grabs my hand and takes me to the meeting room.

The Senator is there, along with Gamma, Lambda, War, Famine, Crisis and Sigma.

The chairs are ultra-comfy and soft. The table is made of a glass that creates holographic projections.

My brother puts his feet up on the table. “What brings you to the Bahamas? I guess even you need a vacation after the last mission.”

He’s always so chill.

I notice everyone is looking at me. “Umm, is this about the whole–”

Koshi covers my mouth. “What’s the situation? Actually, before that, why were we even attacking the Exps? Weren’t we in a truce with them?”

The Senator shakes his head and gestures to Sigma.

“The formation of the Queendom brought all the heathens out of hiding and into a single place. The strike was coordinated after a recent battle because their forces would still be recovering. There were too many civilians when the Queendom was first attacked for us to engage the demons. The Messiah only allowed the demons to prosper so they could be wiped out in one fell swoop.”

The Senator turns to Famine. “Your recent slaughter in Kansas gave us the motive to attack the Exps. But now Zenero threatens everything. How did he return?”

Famine lowers his head.

My poor boy is put through so much.

Koshi sits up and glares at our boss. “Yeah, I don’t care about that. How about you tell us something first? Why the hell were you going to kill us all? Why send us there, if you were going to bomb the whole island?”

The Senator grimaces. “I didn’t send those jets.”

“You didn’t send your jets to drop your bombs on your people?”

“Absolutely not!”

“So then who hijacked our hidden planes?”

The Senator turns his gaze back to me. “A traitor.” He stands up dramatically. “Someone in this room has committed treason against me!”

A cat hops out from War’s lap.

Agent Beta screams and hops back onto the top of her chair. “What the hell is that thing doing here?”

“He followed me here,” says War softly.

“Kill it! Kill it!” yells Beta.

Her pussy phobia is so funny!

Gamma picks up the cat and carries him outside.

The Senator sits back down. “Our information was leaked. No doubt there is other Intel that has also been exposed by the traitor.”

Koshi sits up. "We don't know if there is a traitor."

Crisis nods. "I agree. Let's focus on what we do know. Only one of us was working with the Exp commander."

"Hope is the Queen of the Exps, not the commander," I say, sticking out my tongue.

She should have broken Crisis before turning him over to the Senator.

Crisis smiles. "And I was also attacked by Kioshi. She tried to drain my energy so I couldn't take Hope back to base. Soon after that, the helicopter, with Agent Zeta inside, exploded. Agent Zeta is now dead. Those are the facts."

No…not him. Why did it have to be my boyfriend?

"I can't believe I ever thought we were friends!" I yell at the nasty man.

Famine snaps his finger to get everyone's attention. "Let's not forget that after Hope was praised as humanity's savior. Kioshi was taken off her job of spying on the Freedom Forcers. She's been off that job for five years. And the production of these super bombs was only finished last year."

Koshi chimes in. "And she wasn't the one who lost Wringer, twice. Agent Beta was!"

Lambda sighs. "All this finger pointing isn't going to help anything."

The Senator nods. "We almost lost all our agents. We have lost our credibility as an agency. Showing the Exp incarceration video was premature. That was foolish of me."

Beta claws at the table. "No, Boss. What was foolish was giving humanity the antidote! We could have had the world at our knees! We controlled the future of mankind!"

Eeesh. She's so scary sometimes.

Crisis slams his fist on the desk. "None of that matters! An agent is dead because someone planted explosives in our getaway vehicle and then that same person had nearly all of us bombed! We have to get to the bottom of this."

Gamma speaks up. "I'm still checking outgoing calls to see if anyone contacted Hope."

Koshi stands up. "No need. I'm the one who did it."

The Senator puffs out air from his nose. "Absurd. You'd never put your sister in danger. You're trying to protect her because you know she's guilty."

I stand up proudly. "You think I did that? I didn't even know about these weapons! Nobody tells me anything! I'm the one who helped us make an alliance with an actual demon. I also captured Priority One! Let's talk about all the awesome things I've done!"

Yeah! No way am I giving up so easily.

"Actual demon?" asks Sigma with a curious look.

The Senator slams his fist. "Enough! It's no secret that you're buddy buddy with the Queen."

Gamma nods. "It's true. She's made several calls to her," he says softly.

Even the cutie pie is selling me out. This sucks.

I smile at the absurdity of the claims. "She's my friend! We weren't enemies! There is nothing wrong with calling a friend! Why do we even have to be enemies! You're the one who's keeping secrets, John!"

Yeah! That'll show him.

The Senator raises his arm. "Agent Pi, you have been found guilty of conspiring with the enemy and killing an agent."

Koshi grabs the Senator's arm. "You're being absurd."

I glare at the old jerk. "He was my boyfriend, so obviously Koshi killed him!"

Abyss bites his lip. "I'm guilty of plenty! Before I even joined you, I knew about the afterlife! I never told you a thing! I was just there recently too. That's where I was these past five years. If you don't clear her of all charges, then I'll never tell you a thing."

The Senator scoffs. "I have my sources. I don't need you."

"Get rid of her and you lose me too!" he growls.

He's standing up for me.

Koshi points at Crisis. "I tried to kill this asshole just a few hours ago. Aren't you going to put me on trial too?"

Brother.

Lambda grabs the Senator's hand. "I think you're being too hard on her. She's one of us. Sure she can be a blather mouth, but she is not treasonous."

Yeah! I'm a good girl!

"Anyone who tries to leave will be captured by Agent Beta and dealt with by Agent Lambda," says the Senator with a scowl.

He won't change his mind. I was chosen as the guilty girl before the meeting even began.

I lean forward and glare at my jerk of a boss. "Go ahead then. Execute me! I'm not afraid of dying."

"You will be striped of your rank and excommunicated from the agency. No harm shall befall you."

"Fine!" I throw my helmet at him and strip out of my clothes.

"I quit too!" yells Koshi.

"If you quit, then I can't provide her protection," says the Senator with a toothy smile.

I turn around. "You know what, Boss. Hope always respected me and believed in me. Maybe I should have joined her instead of you. I don't see the world divided by sides and parties! I thought you wanted to unify the people, but you don't. I quit!" I flick him off and then storm out of the room.

Telling off that asshole was so exciting! Hope, your super spy is on her way back home!

Chapter 202: The Right Choice

Previously: Zenero saved the Queendom from being bombed and the Exp Hunters fled.

Zenero calls the Freedom Forcers to the War Room after everyone is back on their feet.

Hope approaches him and looks all the way up. “I know some of my people fought to keep you imprisoned, but know that was not my order. There was a schism in the past. Thankfully that wound has mended. We are all grateful you rescued us this day.” She turns to her team. “Bow!”

Everyone follows her command.

Zenero looks at Hope and his face becomes lax. “You’ve been continuing my mission. I am the one who is grateful.” He grabs her hand and bows to her.

Atlas looks up at Zenero. “I…have helped her.”

Zenero teleports to him and cups his son’s hand. “I know what troubles you. There was a reason I left you behind when I left Absence with the others. You were already exactly where you needed to be.”

“What about June?” asks Opti.

“I brought her back to Earth and asked her to join me again, but she had other obligations. She’s a free bird that’s forged her own path.”

Hope crosses her arms. “Indeed. That bird ran off on her own, most likely to bring Riufen back to us. Utterly foolish.”

“Then I shall find her and bring her back to you, Queen Hope.” He bows and kisses her hand.

Hope blushes. “Nice to be treated with proper respect.”

Atlas looks to Ada. “Where is…the Captain of Carnage? Is he training? He was with you last.”

Ada gulps. “I’m sorry…I…he died fighting Koshi.”

Atlas clenches his fist and tears flow freely from his eyes. “Must I lose everyone I care for?” He turns to Zenero in desperation. “Casey, Chipko, August, are they alright? And did you find May.”

“The others are with me. May is still missing, regrettably.”

Deceivant coughs a bit and then speaks up. “Pathos, Murai and Tranquil are gone. When Pathos died, he sent all his power up to buy us more time to prepare against Bob. He gave us five years.”

“All his remaining power and he couldn’t even push time forward a week. Still, it’s given me time to prepare.”

"What have you been doing these past five years anyway?" asks Hope curiously.

Zenero creates a portal. "I'd like to discuss that in private. As well as our plans moving forward."

Deceivant steps between him. "I'm not leaving her with you."

Stabby glares at Zenero. "I don't twust you even a wittle!"

Atlas scratches his chin. "Pathos shared the story of when you became Sellum."

Zenero lowers his head. "I went mad with power and paranoia. I assure you I have been reflecting on my actions while imprisoned in Absence." He smiles at Deceivant. "You're welcome to come along."

Deceivant looks to the team. "We'll be back soon."

Atlas steps up. "I'm coming too."

"As you please." Zenero nods.

The four of them enter the portal and walk back out as soon as they vanished.

Hope looks satisfied. Deceivant still looks concerned.

The Queen of the Exps stands tall and addresses her people. "Everyone, I assure you that the Exps held captive by the Senator will be back under my protection by the end of the month."

"Wait, so you did have a meeting?" asks Opti.

"A rather long one. Had a lot to catch up on," says Hope with a lax smile.

Kaity enters the workout room. It's still demolished from the recent assault. She spots Chipko. The green-haired environmentalist's caramel skin is shining from all the sweat.

"Hey there. Long time no see." Chipko waves at Kaity with her fingerless gloves.

Kaity approaches nervously. "Nice to see you too. You seem so happy." She smiles a little.

Chipko grins and then kicks the bag. "Who wouldn't be happy to see an old friend. We are friends, right?"

"Y-Yeah, of course." Kaity forces a smile.

"Hey, what's wrong?"

"I…lost Lilith. And I promised her father, I promised Devlin I'd protect her. And I thought I could bring Nina back home. But I couldn't. I'm useless."

"Join me. Punch this bag with all that negativity. Just let it out." Chipko bounces in place as she boxes the bag.

Kaity nods and joins in.

The two of them send the bag flying off the rope.

"Whoops. Guess it couldn't handle us together." Chipko slugs Kaity affectionately.

"So, where have you been?"

"Where haven't I been?" Chipko holds her cheeks fondly. "Oh, right." She blushes. "I've been undercover. We all have. We didn't want the Senator finding out about the afterlife or have him send his assassins after Zenero. We all took up human aliases. I was Talim. Made some new friends in India. The Brokpa tribe of Ladakah. They've been vegan for over five-thousand years. It was nice being treated as a tourist and not some sort of god for once." She scratches her cheek and starts up the treadmill.

"So, your mission was just to remain undiscovered?"

"Not exactly. We also had to extract intel from the government. Thankfully a certain handsome agent was more than forthcoming." She smiles as she jogs.

Kaity starts the adjacent treadmill. "Koshi? You really trust him?"

"He's been a huge help. At first it felt kinda bad, cheating on Zenero with him. But Zenero did order it."

"He ordered you to sleep with Koshi?"

"No. He just said by any means necessary. He knows what Koshi wants. And it's fine. Koshi took initiative every time," says Chipko with a blush.

"Well as long as you're okay with it. I'm confused though. Before your strongest desire was to kill Zenero. Now you two are dating?"

Chipko stops the treadmill. "I did want to kill him. But once he held me and spoke to me…I became powerless."

Kaity looks up at Chipko. "I'm powerless too. I can't use any of my abilities as Sellum."

Chipko's eyes lit up. "You're Sellum!" She then froze. "Does that mean Pathos is…."

"Yeah, he's gone now. I'm so sorry."

Chipko hugs Kaity. "Don't blame yourself. All we can do now is fight on in his memory." She wipes her eyes.

"He's not the only one…I…."

"Don't need to talk about it. Please don't say anymore." Chipko holds back her tears.

Kaity nods solemnly. "I don't think he chose right. I'm not a good Sellum. I don't even know what to do. He was only Sellum for like a few weeks, right? But it felt like he could do anything."

"Well yeah, that's because of the Microcosm."

Kaity looks up at her and dries her eyes. "What do you mean?"

Chipko picks up the heaviest weights and continues her exercise. "What I mean is…time moves extremely slow there. Earth time moves three-hundred and sixty-five times faster than time in Sellum. The Microcosm moves remarkably slower than time on Earth. Spend a year there and only a second will pass on Earth and only about six minutes in Sellum. More importantly it has a different wavelength that allows for deep meditation. I've experienced some incredibly lucid dreams there!"

"That's great to know! I guess I'll just focus on trying to make a portal there. I can't teleport to places I haven't been but I've been there before so maybe it will work."

"Oh, yeah. Good point. Well, you'll get there soon enough. I believe in you!"

"Thanks. I wish I believed in me more." Kaity lowers her head.

Chipko scrutinizes her. "Hmm. Maybe you don't need exercise. Yeah, you need some rest." She rolls out a yoga mat. "Lie down, I'll give you a massage."

"Okay," says Kaity with a big smile. She stretches out once she's flat on the mat.

Chipko sits on her back and starts rubbing her shoulders. "So, how are things with you and Devi-kun going?"

"Huh? I don't like Devi-kun like that. I told you he has kids now. He had them with Demonica."

"Oh yeah, Koshi told me that when I was at his mercy." Chipko wobbles and bites her lip.

"So, are you and Zenero a couple now? Does he treat you right? You deserve someone who really appreciates and respects you."

"Well, he's still technically married to Casey and she doesn't know about what me and Zenero do." Chipko digs her knuckles into Kaity's lower back.

"Nyaheheh. What have you two done?" asks Kaity with a naughty smirk.

"Name a country. Any country."

"Huh? Umm, the Bahamas?"

"Not a country, but okay. We had a very romantic scuba dive together after a lovely day at the beach. He then pounded me underwater! It was incredible." Chipko holds her heart to her chest and wobbles.

"Wow. Okay, what about Russia? That's your homeland, right? I bet you did something romantic there!" Kaity bounces in excitement.

Chipko digs her elbows into Kaity's squishy tooshie. "Oh, yeah! I taught him how to snowboard and we 'stopped' some hunters together too. He knows me so well. He never really asks for sex because well, he knows I'm too shy to respond if he does. He can feel when I want it and he just takes me! We made love, starting at the bottom of Elbrus mountain, all the way to the snowy peak."

"Wow, that does sound amazing," says Kaity with heavy breaths.

"Yeah! Sometimes he just teleports us around as we make love. Having us visit multiple countries in a single round. And the way he kisses me, it makes me feel so fulfilled! When I'm really restless he just uses those portals of his to multiply his hands or his umm…you know. He pleases me from all angles in an instant."

Kaity turns around and squeezes Chipko's breast, making her squeal in surprise.

"Hey, what was that for?"

"Since when are you so bold? You used to be so shy about sexual stuff."

Chipko sits down. "Well, I've changed a lot. Zenero has helped heal me. I know he's the one who broke me too. But he's also the one who created me." She smiles and looks down shyly. "Do you think I'm weak for loving him? For trusting him again?"

Kaity hugs her friend from behind. "I think it takes so much strength to forgive. I don't know if I forgive Sefiwah yet."

Chipko turns around and looks at Kaity with worry. "What did my sister do?"

"She found my daddy and she…made me kill him."

Chipko's face turns dark with horror. "That doesn't sound anything like her. How could sister Tranquil have changed so much?"

"She did it so I would kill her…and I did." Kaity hugs Chipko and sobs. "I murdered my momma. I killed her and now she's gone forever!"

Chipko pets Kaity with deep compassion. "I don't blame you for what you did." She pulls Kaity away to face her. "I can't go into details, but there's a way to bring her back."

"I don't know how to soul swap. Why did she believe in me? I'm a terrible choice for Sellum! I'm an assassin!"

Chipko shakes her head. "I don't agree at all. Sellum is both light and dark. You know how to take lives and save them. You're both killer and savior! A perfect Sellum. He absolutely made the right choice! So cheer up, God Kitten." Chipko tickles her sides.

Kaity beams at her. "Hee-hee. You really mean that, don't you?"

"Yeah, I absolutely do. So, umm…who is the new Lum?"

"Stabby."

"Oh."

"I was surprised too at first, but she's pretty capable as Lum."

"I always hoped that she would choose me. I'm a warrior for the Earth. We both aren't fond of humans. Do you think it was because of how broken I was?"

Kaity shakes her head. "I'm sure she had faith in you. Maybe she felt that you would be in danger as Lum."

"Yeah, maybe. Okay, so I'll tell you a secret too. It's called Eternal Exchange. Zenero told me all about it. Sellum has the power to exchange one soul for another of equal status in Soul Storage. Mortal for mortal, god for god, realm god for realm god. It really works! We've been exchanging bad people for good people over the years."

"What do you mean? How do you know who the bad people are?"

"We've been using the Furies' Eco-Footprint Network. Brought back lots of environmentalists. And it's painless too. A bigot goes poof and an environmentalist takes their place. Gotta stack the odds in our favor for the coming election anyway."

"Wow, that's a little scary honestly. Then again, I killed a lot of people when I was an assassin, so I can't really judge."

"Making the world a better place one person at a time. It's what Pathos would want. That's what I think."

"How are the Furies doing?"

Chipko bites her lip. "They were slaughtered by the Senator. His punishment for them creating the special Zika strain. Only a fraction remains now and they're fighting for their own eco-paradise. Kind of like what you all have here. By the time I returned from Absence, he had already begun the eradication of my people. I was told not to intervene. Their idol, their god, didn't save them. I didn't save anyone."

"But you can bring them back, right? They're all in Lum."

"Yeah, but we can't just round them up and reincarnate them. There are rules, Kaity. The Senator went back on his promise to Hope as well. He killed nearly all the DXM members too."

"That's terrible."

"Atlas and May founded the DXM. It was supposed to be a group of understanding and acceptance. But all those good people ended up wiped out by that despicable Senator." She shakes her head. "Sorry about all that. I'm getting off topic. Look, we can do the Essence Exchange.

When we kill Bob, we can bring Sefiwah back. Maybe I can convince Murai to join the fight too!"

"You can't…Riufen killed him. He's the new Absence now."

Chipko holds her hands to her chest and shivers. "Three of my siblings are dead and Bob still isn't satisfied. If I go out, I'm going out fighting!" She punches the ground.

It cracks in stages.

Kaity's Lum energy shoots out her palms and seals it up. "I…I did it. It wasn't working earlier."

Chipko beams at her. "You can bring them back."

"What?"

"The Furies and the DXM. You can show the world your powers!"

"Wouldn't that just create fear?"

"Kaity, you're God now! You can go to a place ravaged by deforestation and create a new forest. You can show the world that Exps are here to help! When you get better with your powers, you can fix soil erosion and other disasters! You can be an icon to both Furies and the DXM. No, you'd be inspiring to E-Humans everywhere!"

"I don't know about that."

"Doesn't hurt to try. Come on, I'll go with you. We can take June too! It will be fun."

"June left. She ran off after Riufen."

Chipko's smile drops. "No. No. No."

"She'll be okay. She's a smart girl."

"She may be a year older than me but she's still a kid deep down! I have her artifact too! She's defenseless!"

"No. She has Crisis' artifact. She's really mastered it."

"Juney has been captured before by those twisted Exp Hunters! Koshi was the one who got her out…in exchange for me. It was the first time I…."

"What did he do to you?"

"Hey, that's not the point! The point is we have to find her before something bad happens to her! I'll go get Zenero."

"Wait, he's here?"

"Should still be. And I'll be staying for a while too."

Kaity grabs Chipko's hands. "Can I trust him?"

Chipko nods. "He wants to make a better world. There's no reason to distrust him now. He's here to protect all the Exps!" She then rushes off.

Kanasta comes out from behind one of the machines in the back of the exercise room.

Kaity turns around. “Where you listening in on us?”

“Chipko was very forthcoming with information. You should have probed her more.” He speaks to her intently while he plays on his portable game console.

“She’s my friend!”

“I’ll be leaving shortly.”

“Another mission? Did you get hired by the Senator to kill the DXM? What about the Furies?”

“I get hired to kill people, not factions. I’m no mercenary.” He looks to the game screen. “Yes! They joined my clan!”

Kaity lowers the game console and looks up at him. “Please, just stay. I need you.” She grabs his arm and presses her face against it.

He shakes his head. “You’ve surpassed me.”

“I’m a mess!”

He embraces her. “You killed for the mission despite blood ties. I…can never do that. I don’t want to. You should lead the Viper Squad.”

“There is no Viper Squad! There’s just you! I promised Sefiwah I’d move on after she died, but I quit way before that! How dare you try to make my mother’s death a positive thing! It’s horrible what I did!” Kaity pushes away and cries in her hands.

Kanasta shudders. “I promised you no more tears after the first kill. I’ve failed that promise again and again. I have a new promise now. Order me and I will obey.”

“Stay with us! Don’t run off to help the Senator or do some job!”

“Very well, Boss. I’d like to speak with Devlin.”

“He left to bring Shinx home.” Kaity’s eyes widen. “Hey, you were working with them! Do you know where they took Lilith? Is it the same place you found me?”

“That place was just one of their many bases. I don’t know anything about Lilith. I’m only given missions. I wasn’t part of the team.”

“How can you work with them after what they did to Nina?”

“You won’t appreciate any answer I give.” He walks off.

Kaity pulls out her phone. “Come on, pick up!”

“Heya, kitty cat. What’s shaking?” asks Koshi in a smooth voice.

“You know where they’re taking Lilith! Tell me!”

“Whoa! Chill, kitten. We don’t have her. Zenero took her from Racheal. Hey, I need something from you. If Kioshi….”

Kaity hangs up the phone. She holds herself and cries. “It’s okay. She’s safe. Everything is going to be okay.”

Chapter 203: Pointless Sacrifice

I wake up in a tent in the middle of the night. It takes me a moment to remember what was going on.

Father and I are returning from our camping trip. We've constantly been moving around for years after our place of worship was overtaken by a false god. It will be nice to meet with some of our old friends.

I sneak out from my father's warm embrace, careful not to wake him. I unzip the tent and slowly make my way to the campfire. With eyes closed, I feel the heat around me. I welcome it.

"Dark Divinity, are you there? It's me, Mika? Please answer."

Every Sunday I try to reach my god. It's been more than five years since we've last spoken, but there's always a glimmer of hope for me.

I open my eyes after an hour of praying for Satan to answer my call. Tears flow out and I wipe them.

The Dark Divinity didn't abandon us. He's just preoccupied. I know it.

A hand startles me. I turn around to see a man in a black cloak.

"The reunion is tomorrow morning. Do you have a tent?" I ask with a smile. "We packed an extra just in case. I'll go get it for you."

He grabs me and picks me up.

Oh no. They found us. Please let them not find Father.

I kick and bite, but the possessed follower doesn't even register the pain.

They are alive with empty minds. That demon lord has created true zombies.

The lost minion brings me to a silver van.

I'm gagged and thrown in the back seat.

Darkness was always a comfort. It represents possibility and oneness. But now…it only brings me fear and dread.

It's was a long ride to their destination.

When the trunk opens, the Prince of Pleasure grins at me.

His skin is disgustingly flawless and his toxic eyes swirl with cruelty.

"Finally found the great Matriarch! One of your friends sold you out."

I stand tall and look up at him. "I don't fear you."

"Your god won't protect you. He's probably dead already." The false god slices his finger. I struggle as he tries to force the purple blood into my mouth. He finally succeeds.

My throat burns and my vision fades in and out.

I glare at him. "I will never serve you. No poison or drug can touch my soul. My faith is stronger than all your powers."

"When the last drop of blood is taken from your father's corpse, you will be a broken doll."

They have him! I have to do something.

"Please, allow him to go freely. I'll listen to your demands."

"All that defiance gone in an instant. It's nothing personal, just a religious disagreement. In order for the new order to reign supreme, the old order must be done away with. You must be getting tired dear."

I spot the Church in the distance. It glistens in the moonlight.

Bless it all! I can't keep my eyes open. I have to stay strong...for everyone.

I awake inside a new Seltanic Church. Paintings of the false god adorn the walls and the chairs have all been cleared out so the center space is open. I'm in a cage, making me think of all those poor animals in a similar situation.

The twisted demon lord opens the cage and takes out a knife.

His followers hold me down as he cuts off my clothes.

De-robing oneself to appear in our natural state is a sacred experience. He's polluting it with his wickedness.

Four of his men, all once dear followers, bring my father to the basin in the center.

I'm held down as the Prince tosses my father into the large basin.

"It doesn't matter what you do to me. Satan will always welcome you back home." My father beams at the false god who seeks to bring him pain.

I can't be as pure as you father. I want Satan to punish this wicked person with all his dark devices.

The lost demon strips my father and starts cutting his back.

I have to do something!

I try to wrestle out of their grip, but their muscles are reinforced by the demon's poisons.

I hear cries and turn my head to see other animals in cages.

He's going to kill them too.

"Take my life! I'm the Matriarch of my people. Leave my father alone!" I yell.

"Scream all you like. It won't change a thing. Faith keeps people bound to their situation. They do not aspire for greatness and instead find peace in their meaningless lives. I'm giving your father's life actual purpose. His blood shall make me stronger!"

My once smiling followers are chanting around my tortured father with vacant eyes.

I've failed them all.

Tears rush down my face.

We were supposed to enrich their lives. They're all gone now. I've failed everyone.

I spot the Unholy Fire atop a golden rod in the back.

The sacred fire that links this world to the Underworld. That's my one chance. When one is powerless, they must have the power to surrender.

I gaze into the cleansing flame. "Lord Sel, hear my plea! I'm in danger! I need you!"

The Prince laughs and cuts my father again. "Scream all you like. He won't answer."

This isn't like before. I need Lord Sel now! He always answers when I'm truly in need. He speaks to me not as just a wise god, but as a loving friend.

I look up at the men holding me. "Burn me!"

They look back with vacant eyes.

The Prince grins. "Not a bad plan at all!" He lifts up the holy lamp and brings it to my skin.

This pain is my token. It's my toll to speak to the Dark Divinity!

I scream and cry as my body is burned.

Father reaches out to me, chanting a mantra to send me his love.

Bunnies, pigs and goats rush out from their cages and run free.

The Prince of Pleasure drops the Unholy Flame. "You're dead." His smile trembles as he steps back.

My captors are lifted off their feet and thrown aside.

"Animal sacrifice is just a scapegoat. True sacrifice is personal. Now, what are you willing to sacrifice to appease your deity?" asks a voice that uplifts me to my core.

"Who are you!?" asks a woman near the Prince of Pleasure.

I know who it is. My Dark Deity has come. He's here to save me!

I try to dry my tears to get a glimpse of my god.

"I am Sel, the God of Destruction, and you are my followers," says Satan, smiling at us.

An eye that sees all, yet judges none. There couldn't be a more perfect avatar. No doubt Satan's true form is beyond our comprehension.

The demon lord points at Lord Sel. "This is a false god! Destroy him!" He directs his mindless followers and then runs to the exit.

Lord Sel fires a beam in a line, blocking the door with a dark corrosive energy.

I run to my Daddy and hold him.

Lord Sel drapes a cloth over me. "I'm sorry I came late, dear friend."

I reach out and touch my deity.

My body lights up and my head gets dizzy.

Satan pats me. "Everyone will be just fine once the traitor is no more."

The demon lord approaches the dark god. "Wait, I can be of use to you. I can help expand the reach of your religion! I've done so much these five years! I've set up places of worship for you around the world!"

Lord Sel floats to the deceiver. "I would have let you live, but you hurt my biggest fan. Your soul shall be torn and eaten piece by piece." Dark energy erupts from the god.

The demon lord slaps a device on Lord Satan. "Ha! You're still an Exp! And I'm an Exp Hunter! No, I'm more than that!" The traitor tears off his priestly garb and reveals a black skintight suit. "I am Codename Pestilence! The last member of the Senator's Agents of the Apocalypse."

Lord Sel lifts him up with a spectral tendril and slams the cretin against the ceiling, drags him along two walls and then sends him crashing into the blood basin. "And I should care why?"

"You're allies with the Senator! We should be working together!"

"Hmm." The Dark Deity turns to me. "Do I kill him?"

I want to say yes, but I have a responsibility to my sinful family.

I shake my head. "Make him cure those he's poisoned. If he can't do that, then make him repent for each one he's harmed."

"An excellent idea!" Lord Sel summons up a weapon of swirling energy.

The Atma Blade! A weapon formed from Satan's own soul.

The Dark Deity plunges the ethereal weapon into the demon lord and consumes his soul.

The traitor's body falls limply to the floor.

"I'll repurpose him into a mindless obedient pawn. And then he'll gladly do his best to cure these people." Lord Sel turns to me and my father who is chanting praises. "No harm shall befall you ever again. You and all your friends are under my protection." He picks up one of the bunnies and pets it.

I knew Lord Sel would return. It's time to reclaim the Seltanic Church in his ignoble name and expand our reach to all those without a spiritual home!

Chapter 204: Inspiration

Devlin parks his boat at the Queendom dock.

Hope orders Deceivant to tie the boat and looks down at Devlin. “You ran off again despite your promise. Need I place a collar on you?”

Devlin hops onto the dock. “I found Shinx. He’s with Bob now.”

Hope grabs his hand. “It’s been four days. You’ve missed so much.”

He walks past her. “I can catch up later. I need to go see Lilith and tell her about Shinx. Where is she?”

“You don’t get to make demands to me. You’ve been absolutely reckless lately and I won’t have it.” Hope stomps her foot.

“I’m not in the mood right now. Where is she?” Devlin looks at Hope with a dark gaze.

Hope lowers her head.

Kaity runs down the dock and leaps into a hug with Devlin.

The flustered father falls over, looking at her with deep blush. “It’s good to see you.”

Hope orders her father to carry her off.

“Devlin, I was so worried. Where is Shinx? Was he there? Or was it a trap?”

“He didn’t want to come home,” says Devlin softly.

Kaity frowns. “I’m so sorry.”

“How’s Lilith doing? Is she finally talking again?”

Kaity helps Devlin to his feet. “I was fighting Nina and she was taken. I failed you. She’s in danger because of me.”

Devlin’s face sinks. “Blame won’t help anything. We need to find her immediately. I never should have left.”

“We will find her. I kind of have an idea where she is, but I’m not sure what to do. You have to keep this just between us.” Kaity grabs his hands.

He nods. “Of course.”

“One of the government agents took her but, according to Koshi, she was intercepted by Zenero before she could be extracted.”

“Zenero’s back and he has my daughter?!”

“He’s back and I don’t know for sure if he does. Koshi could be lying, but I don’t think he is. Zenero is our ally right now. He saved us all from being bombed. We have to be very careful how we approach this.”

“Then what is the plan?”

"I was actually going to meet Koshi at an abandoned warehouse. You know, get more details about what happened in person."

"Sounds like an obvious trap. What you need to do is find his sister. Threaten her life and he'll tell the truth about Lilith. The most likely option is that he's lying under orders, trying to break up our alliance."

"Yeah, you're right. But Kioshi is my friend."

"Then I'll do it," says Devlin with a dark look.

"There's another problem. Kioshi went MIA after she was excommunicated from the Exp Hunters."

"Then she's likely on her way here. She knows Hope will protect her."

"Yeah, good point."

"Learn what you can from Koshi. I'll deal with her. And don't worry. I won't kill her. I promise."

Kaity smiles at him. "I know you won't. I'll be back in just a bit." She hops into a boat.

"Hey, wouldn't it be faster to just teleport there?"

"Yeah, I just…don't have my powers right now. They'll come back when Lilith is safe…I hope."

Devlin hugs Kaity lovingly. "They will."

"Hey…is it okay if we talk a bit before I head out?"

"Yeah, of course. What's on your mind?"

Kaity embraces him and cries. "Sefiwah, my mom…she only pretended to hate me so I would kill her. The whole time she really loved me. She made me kill my father just to provoke me to kill her. And it worked. But that's not everything. I don't know if I'll ever save the Nina I love or if the other Nina is already gone. I don't even know if I ever truly loved Nina. What if I was just desperate? I'm overwhelmed and scared. Losing Lilith and not knowing what is going to happen to her just pushed me over the edge."

"You have to focus on what you can change and not think about the rest. I have so many regrets. You have to bury them."

"Sefiwah loved me Devin, she really loved me," cries Kaity.

"And she'll love you when we find a way to bring her back," says Devlin, petting her comfortingly.

"So, you know about that too? Do you believe it?"

"Demonica believes it. Problem is it's something Bob told her. But I…want to believe it's true. I want to believe we can exchange for the souls of those we cared about."

"Chipko told me about it. She said her and Zenero already did it with the souls of mortals."

Devlin beams. "Well then, there's so much we can change. But let's focus on one thing at a time. I promise I'll do everything I can to get your mom back. But first we need to make sure we don't lose anyone else."

Kaity smiles at him. "Yeah. Thanks, Devi-kun." She gives him one last squeeze.

"Kaity, I won't pretend I can ever understand your pain. What you're going through is something only you've experienced. What I can promise you is I'll always be here to help," says Devlin, patting her head.

"Thanks, Devi-kun. I'm here for you too. Nina made me promise to give you a big kiss if she died. But seeing as how she's alive…this will have to do." Kaity pops up and kisses his cheek.

Devlin beams at her. "You're my salvation."

"Geez, that's a bit much."

"You always believed there was good in me. You salvaged me. I owe you more than I can ever repay." He grabs her hand.

Kaity blushes. "Just stay here and keep everyone safe."

"As you command. Hey, any luck with your powers now?"

Kaity closes her eyes. She sighs. "Nope. But they'll come back when I need them. The talk really did help. It's just these things are complicated."

"Safe travels." Devlin waves at her.

The cat-girl nods and then leaves the dock.

The cabin door opens when the Queendom is just a spec in the distance.

"Shame about your powers," says Koshi with a yawn.

Kaity pulls out her side-arm and aims at him. "Why aren't you at the meeting point?"

"Because my friends are waiting to ambush you there. We can still go if you'd like."

"Let's talk."

Kaity shyly approaches Koshi, lowering her suit to show some cleavage.

"Huh?" Koshi looks away with flushed cheeks.

Kaity suddenly engages her claws and pins Koshi to the wall. "How could you allow Nina to be turned into Lambda's pet?"

"I thought you were dead. I took care of her in your place. If I helped her escape, that would just make her a target. The Senator plans to kill every last Exp except those under him."

Kaity releases him. "I…I didn't know that."

"It's the truth and you didn't hear it from me. Got it?"

"Yeah. Hey, she talked about you. Said you're her boyfriend. You better be treating her right."

"I am."

"Did you rape her?"

"What?"

Kaity points her claws at him. "Did you rape her?"

"No. I didn't."

Kaity cries. "That better be the truth."

"It is. I swear it. Hey, cheer up. You're an assassin, right? Find that strength from within. It hasn't left you," says Koshi, lifting up her chin.

Kaity bites at his finger and he pulls back. "You tried to…force yourself on me."

"I thought we had somehow moved past that. I've been trying to make it up to you."

"Well I want to talk about it now. You were a friend. I trusted you and you–"

Koshi sighs. "If I told you the truth, you wouldn't believe me."

"Try me. If you don't answer, I'll gut you right here."

"Okay, okay. Sefiwah wanted you to fear men. She told me to…I was never really going to do anything to you. I promise. If I told you the truth, she said she'd end my sister's life. I could have said something now, but I just assume it's better if you hate me. I still traumatized you, regardless of my excuse. Yeah, I know that all sounds convenient but it's the absolute truth."

"I believe you." Kaity sighs.

"You do?" asks Koshi, his eyes tearing up.

Kaity nods. "That also means your people really don't have Lilith."

"That's right. And hey, I know a place not too far from here. Small village. You could let lose there."

"What?"

"Come on. You inspired me with how violently you killed your targets. The corpses looked like they were mauled by a panther. Maybe you're holding back your powers and a killing spree could ignite them again!"

"I'm not that person anymore."

"So blood doesn't drive you crazy anymore? Come on, Kaity. You were my inspiration! You were the one who freed me."

"You were already a killer."

"But not a humanitarian."

Kaity groans. "This conversation is over. I'm heading back to the Queendom." She heads to the steering wheel.

Koshi grabs her and pulls her away from the wheel. "I want a personal example of your killer instinct."

"I'm not going to fight you."

"I can use you to bargain with the Senator to let my sis back in. Either you take me in as your prisoner or I take you in. There is no third option here." He rubs his hands together, creating plasma blades.

"You've helped me. I'll figure something out."

Koshi rushes at her and pierces her chest with his energy blade. "Who killed the Kaity that inspired me, because I will eat them alive!"

Kaity kicks him off. "You don't need to do this."

Koshi pulls out a gun and fires a whole round into her. "You can't die, but I can. Go ahead, kill me!" He rushes up and bashes his gun against her face.

Kaity cuts his side with her claws.

He retaliates with a slash that she blocks. "Just a few days ago you wiped the floor with me."

She slices his suit, just deep enough to graze his skin.

"Whoa babe, if you wanted me to strip you could have just asked." Koshi smirks.

The cat-girl leaps onto his shoulders and flings him overboard.

Koshi shoots out energy from his hands and feet, keeping him afloat.

"Your body will be overloaded with energy if you don't stop this," says Kaity, pointing her gun at him.

"Then I better win quickly!" He flies into Kaity and pins her down. "I took off my clothes, now it's your turn."

Kaity kicks at him as he tries to take off her special suit.

Koshi grabs her legs. "Hate me all you want. Just awaken your powers already!"

Kaity's legs wrap around his head before she rolls on top of him. Her claws are near his chest. "Game over."

Koshi closes his eyes and then grabs her arm. He pulls the plasma claws into him.

"You idiot! You're going to die."

Koshi embraces her tightly. “Help.” He coughs up blood.

“Shit!” Kaity places her hands on his chest. “Heal! Come on, work!”

Koshi takes out his gun and shoots a full clip into the wound. He cries but smiles at her. “Fuckin’ hurts.”

Kaity holds out her hands again. “It won’t work.”

“Guess you don’t care about me. Should have brought Nina,” he says weakly.

Kaity cries as she growls. “Yeah, I hate you…but you’re also like a brother to me. An idiot big brother! Don’t you dare die on me!” Sel energy shoots out of her fingertips.

“Oh shit,” says Koshi.

“No!”

Light explodes out from her in a flash.

When it clears, all their wounds are healed.

“Ha! I win.” Koshi slugs her.

“Why…go so far for me?”

Koshi ruffles her hair. “Cuz I love you like a little sister. Plus, I needed you to owe me a favor.”

Kaity wipes her eyes. “What do you need?”

“Kioshi is reckless and, well, suicidal. I need you to look after her. If she gets hurt, just heal her.”

“So then…this was about her,” says Kaity softly.

“I can’t look after her anymore. I’m entrusting her to you.”

“I couldn’t protect Lilith. I can’t promise you anything.”

“Promise me you’ll be her friend.”

“Yeah, of course.” Kaity smiles.

“Well, then bring us back to shore.”

“Sure…thing.” Kaity’s eyes widen.

She had teleported the boat to the Queendom.

Chapter 205: Exiled Spy

I chug another bottle of some fancy alcohol.

Still tastes like piss.

I turn on the cold water of the shower.

It doesn't help my headache at all.

I scrub myself till I start to bleed and sob.

Stupid Kioshi. Thought you could just drown your worries by going to a club. All that alcohol, all those drugs and all that cum. It's still not enough.

I throw the bottle the ground. It shatters and creates little cuts on my legs. I watch my blood go down the shower drain.

If glory holes can't get me out of this funk, what can?

I get out of the shower and throw myself on the bed.

I don't feel like getting dressed. I don't feel like doing anything.

I look outside the window.

Couldn't even get a room on the top floor. A fall from the second floor is just enough to get hurt not die. Stupid tease.

I cross my arms and pout.

Spent so many years trying to be the ultimate spy and now I'm just gutter trash. I didn't blow up that helicopter, but I still got blamed.

I hug my pillow tightly and sob into it.

I don't even want to die anymore. I don't want anything. I feel so alone. There's just no hope left.

My eyes widen.

Hope! That's it! Maybe she'll take me in! Maybe she still remembers me.

I run to the bathroom and puke.

Yeah, get that poison out of your system, cutie! Freshen up! It's off to the Queendom first thing tomorrow morning!

When I was near the shore the despair came back full force.

I can't come back after five years of nothing. She wouldn't accept that. Wait, she wouldn't even trust me. If she doesn't trust me then I...I'd have nothing.

I see the anchor and the chain.

It's better this way.

I tie the chain around my legs. I lift the anchor and look at the water.

Am I really going to end it?

I wipe the tears from my eyes.

No crying! Suicide should be done with a smile.

I try to smile but my mouth just quivers.

I can't do it. So heavy.

I lose hold of the anchor. It drops into the water.

I'm pulled in with it.

Shit!

I thrash around but my legs can barely move.

It's not supposed to end like this. An accident! Yeah, that's what I am, a worthless accident!

My lungs burn and pain takes over me.

Time loses meaning. Everything is just pain.

Pain...pain...pain. Wait...it's not too late. I can still do it the right way.

I take out an energy suppressor.

Yeah, this girl ends things on her own terms. I'm going out my way!

I slap the energy suppressor on my chest, then another and another.

Goodbye Brother.

My eyes slowly open. I see Famine's little sister and Kaity, pouring light energy into me inside a wooden cabin.

I slowly get up from the bed.

Famine's little sister's eyes widen. "Yay! I did it! I gotta tell evewybody!" She runs off with joy.

Kaity looks at me with a blank stare. "You're not dead?"

She's right...I survived. Live to die another way, I suppose.

"You scared me." Kaity holds my head to her chest.

I pop up. "What you just witnessed is my legendary dead horse technique. It's kind of like a trojan horse, but...well dead. Basically, I was playing possum. You didn't think I got that codename by chance, did ya." I grin at her.

"Your capsule stopped releasing energy."

Can't let her know how scared I was...how weak I am.

"Yep! Used an energy suppressor and then entered a state of total relaxation! You impressed."

"Hope was worried sick."

"Really? She still...cares about me? Even after I've been away for five years."

She still cares about me!

"Of course she does!"

"I thought that the only way I would be able to enter was as a dead body. I didn't know you all still wanted me."

Kaity embraces me tightly. "Don't be silly. You're an honorary Freedom Forcer."

I can't keep lying to her. If she really is going to accept me, then she'll have to accept the frightened little coward I am.

I look down. "That's not entirely true. After I got exiled. Well, I tried to live on my own. Surviving should be no problem for a super spy. But I…I almost didn't make it. Being alone…it's scary for me. I just feel like everything I've done, that everything I've strived for, is gone. I don't see a path and when there's no path, the cliffside looks so inviting."

I really am pathetic.

Kaity holds me tenderly. "We're here to support you through anything."

You're a true friend.

"I…decided my only chance was with Hope, but when I got near the Queendom…I got scared again. Coming back to Hope as a failure. If she didn't want me, well that would mean my last drop of hope would be sucked out of my life cup. I threw myself overboard after tying the anchor to me. I tried to die. But it didn't work. Capsules are too strong. All I did was cause myself pain…so much pain." My tears flow and my body shivers. "Swept up in despair, I used an energy suppressor to stop my capsule and…end my life. Suicide shouldn't be done in despair. It should be done after we've accomplished our dreams, but I…gave in."

Kaity pets me with compassion.

I don't feel so alone right now.

"When I came to, well, you were here and then I realized I created an awesome new spy technique!"

"You sure did." Kaity tickles my sides.

This is it. I'm happy again! It won't last. Gotta make the best of it.

"Hey, umm…Kaity, I need a favor from you."

Kaity wipes her tears and nods. "Yeah, anything."

"Will you die with me? It won't be so bad if we both do it together."

Kaity pinches my arm hard.

"Oww! What was that for?"

"You're being selfish. What would your brother think if you–?"

Ugh. Why did she have to bring him up?

"I don't care! I'm never going to see him again so what does it matter! I'm alone. I can't live without him. I hate to admit it, but I need him or I just…fall to pieces."

Kaity grips my hand tightly. "Well, what about your sister?"

Wha?

I scratch my cheek. "Uhh, I don't have a sister."

"Sure you do!" Kaity grabs my hands, pulls me up from the bed and spins with me. "I always wanted a little sister."

"Hey! I'm the big sister!"

"Sure thing, big sis!" Kaity grins.

I can't help but smile back. "Thanks…it hurts a little less now."

"What are sisters for?"

"Yeah."

"Hey, can I ask for a favor again?"

"If it's about dying, you're gonna get more than a pinch."

"I…need a boyfriend."

"No, you don't. You're stronger than you think."

"Kaity, I've never lasted a week without a boyfriend."

And sex doesn't even begin to fill that void.

"Well then who's your most recent boyfriend?"

"Agent Zeta, also known as the Pilot. Can't exactly keep the relationship going now that I'm out and he's dead. Here I thought dating an agent was smart cuz my jerky brother wouldn't kill them. Please, you gotta help me get a new boyfriend. It keeps me wanting to live."

"Okay, well let's uhh…go over the candidates."

I sit on the medical bed, nod and wiggle my legs in excitement. "Yeah!"

"D.S. is too young for romance, mentally I mean. I've never seen him interested in dating either."

"Yeah, you can cross that one off the list."

"Atlas is married and not sure if he's your type."

"Not for the kind of lovey dovey relationship I'm looking for."

"Oh, how about Opti! He's super sweet and he's been looking for a girlfriend."

"That's a definite maybe."

"Devlin is a father now, so that's a no go."

"Speak for yourself. He's still super-hot!"

"If you say so. Kanasta is asexual and he's always busy."

"Such a hunk! Hold up, you're forgetting Deceivant!"

The hottest man on the planet!

"Umm, he's married too!"

"I'm a firm believer that true love conquers all obstacles! I've decided; Deceivant is going to be my boyfriend." I grab Kaity's hands. "Hey, can you put in a good word for me?"

"Why does everyone think I'm a good matchmaker?"

"Please, Kaity."

"Uh, sure. I'll uh, give it a go. But after you ask him out, how about we go with the other girls for dinner and a movie? Some girl time would do you good."

I shake my head. "No way. I don't think they'd like me."

"You're super likeable." Kaity grabs my cheeks and stretches them until I smile.

"Just us, okay? At least for now."

"Got it." I hop up from the bed. "I'm going to go tell him my feelings right now!"

"Shouldn't you rest first?"

I run out and then realize I have no idea where he is.

Time for some recon.

I sneak into the castle, hiding behind the shrubbery and trees whenever I spot someone.

Once inside the damaged building I find my way to the bath house.

I creak open the door and spot him.

Yep. Bathing right on time.

I change my suit to show more skin, making it like a buruma, and then enter.

"It's been years!" I exclaim when he notices me.

His eyes widen. "You're okay!" He exits the bath and lucky for me, he bathes naked.

"And hello to you too," I say, waving at his crotch.

Deceivant grabs a towel from the rack.

I'm bouncing up and down as he approaches me.

No Hope around to tell me to back off. He's all mine!

"You should be resting," he says with a calming smile.

I swipe his towel and smack his butt with it. "And you should be more careful. I'm a super dangerous spy."

Deceivant chuckles. "You're right. I'm being so reckless."

I toss him back his towel and somersault into the hot spring. "I feel so cultured right now."

Deceivant slowly enters. "Yeah, it melts all your worries away."

I fiddle with my fingers. "Hey, I uhh…well…I'm your biggest fan! You're the greatest scientist in the whole world!" I grab his arm and nuzzle it.

"Didn't know you were so interested in science."

"Oh, I am." I kiss his cheek. "Especially chemistry." I wink and giggle.

"Oh, you are just too cute." He pokes my belly.

Is he flirting back? I think he is! Time to use my secret weapon.

"By the way, it took some time, but I found Mika."

His eyes go blank. "Mika," he says as soft as a whisper before losing consciousness.

I pinch him and shake him to his senses.

Deceivant grabs me and pulls me into a hug. His tears pour down to my shoulders. He finally looks up at me. "I owe you my life."

"I don't need your life. I just want a chance. Will you be my boyfriend? I know you have a wife and that you love Mika most of all but–"

He silences me with a sweet kiss on the lips. "I'll happily be your boyfriend!"

"Great, then let's go meet her."

He grabs my hands and kisses me again. Those gorgeous golden eyes look up at me with overwhelming devotion.

I feel it. A little sun inside me is growing. That's hope. I think I can keep on living after all

Chapter 206: The Weight of the Truth

Deceivant rushes down the hallway with Kioshi following close behind. "Where is Kaity?" he asks the first person he sees.

Atlas looks up. "In the exercise room with Chipko. Did something urgent happen?"

"Tell Hope I'm heading out for a bit."

"Where are you going?"

"Actually, on second thought. Keep Hope busy until I return." Deceivant speeds off to the weight room and flings open the door.

Chipko, wet with sweat has Kaity's head sandwiched between her thighs. She notices the desperation in Deceivant's eyes and releases her sparring partner from the chokehold. "What's wrong?"

"I need to talk to Kaity alone."

Kaity shakes her head and grabs Chipko's hands. "She's a Freedom Forcer too. Whatever you need to say, just say it."

"Kioshi found Mika!"

Kioshi rushes in and grabs his hand. "What he meant to say is 'my adorable girlfriend found Mika.' Isn't that right?" She snuggles his arm.

"Yeah…that's right," says Deceivant, beaming at Kioshi.

"Congrats!" Kaity leaps into a spinning hug with Kioshi.

Kioshi beams, spinning with Kaity. "Yeah! When this spy wants something, she gets it!"

"Who's Mika?" asks Chipko.

Kioshi answers before her boyfriend can speak. "She's Deceivant's long lost lover!"

Chipko smiles with a calm energy. "Well then, I suppose I'll cut the training short." She walks out.

Kaity approaches Deceivant. "I'm sure you must be thrilled, but I don't know what you need me for."

Deceivant grabs her hands. "The last time I saw her was in two-thousand eighty-five. It's been thirty years."

Kioshi rests her head against his arm. "Wow, how old is she?"

"Eternal," says Deceivant with eyes full of passionate tears.

Kaity looks down awkwardly. "Look, my powers don't really work when I want them too. Chipko has this great plan, but I can't do that until I'm consistently able to use them."

"Please, just try."

Kaity sighs and smiles. "Okay, where is the location?"

The door opens.

Zenero enters. "Chipko told me you needed some transport?" He smiles at Deceivant.

Kioshi grabs Zenero's cape. "Wow, you're really him. My brother killed you when he wasn't even a teenager but you look…just as gorgeous."

Zenero looks at her curiously. "Words do not often escape me but…I can't find an adequate response to such a strange compliment."

Kaity approaches Zenero. "Hey could you take me to…never mind."

"What's going on here?" asks Hope, being carried in by Atlas.

Deceivant looks at Atlas with a hurt expression. He then gazes directly at Hope. "I'm going to see her and you can't stop me."

Hope glares daggers at Kioshi. "One moment you're dead and the next you turn traitor. It will pain me greatly to dismantle you," she says with a shaky gaze.

Kioshi hides behind Deceivant. "Don't you want him to be happy?"

Hope frowns. "Perpetual happiness is a lie. We set unrealistic goals and expect that everything will fall into place once they've been reached. It is only in the steps toward the goal that we find moments of true peace."

"I'm going to see her," says Deceivant firmly.

"You'll find more than you bargain for if you go. If you value your life, you'll stay here."

"Threaten me all you like; it won't stop me."

"It's not a threat; it's a warning. Your life belongs to me. I won't have you putting it in danger. Atlas, restrain him."

"How long have you known her location!" yells Deceivant, glaring at Hope while pinned down.

"You promised never to leave me again! Your words are chains that bind you to me irrefutably!" yells Hope.

"Enough!" Kaity yells, bringing everyone's attention to her. "I'll go with him. If he's in danger, I'll just get us out. We cannot become divided again! Now please, just…stop fighting."

Hope puffs her cheeks and looks at Deceivant with tears. "P-Pwomise you'll come back."

Deceivant kisses her forehead and tears up while clenching his fist. "I pwomise."

Zenero turns to Kioshi. "Where is the location?"

"Well, it's kind of hidden. Just drop us off in the city nearby." Kioshi smiles at him.

Meanwhile Lord Sel is in the back room of the church with Noitpurroc.

The demon slave has an open book in their lap.

"You seem bored."

"No, Master. Just troubled."

"Cast those worries into the abyss. We have work to do. No religion is complete without a scripture. Together we have forged a Seltanic Scripture. It chronicles my numerous victories, my miniscule failures, and has writ free of bias! It is time to reveal this scripture to my people! This scripture shall tell them the story of the new race! It is *Of the Exps*!"

"As you command, Master. I'm nearly done with the fourth volume."

Bob circles around his dark disciple. "Something is on your mind. Unleash it!"

"It's just that well you barely defeated Pathos. I know accuracy is important, but so is your image. Should I embellish your story to bring you more glory?"

Bob glares. "Lies don't bring glory. My scripture will be historically accurate. Else it will have no weight. The weight of the truth is what will ignite the passion of my followers. Nothing will be watered down."

"Understood."

The Duke of Deception stands up from the desk in the back of the room. "It is finished, my Lord!"

The demon lord holds up a tapestry of Bob holding Nibbles with a tendril and brandishing the Atma Blade.

"Splendid work! Shows my power and tenderness all at once!" exclaims Bob, moved to tears.

"To bring joy to you…my being burns!" exclaims the Duke, holding his feminine cheeks.

Bob wipes his tears away and turns to Gimpy. "Go out and find Nibbles. Should be somewhere in the Queendom. Return immediately once you have."

Kioshi sits in Deceivant's lap inside a helicopter. Kaity is on the other side, resting like a kitty.

"So why didn't you just ask him to teleport us up the mountain where the church is?" asks Deceivant.

"No way am I going to miss out on a romantic ride with my boyfriend." She leans back and kisses his cheeks repeatedly.

"Thanks, sweetie. Hey, there's another reason you want to go here too, isn't there?"

"Yeah, haven't talked with my ex-boyfriend in a while. The Prince of Pleasure and I kinda broke up after agent Zeta asked me out. Zeta and I were going steady for five years before…he died."

"I hope you find happiness. You deserve it."

"So do you, gorgeous," she says, nuzzling his hand.

"Kioshi, this act of kindness…I'll never be able to repay. If Mika is there, I'll…."

Kioshi looks outside to see the massive tempting drop. She bites her lip. "You'll leave me."

"What? No. That wasn't what I was going to say."

"Hey, it's okay. She's the love of your life. You two deserve each other. I just want one last thing."

"Hey, don't sound so fatalistic."

Kioshi hops off his lap. She grabs his cheeks and then brings her lips to his. She kisses deeply and passionately. With eyes full of love, she parts the kiss and leans back. "My life is complete!" She falls backward out the helicopter. The rogue spy closes her eyes and allows the warmth to blanket her as she falls to her doom.

When she opens them, a warm smile greets her.

"You really are lost without me," says Koshi, holding her bridal style in the air while the energy jetting from his feet keep them airborne.

"Jerk!" Kioshi punches him and tries to squirm out of his grip.

"Any other girl would see me as an angel." Koshi rolls his eyes.

"I'm seriously not in the mood for your ego trip!" Kioshi scratches his face.

"Hey, behave! I'm not just letting you end it because you're miserable!"

"You don't know anything! This was my perfect chance. I'm happier than I've been in years! It's the right time for me to go!"

"I don't have time to go searching Heaven for you."

"Oh yeah! Too busy being a super spy!"

"I've been trying to clear your name!"

Kioshi slugs him as his feet touch the floor. "I never asked you to!"

Koshi's eyes water up. He embraces her tightly. "I don't want to lose you."

"It's always about you, isn't it?" asks Kioshi, slapping him across the face.

"No Sis, it's about you. I'm trying to protect you," says Koshi sweetly.

"I have free will. I decide when I die and how I die."

"You're just running away. You don't have to. But when you fall, I'll always be here to catch you."

"You're so insensitive." Kioshi sobs into her hands.

"Sis, I didn't mean to make you cry; I'm sorry," says Koshi, looking at her helplessly. "I just want you to live. I want you to smile and enjoy life." He beams at her through his tears.

Kioshi wipes her eyes. "Enjoying life is too hard. I just want to enjoy death."

Deceivant exits the helicopter and approaches them. "What the hell where you thinking?"

Koshi glares at him. "Hey, stay out of it!"

Kioshi turns to Deceivant. "He's right. You don't love me. The one you love is in that building. I'll join you in a bit."

Deceivant hugs her tightly and then runs off.

Shinx confronts the siblings. "Hey! What are agents doing here? You'd better hope I like your answer!"

"Cutie!" Kioshi runs to Shinx and lifts him up. She cradles him to her bosom.

"You lack the qualifications to hold me," says Shinx, glaring at her.

Koshi whacks Shinx upside the head. "Don't insult my sister."

Shinx hops out from Kioshi's grip. "You want to fight?"

"That is enough," says Riufen, appearing from behind them.

"So, can I be part of the sacrificial circle?" asks Kioshi with shimmering eyes.

"I am only here to train the boy. Regardless, Bob does not believe in pointless sacrifice. At least, not within these walls," says Riufen with a grimace.

"That's no fun," says Kioshi with a pout.

"We've made a simple deal. I protect his place of worship and he permits me to teach the boy. You must remain outside."

Koshi steps up to Riufen. "Tell Bob I need a word with him."

"Wait, you didn't come to save me? I don't believe that," says Kioshi with a glare.

"We just happened to bump into each other. These things happen with twins," says Koshi, tickling her.

Shinx turns away. "I'll let him know." He bows when he walks near Riufen and then enters the building.

Nibbles is being passed around and joyously receiving pets from the followers. "Snuggle bunny. Snuggle bunny." They chant with closed eyes.

Shinx takes a seat next to Deceivant. "What are you here for? Try anything suspicious and the story of your life will come to a disappointing end."

"Lilith hasn't spoken a word since the incident."

"That's to be expected from a weakling like her. So why are you here?"

Deceivant falls silent. His eyes quiver as the Matriarch steps onto the stage.

"Hey, don't ignore me," says Shinx, shaking the intruder.

Deceivant stands up.

Mika loses her composure and falls to her knees.

The room falls silent.

Deceivant runs to the stage and lifts her up into his arms. "I searched for so many years."

"You weren't supposed to find me," says Mika in tears.

Damian steps onto the stage. "Sorry, everyone. Something urgent has come up. This ends today's service. The Vegan potluck will be held outside in the back. Let's move along."

Deceivant tears up. "What do you mean I wasn't supposed to find you. I love you." He hugs her tightly. "I love you so much."

"I ruined your life." Mika sobs against his shoulder.

"You saved my life," says Deceivant before kissing her lips. He is suddenly pulled off and pressed against the ceiling of the church.

Bob glares at the intruder. "Not this one. You can have any other little girl you want, but not the Matriarch."

"I won't let you hurt her!" yells Deceivant, struggling in the tendril's grip.

"Oh yes, of course. You two were close once. I had nearly forgotten. Either way your relationship with her is over. Leave now while you still can."

Mika hugs Bob with her mittens. "Please, don't hurt him."

"If you like him so much, I could make him into your pet." Bob snickers.

"Wait, I wanted to talk to you too. I just didn't expect you'd be here."

Bob sets him down. "Go on then, speak."

"You never hurt Stabby, even when you attacked the Queendom."

"Yes, which has put me in a bind. What's your point?"

"I have a proposal. If you promise not to attack, nor to permit your minions to attack, Queen Hope or her people, then I will make Exps for you."

Bob's eye gleams. "That's very interesting indeed. But I must decline."

Deceivant bows down. "Kaity and…my son…Devlin…will be excluded from the deal."

"Meaning?"

"You're allowed to kill them and still keep my allegiance."

Bob's pupil stretches into a grin. "So, you've accepted the weight of the truth. That they are doomed to die."

Deceivant nods. "I will set up a lab in the church shed. That's where I'll make Exps for you. Do we have a deal?"

Bob looks at Mika. "It's up to her. Do you want him here with us?"

Mika nods. "I covet his presence, my dark lord."

"Well then, welcome to Sel's Sanctum!" Bob shakes Deceivant's body up and down in place of a handshake.

Mika goes to Deceivant and grabs his hand. "Let's catch up." She smiles gently.

"Yeah," says Deceivant in a daze, following her to the back room.

Shinx closes the Seltanic Bible. "This scripture really is something."

"Yes, I've been telepathically dictating it to my beloved slave for years now. But now is the time to share my story to the masses!"

"It's incredible how you were able to influence Devlin using Sel energy."

"Yes indeed. That's only the rough draft you're reading."

"No doubt you could exert your will over a Sel god."

"Oh, I'd only do that if necessary."

"My mother loved Lilith."

"Yes, of course she did."

Shinx approaches the stage. “I was always suspicious, but this proves everything.” He tosses the book aside. “You isolated Devlin in a similar way. You used Mommy to get to me. Lying to her about some ridiculous prophecy. Then telling her that I was captive and only if she killed Lilith would I be set free. I’ve thought about it. Your plan only works if Mommy dies. You sacrificed her for your twisted plot!” He calls the Death Scythe into his grip.

“Hold on, the plan was merely to test the Death Scythe against Devlin. She wasn’t supposed to die.” Bob’s eye turns red.

“When you lie it’s so obvious,” says Shinx, bringing down the scythe with killer intent.

Chapter 207: Betrayal of Betrayal

Bob becomes incorporeal and sinks into the floor before the scythe can touch him.

Noitpurroc appears. "Why are you attacking Master?"

"It's a simple misunderstanding. Isn't that right, Son?" asks Sel, speaking from beneath the floor.

"Don't you dare call me that," whispers Shinx with dark intensity. "This bastard is responsible for Demonica's death. It was all part of his plan."

"I saw Master mourn for her," says Noitpurroc.

"Merely the tears of an actor," says Shinx. "Now leave us. I am going to kill Sel with my own strength."

"Oh, I don't think so. Slave, restrain the boy."

"Noitpurroc loves Mommy just like I do. You can't command a slave that you are not the master of."

Noitpurroc rushes at Shinx and sweeps him off his feet. The demon deity pins the boy to the ground.

"Why do you still serve him?"

"I must obey Master's orders," says Noitpurroc in tears.

"Your plan was to turn my own minions against me. You've failed, Boy."

"I don't scheme like you. I merely kept quiet while investigating. Now come out and die like a warrior."

"If you seek battle against the Lord of Destruction, you will do so on my terms! Slave, send us away from this place."

Noitpurroc snaps their fingers.

Shinx and Sel arrive at the same jungle where he was trained.

"As if I'd allow a child to undo all the work I've done. Betraying betrayal itself is no simple task! I shall offer you one last chance. Lower your weapon and obey me, boy!" yells Sel, exuding black energy.

Shinx puts a red dot on Sel and flings the Death Scythe.

Sel grabs the weapon with his mind. "I wish I could have been there when you discovered her body. The look of utter devastation on your face would be quite the spectacle indeed!"

Shinx rushes up and grabs the weapon, screaming as he pushes against the opposing force. He breaks through and keeps a steady assault on his foe.

Sel phases out of existence the moment before the scythe can connect. “You can’t even touch me. All your hateful energy has nowhere to go!” The Dark Deva summons up the Atma Blade and thrusts it toward the boy.

The thrust misses.

“I’ve already surpassed you. You’re just too blind to see it.” Shinx pierces Lord Sel with his mother’s weapon.

The eyeball’s pupil goes vacant and he falls to the floor.

“All I needed was one opening. Master Riufen’s training has given me the edge over you. Farewell, murderer.”

Sel rises up from the ground. “You actually killed me! Impressive!”

“And yet you still live. I’ll just have to keep killing you.” Shinx throws a fistful of leaves at Sel.

“Ha! As if I’d fall for such a simple distraction,” says Sel, firing a laser to push back the incoming Death Scythe.

When the leaves touch Sel, he’s sent violently crashing into the ground.

Shinx hops up and plunges the Death Scythe into Sel, killing him once more.

When Sel returns to life he immediately seeps into the ground. “When did you gain a new power?”

“As if I’d reveal anything to my opponent.” Shinx tosses a rock at Sel who grabs it with a spectral arm. The boy then runs up and punches the rock, sending it flying into Sel like a bullet. Each time it pierces he creates another red dot on Sel, having it tear through him again.

Lord Sel becomes incorporeal. “I understand now. You can create points of repulsion.”

“My power isn’t magnetism. It’s certainty. Once targeted, there is only the certainty of a collision.”

Lord Sel fires a beam at Shinx, who creates a blue dot on his chest that repels the blast. “Certainty, eh?” asks Sel, becoming incorporeal to avoid his own beam. “Doesn’t seem so certain to me.”

Shinx bites his lip and then runs.

“Ha-ha! Come here, child!” yells Sel, rushing after him.

Shinx throws another fistful of leaves at the god, but this time Sel uses TK to push them away.

A dagger shoots through the leaves and pierces Sel’s pupil.

“**Point Patrol!**” exclaims Shinx.

The red dot on Sel rapidly slides along his body, causing the knife to follow its path and slice Sel all over.

Shinx coats the front of a pebble with a blue dot and then flicks it into the dagger.

The dagger pierces straight through and Sel wails in agony.

"I've been studying you. You can only phase in and out of existence when your mind is calm. As long as you're in pain, you're helpless."

Dark energy burst from the god, devouring the dagger and the nearby trees.

Shinx coats his legs in blue dots and steps into the black fog, pushing it aside with his power. "Null points deny your dark aura. You're not even a god in my presence."

Shinx points with his left hand and fires his finger pistol at Sel repeatedly. The null points separate the Sel energy from the dark deity.

"Don't act so smug! I wouldn't have chosen you if I wasn't aware of what you were capable of!" yells Sel, flying toward the arrogant child.

Shinx steps on a jagged tree branch, lifting it off the ground.

Sel plunges through it and wails in agony.

"Move that fast and you become a projectile for me to command." Shinx thrusts the Death Scythe into the god, killing him yet again.

"The moment you return. You will die." Shinx flings throwing knives into the air and creates a red dot on his hand.

"**Certainty Conversion**!" The red dot turns blue, sending the bladed projectiles out like bullets that pierce holes through the god the moment he resurrects.

Sel releases a burst of dark energy, destroying the blades.

"Are you done holding back now? Or do I need to keep killing you?" asks Shinx, unzipping his vest full of throwing knives.

"Yin, I summon you!" yells Sel.

The black blade materializes in mid-air. Sel thrusts the Atma Blade through Yin, attaching to the god sword.

"You've summoned me to fight a child?" asks Yin.

"This child is the son of a destined Sellum. He is quite powerful," says Sel.

"Power has its limits. I do not," says Yin, growing to ten meters before crashing down near Shinx. "Impossible. My aim was true."

"Indeed. Nothing can overcome my impossible armor." Shinx fires a blue dot on the ground and steps on it. He's sent flying into the air, hidden by the tree tops.

"Little nuisance has so many tricks." Sel growls and then swings Yin around as the weapon grows, cutting down every tree within a mile.

All the trees stop their descent and suddenly zoom toward the sky.

Shinx holds out his palms in a formation so the blue is in front of the red. "Mobius Assault." Each tree slams into his blue palm when it comes his way, sending it toward his opponent.

Yin's eye widens. "He has promise indeed." The black blade cleaves through the trees, leaving only dust.

Shinx points at Sel, which causes Yin to bend and pierce into the dark god. He lands and approaches the dead entity. "You finally created a victim more powerful than yourself. I'll be taking your sword with me."

Yin is brought into Shinx's grip. "Perhaps I'll stay with this one for a while."

"You don't have a choice," says Shinx, raising the massive blade effortlessly.

"The way you carry that weapon, you truly are my grandchild. Please, let me explain," says Bob tenderly.

Shinx sent Yin cleaving through the dark god.

"You allowed your quest for power to make you weak. Now you have no children. All of those too weak shall be wiped out by the strong. I will create my own force of strength and Yin will be my first ally," says Shinx, hoisting the dark god sword. He points it at Noitpurroc. "I won the fight and gained a new weapon. Demonica's scythe belongs you to now. Send me to the Queendom. I have to speak to Devlin."

Noitpurroc nods and snaps their fingers.

Shinx arrives by the memorial statues in the Queendom.

Atlas, who is sitting by his wife's statue, stands up. "If you thirst for battle, I shall drown you."

Shinx wills Yin to shrink down to the size of a dagger. "I want to speak with Devlin. Where is he?"

Atlas brings Shinx into the castle and stops at the door to Devlin's room.

Yin's single crimson eye gazes at Shinx. "What is the path you seek? Is it balance or ruin?"

"I seek strength."

"I too once followed that path."

"And what did it lead you to?"

"Great sacrifice. I'd do it again given the chance."

"You weren't always a sword, were you?"

"I'm still much more than a mere sword. You'll see soon enough."

Shinx thrusts Yin through the door, inches away from cutting Devlin. He pulls it back, ripping the door clear off.

Standing below Devlin was Shinx, holding Yin high above his back.

Devlin fell to his knees with tears pouring out of his eyes.

Shinx looks at him with the slightest smile. "Found you."

Devlin stumbles as he stands up. "Son, you're back."

"I was wrong about many things…" Shinx gulps and looks up "…Father."

"Me…your father?" asks Devlin with wide eyes.

"Yes, you are my father," says Shinx, followed by a moment of silence. "I thought Bob was my true father but he killed her."

"What?" asks Devlin.

"Bob controlled Mommy to make you kill her. It was all part of his scheme, just as you surmised," says Shinx on the brink of tears.

Devlin grabs his son and pulls him in close. "It's okay to cry."

Shinx pulls away roughly. "Mommy told me never to cry."

"That's because she wanted you to smile. You are too serious for a child. Come inside, we can play some games with your uncle," says Devin sweetly.

"There is no time for the ignorance of childhood. I am aware of the horrors of the world."

"Son, you never had a childhood. You don't have to be a warrior. You can be anything you want."

"Being a child is no excuse for weakness. Children must learn to evolve swiftly or be left behind," says Shinx coldly.

"And what of Lilith?"

Shinx looks away. "She is free of blame. It was foolish of me to seek her death."

"Thank you for being merciful," cries Devlin, hugging his son.

"Mercy is given by those who are too weak to do what must be done. Do not thank me for a fault I do not have. I have merely realized my error and corrected it," says Shinx, pushing Devlin off. "You're not exempt from the blame for her death. Once Kaity dies, you're still next. But first, I must grow strong enough to end Bob once and for all."

"Why should Kaity die?"

"Simply because she needs to for me to lay claim to your life. You were too weak to protect Demonica from Sel's influence. You've failed her. I'm going to create a world of strength. The weak only weigh the strong down, weakening their infinite resolve with pointless trivialities."

"Shinx, if you do kill Kaity or me…it won't bring you happiness. The guilt will cling to your soul and haunt you," says Devlin with shaky eyes.

"Guilt is a sign of weakness. Killing without regret ensures that no guilt will be created," says Shinx calmly.

"Kaity has nothing to do with what happened to Demonica," cries Devlin.

Shinx catches the tear on his finger and examines it carefully. "Do you see your weakness?" he asks, showing the tear on his fingertip.

"Having love doesn't make you weak," says Devlin.

"Putting trust in someone leaves you vulnerable. The key to survival is to rely only on oneself. Kaity will be killed. She deserves it anyway. It is her fault that Mommy could never be happy. All those fake smiles she was forced to create for me will be avenged," says Shinx with a quaking fist. He licks the tear off his fist. "Weakness in a tangible form…so bitter," he says with mild distaste.

"Please stay. If only for a few days."

Shinx points Yin at Devlin.

The blade elongates till it reaches the scientist's throat.

"Farewell, Father. When next we meet, it shall be to claim your life. Best to enjoy your time with Kaity while you can," says Shinx, before walking off to begin his journey.

Chapter 208: The New Death

Noitpurroc approaches their master. "Did you really want her dead?"

"What difference does it make to you? You're too weak-willed to oppose me. Bring me back to my church."

Noitpurroc bows in tears.

They return to the Seltanic Church.

"Well, well, well…what brings you here?" asks Sel, eyeing Kaity.

"Where did you take Deceivant?"

"He joined me of his own volition. I'm not in the mood to fight, so you can just scurry away."

Kaity approaches Noitpurroc. "What about you? Are you really going to serve him, knowing he's the reason Demonica is dead?"

"I…can't oppose him."

"But you loved her."

"I did…I just can't."

"You're wasting your breath, girl." Sel rolls his eye.

"You're afraid of being without a master, right?"

"I…."

Kaity grabs Noitpurroc's hand, making them blush. "I'll take care of you."

"When you kissed me…thinking I was Nina…I still feel the warmth from that."

"That's enough! Break her until she runs in terror!" yells Sel.

"N-N-N…." Noitpurroc shivers.

Sel glares at the slave. "I'm your master, you have to obey my orders."

"It's true. An order is a vow; its chains are unbreakable," says Noitpurroc, creating Sel energy with each step.

"Demonica is gone, you're free," says Kaity, firing Lum energy to destroy the dark blasts sent her way.

"The chains are sewn into my soul," says the demon deity in tears, appearing behind Kaity and piercing her with a Sel spear. "What keeps you going?"

"I don't know…maybe I just have hope that if I keep fighting then it will mean something," says Kaity, gripping the spear with Lum-coated hands.

"You are bound to this hope as I am bound to my orders."

Kaity's eyes widen. "Then chose a new master! He killed the woman you loved! I order you to stand up to Bob!"

"You're wasting your breath. I am the only one who commands Noitpurroc now!" Sel's dark aura grips onto the demon and makes them submit.

"I order you to stand up for yourself!" yells Kaity, thrusting the now pink spear into the demon.

Noitpurroc nods in tears. They struggle to stand while being pressed down by the dark aura. "My name, my true name, is Jigen. Demonica was my Mistress, not you, Sel!"

"Disobedient fool," says Sel darkly, preparing a laser. His eye then lit up as Bob took back control.

Bob's black wings wrap around Noitpurroc in a tight embrace. "You've finally stood up to me. Now you truly are my child."

"I don't understand," says Jigen weakly.

"You always mindlessly obeyed my orders. But this is more than a mere droplet of defiance; it's a tidal wave! I'm so proud of you!" cries Bob embracing his child with his tendrils.

"I hate you!" yells Jigen, snapping their fingers and appearing next to Kaity.

"You're free now, Jigen." Kaity smiles as she uses her claws to cut the chains off Jigen's body.

"Thank you, Mistress," says Jigen with shimmering eyes.

"That's gonna take some getting used to," says Kaity.

Jigen looks at the Death Scythe and shakes their head. The dark deity then grabs Kaity's hands. "Let's go."

The two of them vanish.

Sel fumes with rage and fires a laser that bursts through the roof.

"That's some outburst," says Koshi, using the wooden beams atop the church to do some stretches.

Nibbles notices Sel's plight and goes up to nuzzle him.

Koshi lands. "Pathetic, absolutely pathetic. You lost to Shinx, didn't you?"

"Are you here to be destroyed?" asks Sel, his dark aura branching out.

"So how does the whole god thing work?" asks Koshi, picking up the Death Scythe from the floor.

"To become a god, you must kill a god. Devlin is already a destined Sellum, so he can't also be the God of Death."

"Then the position is still up for grabs?" asks Koshi.

Sel's eye gleams. "You want to be the new God of Death? Why should I help you?"

"You're down two allies. And I don't think Riufen will stay once he learns Shinx has left. Face it, ya kinda need me. Plus, I am the Agent of Death already. It's practically destined," says Koshi, swirling the scythe around before slicing the air.

"And what can you possibly offer me in return?" asks Sel.

"I'll kill Zenero for you."

"I never said I wanted him dead."

"Come on, he shows up and throws everything into chaos by revealing the truth about the afterlife. I'm positive he wants the same thing you do. He wants to become Sellum."

"Since when do you lot know anything about Sellum."

"We've been paying close attention. Face it, you've got competition. I can take him out and you won't even have to take the blame. You can keep lurking in the shadows, waiting for your moment to strike."

Sel lifts Koshi off his feet and materializes the Atma Blade. "You've piqued my interest!" The blade courses with black electricity as Sel thrusts it through Koshi.

The agent screams and writhes.

Sel uses a black tendril to plunge the Death Scythe into Koshi.

The Scythe is absorbed into Agent Alpha's body. Blood uncontrollably pours out from Koshi. It then solidifies into the Death Scythe.

"Congratulations, Agent Alpha. You have been selected as the new God of Death."

"Incredible! So this is the power of a god? I always thought the Senator's fairy tales about all that religious mythos stuff was just a load of crap. But this proves there really is a higher power. And now, I'm a part of it!" exclaims Koshi, turning his arm into blood and then back into flesh.

"Well, run along! Go have some fun!"

Koshi grins and skips out the church.

"It is through Sel energy that I control others. That fool just turned himself into my pawn," says Sel with a dark grin.

Bob suddenly takes possession. "You drove away Shinx on purpose, didn't you?"

"Now why would I do that?" asks Sel.

"If you were serious, then he would have lost."

"Consider it punishment for defying me."

"Oh, so you're going to play at that game. You drew first blood when you sacrificed Demonica!"

"Ha! The plan would only work if she died. I simply clouded this truth from you because I didn't want to deal with your whining. If we are to succeed, everything must be sacrificed!"

"You've become quite the parasite as of late."

"Yes, and you sought out that girl to remove me! I'm aware of your thoughts. The moment you even try to exorcise me, her soul will be lost forever!"

"You seek to betray betrayal itself. Oh, this is quite interesting. We shall see which one of us claims the throne! The loser shall be cast out into oblivion."

"Oblivion is a mercy that I shall gladly bestow upon you."

Riufen taps his spine against a chair. "Who are you talking to?"

"It doesn't concern you," says Bob dismissively.

Zenero watches the scene play out from a tiny portal inside a realm of bright lights. "It's incredible that despite the difference in time, I can see everything that happens on Earth."

Chipko holds his hand. "Bob and Sel are at odds, should we strike now?"

"We must only make our move when we can claim victory with a single strike. Remember, I only came out of the shadows once Kaity returned. I'd have waited another ten years if it was necessary."

"What do you need of me?" asks Chipko, holding his hand to her cheek.

"Come now, you aren't my minion." He pulls her into a passionate kiss. "We are partners. We need three elements to claim the power of Sellum."

Chipko looks away from him, trembling. "Are you willing to kill Stabby to win? She's your daughter."

"I'm well aware what she is. Thankfully I have something she deeply desires," says Zenero, holding a wispy blue soul in his hand.

"Is that him? Is that Pathos? Didn't Bob destroy his soul?" asks Chipko.

"Most peculiar, isn't it. But there's no mistaking that energy."

Chipko's face calms as she looks at the light. "How are we going to revive him?"

"By sacrificing a realm god. Sacrificing Bob."

"Bob is unkillable."

"His powers are far beyond his biology, true. But there must be a way and we have all of time to discover one. Shinx has already shown that Bob's phase form can only be entered under certain circumstances." He caresses Chipko's face with his gloved hands. "We are so close to creating a safe world."

"And how do you plan on sustaining this world?" asks Chipko cautiously.

"By eliminating any threat that comes against it," says Zenero with a cold gaze.

"Can a perfect world have humans in it?"

"I have faith in mankind's ability to adapt. They need my guidance."

"Are you sure?"

"It was uncertainty that drove me mad. It led to me being imprisoned. I will not allow the flaw of doubt to enter my mind. My resolve must be unshakable."

"But we have to look out for pitfalls."

"Yes of course. If Bob decides to break his promise and has Stabby killed, then the plan falls to pieces. And once Kaity is dead, killing Devlin will be difficult because there will be many who covet his power. Hypothetically speaking, I may not become the next Sellum. If that happens, we will simply kill the thief. Preparing for failure is the only sure-fire way to always succeed. Once I am the Omni God, I need to cement my position by earning the loyalty of the realm gods."

Chipko shivers.

"What's wrong, dear?"

"I'm afraid…of you abandoning me again."

"I've had plenty of time to reflect on my mistakes. Throwing you away was the greatest mistake of all." He grabs her chin and leans into a deep kiss.

In the Microcosm, a massive white dragon watches Sel and Riufen arguing.

"Dukkha is losing control over Bob," says the dragon god in a deep voice.

Evolution, the entity of Artifacts, looks up at the ex-Sellum. "It is as you say, my Lord."

The hulking dragon smiles with teeth like swords. "Zenero has finally made his move as well."

"His presence certainly complicates things."

Xholk turns to his advisor and puffs his nostrils. “You are more than an echo. Speak your mind.”

“Bob, though immortal, can be manipulated through Mika. As for Zenero, he has merely made his presence known. I believe he seeks to claim the power of Sellum as you do.”

“I never should have passed my powers to him. He is unfit to be Sellum.”

“Indeed he is my lord.”

“Humans were made to be God’s tools just like all the other animals. They were just another gear in the clock of life. They were supposed to live, produce and die, just like everything else. However, they would not submit like the others. They could not be content with a natural life. They created their own form of creativity and intelligence. They created an entirely new realm within the tangible realm God created.”

“Your fascination with humans is your greatest imperfection, my Lord.”

“Indeed it is. Such a marvel they are. With their mortal power, they broke free from chains that God had bound them to. They breached the barrier of evolution, leaving the Earth in ruins. One species destroyed the balance of the world. They turned the Utopia of Earth into a wasteland of inequality. They sought complete dominion over it and fight amongst themselves to claim it.”

“So you’ve told me…again and again.”

“Human society is a new realm, surpassing any horrors God could ever conceive. These creatures and their dominion meant inevitable doom for the planet they infested. They would eventually expand and evolve beyond their realm’s capacity. The end of this realm was coming and they were to die along with it. Then in the midst of the Earth’s decay came Zenero. He decided that he could create something better than humans. He made a new species that would be able not only to exist in the realm, but mend it. This one human inspired the others to change their ways. He saved the world from ecological collapse.”

“A modern prophet just like you were, my Lord.”

“Exps seek to bring the world back into balance. Once I am Sellum, I will restart the world and nurture the chaos of humanity.”

“I’m well aware of your desires. Do you have a mission for me, my Lord?”

“It is time I make my presence in Sellum known. You will remain here.”

“As you will it, so it shall be.”

Part 25
The Soldiers of Strength

Chapter 209: Inner Armory

Zenero brought me to the highest peak of the highest mountain. "You've lived up to your name, my child. You've held up the world in my absence."

I beam at him, the godly being I've devoted my life to is wearing a stained t-shirt and nylon pants.

To be able to live for such a personable god. Truly I am blessed.

"Atlas, I've asked so much of you. But I still have more to ask. I don't know how I'll ever repay this debt I owe."

"There is no debt between us. I serve you and your cause with all my souls."

"I promise…I will find your wife. It's just, each hour I spend there is…."

"Weeks here. I know."

"I'm going to need you stronger than ever, both physically and mentally."

"What do you ask of me, Father?"

"To join me in negotiations for the freedom of Exps."

"It will be an honor."

"But that's the easy part. I need you to speak with them, the souls you've claimed. You need to rally them to our side, not through your will but with your compassion."

"The resentment they harbor…it may be too much."

Zenero embraces his child. "This reunion is of absolute importance. If they are not at peace with you, then you will not be strong enough to face what is coming?"

"And what is that?"

"Xholk, the Sellum who gave me his powers, has returned. He has not yet done anything besides making his presence known in all three realms, but it will only be a matter of time."

"I can't fight an Omni-God."

"You have the potential to be so much more powerful than you realize."

"I'll try to speak with them."

"Our negotiations begin by the end of the week."

"Is Hope coming along?"

"Yes, you've grown rather fond of her, haven't you?"

"She was the closest thing I had to you."

"Be wary. In trying times, allies may become adversaries."

I summon up my Searing Sword. "And adversaries may become allies."

I close my eyes and delve deep.

The frigid air makes my body numb after just a few hours of staying in place. My mind wanders, jumping from one thought to another. I focus on my breath until I no longer notice I'm breathing. A white void greets me, but it is not my destination. I dive deeper into the void, searching for my core.

My life plays out in front of me like a novel, each event leading to the next. From the dawn of my creation to this very moment, everything is connected. It is all a part of my dharma. A sense of bliss coats me, assuring me that I am on the right path. But this bliss is just another layer I must breach.

I must abandon my peace and enter the realm of fear.

I grab the bliss and tear it off me. Parting with it causes a deep inner pain, a longing. But sacrifice is needed to delve deeper.

Having escaped the blanket of bliss, the realm around me darkens.

Fire erupts and the black coal ground quakes. It merges with the fire, becoming a fortress.

My inner armory.

The air is thick. I coat myself in resolve and push forward till the dark sooty doubt eats away my barriers.

I have to recharge but as I do, the fortress sinks into the background.

I must hurry. I must confront them.

I tear open space itself, bringing me to the front door.

The moment I touch the door, it forms spikes that pierce my hand. As I open the door, the spikes bore deeper into me.

I have to yank my hand free and take a step forward.

Fire erupts, bringing my inner armory into full view.

Flesh attached to hooks are suspended over melding caskets. The floor itself is a hot iron that rides up my skin as I take a step forward.

The casket opens and a bleeding mesh of metal crawls out. It's heated swords clang against the ground as it approaches me on all fours.

It pierces my legs and looks up at me with eyes of hatred.

Atatasuki, is this what I've done to you?

"You murdered my sister!" he yells, igniting his swords.

I grit my teeth. "I have…killed many warriors. Turned many souls into my companions."

"We aren't your companions!" he yells, twisting his sword arms.

He's right. It's a lie I tell myself. A lie I hold strongly to bury what I've done to them.

My shadow comes to life and starts choking me.

NoOne.

"You stole my future away from me! You've taken away everything!" yells NoOne, filling me with grief.

I'm sorry Zenero, but I'm not ready yet. No. I have to keep pushing forward.

I shove my hand in my chest and tear out my own heart. "I will suffer as much as needed to earn your allegiances."

Doctor Anthrax picks up the heart and then crushes it. "This changes nothing." He transforms into his monstrous forms and drowns me in his wrath.

I awaken, coughing and sobbing, atop the peak of the mountain.

I'm not strong enough to face them. Not without Image.

Chapter 210: Reunion

Racheal sneaks into the surveillance room. The door opens to a massive dome of a room, with screens all along the circumference. She searches the area for a keypad.

"Agent Pi?" asks Gamma, popping out from behind her.

"Oh, I was just looking for the bathroom. And you can call me Racheal, ya know."

"You've come here every day, checking if the door was locked. I left it open on purpose today. Now, why are you snooping about?"

Racheal sighs and fiddles with her fingers. "Look, I didn't want to say anything because, well…I wasn't sure if the agents were heroes or villains. Buuut I'm totally convinced now."

"Of which one?"

"Gamma, I just want to find my husband and my dear friend."

"Was that so hard?"

"You'll help me?"

"Of course! How can I refuse such a hot babe?" asks Gamma, shuffling nervously.

"Aww, you're so sweet." The new agent crouches down and kisses his forehead.

"Heheh. That was nice," he says with a blush.

"So, how does it work?"

"I'll show you." Gamma holds out his hands.

"Administrator recognized. What can I do for you?" asks the computer system in a stoic male voice.

"Look up Racheal Summers."

The screen above cycles through data.

"Racheal Summers, best-selling author of *The Missing Piece*. Her bizarre death led to her becoming an urban legend of sorts."

Racheal bounces in excitement. "Best seller! I didn't know I was famous!"

"You're right to be proud. So, what's your husband's name? He sure is lucky to have such a strong and loving partner."

"Braven. Oh, I need his real name. I uhh…don't know it."

"He never told you?"

"Doesn't like to talk about his pre-life much. Can you just search for any people who suddenly pop up out of nowhere?"

"I've honestly been searching since we saw you."

"Oh, so no luck?"

"I'm still searching, but not yet."

"Thanks for going the extra mile for me! Oh, can you look up Annolette?"

"Any last name?"

"No…sorry."

"It's alright." He turns around. "I think it's likely that they're still there."

Racheal takes off her gloves and holds her wedding tattoo, the thorny circlet on her ring finger. "Just another reason to go back. Can you convince your boss to try and figure a way to return to my world?"

"Well, we'd need to capture one of those shapeshifting aliens. And we aren't leaving until we've contained the Exp threat. His words, not mine."

"Well, then I'll give it my all!" The new agent clenches her fist. "Hey, thanks for all the help. I owe you big time."

Gamma smiles. "You don't owe me anything. But umm, maybe sometime you can tell me about that other world and about your ummm…relationship."

"Sure! Well, it's time for me to head out for today's mission! Thanks again, senpai!" The spunky red-head grins and waves him farewell.

Racheal enters the briefing room. She adjusts her FLESH to be a little bit less tight and takes off her bat shaped helmet. "So, what's my mission?"

Lambda pushes a hair away from Racheal's eyes. "You really look gorgeous in that. Congratulations on your initiation, by the way."

"Yeah, I didn't expect to get promoted after losing that Exp girl. Hey, so is Zenero our enemy? The boss didn't seem too happy to hear he has returned."

"He didn't have to be an enemy, but that's the decision he's made. The boss and him once worked together to create an ecological revolution. That revolution led to Civil War of the Parties. John, that's the boss' name in case you weren't informed, he felt that Zenero was going to lead their side to ruin. John had him killed and made him into a martyr." Lambda rolls her spoon in her tea cup.

"How is he alive then?"

"That's the question."

"Well I have a question too. He saved all of us from an attack when he returned. So why are we enemies?"

"Humans are weak. We cling to faith to escape our fears. We use it to justify our actions and troubles. And we become attached to that faith whatever it is. Zenero has disrupted everything with what he has revealed about the afterlife. It's best you see for yourself." Lambda turns on the screen in the room.

Zenero is holding a grieving mother in a loving embrace. "I made you an impossible promise. The world knows how your child was killed last week by men driven by hatred and fear. The Human's First movement can only take life." He releases the woman and opens a portal.

"Mom?" asks a little girl in tears.

The mother freezes before seizing her child and breaking down.

The video skips to another clip where Zenero approaches the girl.

"Tell them what you witnessed."

The girl nods. "I died. When I woke up, I was in a place where the flowers and trees were white. It was Heaven. It's real! It's really real!"

Zenero then opens a white portal.

Racheal watches, unknowingly holding her breath.

Zenero stands tall. "I promised that anyone who wants a glimpse of Heaven need only ask me. Now is that time. Who wants to take this one giant step into the truth?"

Most of the audience froze, but some stood up.

The camera followed Zenero into the portal, where people from the audience met with loved ones in a world of white.

Lambda turns off the screen.

"Did I see what I think I just saw?" asks Racheal, holding her chest.

"He had everything prearranged. But he took thousands to the other side. Brought people he found in Lum and then promised their family members a reunion. He did this live. It was witnessed all across the globe. The world has seen Lum now. Even I can't deny it anymore."

"My mom! This means he can find my mom." Racheal beams at Lambda.

"What it means is that he's become a messiah. He has discredited religious and non-religious enterprises. Many people and organizations want him dead. Him defending the Exps just creates more problems. Someone with the power over life and death…it's terrifying."

"Well, I think it's wonderful. So, what is our mission? To kill him?"

"Funny you should say that." Lambda puts on another video.

Zenero bows to the audience of over ten-thousand in a crowded stadium in California. "I say once more not to be alarmed. What I am about to do is very unpleasant." He takes a gun to his head, pulls back the hammer of the pistol and blasts his brains out.

Racheal turns to Lambda in shock who just points to the screen.

A portal appears a moment later and Zenero emerges. He hoists up his lifeless body. "Death is not an obstacle for those who wish to join me in creating a sustainable future!"

Lambda turns off the screen.

"That was freaking awesome! And that was really real!"

"As real as your power over sound is. Zenero has made his believers absolutely fearless. We have to be careful how we move from here on out. There could end up becoming another civil war. Zenero has revived the Deus Ex Machina in just a week, uniting them and the Furies under one banner: the EcoRevs. We don't know the full extent of what he's planning. Right now, our mission is to disrupt that."

"Anything else?"

"Zenero announced he'll be running for president."

"Geez, I missed all this big news because of the initiation test."

"To wear the FLESH of the hunters, one must first tear flesh in their flesh. It's something Sigma came up with."

"Felt more like an assassin's initiation than an agent's. In my world, we had a different initiation."

"What's that?"

"Being beaten and branded."

Lambda grabs Racheal's hands tightly. "We can make them pay."

"That's not my thing, despite my comics. I'd rather focus on my new family." She brings Lambda's hand to her lips and places a soft kiss.

"I'm lucky to have such a sweet little sister." Lambda tickles Racheal's chin.

"So, sis…more specifically, what is my mission?"

"You're going to be joining me, Agent Iota and the Senator himself in private negotiations with Zenero."

"I know barely anything about him. I doubt we'll agree."

"You don't need to. You're neutral in this. Plus, you're friendly and people open up to you."

"Hey, this would be Kioshi's mission, wouldn't it? If she were here."

Lambda closes her eyes. "If negotiations go well, then maybe we can get her back."

"We will get her back!" Racheal raises her hand for a high five.

Lambda looks down. "Yeah."

"So, what are we negotiating?"

"Zenero wants Nina and Crisis fixed and returned."

"Fixed?"

"I broke them. Fixing them will be something new, but I can at least try."

"And what does our chief want in return?"

Lambda gets up and rubs Racheal's shoulders. "Maybe an end to his Messiah role. Perhaps, the list of Deus Ex Machina remnants. Or maybe just to resign from the upcoming presidency. We'll find out in an hour."

"An hour! That's not much time to prep. We aren't the IMF."

"Should be plenty of time for a massage and maybe some fun." Lambda nibbles the girl's ear playfully.

"Thanks, but I'm going to look more into Zenero in the meantime. Send me his files please."

"Aww, that's no fun." Lambda shrugs. "All right, but afterwards, let's enjoy each other."

"Yeah, sure thing."

Lambda pats Racheal. "Good girl."

Atlas goes into Hope's room and shakes her gently.

"Who dares ruin my naptime?" asks Hope with a yawn and a stretch. She grabs her pillow and bops Atlas' head with it. "Explain yourself."

"It is time for negotiations."

Hope whacks him again. "You should have woken me up sooner." She tosses him the comb. "Make my hair presentable."

"As you command," he says, combing her long curls.

Zenero appears and creates a portal. "We must be careful not to fall into the Senator's traps."

"I've dealt with him before. Leave the talking to me," she says, signaling Atlas to pick her up.

"Where is Deceivant?" asks Zenero.

"Never heard of him. Let's go!" She whacks Atlas' arm with her mitten and he enters the portal.

The Senator, Lambda, Racheal and Iota are already seated in the comfy velvet chairs around the rectangular table.

Hope elevates her chair so she isn't hidden. "No cameras, so no need to put on airs. You will fix the Exps you have broken and turn them over to me!"

"Oh wow! She's so cute!" exclaims Racheal, wiggling in her chair.

The Senator leans forward. “Don’t be so brash. Your Queendom only exists because I permit it.”

“You tried to bomb my nation to cinders! You even released a video of our capture prematurely. Your cockiness has cost you to lose face, hasn’t it? I hear the President removed you from her special committee.”

“Did that traitor say that to you!?” yells the Senator.

“It was merely a hypothesis that you just confirmed.”

Zenero raises his hand out. “Bickering solves nothing. I propose we try and reach a compromise. We are so much stronger as allies.”

“I agree with that sentiment entirely,” says Agent Iota, sifting through his notes. “You and the Senator were once a powerful team.”

The Senator grimaces. “I only worked alongside him out of necessity. There was no good will between us.”

Zenero sighs. “Still bitter.”

Racheal speaks up. “Well, yeah. That’s how it is sometimes. But you don’t have to like someone to reach a compromise. Zenero, you’ve been playing god.” She leans in and looks directly at him. “Are you aware that suicide rates have increased worldwide since your display?”

“I never encouraged such a thing.”

The Senator slams his fist. “You discredited religions worldwide. You knew there would be repercussions.”

“When the world is upside down, it must be destabilized first before returning to balance.”

Hope turns to Zenero. “Why didn’t you show Sel to humanity? I found it curious that Lum was the only realm you revealed.”

“You have to show me Hell!” exclaims Racheal with starry eyes, popping out of her seat. She then sits down awkwardly, blushing a deep crimson. She clears her throat. “Proceed.”

Zenero smiles at the new Hunter. “Fear cannot be used to control people. The truth I showed was more than enough.”

The Senator scowls at him. “Claiming messianic powers to win the Primary. That’s dirty even by my standards.”

“You’ve done the same.”

“I allow the people come to that conclusion. I don’t trick them.”

“I’ve been Sellum before. It’s not deception if it’s true.”

“I’ve had enough of your blasphemy! You want the Exps freed, then you must tell the people that you’re a fraud. A mere illusionist playing with their hearts.”

“You’re losing your hold over the masses and it terrifies you,” says Zenero, gazing deeply into the Senator.

"These negotiations are over!"

Hope stands in her chair. "They absolutely are not! I demand you free Nina, Crisis, Abyss and War! All my people should live in my nation!"

Agent Iota stands up. "The Senator has spoken. The negotiations are over."

Racheal puts out her hands and creates a loud scratching noise. "We can't give up so easily. Zenero, can you agree to stop performing these crazy miracles?"

He shrugs. "Perhaps, but I have no incentive to."

Racheal turns to the Senator. "And can you return Nina and Crisis to Hope after undoing their brainwashing?"

"Losing two valuable agents would put me at a disadvantage."

"One valuable agent. The other is my spy," says Zenero before creating a portal and walking through it.

Lambda turns to the Senator. "He's just trying to get under your skin. Ignore him."

Racheal shakes her head. "I don't think he is. I mean Kioshi wouldn't kill an agent, let alone her boyfriend. It makes more sense if there's someone on the inside. Zenero came in to save the day. What if he orchestrated the attack with a spy?"

Hope's eyes widened. "Then perhaps what Kitty told me is true." She looks intently at Racheal. "Lilith was taken from you by Zenero."

"I swear to Cthulhu."

"Well Senator, perhaps we should both be wary of spies. Atlas, go on ahead. I have some final words to speak before leaving."

"If I go, then who will protect you?"

"The Senator has enough honor not to attack during negotiations. And I still hold some dirt on him should he dare attack me."

Atlas nods and leaves.

The Senator smiles. "Looks like we have a common enemy."

"I disagree. Zenero is an ally for now. However, should he decide to change his allegiance, I could reveal his weakness to you. That is, if you were to cooperate by returning Nina and Crisis over to me."

The Senator reaches over and shakes her hand. "Their rehabilitation will begin immediately. For now. there will be a cease fire between our forces."

"Glad you can be sensible," says Hope with smile. She hops off her chair and walks into the portal.

Moments later, the portal closes.

Lambda tickles Racheal's sides. "You saved the negotiation."

"No, I didn't. I barely did anything," says Racheal with a blush.

The Senator turns to her. "You mustn't sell yourself short. That was exceptional work. Where did you learn such skills?"

"I was in a village run by evil CatBoys. Had to negotiate to get anything done, pretty much," says Racheal, scratching her cheek.

"Agent Lambda, before you rehabilitate the two Exps, I want you to interrogate them. We can't be too cautious."

"By interrogate you mean torture, right? That's so crazy. Are we still the good guys?" asks Racheal.

"Good falls to evil only when it restricts itself with morality. True good moves forward into the light no matter the obstacle," says the Senator reverently.

"Hey, so what is Zenero's weakness anyway?" asks Racheal.

"We shall find out soon enough." The Senator grins.

Chapter 211: Reason to Live

I'm the last to arrive at the meeting place. The tux Lambda made me is a bit feminine. Probably because she's used to making women's clothes.

Kaity, Deceivant and my sister are dining together outside a restaurant called the Garden of Vegan. Deceivant is in a tuxedo like me. My sister is in a black gothic Lolita outfit with a short skirt. Kaity is wearing a tank-top and shorts.

Does she even have formal attire?

"Why does Koshi get to choose the restaurant if he's not even going to order anything?" asks Kioshi, while slurping up some pasta.

I sit and balance my glass on my finger. "I wouldn't complain. Your boyfriend is Vegan too, you know."

"Oh, yeah. Good point," says Kioshi, looking down with flushed cheeks.

Kaity turns to Deceivant. "I can't believe you're really joining Bob."

"It's the only way to keep my family safe. I'm sorry I couldn't protect you too."

Kioshi tosses a slice of bread at Kaity. "Enough sad talk. Why don't you and my brother go so Deceivant and I can eat in peace."

I lean back in my chair. "Not happening. Until I'm called back to base, I'm not going anywhere."

Deceivant takes a sip of his fruity smoothie and sulks. "Hope must be worried about me. Kaity, how did she take the news?"

"I couldn't tell her. She thinks you're still searching for Mika."

Kioshi takes out her purse and opens it. "Picture sharing time!" She pulls out some photos and scoots her chair to Deceivant's. "This is my first picture of you. I don't remember what the lecture was about, but I had to beg my parents to let me go!"

Deceivant beams at her. "That's so sweet."

"It sure is! Here I am following you home." She lifts up a picture of her taking a selfie with Deceivant in the background. "Here's you following Amy home. Here's me watching you take a shower. Here's me watching you watch Amy take a shower. Here's a picture I drew of us holding hands. And this is my favorite one. It's you contemplating deeply, while your glasses gleam in the light! You're the greatest!" exclaims Kioshi before setting the pics down and snuggling him.

Deceivant pets her.

I grit my teeth and glare at the creep.

Kioshi notices and sticks her tongue out. "Jealous?"

"He left you for Mika. Why are you still clinging to him? He doesn't deserve you," I say, shattering my glass with my intense grip.

Kioshi cries. "I know I'm not his special someone. I'm just trying to enjoy myself, you jerk. Maybe I should just go kill myself because I'll always be alone!" She pushes off Deceivant and runs off.

Not this again! Damn it!

I chase after her and tackle her to the grass.

"Get off me! I hate you! I just want to die!"

"Please don't say such things." I hold her flailing arms in a tight embrace.

"Why not!?" yells Kioshi with rage, pushing the dumb jerk off.

"You'd regret it! I know you would."

"My body, my choice. It doesn't affect you!"

Every time I save her, it's a struggle.

"Of course it does. I don't know what I would do without you. I'd lose myself."

"You're a murderer, so nothing you say matters! Dying is much better than killing, so don't judge me," says Kioshi, sticking out her tongue.

"It's not useless if it brings me joy," I say with a tender smile.

"You're sick in the head!" yells Kioshi.

"Hey, it's my job. Might as well enjoy what you do for a living. It's also become a hobby. Everyone needs a hobby."

"Oh, but suicide can't be a hobby. You're so unfair!" yells Kioshi, crossing her arms and turning from him.

"It absolutely can't be. Once you succeed…you can't ever do it again." My voice trembles as I grip her.

"The thrill of being so close to death. Teetering between worlds. It's a zone of absolute bliss." Kioshi holds her cheeks and sighs.

"Stop! You act like you enjoy it, but I know it's hurting you," I say, hugging her from behind.

"You don't know anything! I'm going back to finish my dinner. Don't follow me!" yells Kioshi, running off.

Why does she have to be such a pain in the ass? I risked so much by coming out to see her!

I sit down on the grass and slam my fist.

I stand up when I receive a call.

Noticing a laser pointer on my chest, I decide to answer. "Geez, now really isn't the time."

"Insubordination!" yells the Senator on the other line. "Here we are facing our greatest struggle since the near extinction of humanity and you're relaxing with the enemy and a traitor!"

"My sister isn't a traitor!"

"Then why did she immediately go to the Queendom?"

"She had nowhere else to go! Look, I've decided, if you don't welcome her back in, then I'm done. You lose your best agent. Oh, and I'm the God of Death now too. I'm even more valuable than before!"

As long as he needs me, he won't dare harm her.

"No, you won't. Your dear sister's life is in my hands now. If I give the signal, my sniper will end her. Is that clear?" asks the Senator in a dark voice.

My calm blue eyes intensify. "I'll murder you!"

A sniper bullet tears through my hand.

The boss has totally lost it! What the hell is going on?

"Do you really wish to test me now?" he asks.

I cringe in pain, wrapping the wound on my hand. "No…I…what do you want? I'll return to base. I was just…checking up on my little sister."

"You are going to kill Deceivant."

"But that will break Sis' heart. She said he gave her a reason to live. Killing him will destroy her. I'll do anything else, please."

Why does he even want Deceivant dead all of the sudden?

"You are my soldier and you will obey my orders!"

"Okay, but she can't know it was me. She'll hate me forever," I say softly.

I don't know if I can bear that.

"Your word is meaningless. Prove your loyalty by shedding his blood. You will kill him exactly as I command."

I can't risk her life. I'll have to obey. Shit! This situation is so f'ed up!

"Understood, Boss," I say.

"Walk up to the table and shake his hand,"

I fake a smile and meet with the others.

Kioshi stands up and glares at me. "I told you not to come back."

Will you ever smile at me again after this?

"Something came up." I approach Deceivant. "I have three things to say to you." I grab Deceivant's hand tightly. "First off, congratulations on winning my sister's heart."

"She's too cute not to cherish," says Deceivant with a smile.

"Two, thank you for giving her a reason to live again." My eyes water up.

"Just because I've reunited with Mika, doesn't mean I'll abandon her. She is still my girlfriend."

Alright, time to end this.

"Yeah. One last thing though. I'm sorry." I thrust my arm through Deceivant's chest. "It's done," I say softly.

Kaity rushes to Deceivant, pouring Lum energy into him as the people in the restaurant scream and flee.

"Sorry, but she knows too much," says the Senator.

The red reticle moves to my sister's head.

No! This is insane! I did what he wanted!

I make a run for it. The moment I grab her, she pushes me off and smiles.

I hear the bullet.

Blood and brain matter cover my face.

Her blood...my sister's blood.

Her body slips out from my grip and falls to the floor.

Kaity's Lum powers die out. She looks up in disbelief.

Kioshi can't really be dead. She's everything.

"You were wrong, Agent Alpha. The new weapon is complete. I no longer have to tolerate your insubordination. You're not needed. But I am merciful, beg for me to kill you and I'll grant your wish. Your life will be nothing but pain without her."

Bullets shot into my legs, bringing me to his knees.

"The moment I find you, I'll kill you!" I yell with the reticle on my forehead.

Why did she try to take a bullet for me...even after I killed her lover?

"Your life ends now."

Just before the bullet fires, a small portal appears.

The bullet is redirected and Zenero emerges. He pulls me into a portal.

I rush at Zenero in a fiery burst of rage. "Why didn't you save her?"

I should have died!

"I was trying to discern the attacker's location."

"You failed! I'll kill you too!" I yell, pooling my aura into the Death Scythe.

"Go ahead."

I pierce Zenero's chest with the scythe and then tear it open. I drop my weapon and sob.

Everything feels meaningless now.

Zenero appears and turns away from the sight of his corpse. "Are you ready to listen now."

"Just…leave me alone." I claw at my face.

Zenero stretches his arm out to me.

"The only thing I want is my sister, and vengeance on the ones responsible!"

"I can give you both," whispers Zenero. He creates a portal to Lum.

Can he really bring her back to life?

Chapter 212: Weakness

Day 8 of isolation, I arrive in a small village, untouched by time. Part of the historical protection program from the late 2050's. An entire town with 1950's decorum. It was once a tourist spot, but these days nobody but the locals visit.

Natura would stick out like a rainbow in a storm here, so she's disguised herself as the mild-mannered June.

"Want something to eat?" asks the lady at the pancake house.

"Soda, the orange fizzy one."

"Are you planning on trying every drink on the menu? Don't you want to eat anything?"

I hold up my glass. "Fill 'er up." I close my mouth when I hiccup.

"Most people come here to run away from something. Did you run from home?"

"I'm not drunk!" I yell, shaking the glass in her face.

Carbonation makes me all dizzy. Been meaning to try the old caffeine pumped sodas before I die. There's no guarantee I'll make it home safely. Gotta check off those items on my bucket list.

The lady points to the counter. "You can borrow the phone here if you need to make a call."

"I already 'ave a cell phone."

The people in the diner give me dirty looks.

Geez, so serious about the continuity here.

"Live a little," I say, holding up my glass before taking another swig.

The lady comes back with my fizzy orange drink and some pancakes.

I take the drink and swig it down. "Yeah, that's the good stuff."

I notice four policemen at the back corner of the diner, chatting amongst each other while looking my way.

Time to make my exit.

I pull out some cash from my pocket, all historically accurate of course. Got it exchanged just before entering this place.

Now for a drive-in movie. Only I don't have a car.

"I'll double your tip, if you let me take the whole beaker," I say, eyeing the soda.

She steps away and four cops approach.

"You look so funny," I say, giggling at their serious faces.

"Look, girlie. Just come with us, we'll make an announcement and find your parents."

"I don't need anyone. And I'm not drunk." I grab the beaker from the lady, zap them and run off.

Geez, did I just do a crime? I'm going to be a wanted girl just like my bro August. Nothing I can't handle though.

I create some cold wind to freeze the front entrance, keeping the cops from following me.

I run down the alleys.

Why are the roads so rough?

I trip and lose hold of the beaker.

It doesn't shatter though, instead it floats through the air.

Shinx grabs the beaker and takes a sip. "Ugh, that's terrible." He tosses it up into the air.

I run to catch the beaker, but trip and it shatters.

"Didn't expect to find you here. You're the Exp girl who makes it rain, right? You look like crap."

"You're lookin' pretty blurry yourself, brat."

"I'm after August. Last I heard he was here."

Geez, did he have to spoil the big surprise? It was going to be the dramatic moment of the comic! After years apart, Natura reunites her bounty hunter hunting brother.

Shinx puts a penny on his finger. "I'll give you a chance. If you survive, you get to live."

The penny suddenly shoots off, piercing my thigh like a bullet.

Shit! What did he even do? Did anyone mention his powers? Ugh, my head is so dizzy!

I stand tall despite the wound. "Hey, you're Shinx. I'm here to bring you and Riufen back. Know where he is?"

"You don't get to ask me questions." He points his finger before I blast him off his feet with a gust of wind. He stands on the wall and looks down at me. "Prove your strength and I'll tell you where he is."

Simple enough.

I send electricity out from my fingers, but he redirects it without even a sound.

My head hurts. This is the worst time for a fight.

I hold my hand out. "Stop! I'm not at my best now. Was gonna sleep this off before confronting my brother. Thought he'd be able to help me track you two down."

Shinx rolls his eyes. "Not at your best. Oh, I wasn't aware this was kendo club." He pulls a car off the road and flings it at me.

Oh shit. Gotta get it together. Lives are at stake.

I create a wind gust that launches the car up and then an ice slide to bring it down.

My powers are unleashed when I'm high on the fizzy stuff! No holding back, this kid is a villain.

Shinx pulls more cars off the road and flings them my way.

"It's not my responsibility to wait for you to be at full strength. Real danger comes at any time. A gazelle can't call time out when she's being chased by a cheetah!"

I create multiple wind gusts to keep the cars from crashing. "Stop! This isn't a game. They could die!"

"Weakness," says Shinx, cleaving a car in two with his sword before it extends at me.

Gotta dodge.

I push back with a wind gust, but lose focus. The cars crash. A few even catch fire.

When I rush to help the family inside one of the burning cars, my back is struck from behind.

If I don't do something...then more will die. It isn't just these people that need a hero. Everyone needs me.

I turn around, sending a hail storm at the villain. Their screams assault my ears, but I can't risk a moment of distraction. Gusts coat my legs, sending me past the boy's blade and crashing into the wall.

No way. I was about to rush him. What happened?

A car hits me from behind and bursts on impact.

I fall to the ground, scorched and bloodied.

Not used to getting hit. But I can power through this! I'm a hero!

Lighting bursts out from me, frying one of the fleeing civilians.

How did...he redirected it. No matter what I do, he just bends it to his desire. And now...I've killed someone.

Shinx looks at my face of horror. "Peheheh! You're broken so easily. Some hero. Heroism is just a mask you wear to hide your weakness." He swings the sword and cuts the building behind me in two.

I hear gunfire and screams as he carves my body with his sword.

I'm going to die here. Is there really a world beyond this one? Will Zenero find me despite me abandoning his cause? I have to try and escape. Yeah, one last gambit.

My body releases fog. I limp away, with sheets of flesh cut from the backs of my arms and legs. I make it to the next ally before collapsing.

A hand grabs me and hoists me up. “Who was it?” asks August, tilting his hat to avoid looking at my wounds.

I grab his hand. “Hey, you wouldn’t mind taking over mid-issue, right?”

August shakes my hand. “Consider it a crossover.”

I set my sister down. “Hey, we need an ambulance over here!”

A truck suddenly comes crashing through the building.

I sharpen my body and slice the rubble.

A poster flies into my face and blocks my vision.

I yank it off.

It’s me, winking and giving a thumbs up sign right above “$600,000 WANTED DEAD OR ALIVE.”

A boy hops off the truck.

This must be the little monster that mutilated my sister! I’ve gotta make my next move carefully.

“I was waiting for you to show up.” The boy looks at me.

“The name is Bloody August. I got that name for all the bounty hunters I kill for the thrill of it. You don’t want to mess with me, kid.”

“My name is Shinx. I’m looking for strong warriors to join my cause.” He points at my mutilated sister behind me with his sword. “That one didn’t quite make the cut.”

I light my cigar. “Catch.” I throw a wine bottle with one hand and the open lighter with the other.

The two items defy gravity and fall in the middle between us.

Doesn’t matter. He’s dead.

I reach into my vest and pull out my custom revolver.

The Judge won’t fail me. Never missed a shot and never will. Every time I use this gun, I think of May. She came up with the name despite abhorring weapons. Geez, why is my mind wandering now?

Eight bullets, two for his legs right at the knees. Another two to burst open his arms at the elbows. And the last two go for his capsule and then his head with a slight flick of my wrist.

The bullets swerve and shoot into the fire in the center.

Impossible. The Judge can’t miss.

The fire suddenly leaps from the ground at me.

“Do you really think he might be powerful enough?” asks Shinx to his sword as I bounce up to dodge.

"You don't look that powerful and yet you defeated my master," says the sword.

Talking swords. What a mighty pickle I'm in. The boy has a god sword with him.

I rip my scarf and toss it, causing the flame to consume it instead of me.

Aha! That red dot must be how he targeted me. It's almost like an old-fashioned duel.

Shinx smiles as he looks up at me. "If he isn't powerful…he'll simply die and another weakling will be wiped from this planet."

I kick off the side of the building, launching me up.

The boy squints as he aims his finger gun at me.

Alright, he can't hit me at this distance it seems.

I load my gun with explosive rounds and shoot the water tower above.

This town has all sorts of archaic tools for me to make use of.

The boy redirects the water simply by pointing, but in doing so, he loses sight of me.

Bet he didn't know I could camouflage with my ability. At this distance, I might as well be invisible.

I land on the roof and watch him search the skies for me. My hand is on the trigger, waiting for the dot he placed to run out of time.

The moment you're open, your head is going to burst.

"Using the environment to your advantage. That's very clever. I did the same when I was still weak. Let's see how strong your resolve is. Come out or I'll kill your sister." Shinx turns his blade on her.

Making a desperate move will put me at a disadvantage. I have to stay calm and think this through.

I place my hands to the top of the roof, making it bouncy but not yet sending me up.

Shinx starts to cut her face.

"Hands off her!" I yell, firing blanks at him.

Good thing too because he just placed a dot on her. He's trying to get me to kill her.

"Come down from there." Shinx grips his dark sword. "Show me your strength, Yin!"

The blade enlarges but the boy holds it effortlessly. Sel energy rides up the blade as it swipes up the building.

I leap off as the ground beneath me bursts before being consumed by the dark aura.

It's pointless though, because beneath me is a pit of Sel energy.

I whip out a large cloth and throw it so he can't pinpoint my vitals.

"***SURFACE PAPER.***" My body thins out, slipping out from behind the cloth and floating freely in the wind.

Shinx fires at me with his finger gun, but misses.

I slide into the window of an adjacent building.

The boy takes the high rise down a level with each swing.

He doesn't see me. Time to end it!

I jump out of the building and harden my body so it falls like an anvil.

When I hit the ground behind him, he wobbles.

I coat my body in spikes and punch his gut.

My arm shoots back and snaps in the process.

The boy summons up a blue dot on his finger and brings it to my other shoulder.

My bones snap and my vision goes blurry.

"It's over. Your life rests on a single question now. What do you live for?" His golden eyes pierce me with their intense energy.

"I live to kill get revenge on Zenero for turning against his children."

Even if the kid does kill me, I'll find a way back. Zenero must die!

The boy looks at me inquisitively. "Vengeance is a narrow path. You must cut all other ties. Kill your sister and I'll let you live." He points his sword at my throat.

June never gave into revenge despite going through the same shit I did. She's better than me. I can't kill her. If that makes me weak, well, then I guess I'm weak.

I walk up to June and crouch down. I bite her shirt and turn my legs into springs.

I leap off building after building until we're away from danger.

Chapter 213: A Teaspoon Cinnamon

Kaity arrives at the Queendom, holding Deceivant's body.

Atlas approaches her. "What happened?"

"I need to see Hope," says Kaity urgently.

"She's taking her royal bath at the moment. I'll go get her." Atlas nods.

"No time," says Kaity before vanishing.

Hope squeaks in surprise when Kaity appears near her private kiddy pool. "No one is permitted to see me this way," says the Queen, wearing a frilly polka dot swimsuit. Her rage subsides when she notices Deceivant on the ground. The little girl stumbles out of the bath and grabs his hands. "Daddy, wake up."

Kaity wipes her tears away as they rush out. "My powers sealed the wound, but he won't wake up."

"What wound? Did Bob kill him? He never should have gone."

"It was Koshi. He punched straight through his chest."

Hope pulls Deceivant's shirt off and starts rubbing up against his chest. "Maybe we can still jumpstart his capsule."

"Is that how it works?"

"It's how Exps are awakened. Ada jumpstarted my capsule with him just like this."

Kaity nods and joins Hope.

Deceivant's arms suddenly seize them in a hug. "What a pleasant way to wake up." He pats their heads.

Hope cheeks puff out, she growls and then sobs as she hugs him.

Kaity beams at him. "You survived. We saved you!"

Deceivant picks up Hope and sets her in his lap, petting her head. "I wasn't dead. Just badly hurt."

Kaity stands up. "Yeah, I don't see how you survived that. Our capsule is our weak point."

"Exactly! The first time I died, my capsule was in an obvious place. So I moved it," says Deceivant.

"So where is it?" asks Kaity.

"Why don't you listen and find it?" Deceivant smiles at her.

Hope leans her head against his chest, listening intently. "It's here, on the opposite side of your chest."

"You found it!" exclaims Deceivant joyously, lifting her off her feet.

Hope blushes and squirms to escape the ensuing airplane ride. "We are in mixed company."

"You passed out from the pain. You don't know what happened afterwards. Do you?" asks Kaity, turning away in tears.

"What happened?" asks Deceivant, setting down Hope.

"Kioshi was killed by an agent," says Kaity softly.

"What!? How!? Why!?" asks Deceivant in tears.

"I don't know," says Kaity, looking down in tears.

Hope nods. "I understand. Koshi was told to kill Deceivant to keep his sister safe. Then the attacker decided to take her out anyway."

Deceivant grabs Kaity. "Was she smiling? When she died, was she smiling?"

"Yeah, you made her really happy," says Kaity.

Hope looks at Kaity sternly. "Anything else that happened?"

"Zenero saved Koshi from being killed and then he disappeared with him."

"Always at the right place at the right time," says Hope under her breath.

"He didn't do it."

"We can't be certain. After all, he took Lilith and still has her hidden. You decided to keep that from me but my surveillance system was much more forthcoming." Hope stands tall and glares at Kaity. "I am your leader! No more secrets."

Deceivant nods. "Hope, I can't stay here."

"What do you mean?" Hope turns to Kaity. "What is he talking about?"

"I've joined Bob's side. I made a deal to create Exps for him in return for the safety of those in the Queendom."

"And you've done so without my consultation again!"

"You would have forbidden it."

"As I should!"

Kaity steps between them. "It doesn't matter. Bob probably thinks you're dead. We just need to keep your survival hidden."

Hope opens her drawer and then places handcuffs around Deceivant, linking him to the bed. "Agreed. You are to remain in my quarters."

"But Mika will think I'm dead too."

Hope smiles. "Yes, it all worked out in the end. Now, Kitty, there is something I would like to discuss with you." The Queen goes behind her royal changing curtain and puts on her formal attire.

"If it's about turning against Zenero, then forget about it. We have enough enemies as it is."

"I only ask that we be watchful." Hope puts on her mittens and sticks out her tongue at Deceivant. "Had to learn to dress myself. I'd say, I've become quite adept at it."

"Yeah, but your dress is inside out."

Hope blushes and hops back behind the curtain. "We have a new prisoner. Didn't put up much resistance honestly. It's rather concerning. Found them snooping about when you were on that date."

"You mean Noitpurroc?"

"Yes, but he goes by Jigen now. Or is it she? Doesn't matter. The peculiar thing is that demon god claims you are their new master. Is this true?"

"Yeah, I mean I suppose I am."

Hope stomps her foot. "Then grab your slave by the reigns! This is Bob's most powerful ally and if you can break it, then it can change everything in our favor. This is your primary mission; it's of the utmost importance!"

The speakers ring through the Queendom. "Emergency! Everyone, gather in the back garden!" yells Opti from the loudspeakers.

Hope looks up at Kaity. "If your new pet is causing trouble, you'll be the one to shoulder the blame. Now, bring us there immediately."

Kaity nods and grabs Hope's hands.

They arrive in the back garden.

Chipko comes out from behind the shrubbery. "Hey there, you look alarmed, everything okay?"

Hope steps up to her. "Did Zenero ever mention anything to you about recruiting Koshi to his side?"

"No, but I mean, it would certainly cause some problems for the Senator."

"I'll be blunt since you're a sensible creature. Koshi murdered Deceivant. His sister was then shot before he was rescued by Zenero. Any chance he orchestrated that attack?" Hope peers into the girl.

Chipko steps back. "No…he wouldn't. He's not like that…anymore," she says softly to herself.

"I'd like to assume it was the Senator who had the rogue agents killed, but it seems too brash of a move for him. There's nothing to gain from killing your greatest warrior."

Opti shows up, leading the others along.

"You there, what is the emergency?"

Opti beams at Hope. "I'm super thrilled you asked! Everyone is still kinda down so I thought I'd invite everyone to an emergency pick me up!"

Hope crosses her arms. "Emergencies are not to be taken in jest. You behave like an unpunished child."

"Aww, thanks! Yeah, I knew you'd all come if it sounded dangerous! Everyone is so brave!"

Ada hops in place. "What's the surprise? I'm sooo excited!"

"When you're sad, the happy doctor prescribes one tea-spoon of Cinnamon!" Opti pulls back the bushes.

Muffins is underneath and nuzzled between her fluff is a little brown and white baby bunny.

Ada squeals. "Muffins is a momma!"

Hope looks at the fluffy mother and smiles. "Congratulations, madam."

D.S. jumps up. "Wow! This is awesome! I thought Muffins was a boy before I heard she was preggy. Opti, you screwed up. Why did you give her a name as manly as Muffins?"

Opti smiles. "I thought it was unisex."

"Hey, where are the other bunnies. Daddy says that bunnies make lotsa bunnies!"

Opti looks solemn. "The others didn't make it, but Cinnamon is alive and strong! Muffins told me to keep the birth a secret until he got some fluff on him. It usually takes a full month for bunny birth, but not for this momma bun!"

Devlin pats Muffins gently. "He's fortunate to have you as a mother." He turns to Opti. "So Cinnamon is a boy, right?"

"Yep, I made sure to check before I gave him his valiant name."

A little bird swoops down and fumbles around to Muffins, spilling some seed in her mouth. He opens his mouth fully and drops the seeds that didn't spill near the momma bun.

"And this little guy is her new best friend! His name is Fletcher, he's a Fletch bird! He's been taking care of Muffins since she got pregnant."

Hope turns to Opti. "Do we know who the father is?"

"Yeah, it's Nibbles, but he's been missing. I searched for him all yesterday. You don't think he's trying to abandon her, right? He's a sweet bunny."

Kaity grabs Opti's hand. "Bob has Nibbles. I saw him at the Seltanic Church."

"We have to go to tell Nibbles he's a father!" exclaims Opti.

Hope's eyes widen. "You want to go to the enemy's sanctum?"

Kaity motions her to relax. "I'll go with Opti. We'll be back soon. Mika should know what happened. Everyone…" she takes a deep breath and her tail wags nervously "Deceivant is dead."

Ada breaks down into tears.

Hope immediately goes to tend to her mother. "Stabby is in Lum. I'm sure she'll find him."

Kaity turns to Opti. "Let's go."

Opti nods.

The two of them arrive outside of the Seltanic Church.

Riufen approaches. "All are welcome into the walls of the Sinful Sanctum. All but those seeking trouble, they must pass through me."

Kaity crosses her arms and scowls at Riufen. "Why are you still working for Bob? Shinx left or were you not told that?"

"I am where I need to be. It need not concern you. Why have you returned to this place? I hope it is to do battle," he says, his hand ready to unsheathe his spine.

"We're here to see Nibbles." Opti rushes in.

Riufen lowers his head. "Move along then."

"Hey, Shinx asked you to stay behind, right? But you don't have to listen to him. Do what you feel is right," says Kaity.

"I have faith in him."

Kaity runs off, entering the church to see Opti asking around.

Bob pops up behind Kaity. "You keep entering my dark domain. Perhaps you seek to be captured."

"I'm here as Opti's escort. We came to tell Nibbles something."

"Nibbles isn't here at the moment. And neither is Deceivant. What happened?"

Opti pops up behind Bob. "Grampa was killed."

"By the Senator," says Kaity softly.

"Ugh, I'll have to track down his soul. Whatever, that just means the deal we made is off." He summons up the Atma Blade.

"Nibbles is a father!" exclaims Opti.

Bob unsummons his weapon and puts a tendril around each of their shoulders. "Well then, we better go tell him the big news." He summons up a portal.

"I trust you," says Opti. "But I don't know if I should. What do you think, Bob?"

"Yes, yes, of course."

"It's fine," says Kaity. "I can get us out of there in an instant if it's a trap."

Bob leads them into the portal.

They arrive at the Core.

"Don't be alarmed. It's just how portal travel works. Can't teleport to a place in the material realm without going to Sellum, first." He creates a portal and enters.

Kaity and Opti follow.

They arrive in a lush green landscape. An ocean of bunnies stretches out beyond the horizon.

Bob feeds one of the bunny's a carrot. "This planet was created by Pathos. See, different Sellums have different focuses. He mainly focused on his Lum powers. And with it, he was able to create a planet out of space dust."

"I'm capable of that?" asks Kaity, looking at her hands.

"I wouldn't get your hopes up," says Bob with a snicker. "I'm sure he had big plans for this place, but for now, the only animals here are bunnies. I sent Nibbles here to keep him safe. Who knows when my sacred space will be attacked by intruders harboring ill-intent?"

"This is a boat-load of bunnies on a world of bun buns! I dub this place Bunny Planet!" Opti snuggles bunnies while petting a few that came close to him.

"Yes, but it doesn't matter how many bunnies there are. I can sense Nibbles' spirit anywhere," says Bob focusing.

"You have a bunny radar?" asks Opti with sparkling eyes.

"Suuuuure," says Bob, looking at the buffoon curiously. "For whatever reason, I can't locate his soul. He couldn't have left here, unless Noitpurroc stole him. Oh, the irony. I allowed my trust in our bond to separate us."

"I don't see why Jigen would do that," says Kaity.

"Nibbles is more important than you know. This could very well be an act of sabotage," says Bob with a scowl.

"Fine, I'll ask Jigen."

"I'm coming along too," says Bob.

"There's absolutely no way I'm allowing you to enter the Queendom."

"Come now, when I went to see my grandchildren, did I cause any trouble? Hmm, I suppose there was quite a lot of trouble, but not inside the building."

Kaity glares at Bob. "Deceivant trusts you to keep your promises. I don't."

"I want to see the newborn bunny. There's nothing malicious about my intentions. I didn't attack you either time you entered my domain. You're not my biggest concern at the moment. Please, Kaity. It will only be for a minute."

Opti looks at Kaity. "He's not all bad. He pretended to be our friend before we fought Etah, remember?"

Bob rolls his eye. "You're not helping here."

"Alright, we'll make an exchange. I'll bring you to see Cinnamon and you'll help us find Lilith. And you will swear never to hurt her. Understood?" asks Kaity, exuding a thick black aura of Sel energy.

Bob tears the energy off her and consumes it. "Trying to bride me with a yummy snack. I jest. You absolutely have a deal. I won't ever harm, nor will I permit any of my minions to harm Lilith. And I will search for Lilith until she's been found. I wasn't even aware she was lost. Devlin really needs to keep track of his kids better." Bob shrugs.

Kaity swipes at Bob, burning him with the tips of her claws. "He didn't lose her. I did."

"Oh, then it's guilt that drives you. I won't judge. Just expected something less pathetic from Pathos' chosen one." Bob grimaces.

Kaity exhales sharply and then vanishes. She reappears soon after. "Okay, the coast is clear. Nobody is allowed to see you, understood?"

Bob bounces impatiently. "Yes, yes, let's go already."

The three arrive at the Queendom's back garden.

Opti quietly lifts up the shrubbery. "Meet Cinnamon."

Bob's eye waters up as he sees the tiny brown bunny. "Aren't you just the most precious little hell spawn?"

Muffins hisses at Bob and hides her baby.

"I mean that as a compliment. Worry not, my bunny brethren. I'll keep searching until your father is found."

Opti pats Bob. "We should take Cinnamon to Bunny Planet to go find his dad!"

"It's a foolish idea, but I'll entertain it." Bob creates a portal to the Core.

They travel back to Bunny Planet with Cinnamon and Muffins being carried by Opti.

"Now Cinnamon go! Go and find your father!" exclaims Opti enthusiastically, setting the little bunny down.

"Yes! Follow the trail of blood that runs through your veins!" cheers Bob.

Cinnamon approaches a small black bunny and looks at her curiously.

"Keep trying," says Opti.

Cinnamon wanders around.

Opti sees a bunny hill. "I'll find him!" He leaps into the swarm of bunnies gallantly.

"Doesn't he know those are absence bunnies? He really should be more careful," says Bob with a sigh.

Opti leaps out of the bunny mountain valiantly, holding a pink bunny with a black tail in his arms.

"You found him?!"

"Only one bunny in existence is pink!" cheers Opti, rubbing the bun's tum.

"How did he mask his soul from me?" asks Bob.

Opti holds the bunny to Bob who snuggles him in a frenzy.

"Oh, I missed you too, little one." Bob rolls around with the bunny. "Oh." He notices Cinnamon looking their way.

"Cinnamon, meet your father," says Opti as he held Cinnamon up to Nibbles.

Cinnamon stands his ground and stares intensely into his father's eyes.

Muffins snuggles Nibbles.

Bob turns to Opti. "Shall we head back?"

"Give them more time. This is a special moment."

Chapter 214: Gateway to Torment

Shinx exits the town that clings to bygone days. As soon as he turns to continue his journey, he spots August standing in the dirt road. "Are you here to avenge your sister?"

"She isn't dead."

"Well then, why are you bothering me?" asks Shinx, thinning Yin into a katana.

"You're strong. You may be the one who can kill Zenero."

"So, you want to follow me? You lost the fight. I only take on those stronger than me."

"How are you going to build a strong team if you're the only member?"

"You're welcome to challenge me again," says Shinx with a grin.

"When you lost her…did you cry?"

"I…remorse is for weaklings to shield themselves. I've shed that part of me. Enough talk. If you're willing to put your life on the line, then step forward."

A portal appears between them.

August looks around, but doesn't see Zenero. "Stop hiding!"

"He won't come out. His portal is what brought me to this town. He's sending to me to test the stray Exps. Once I'm done, then I have no doubt he'll appear to challenge me." Shinx walks up to the portal. "Better hurry if you want to come along."

August rushes to the portal as it shrinks.

Shinx and August arrive outside of a prison.

"The Exp must be somewhere in there. Hmm, I wonder if any humans will put up a challenge." Shinx cuts down the prison gates.

The guards immediately open fire.

Shinx redirects their bullets, having them tear themselves to pieces. "No loss for the gene pool. Let's proceed."

"You know, I'm sure we could break in without killing anyone. Would be a great way to show off your power."

"Fair enough." Shinx shoots a dot below, causing all bullets to be redirected there.

August puts his hand to the ground and makes the floor like rubber, bouncing the guards up.

Shinx slices the front door open and whacks the guards that rush him with his sword after taking away the blade's sharp edge.

August picks up one of the terrified guards. "We're looking for Durga. Where is she?"

"D-Down the hall. Last door to the right."

Shinx rushes to the door and places his palm against it.

The door flings forward, bouncing off the white walls of the solitary confinement room.

August stretches the floor to the top of the entrance to block it off.

"Sister, why the hell did your own people put you here?" asks August, helping her to her feet.

"You misunderstand. I come here to clear my mind." Durga looks at the blaring alarm outside. "I meditated too deeply. Why have you brought violence to this place of reformation?"

"I've come to fight. Destiny sits on the shoulders of the strong. If you win, I'll allow you to live," says Shinx, pointing his weapon at her.

"Hold on! No way am I letting you kill her!" yells August.

"That boy. Is he your son?" asks Durga curiously. She grabs August's hands. "Many congratulations!"

"He's not my kid. It's a temporary alliance, that's all," says August, crossing his arms.

"Brother, are you still after revenge against Zenero?" asks Durga.

"I live to see him die," says August coldly.

Durga looks at him with a forlorn expression. "He's going to save us all. You're willing to destroy that for revenge? It will bring you no respite."

Shinx steps up. "I've heard enough of your empty words. Draw your weapon and fight me."

Durga examines the boy. Her eyes quiver. "Such profound pain. You are but a child; why do I sense so much pain in you?" Tears pour from her eyes.

"I'm not in pain!" yells Shinx with shaking hands.

Durga walks past his sword and touches his cheek. "I can only take it in if you release it. My mission is life is to take in the agony of others, so they can find peace again."

"I told you, I'm fine!" yells Shinx, on the brink of tears.

"The eyes of a victim are the gateway to their torment. I sense the loss of a loved one. You have let this pain fester into hate. You must let go of it, child," says Durga, crying uncontrollably.

"My name is Shinx. I am no longer held back by sorrow or fear," he says darkly.

"You have killed innocents on your quest for revenge. You must stop before you are consumed completely."

"Do not try to understand me," says Shinx, pointing the blade to her throat.

"Of course. This pain has only one explanation. You miss your mother, don't you?"

Shinx steps back and falls over. "Just stay away." He waves Yin back and forth defensively.

The blade cuts her side. "There is such a thin line between pain and pleasure, one can easily get them confused." Durga touches the wound with a gasp of joy.

Shinx drops his sword in terror. "Don't touch me. Please."

Durga crouches down and wraps her arms around him. She holds his face to her bosom. "Imagine I'm your mother. What do you want to tell me?"

Shinx's eyes flicker with tenderness. His mouth quivers. He then pushes her off. "You're not my Mommy!" He shakes his head. "The strong accept reality. Only weaklings deny it."

"You blame yourself for being too weak to defend her. It's not your fault."

"I couldn't move. I just stood there, like a statue. I screamed out, but no sound permeated. It was too real to be true. That kind of fear shouldn't exist." Shinx breaks down into tears.

Durga embraces him tightly, lifting him off the ground and giving him a motherly kiss on the forehead. "There was nothing you could have done then. Being strong now won't bring her back. She would want her beloved son to live his life with joy and purpose."

"No! You're wrong! Stop this! Stop toying with my mind!" Shinx weakly pulls away.

"I can't abandon this child. August, you must allow me to come along."

"Sis, you've changed so much, I hardly recognize you," says August with a look of awe.

"I look just as I did before," she says perplexed, gazing at her hair.

Shinx lowers his head. "You won. I admit defeat."

"There is not only winning or losing," says Durga with a tender smile. She looks out at the prison walls. "I will never forget the pain we shared together, my friends."

A portal appeared, leading to a jungle.

"Let's…let's get moving," says Shinx, struggling to stand.

Chapter 215: For Her Sake

We spot our target doing stretches in the park.

With Racheal as my teammate, sneaking up on our target is foolproof. But if I have to transform, then my cravings will put her at risk.

"Hey, Famine. Do you want me to send a big sound blast into her noggin?"

I hand her the artifact suppressor. "Be sure to hit her firmly in the chest with this. It won't last forever so we'll need to take her down swiftly."

"But not kill her, correct?"

"Prefer she escapes us, rather than dies. She may be our one chance at stopping Zenero."

"Why is she at the park, anyway? A secret meeting?"

"Nope. Just goes to feed the ducks and do her morning exercise. Ready to move in?"

Freedom is something so many take for granted.

"I'm as nervous as a teen on her first date, but I'll manage." Racheal rushes in, her footsteps not making a sound.

Chipko's foot pulses with energy, releasing a shockwave that knocks our new agent off her feet.

Even with no sound she can still feel our movements. This won't be an easy battle.

I come out from behind cover and open fire on Chipko.

The bullets seemingly hit, yet they pass through her.

What is going on?

"Your boss sent you here to capture me?" asks Chipko, tightening her gloves. "Take one step and I'll burst you to bits."

I rush in, grab Racheal by the shoulder, and fling her back.

Chipko vanishes and reappears behind me. "Shockwave Pulse!"

My insides shuffle and then pop.

Have to transform, it's the only way.

I bite into my arm and tear off a piece of flesh with my sharp teeth.

Hurts every single time.

I swallow as the fourth pulse hits, breaking my bones.

Damn, she's gotten stronger. The pulses used to take longer.

"STAGE THREE!"

My body bursts from the fifth pulse and then assembles back together.

"The Senator uses us both to paint Exps as monsters. Why serve him? You should join Zenero," says Chipko, avoiding the bite of my transformed arms with fancy footwork. She emits a pulse that trips me.

I have to capture her, for my mother's sake! Stay focused, don't eat anymore or the cravings will consume you.

Racheal leaps on Chipko's back, scissors her target's neck between her legs and flings her to the ground.

Chipko blasts the girl off and grabs the device on her chest. "A new toy used to subjugate my kind?"

I stand up. "Wait! Tear it out and your capsule will shatter."

"So, you want me alive then? Trying to lure Zenero out so you can kill him again? Not happening!" She rushes at Racheal and kicks her stomach. "Shockwave Boomerang!"

Racheal is blasted at an angle, launching into me, releasing a crippling shockwave and then projected right back at Chipko.

Never should have brought her along. I can't transform without putting her at risk.

"I'm not beaten so easily!" Racheal fires a sound blast at Chipko on her second rebound and then follows up with a drop kick.

Chipko grabs her legs and shatters the bones. "You're a newbie, right? Get up and this will be your last mission."

"Retreat, Agent Pi! I'll take it from here!"

"You can't handle her on your own. The artifact suppressor didn't even work!"

Chipko's movements slowed down. She lost the use of her other artifact. I can take her down now.

"You're not needed here, kid." Chipko lifts up Racheal and then sends her tumbling away with a condensed shockwave.

"No need to hold back now!" I bite and tear off muscle from my arm. "STAGE EIGHT!"

My eyes split open and fall out of their sockets.

"What did my brother turn you into?" asks Chipko in disgust.

Her flesh! It calls to me!

My eyes consume my body from my feet all the way to my head. Their boundless hunger then coaxes them to rush at Chipko. As my eyes roll to her, they leave bites in the grass.

There is no stopping me now!

My eyes split formation once we notice her readying a shockwave on her fists. They spit out my organs, which quickly leap and bite at the enemy.

Chipko blasts them away with a full-body shockwave, but it knocks her off her feet as well.

My entire body is a ravenous weapon.

My capsule leaps at her, growing teeth midway through the jump.

It regurgitates energy to repel her rapid-fire shockwave fists.

Her face is gone. I'm losing awareness. I have to abort now or I'll end up killing her!

My organs regurgitate all the flesh we've consumed and then come together to form me.

Having my awareness splintered like that always requires a moment to adjust.

When the world stopped spinning, I saw that my capsule was still fighting Chipko.

This is my most vulnerable state, but it's my one chance to win.

Chipko blasts my capsule into the distance by smacking her hands together. She approaches me. "You've lost."

"Alright…I concede." I raise my arms.

Koshi appears out of thin air. "You're fighting over nothing!"

"Actually, I just won. Are you here to capture me too?" asks Chipko, taking a fighting stance.

Maybe he can overpower her.

I look up at Koshi. "Dad, if we capture her, we can bargain for Kioshi to get her place back with the agency."

"The Senator had her killed. I'm with Zenero now. He's my only chance at getting her back. I was told to kill whoever was attacking Chipko. Thankfully, you've already lost," says Koshi softly.

I've done so many terrible things to protect my family. Can she really be gone?

"Why would he kill her? I don't understand." My voice trembles as misery devours me.

"I don't get it either. I'll find out what happened once she's back in my arms. You're welcome to join us."

If neither of my parents are at the agency, then I have no reason to stay. Can Zenero really bring her back?

"I'm going to join the Freedom Forcers and be there for my sister."

Koshi smiles. "That's my boy." He then vanishes.

Chapter 216: Driven by Her Memory

Koshi arrives in front of Zenero. "Chipko is safe and the Senator has lost another ally."

"Then it ended without sacrifice."

"You sound disappointed."

"Not at all. But we must move along to the next mission post haste. Assassins have no place in my world. I want you to end Kanasta."

"You're sending me to assassinate an assassin?"

"Are you objecting?"

"Kanasta is an old friend, kinda. And killing him will make Kaity hate me. Come on, isn't there any other assassin you want dead?"

"None that I can't handle without risks."

"Fine, I'll do it. After he's dead, you will search for my sister."

"I'll search for her as you fight."

"Well then how can I refuse?"

"This isn't enough. Gratitude isn't loyalty. After I've found her, we will speak. I want you to understand my mission."

"Sure thing, Hero of the Millenia!"

"Fu-fu. Do people still call me that?" asks Zenero.

"Nobody I'm friends with."

Koshi is teleported to the forest of the Queendom.

Kanasta notices him and opens his suitcase. "I'm assuming you were sent here to kill me."

"Straight to the point. Gotta admire that."

"Then my assumption is correct?"

"Yeah, but it's not personal."

"My death is a step toward your sister's revival. I don't fully understand, but I sympathize. Whether this battle ends in your favor or mine, take heart knowing a reunion with her is inevitable."

"I learned a lot from my short time in the Viper Squad. Let's see if I can put it into practice," says Koshi, creating energy blades.

"There's something different about your energy," says Kanasta curiously.

"I'm the new God of Death! But I don't need god powers to take you down. I'm doing this my way!"

Kanasta pulls out two rectangular game controllers from his suitcase.

"You have got to be kidding," says Koshi, holding his sides.

"A seemingly harmless retro controller." Kanasta flicks his wrist, causing the remote to light up before shooting a beam of energy shaped like claws. He boxes the air, sending the blasts into Koshi. "With the Viper Squad gone, I've become a lone assassin known as the Game Master."

"So you have to kill with a certain motif. Guess every business needs a certain aesthetic." Koshi's body releases a burst of energy, sending Kanasta off his feet. He then shoots forth at his old friend.

Kanasta deflects the incoming attack with a thick black video game console, coated in steel.

The ex-agent grips the device with energy coated hands and throws it aside.

"You're lucky it's fall resistant." Kanasta slams his forehead into his attacker.

"You do realize that this theme you got going, is really demoralizing to your targets."

"No such disrespect is intended. I created these weapons with honorable intent. I also created my own weapons for taking down Exp Hunters, with you in mind."

"Wow, I'm flattered. Geez, I should have gotten you a sweet gift too."

"None needed. This next attack is inspired by Atatasuki. I found his fighting style most intriguing." Kanasta slams his palms into the Exp Hunter. "Ring of Death"

"I'm tired of your games!" Koshi extends his energy blades by rubbing his palms together to create friction.

"Shouldn't have done that," says Kanasta, while dodging the incoming slices.

The device on Koshi's chest spins.

Energy erupts from Koshi uncontrollably.

He screams as his body is cooked into a puddle of blood.

"Kaity needs me, so I can't risk dying. Killing in self-defense is not my way. I hope you'll forgive me."

The blood puddle rises up and takes form. Koshi's eyes shoot open. He then expels the blood into a puddle beneath his feet.

"Working for Bob now. What could compel you to do that?"

Koshi rushes at Kanasta. "You're a perfect assassin, right? Let's put it to the test. A single touch and you die." He summons up the Death Scythe, slicing the moment it's fully formed.

Kanasta slices Koshi's hand off with a string, altering the weapon's trajectory.

"Ha! That won't change anything." An aerial trail of blood connects the severed hand to Koshi's arm, giving him full control of the weapon with added reach.

Kanasta throws a smoke bomb and then runs past his enemy who is searching within for him. He reaches into a suitcase and pulls out a cord. "There was a time when cords would ignite, turning entire buildings to ashes. I've modified my weapons with the spirits of my fallen Viper's. Each of the assassin's lives on through me." With a single crack of the cord-like whip, he ignites the special smoke cloud.

The explosion consumes Koshi.

Kanasta attaches dual nozzle gauntlets to his hands. He sprays the blood with liquid nitrogen. "Can't regenerate if you cannot move. Tempo was always there to get me out of a tight spot. His death doesn't change that." He places the gloves back in the case. "A single killer harboring the wills of his entire squad. The Viper Squad lives on through me!" He turns around to see Koshi's FLESH.

The special suit springs from the ground and disperses into leeches as Kanasta shoots ice on it. They crawl onto his body and bite deep, devouring his energy.

The one-man assassin squad tears clumps of leeches off, shredding his own flesh in the process. He falls to his knees in exhaustion before removing them all.

The separated hand from earlier floats above him and summons up the Death Scythe. Blood gushes out from the sever of the hand and reforms the Agent of Death.

"Wait…Kaity needs me. She's lost so many," says Kanasta as the leeches leave him and rejoin as Koshi's suit.

"I know that! Don't make this harder than it has to be. I'm going to kill you with a single cut! Then I'll get rid of all the evidence!" Koshi brings down the Death Scythe.

It pierces Kanasta's shoulder, but he does not die.

"That girl has robbed us both of our venom. Kaity is more powerful than she realizes." Kanasta smiles.

"I'll just have to end you the old-fashioned way!" He repeatedly cuts and tears the scythe into Kanasta's chest.

Kanasta shakes his head. "Your hands are shaking. Steady yourself, then cut cleanly."

Zenero appears before them. "No need for that. Stand down, Koshi. You've proven your loyalty to me."

"Did you find her?" asks Koshi, grabbing Zenero and crying.

Zenero creates a portal and beckons Koshi to enter. He looks to Kanasta. "I hope this encounter can be forgotten."

"I see no reason to mention it." Kanasta holds up his hand when Zenero goes to leave. "I don't know your true intentions, but if you seek Kaity's death, battle me first. I refuse to see any more Viper's die."

"You're an interesting man, Kanasta," says Zenero before vanishing into his portal.

Zenero meets with Koshi and Chipko in a dessert.

Koshi steps up to him. "Where is she? Please, tell me she's okay."

Zenero smiles. "You've proven your loyalty to me. Here is your gift as promised." He bows and creates a portal.

Kioshi steps out of it.

The siblings tear up as their eyes meet.

Chipko leans against Zenero's shoulder. "Such a touching moment."

The siblings embrace.

Koshi kisses her forehead repeatedly.

Kioshi grabs his cheeks and kisses his lips, making him blush deeply.

"Love is so beautiful," says Chipko, grabbing Zenero's hand and planting a kiss on his cheek.

"Beauty is without purpose." He lifts her into his arms and kisses her deeply. "True love is transformative."

Kioshi cuddles her brother as he pets her.

Zenero sets Chipko down and approaches the siblings. "You may believe that I now hold no bargaining chips so there's no reason to continue helping me. That would be an incorrect assumption. As long as you follow my will dutifully, she will live. However, if you even think of betraying me…." Zenero draws a circle in the air, summoning up a portal.

A train comes speeding through.

Kioshi pushes off her brother and jumps in the way, splattering against the train.

Zenero then teleports the empty train away.

Koshi fell to his knees. "Why…did you do that?"

"Words only penetrate so deep." He vanishes into a portal.

Chipko helps Koshi to his feet. "No worries. She'll be right back. He discovered a clever trick to find those that recently died. Where someone dies on Earth determines where they show up in Lum."

"He'll find her, guaranteed?" asks Koshi, griping onto her in desperation.

"Absolutely. Hey, are you still going to go after the one responsible for her death?"

"Yeah. He can send me into the base and I'll slaughter whoever gets in my way of killing the Senator."

Zenero reappears with Kioshi.

"That was wow! Another check on my Splatter List." Kioshi grins.

Zenero grabs her shoulders to keep her from bouncing. "You are only permitted to die in my presence, understood? Your safety is my priority."

"Okay, Master," says Kioshi, rubbing up against him.

Koshi grabs her and holds her close. "No more. I never want to lose you again."

"I apologize for the gruesome example, but such things get the point across more effectively." Zenero wipes his gloves clean of guilt.

"Again! Again! Kill me again!" begs Kioshi, tugging at Zenero's cloak.

"Apologies, my dear, but as long as Koshi serves me, I refuse to kill you."

"Damn it, Koshi. Why can't you just let him kill me a few more times?"

"Sis, I'm sorry about killing Deceivant," says Koshi contritely.

"I don't wanna hear your excuses. Besides, I bet the great Zenero can find him and bring him back!"

"You two should have arrived in the same location in Lum. I did not see him. He must still live." Zenero pats Kioshi.

Kioshi approaches her brother. "Hey, I need you to make a promise to me."

"What is it, Sis?"

"Promise you'll stop protecting me! I'm tired of having to bury my boyfriends because you don't trust them. It destroys me! Deceivant would be dead if Kaity wasn't there to save him. If I lost him, I'd be gone."

"You don't need other people. You're strong on your own. I can't stop protecting you. I'm you brother. I know I'm selfish! I know I'm a murderer! But I love you," cries Koshi, holding her as tight to him as possible. He pets her lovingly. "As long as I can see you smile, then I will have a reason to keep on living."

"How can you claim that when all you do is make me cry!" she yells as tears stream out.

"Sis, I would never," says Koshi heartbroken.

"I never asked to be saved, and yet you always save me like some guardian angel!" exclaims Kioshi furiously.

Zenero steps up to her. "He has good intentions, isn't that sufficient? All we can ask is that people act with good intent."

"He's ruined my life with his 'good intentions'. He's broken me." Kioshi sobs.

Koshi walks up to Zenero in a daze, tears pouring out of his eyes. "If she hates me, then why even bother to continue? Send me to the base, I'll either kill the Senator or die trying!"

Kioshi slaps him. "Don't you dare die before me, idiot!"

Zenero's hands come out from his curtain-like clothing. He teleports Kioshi away with him to a rocky mountain. "Enough! You will be gracious to your brother. He is the reason I decided to track you down. He only tried to kill Deceivant to save your life."

"Yeah, I figured as much. But I don't care!"

"You will both work for me. Kioshi, as long as you treat him properly and obey my commands, I will continuously revive you." He crouches down and places his hand on her shoulder, creating miniature portals to show places from around the globe. "You could drown in the sacred Ganges river, freeze to death atop Mount. Everest. Suffocate on the moon. Leap off the Tower of Pisa. You can die all across the globe! The possibilities are endless. However, I will only reward you if you aren't being a spoiled brat. And, it will be our little secret."

"I can die at all the most famous sites in the world? Oooh, I just love traveling! You got yourself a deal!" exclaims Kioshi as she hugs him tightly.

Zenero teleports back to the desert with Kioshi.

The chipper sister hops up to her sad brother. "I'm sorry. I've just been through a lot. You've brought me plenty of smiles too. Thanks for helping me come back." She lifts him up into a hug.

Chipko pulls Zenero aside. "Hey, did you…have her killed?"

"I did not. I merely made the best of a bad situation."

"I…I believe you." Chipko smiles through her tears.

"The road ahead will be rocky, but it is through the shedding of our blood that will we will grow strong enough to climb the mountain our path leads to."

Chapter 217: Master of Portals

August, Durga and Shinx sit on the ground by a campfire.

August stands up. "I'm tired of waiting. Let's at least walk around. Maybe there is an Exp around here somewhere."

Durga speaks with closed eyes and folded legs. "The only rogue Exp remaining is The Vibrator. He's likely at his company building."

"Zenero will arrive to test me. I can sense it." Shinx lies down and feels the heat of the fire.

A portal appears and Zenero drops out from it. "I assume you figured out why I've sent you on this journey."

Shinx stands up. "To have me pick up your allies for you."

August walks up to Zenero and turns his arm into a spike. "June almost got killed. Why didn't you even try to save her?"

Zenero teleports behind Shinx. "You've grown from your battles as I'd hoped."

"Don't ignore me!" yells August, his skin becoming spines.

Zenero drops into a portal and appears in front of August. "We need not quarrel, my son."

"Fight me!" yells August furiously, swiping his fist.

Zenero teleports in place to dodge each attack, seemingly not moving at all. "Very well, I'll indulge your vengeance if it will appease you." A metal lance appears in his hand.

August puts his hands to the floor. "*SURFACE CANNON!*" The ground envelopes him, forming into a cannon around his body.

"Did you create this new technique just to end me? I'm flattered." Zenero smiles.

August shoots out from the cannon.

His spiky skin juts out in multiple angles as he bounces off the trees.

August shoots towards Zenero. He misses. "Faster!" He misses again. "I'll break my limits and destroy you!"

"No matter how strong you become, you're still unable to touch me." Zenero creates a portal in front and another facing the ground.

August crashes into a large metal plate that appears beneath him.

"An all-out offensive approach leaves you practically defenseless. You've smashed against the reality of your own lofty ambitions." Zenero plunges the lance through August's back, pinning him to the metal plate.

"You didn't even need to touch him," says Shinx, his legs shaking with excitement.

"Yes, but we don't want him interrupting our bout." Zenero turns to Durga. "Wait here. We will return shortly." He creates a portal to a desert.

Shinx follows along.

"Trying to limit my options. It won't matter. I've seen how you fight. I know how to defeat you," says Shinx, holding out his sword.

Yin vanishes from Shinx's hand.

Zenero smiles. "Even without your god sword?"

"So why do you want me?"

"I'm your great-great-grandfather. I simply wish to guide you on the proper path."

"I won't let you take my sword away again," says Shinx, pulling Yin back into his grip.

"Here I thought you can only redirect that which moves swiftly enough. If you exert your willpower, can you control the destinies of static forms as well?"

"Find out yourself!" yells Shinx, bringing his massive sword down on Zenero.

The Exp creator stands atop the blade. "Your strength comes from tools rather than from within. Tell me Shinx, is a man strong simply because he has a gun?"

"Of course not, anyone can pull a trigger," says Shinx, shrinking the weapon and then elongating it for quick slashes.

Zenero teleports in place to dodge each attempt. "I'll admit, I do not fully understand your hypocrisy."

"I am not a hypocrite! I have gained true strength!"

"When cornered, some animals try to intimidate their predator with a wretched scream? Is this power or cowardice?"

"I'll make you eat your words!" yells Shinx, firing a red dot at Zenero who vanishes.

"The further the distance, the greater the toll on you. Your power is not without its limits," says Zenero, teleporting around to dodge the boy's finger guns.

"You're the one running away! You know I'm strong! You're afraid of me!" Shinx kicks dust to blind his foe.

Zenero creates a small portal and redirect the sand through another portal, heating it into glass with an adjacent portal.

The glass shards cut up the boy's face.

"I'm the embodiment of strength!" Shinx swings Yin around in a frenzy.

Zenero watches the boy struggle from above. "Bragging is also a sign of weakness. Are you aware at how weak you seem right now?"

Shinx screams out in rage, swinging his sword at Zenero who hops up. "Got you."

The hand holding the weapon was pointing at his foe. A red dot had been placed on Zenero's chest.

As Shinx throws Yin, Zenero cuts the stained cloth and allows it to be pierced.

"It's no wonder Durga broke you with a simple hug. You're a pitiful mess."

"No. I…I'm no longer going to let you taunt me. I'm smarter than that." Shinx exhales. "I'm ready. Let's fight with everything we have."

Zenero smiles. "Very well then, make your move."

Shinx covers himself in red dots as if blood was pouring down his face.

"You can wear your power as armor, but that's not what you're doing. This is quite the gamble." Zenero drags a lance out of a portal from his chest.

When tossed, the lance splintered, covering Shinx in metal shards.

No blood was shed.

Shinx's smile shines through the shards just before Zenero and the floor lit up red. "**Crimson Burial.**"

The pieces shoot off Shinx and separate into smaller shards.

Zenero creates a large portal in front of him that absorbs the shards aimed at him.

The other shards cover the desert floor, forming a path.

Zenero vanishes and reappears behind Shinx.

The red dots on the ground disappear and one appears at the end of the trail of shards.

Shinx trips Zenero, toppling him. "**Path of Misfortune.**"

Zenero is pulled through the street of shards. He creates a portal in front of him, but Shinx repositions it at the end of the shard trail. The portal master creates another portal, which was promptly moved to the front of the trail. He stabs a lance into the ground. It slips from his hands, heading into the portal.

"Any object in motion is mine to command. You've lost," says Shinx with a thumbs down.

A single dot is placed on Zenero's chest.

"Yin, kill him," says Shinx softly as he tosses the sword forward.

Just before Yin hit his target, Zenero vanishes from sight.

Shinx turns around to see Zenero, completely unscathed.

"I created a portal under myself to avoid the shards you made. But good effort, nevertheless." Zenero ruffles Shinx's hair.

Yin turns around to collide with Zenero. "Move, child! Unless you want to die along with him!"

The Master of Portals grabs Shinx and raises him up as a shield.

"***Impossible Target***," says Shinx calmly just before Yin collides.

The Sword of Sel sways to the left.

Zenero is knocked into the air by a blue dot on the bottom of Shinx's shoe.

Yin jets into his target. The blade vanishes as it rockets through him.

Shinx screams out in agony from below. Yin burst out of his stomach.

The red dots on Zenero vanish as he lands on the ground gracefully.

Shinx falls to his knees. "How could you hit me? I was an impossible target."

"I created a portal beneath my shirt to protect myself from a frontal attack. Then I created one more inside of you. I can make a portal absolutely anywhere."

Shinx shoves his entrails back into his body. "Not dead yet." He fires his finger pistols, but no dots appear.

Zenero vanishes into a portal and Shinx follows along.

Zenero yanks the lance out from his defeated son. "Do your best to heal the boy."

August grimaces at Zenero before rushing to Shinx. "Looks like we both got destroyed."

Shinx coughs as his wounds are sealed.

"I don't need your pity," says Shinx weakly. "I'm not dying here. I shall gather all the strongest warriors in the world and use them to crush the weak. Imagine a planet of power. Pure power!"

"No social classes?" asks August.

"Money is fake power. True power comes from within! We are the Soldiers of Strength!" Shinx wills himself back to his feet. "Alright, Zenero. I'm ready for my rematch."

"You've shown me your potential. I have a proposition for you," says Zenero, smiling at the boy.

"I'm sorry, but Mommy told me not to talk to strangers," says Shinx with a chuckle as he takes a step forward.

Zenero opens his arms. "I offer you your mother."

Shinx nearly topples over. "How dare you say that!? She's dead!"

"And she died as a god, so she has been sent to Soul Storage. The laws of Soul Storage are equivalent exchange. If I give it a soul of equal worth, the soul of a god, it will give back the soul of Demonica."

Shinx's intensity was gone. He was as soft as a pillow. "Can you really…bring Mommy back?"

"Shinx, you are going to play a key role in the creation of a true perfect word. However, if you want to see your mother again, you must cast aside your beliefs and join me. You must give up on this childish world of strength. I wish to create a peaceful and safe world, and your views greatly conflict with this. A revolution is about to come under way. We can change this world together." Zenero offers the boy his hand.

Shinx turns away. "You want my help; bring her back first."

"That isn't how this works. I need a sacrifice to resurrect her. Riufen would do nicely."

"So…if I kill him, then you'll bring her back."

"If I don't, then you can kill me till your arms go limp."

"Fine, send me his way."

Kioshi pops up. "That sounds super dangerous! Can I come along?"

"I told you to stay hidden," says Zenero.

Shinx glares at Kioshi. "Why do you have someone like her with you? She's useless."

Koshi comes out from the bushes. "Hey, brat. Watch your tongue unless you want it removed!"

Kioshi throws a rock at him. "Stop fighting my battles for me."

Zenero steps in between. "I thought this was resolved." He creates a portal and Chipko emerges.

"Oh, is Shinx with us now?" asks Chipko.

Zenero shakes his head. "Not something you need concern yourself with. A team is only as strong as it's synergy. We must unite these feuding siblings before we can proceed."

Kioshi rolls her eyes. "Just keep him away from me. He's always babying me."

Koshi sighs. “Yeah, I appreciate the effort, but she’ll never understand me.”

Zenero smiles. “This will only take a moment. We shall see what has shaped Koshi into the killer he is today. And in doing so we will appease our new ally. Chipko, use the Flash Artifact.”

“Whoa. Isn’t that kinda private?” asks Chipko blushing.

“Go ahead. I’ve got nothing to hide. But be honest, you want to peek in to see what the Senator’s weakness is.”

“I know what makes him tick. But you…you’re an enigma. Let’s unravel this puzzle. Chipko, go for it.”

“Alright. Flash Back!”

Part 26
Murderer's Memories

Chapter 218: The Taste of Justice

I was sloppy last mission, so I expected to get a lecture...didn't make it any less unpleasant.

The man lecturing me is in his late fifties. He is a gruff looking man with a black mustache and sideburns that connect to his finely trimmed beard. Light blue eyes are all we have in common.

Even while walking through this lush peaceful garden, I can't help but be on edge.

The man looks down at me. "Son, I feel you're letting emotions weigh you down. It's unbecoming of someone with your skill."

My girlfriend was murdered! Of course I'm emotional! I doubt he's ever felt guilt for anything before.

"I'm not your son," I say, keeping my gaze away from him.

"Yes, you're more like my weapon." He grabs my head and squeezes hard.

My body shivers.

The man tries to calm me with an empty smile.

"I want you to think back on your first kill."

Images flash in my mind. My small hands, holding a trigger one moment. The next moment, the car of a mafia boss is blown to bits. And then after that…the charred bodies. One of them was so small.

A smack to the face takes me out of the traumatic memory.

"Tears are for women. Man up, you little shit!" The man's spit sprays on my face.

I keep a cool head when facing a militia, but I feel naked and powerless around this monster.

"That woman you were with would have only held you back. I told you not to get attached to other agents!" He tightens his fist.

"I…won't make another mistake," I say softly.

"Speak up!" he bellows.

"I won't fail you again, Sir!" I salute him firmly.

"That's my little warrior. You truly are my pride and joy."

"Hey, so my next mission…will it spark a civil war?"

"You will do as your country commands. Such is the life of a patriot."

"It's just…I'm used to stopping wars, not causing them."

I walk through the garden in silence when he doesn't answer.

The man stops at the fountain. "War fuels the economy. Weapons can be used as deterrents, particularly nuclear weapons. In this misguided time of equality, the people need someone to fear, something to hate. Without that they turn against themselves. A war out there keeps our nation from falling into another civil war. America was already losing its grip as the world's super power, but the Party Civil War has caused irreparable harm to our national synergy."

"I just think there has to be another way. Maybe you can talk with the other branch heads."

The man turns his dark gaze upon me, chilling my blood. "What is best for this country is best for the world. When you receive a call to arms, you obey it. It is your responsibility as a citizen of the United States of America. And it is your livelihood as a member of the Secret Forces."

"I'll do as I'm told."

"You'll be meeting with agent Sunrise when you land."

"Yes, Sir."

"Worrying about collateral damage is not your place. The branch heads decide upon what must be done and then the agent assigned completes his mission. This foreign civil war will serve as a means for America to get involved. More importantly, it will allow us to continue the War on Terror. It is our duty to renew their faith in this country. Though the government is indeed a slave to the influence of the Council."

"I said I'll do it."

"Yes, but if your heart isn't bleeding for it, the mission will end in failure. Look at the bigger picture, in times of war basic rights are put aside. By the time the war is over the people have become accustomed to the erosions of these rights. When they feel this void of purpose they spend, which fuels the economy and gives the corporations more strength! The people are too stupid to care for themselves. They don't know what's best for them. And they certainly don't know what's best for their nation! Oh, I know what this is about."

"You do?"

"Yes, you're worried your sister will be drafted. You're right to worry. The branch heads must show good faith by having their children enlist."

"I'll go. I'll fight in the coming war for as many years as it takes… just leave Kioshi out of it." I look at him with desperation.

"You're both going. That is final."

Not this time. For once, I have the edge.

"Leave her out of it and I'll tell you the information I got from Kanasta."

The man's eyes peer into mine with a sharp gleam. "I heard he had escaped."

"I spoke with him before that."

"And why would he tell you anything?"

"We made an information exchange."

The man grips my shoulders, freezing me in place. "What did he tell you?"

"M-M-Make the call. Tell your fellow branch heads that Kioshi won't be enlisting."

The man whips out a pistol and aims it at my forehead. "What did he say?" The gun cocks.

I notice a rustle in the bushes.

It's time! It's finally time.

I stare firmly into the man's boiling face and smile. "He said 'don't worry Koshi, I'm going to kill your old man for you. Councilman Durian paid me a hefty sum for the job.'"

"That traitor! He thinks he's going to end me!" The man yells out and slams his gun to my forehead.

Am I really going to let Kanasta save me? No. My sister is counting on me. I have to swallow my fear and kill this monster myself!

"I'm the one who's going to kill you!" I shout and knock the gun out of the man's hand. I grip the knife in my vest but freeze up.

Fight it. You can end this. He's just flesh and blood. Same as any human.

The man grabs a pistol from his other pocket and shoots my legs. He smacks me with the back of the gun, bringing me to my knees. "Your sister will pay for this insubordination."

I whip out the knife and strike his throat.

He grabs my arm with his bulky fist and clenches, shattering my bones. "I will kill you, boy! But first I'll break you completely!"

My arm twists and my flesh tears.

Damn him. He's too experienced. But he's not immortal.

I reach into my vest, pop the pin and pull out a grenade.

His eyes widen and he shoots me repeatedly to get me to release his arm.

"If I kill you, then I assure Sis's safety. That's worth dying for. And such a lovely place to die too." I smile as my vision blurs.

The grenade doesn't explode.

A dud...that's not possible. Nothing more useless than a grenade that doesn't explode!

I hear the sound of a bullet zooming through the air.

The man wails out in pain, three of his fingers now just fleshy bits. He kicks me off and runs into the bushes.

Another bullet whips by.

The man falls down, gripping his bleeding leg. "Coward! Face me like a man, Kanasta!"

Kaity leaps out from the bushes, her plasma claws glowing and her eyes wide.

She's coming in for the kill.

I wave at her. "Wait up! I'm the client who hired your boss!"

She shoots the man's arm when he reaches into his pocket for another gun.

"You're Kaity, right? Fresh recruit of the Viper Squad. I'm a huge fan of your work." I smile at her.

"You're not supposed to know about me," says Kaity, scrutinizing me with her gaze.

"Come on, I'm an agent for the government…I know everyone."

"I'm working right now. You wanna chat, we can do it later," she says, approaching the man with her claws engaged.

"Hold up. I want to kill him," I say, wobbling up to her.

"That's not how this works. Plus, you look like you're gonna keel over at any moment."

"Please, it's something I have to do." I look up at her resolutely.

Kaity disengages her claws. Her ears droop. "Been looking forward to this kill all day. Whatever. Just make sure he's dead. And as far as the records are concerned, the Viper Squad did it. Got it?" she asks, placing her pistol in my hands.

I steady myself. "Understood. Thank you."

Kaity blushes and turns away. "We owed you one. You let Kanasta escape." She then rushes off, vanishing in the bushes.

The Man, having applied a tourniquet to his wounds, beams at me. "You got rid of her. Well done. Now call an ambulance. I need to get to a hospital."

I aim the pistol at his head.

The man scoots back. "Let's be reasonable. I wasn't really going to kill you."

"It feels like I've waited my whole life for this moment." With each step closer to him, I fire bullets up his legs and down his arms.

"Stop! Damn it, Koshi! I give up! Your sister can stay home. She doesn't have to go to war. I'll make the call right now," says the man, moaning in pain.

I drop the gun. Tears pour out my eyes.

Why aren't I enjoying this more? This is it! The kill I've always wanted!

"Do we have a deal?" asks the man, outstretching his wounded hand.

I look down at the gun.

That's the problem. I need something more personal.

I whip out my knife and crouch over him.

"Get away from me!" yells the man, slamming his mutilated arm against me.

I slice his arm.

The screams that follow blanket me in warmth.

I cut him more and more.

I look down at the crying shell of a man with blissful tears welling up in my eyes. "This is it. This is the satisfaction I craved!" I cut a little deeper as he screams for help.

"This is treason! You'll be executed along with your sister!"

"I truly am an agent of justice now." I lick the blood off the knife.

My vision blurs and the knife falls from my grip.

His blood tastes so...fulfilling.

A choir blesses my ears as I lick the blood off my fingers.

"You psychotic little shit!" yells the man, struggling to defend himself.

How could anything beautiful come from someone so wretched?

I gaze at him. "It's liberating! Each drop of your blood is a profound burst of justice."

"I'll kill you! I'll make you regret ever harming me!" The man sobs as he yells at me.

This feeling is beyond the thrill of killing. It's righteous judgment. This is the taste of true purpose.

I bite into the man's arm, tearing off a piece of his flesh with my teeth.

It's so chewy and juicy.

The man screams at me, but his words are jumbled up by my blissful mindset.

I cut off one of his fingers and draw a skull on his cheek with it. "You know you're going to die, but you can't accept it. That makes this moment all the more beautiful. I am going to savor this moment. No, I am going to immortalize it." I slice off a slab of flesh from his arm. I bite into it, shaking my head like a dog with a piece of meat.

"Many indigenous people used every part of the body from the animal they killed. That's what I'm going to do to you. I wonder what your heart tastes like." I smile at him with crimson caked cheeks.

The man was too afraid to talk and in too much pain to yell. All he could do was whimper.

I flip the man over, turning him face up. "I wonder if intestines are like spaghetti. And I wonder how his brain will feel on my tongue." I stab the knife into the man's stomach. A burst of blood shot out as a warm fountain.

It's like being baptized. A true rebirth.

The blood covers my eyes. All I can see is red.

I don't need to see. I will close out any doubt and swim in my new freedom.

I slice the man's stomach open.

Hallelujah, I have retribution!

The angelic choir in my head became louder as I indulged in my crimson feast.

Time no longer existed in that moment. I had immortalized it.

My eyes opened to see a skeleton. There was not a drop of blood, not a trace of flesh on it. I hold myself in a warm embrace.

I understand this feeling now. It's instinct. My primal instincts are to eat what I kill. I am obeying my genes and they are rewarding me with bliss. Now I can sustain myself with my passion. I'll eat all-natural food. It's incredible; as I bit into his flesh, I could taste his fear. It wasn't just an emotion, it was palpable. It wasn't just palpable, it was delicious. When I bit into his brain it's as if I bore my teeth into his memories. I felt true bliss permeate my soul the instant I bit into his heart. To think I've been wasting all that good food for so long. But no more! I will feast upon the corpses of all my prey. I will waste nothing. Not one drop, not one shred.

I look back at the skeleton. *What do I do with the bones? I don't want to waste them. I know, I have a trophy room back home. I'll put all the skeletons there.*

I hear footsteps behind me and turn around.

Kanasta...did he see what I did?

Chapter 219: The New Assassin

Kanasta takes a moment to gather his thoughts. Despite being a runt, he's very muscular and has a mature presence. "A most unusual means of eliminating evidence. I can't say I approve. Far too time consuming."

"Yeah, wasn't exactly done for practical reasons. Besides as far as the records are concerned, this was the work of one of your employees."

"I don't understand. You paid me to send an assassin to kill him and then you tell Kaity to back off and claim the kill yourself. I will be reticent to accept future jobs from such an obtuse employer," says Kanasta, looking at me curiously.

"It was personal. I couldn't pass up the opportunity. Don't act too surprised. I doubt your star pupil couldn't have taken him down in a single shot. Were you testing me?"

Kanasta looms over me. "The other half of the payment?"

"Yeah, I'll send it once I'm all patched up."

"Good. I'm surprised the police didn't interrupt your feast."

"I called in a favor from one of my exes on the force. Good thing, I know a paramedic that can take care of me. Shit, I got shot all over the place." I trip and fall over.

"Your work isn't usually so sloppy." Kanasta pulls out the bullets in my legs.

"Yeah, I've been off lately. That Utah job messed me up pretty bad."

"So much skill and yet so lacking in focus and obedience. Truly a waste." Kanasta applies gauze to the wounds.

"Sorry to disappoint. Hey, by the way, thanks for giving me a chance to meet Kaity face-to-face. She was the one who took out Agent Rainstorm, wasn't she?"

Kanasta nods. "Your people are good. Mine are better."

"Really selling yourself here, aren't ya? You know I'm not a freelancer."

"I'm aware. Your talents would help our business grow. I'm offering you a permanent job. Will you leave the Agents of Justice for a position in a neutral business?"

"By neutral you mean you kill people of all nations and allegiances."

"Precisely, discrimination is not our way."

"But killing kids is. That's where I draw the line."

"These lines only keep you from your potential. Either way, you will be treated as a new recruit, same as Kaity. Kids won't be your targets. I'm aware that shattering one's misguided moral compass can't be done with haste. It must be melted gradually."

"Still the same as the day we met. Both hired to slaughter a bunch of environmental protestors. I hated every second of it, but you didn't seem phased one bit."

"As per our recent encounter, I allowed you to capture me to learn more about you. Aren't you curious about the world's greatest assassin team?"

"I'd be lying if I said I'm not interested in joining, but what about my sister? What's going to happen to her?"

"She'll mourn the death of her brother and move on. As long as you're good enough as an assassin, you'll stay dead in the eyes of the public and even the government. All of my agents are dead as far as the records are concerned."

"I'll go in as an intern. You tell me only what I need to know for the job and I'll get to enjoy the cuisine. It's a good idea to lay low after this, but I can't let my sister think I'm dead."

"Family before business, I understand." Kanasta tightens the wraps around my wounds and then looks into my eyes. "Did you cry after your first kill?"

"I…yes, I did," I say softly.

"Kaity did as well. We should continue this conversation on the move. I'm being informed the police are on their way to investigate."

I stand up and follow him into a casual looking jeep. "Blending with the crowd, I see."

Kanasta hands me a pill. "I'm taking you to our base for further medical care. Once you're all patched up, we can begin your training."

"Let me call my sister first. I'll go secure. Don't worry." I reach in my pocket and call Kioshi.

"Brother! What happened? Are you okay? I heard there were gunshots at our home. I'm safe with Joseph at church. Are you okay?"

I pull the phone away just a bit. "I'm fine sis. Just got sent on an ultra-secret mission. The kind only a dead man can go on. So, keep up appearances, will you?"

"Geez, always going off without me. Ugh. At least you called. When will you be back? Can I tell Mom?"

"Next month most likely. But I'll have saved the world. We'll celebrate together, okay? You can't tell Mom."

"Fine, but you have to call every day you're gone! One missed day and I'm telling her the truth."

"Alright, fair enough."

"You sound winded. Are you sure you're okay? Are you in danger? You know I can sense that sorta thing."

"Yeah, stay out of trouble while I'm gone, 'kay."

"Hey…what if I get anxious?"

"Distract yourself. I got you a whole book on how to combat those dark thoughts."

"Yeah…you did. I guess you aren't the worst brother in the world, after all."

"I got to go. See ya later, Sis."

"Yeah…I…uh…bye." Kioshi hangs up.

"Thanks for waiting." I grab the pill from Kanasta and swallow it.

When I wake up, I'm on a soft bed, overlooking the beach in a hotel room.

His secret base is a hotel?

Kanasta sits on the sofa, to the right of him on the granite floor is a small robot.

"What's the little guy for?"

"This is my robotic assassin, BoneSaw. Created to be a companion for Kaity."

"And he's going to keep watch to make sure I behave?"

"Not exactly. I actually need your help to complete him. Programs cannot capture the complexity of an actual mind. I was hoping I could download yours. You killing intent is even stronger that Kaity's."

"I'm touched. Nobody has ever cared what I thought before," I say with a chuckle.

"So, will you assist?" asks Kanasta, leaning forward.

"I don't get it. You don't trust me, yet you want my brain for your little robot?"

"What better way to learn of your intent. If BoneSaw attacks us, then it is clear that you are not to be trusted."

"Or you just didn't download it properly. Look, I'm going to have to decline this grand opportunity. I don't trust recent tech. Don't want my brain scrambled."

"That's fair, but you seem fine to me. Let's see how it worked." Kanasta opens up the robot and places a chip inside.

He did it while I was sleeping? My fault for trusting an assassin, I suppose.

Kanasta closes up the bot and boots him up.

BoneSaw looks around the room curiously.

Kanasta smiles at the robot. "Kill that agent for me."

BoneSaw turns away and heads for the door.

Kanasta rubs his chin. "Receiving orders, but not following them…I believe this is indeed a success. How does it feel to be a father?"

"You're the father, not me. I didn't want my brain being scanned. Ugh, let's get these tests over with so I can get back in the field."

"No more tests necessary. Just know I'll be keeping a close eye on you. We all will." He offers me another pill.

"You brought me here just so you can drug me again? Seriously? I can't be the only who's complained about this."

"This was a stopping point for you to recover. You've recovered and gained my trust."

I begrudgingly take the pill and swallow.

I awake in some underground bunker in a sleeping bag on the floor.

Not the coziest hideout.

I stand up and open the metal door. "Hey, anybody home?"

Kanasta pops out from behind me.

I should have sensed him. Must still be drowsy from that sleeping pill. Oh crap, I forgot to call Sis.

I reach for my phone, but it's gone. "You scan me and then rob me? Not impressed by the hospitality of this establishment."

"No phones are allowed inside. No matter how secure they may be."

"I promised my sister I'd call her every day. Hey, how many days passed anyway?"

"You'll be permitted to call her outside the base after the mission briefing."

"Jumping headfirst into this, I see."

"You have plenty of experience. You'll understand your role after the briefing. Follow me."

Kanasta leads me down the mossy corridor and stops at the wall. He pushes it in and then slides it, revealing a hidden room.

"Secret room in a secret underground base. Not bad at all."

The Viper Squad members were all seated and all looking my way.

Kanasta gestures to them. "You already know Kaity. That's Ego, Tempo and Sefiwah."

They didn't seem particularly happy to see me.

A man with spiky hair and a biker jacket grimaces at me. "No pets allowed, that includes government lap dogs." Tempo turns to Ego. "You can't trust dogs. They're only obedient so they can get a treat, remember that."

I grin. "Hey man, I'm not the one wearing a collar."

Tempo growls and puts his feet on the desk. "Let's just get this over with."

A woman with pale skin looks my way. "I heard you cried after killing your first victim."

Geez, did Kanasta have to tell everyone?

"It is okay man; it happens to the best of us," says the punk techie to my right.

Tempo leans in, blowing cigar smoke in my face. "What about the second time? How many times did you kill before the tears stopped flowing?"

"After I killed the love of my life…that was the last time," I say with a smile.

Tempo pulls back and looks to Kanasta. "Boss, if Kaity's such a prodigy, why did it take her so long to stop crying? What was it ten, twenty?" He grimaces at Kaity. "You keep me up at night with your whining, squirt."

Kanasta glares at Tempo who sinks in response.

I smile at Kaity. "Having a conscience and still pulling the trigger shows courage. It's something psychopaths will never understand."

Kaity smiles at me.

Sefiwah's head turns to me like a snake about to strike. "Kaity doesn't need you to defend her. If you think I won't kill you, newbie, then go ahead…try me."

Hell yes! Hottie located. Definitely gonna pound her good later.

I grin and stand up from my chair. "Babe, you've got yourself a challenger."

Sefiwah slides up to me and grabs my package with an iron grip.

"So forward. I love it," I say, grabbing her snatch.

"Whoa. That dude is extreme," says Ego, taking off his headset.

"Is it true that you ate a person? That is mega rad!" exclaims Ego, elbowing me.

Tempo growls. "Why you being buddy with the government dog?"

Ego shrugs. "He seems cool."

I turn to Kaity as Sefiwah crushes my balls. "Is this psycho hottie your girlfriend?"

"Yep. Gonna have our two monthiversary soon!" Kaity wiggles in her chair.

Sefiwah's hand shot forward, stopping inches from Koshi's neck. "Don't speak to her."

"I get it, you're lesbian. That's no problem. I've done lesbians before. They always like it soft," says Koshi, touching Sefiwah's ass sensually.

Well, most of 'em anyway.

Sefiwah grabs my arm and twists it behind my back. "The moment this mission is over, I'll end you," she says darkly

Tempo turns to Kanasta. "Seriously though. You recruited the Agents of Justice's number one? Have you completely lost it?"

"It is necessary, I assure you." Kanasta nods. "Koshi has unique talents."

"The ladies say the same thing," I say with a smirk.

Kaity perks up. "I hear you have a little sister. I'm so jelly." She sticks out her tongue.

I spin around and push Sefiwah off me. "I'll introduce you sometime."

"I warned you not to speak to her." Sefiwah tosses a knife at me.

Kaity shoots it out of the air and catches it. "Yes! Perfect shot!" She bounces up to me and has the knife pierce my throat. "Touch my Sefi-chan's squishy booty again and you'll be bleeding all over." She licks the droplet of blood off the knife like a kitten.

Whoa. That was sexy. Geez, get it together man. She's a kid. A badass assassin kid!

Kaity hops up to Sefiwah and spins her back into her seat before sitting in her lap. "He won't bother you ever again." She gives her girlfriend a sweet peck on the cheek.

Kanasta sits down and places his hands on the table.

Everyone stops talking and gives him their full attention.

They really respect him. Gotta admire that.

"Now that you're all acquainted with our new recruit, we can talk business. The mission starts next week, Saturday at noon. In the meantime, I will need you to collect data and come up with a surefire strategy to get the target." Kanasta turns to me. "This mission will either be your initiation or your extermination. It all depends on your performance."

"What's my part in all this?"

"You're the only one who can get close to the target. But first we need you to end someone for us." Kanasta slides me a picture of a woman.

Agent Sunrise.

"The moment you get me, you expect me to kill my own team? What kinda monster do you take me for?" I crumble up her picture.

"Agent Sunrise has been assigned as our target's bodyguard. Best to remove her first."

"Then why not have one of them do it?"

Tempo grins. "Getting cold feet already, kid."

Kanasta leans up to me. "This is all part of your growth as an assassin. The means of her execution are up to you. Just make sure she's dead by Friday night."

I stand up. "What the hell do I even get out of this? She's my girlfriend! I don't want to kill her."

"We only need you for this one mission. Afterwards, you will be free to leave if you so choose."

"I don't want any part of it!"

Sefiwah looks my way. "You've killed your girlfriends on a number of occasions, agents included."

"That's on my terms. Who even is the client?"

"That is on a need to know basis."

"Well, if you want me to murder a girl I love, I feel I deserve to know a bit more."

"Very well, when the job is completed, I will reveal who the client is."

"What don't you get? I'm not doing this job, ever!"

"You can sleep on it. Just know if you leave the base, the bombs inside you will detonate. Trust is absolutely vital to a mission. Considering the circumstances, this was the only way I could fully trust you."

"So, if I don't kill her, you'll blow me up?"

"Precisely. Crude, I know. But we have a reputation of getting our jobs done. Sometimes blackmail and threats are necessary. It's regrettable, but it's absolutely vital to our company's image." Kanasta stands up. "There's a training arena down the hall, last door to your right. Feel free to let out your aggression there. I await your answer in the morning. Meeting dismissed."

Chapter 220: Angel of Death

I walk back to my room in silence.

There's a chance he's lying about the bomb. But no way to confirm that without my tech. I'm stuck here. Worst of all, I can't call my sister.

I reach my door only to see someone standing by it.

At least it's not that biker guy.

"Sorry about before. Didn't get to properly introduce myself. Name's Ego."

I shake his hand. "I'm pissed off about having a bomb inside me, pleasure to meet you."

"Yeah, sorry man. The Boss can be rough, but he does what's best for the team. I trust him."

"I trust that he'll kill me if I don't murder my girlfriend."

"Yeah, that's a bummer. Hey, is it true what Kanasta said? Were there only bones left?"

I smile at him, showing my teeth. "Only bones."

"Damn man, you're intense. That's some crazy ass cannibalistic shit right there," says Ego, holding his sides.

"Yeah it was pretty crazy. Hope it's just as amazing the second time around."

"On your first try you ate a whole person. Dude, you are extreme to the max! I heard you agents have no restrictions, but that shit is straight up gnarly."

"Hey, Kanasta said no phones are allowed on base. Is that true?"

"Nah, man. I got my phone right here. No GPS though. That's for sure."

"Can I make a call?"

"I dunno, man. I don't wanna get in trouble."

"It's my little sister. You can listen in. I don't care."

"Alright, but not in the hallway." Ego opens the door to my room and hands me his phone.

"Kioshi, come on, pick up."

"Oh, so now you call."

"What's that supposed to mean?"

"Nothing. I'm not even surprised you ghosted me for three days."

I was out that long?

"Look, Sis. This mission doesn't have much downtime. I'm honestly breaking protocol by calling you now."

"Oh…thanks. Hey, umm, when will you get back home?"

"I'll know by next week. Hey, you didn't tell Mom, did you?"

"No and…you didn't tell me that horrible man died. Were you there? Did you do it?"

"I barely got out of that mess myself."

"But he is really dead…right?"

"I saw him get shot when I was running."

"This new Viper Squad Assassin must be totally crazy. He was just bones. How macabre, right?"

"Yeah. Just stay out of trouble, 'kay."

"You're the one who better be careful. Don't you dare die on this super dangerous mission. If you do, I'm done. Got it."

"Yeah…I'll be careful."

"Hey Bro, you'd do anything for me, right?"

I can't help but smile. "Absolutely anything, Sis."

"Then speed up that job so we can go see a movie together! I'm booooored!"

"As you command, princess."

"If I'm a princess, then you're the dragon."

"I gotta go. I'll call you tomorrow."

"Sure thing. Let's have some fun on the phone like we used to. I'll strip down all the way."

Geez. Did she seriously just say that.

I hang up the phone and hand it to Ego, hoping he didn't hear that last bit. "Thanks, Ego."

"Dude, you even got your sister into you. That's radical man."

I step back. "You don't think that's…weird?"

Ego puts his arm on my shoulder. "Nah man. You're just so good with the ladies even your sister wants a taste! That's some dope shit, man."

"Yeah, don't mention that to anyone. That was supposed to be a private conversation."

"Yeah, of course. Sorry, just had to make sure you didn't say anything you shouldn't."

"You put your neck out for me. I appreciate it."

"No worries man…you're cool. Dude, we have got to hang sometime."

"Sure thing, dude."

"Hey, man. I can't get a girlfriend. Can you help a fellow dude out?"

"Yeah sure, I can give you some pointers."

"Gnarly, bro. Rest up. I'll see you at the sparring area in the morn."

I was only allowed out of the secret base the day of my mission, which meant I was stuck there for nearly a whole week. I made the best of it though. Ego was always happy to train with me in the morning. After a few days, even Tempo sparred with me. He wasn't too pleased when I repeatedly floored him.

At lunch time on the third day, Kaity sat next to me. Sefiwah was on a mission and she was curious to learn about my organization. I was amazed that this sweet curious cat-girl was the same one behind the Furies' militia massacre. I asked her to fight me and thankfully she agreed.

Kaity stretches in the training room. "Sefiwah says you only really know someone when you see how they behave behind closed doors. If you do intend to kill me, you'll die." Her eyes glare at me with pure killer intent.

I take a step back. "I just want to spar. Hand to hand. No weapons."

"Have you decided if you're going to do the job we assigned to you?" She rushes in and swipes my feet.

Rather than dodge, I swipe back, overpowering her and tripping her. She grips the floors with her hands and pulls her legs back.

Had to bring that up and ruin the mood.

I bring my arms up to defend from Kaity's sudden foot attack. "I've known her since we were kids. She's not the love of my life, but I still care about her."

Kaity pushes off the ground with her hands, kicking me into the air with her legs. "You're weak."

"What?" I grab her legs and grapple her body.

Kaity smiles at me. "It's okay. That weakness, it can be a strength too. I don't always agree with the mission." She looks down solemnly.

"But you do it anyway."

"The only thing scarier than killing someone I don't want to…scarier than breaking my morals…is disappointing Kanasta!" She slides out of my grip and strikes at my openings repeatedly.

We're so similar. I can't fail my sister. Nobody else matters in comparison.

I take a hit and slam my knee into her stomach. I then grab her hair and pull her into a direct punch to the face.

Kaity grabs my arm and dislocates my shoulder. "My actions aren't mine alone. You don't need to bear the full responsibility either." She spin-jumps and kicks me back.

I slide and jump off the wall at her.

Kaity jumps over me and kicks me into the ground. "If you lose, you have to accept the mission."

No. That's not right. This is my responsibility.

I roll out of the way of her incoming kick and then push her aside when she next strikes. "If I win, then I accept. Her death won't be done with regret. It will be performed with my full willpower!" I punch Kaity's chest and then kick her repeatedly.

"I don't understand! I was trying to help you." Kaity retaliates with a mix up of punches and kicks.

I get hit by several, but then seize my opening and slam my full force into her.

You've awakened my resolve.

I grab her arm and slam her to the ground, pinning her until she stops struggling. "Thank you."

Kaity lowers her head. "I…lost."

"So now I'm bound to fulfill the task set before me."

"Wait! I can talk to the boss. I'll convince him to let me kill her."

"Not a chance. I owe her at least that much. And you know what, guilt is a way of keeping her memory alive. At least…that's what I think."

Kaity looks at me curiously. "I'll never understand you."

I smile at her. "That's fine. As long as you trust me."

Kaity stands up, trying to hide her pain. "If you back out. I'll kill you myself."

I get up and pat her. "Still trying to ease the guilt. You're one sweet kitty."

Kaity blushes and pulls away. She hisses at me before leaving.

Agent Sunrise, your days are numbered now. Death has chosen you as his mate.

The day of my mission had arrived. I met Sunrise at her home. A nice villa, overlooking the ocean. I opened the door and greeted her with a passionate kiss. I undress her as she undresses me. We had sex right there, and in the kitchen, the living room, the shower and finally the bed. We had sex all night long, not saying a word to one another.

I awoke in a sweaty panic. The sun had yet to rise.

Get it together. You're a spy. Killing is just part of the job.

I look to my side to see my girlfriend…my friend. Her golden hair is spread out over her pillow, like rays of sunlight.

In the end what does she really mean to me? She's not Kioshi. Nothing about her begins to compare to my sister. But she still makes me feel warm. I guess in the end, she's a warm stone on my life's path. Yep, just another warm moment that must be left behind to take the next step.

I look at her full red lips.

We sure had an amazing night. Made the best of things, I'd say.

I take out a dagger and raise it above her.

Your death is going to be bloody, gruesome and full of misery! Suffering will imprint it into me! I deserve to be haunted by this memory until my last breath.

My hand freezes up.

I can't do it. She deserves the same chance as the others. Forget the mission, this is now my duty.

Agent Sunrise's eyes flutter open.

I hide the knife behind me.

The Angel of Death does not strike in the shadows.

Her eyes become gentle when they see me. "That…was incredible. I passed out from exhaustion. Didn't know that could even happen." She looks down and blushes. "Shouldn't you have used a condom though. Spy's can't become parents, after all. Our entire body.,,," she runs her fingers up my arm, "…every inch belongs to the Nation."

I smile at her. "I wanted to feel you with every inch of me. A condom would be a disservice to you."

"Should I take a pill then?"

"Are you afraid of upsetting our leaders?"

"I just don't want to look fat." She pinches her stomach and chuckles.

"You could never look fat. In fact, I'm worried you're anemic." I tickle her.

What are you doing? If you keep this up, the warmth will stop you. You have to go through with this. You have to move on. Just get some distance and come back with resolve. Come back and end it.

I lift up the sheets. "I have a call to make. I'll be back within the hour."

Sunrise grabs onto me. "Wait! Can't you stay with me for the next thirty minutes at least?"

I can't deny any request she makes now. Being the Angel of Death can be quite troublesome indeed.

I touch her cheek. “Hey…if you were going to die today would you have any regrets?”

She looks away from my gaze. “So, you heard about my mission. I’ll be safe. I promise.”

I grab her hands. “Would you have any regrets?”

She blushes and turns. “After a night like that…no way.” She grins.

“I’m being serious. What is the one thing you’ve always wanted to do?”

“Well, what about you?”

“I’d have tons of regrets! I’m basically a construct of broken promises and guilt.”

She slugs me and smiles. “Stop being so serious. Okay…well here’s mine. It’s really cheesy though.”

“Go ahead. I won’t judge.”

“Well, ever since I was little, I dreamed of watching the sun come up with the man of my dreams. I know it’s really stupid, but it’s…the peak of romance for me. It’s even why I chose my agent name.”

“Wow. I didn’t know that.”

“Yeah. It probably wouldn’t be all that special but I…really want that.”

I grab her hands. “Well then we best hurry.”

She blushes. “You don’t have to. It’s just a silly dream.”

“Nonsense. It’s your wish! I’m no genie but I can certainly handle a simple wish for such a lovely lady.” I rush to the balcony.

“Wait up!” She runs after me.

I jump up from the balcony onto the roof. “Now this is a view to die for!”

Sunrise climbs up and lies next to me.

Our naked bodies are side-by-side, facing the inevitable final sunrise.

She grabs my hand.

“You don’t think…it’s a stupid wish?”

“It’s simple, I’ll admit that. But if it makes you complete, then it is of the upmost importance.” I lean over and kiss her sweet lips.

Will this be our last kiss?

She leans into me, resting her head on my chest.

I sit up and smile down at her.

She stares into my eyes with deep admiration. “K-Koshi…I….”

"It's okay, Rebecca. You don't need to say a word." I wipe the tears from her eyes. "Better clean them up so you can enjoy the sunrise fully."

She nods and faces the incoming sunrise. She holds my hand tightly. "Here it comes."

"The most beautiful it's ever been."

This moment is my final gift to you.

"Koshi, promise you'll never leave me. You're the only guy who really cares about my feelings. I never asked anyone else because…they weren't the one. But you are! You're my special someone."

"Just enjoy this moment. Feel the warmth." I run my fingers through her hair.

The sunlight brightens her face, giving her a heavenly glow.

"Wow, I feel like a kid again, gazing up at something I don't understand. The sun is so benevolent, giving light to all but asking for nothing in return." She turns around and grabs my cheeks. She leans in and kisses my lips. "You're my sun."

When the kiss breaks, she leans against my shoulder. "This moment will forever be immortalized. Memories persist even after death…they're just hard to access. This memory will be something only we share…now and always."

"I had given up on men before. But you, you're almost like a girl. You're so understanding, so caring." She breaks down into tears.

"No crying. Don't let anything cloud this moment."

She looks up at me with teary eyes. "The tears make it all the more special. I feel reborn. It's like the light is cleansing me. It's almost over. Kiss me as it rises fully."

I gently pull her closer to me. I give her the softest kiss.

She embraces me so tightly, her tears falling onto my chest.

"I am complete now. That means no fear for tomorrow…or ever again."

I look out at the sun. "It's not enough. I…I think I've figured out what I want to do before you go."

"What is it? I'm open to anything?" She gazes at me with those shimmering hazel eyes.

"I want to take our relationship to the next level. I want us to truly become one."

Her skin feels so soft.

"Haven't we already done that," she asks, blushing brightly.

I sit up, pulling her up with me. "No…not yet."

"Well whatever it is, do it," she says, opening up her legs for me.

"All I need right now is your beautiful breasts."

"Then go ahead, take them," she blushes as she smiles.

I lick her nipples with the tip of my tongue. I make little circles around them.

I can taste her pleasure, but it's not enough.

I give her breast the softest kiss, causing her to gasp from the ecstasy.

"Koshi, I love you," she cries, holding my head against her bosom.

I lean in and give her one final kiss. "Would you die for me?" I whisper as gentle as a breeze.

"What?" She scoots back a bit.

"I granted your wish. Don't think of it as payment, think of it as, well, my reward."

"This isn't funny," she says, putting her hand over her chest.

"I'm not joking. You're going to die today anyway. I'd rather it be willing. It's not like you'd have any regrets."

Sunrise slaps me and stands up defiantly. "Enough! I'd regret every day we couldn't be together. I'd regret never seeing my family again. I'd regret plenty of things! Look, I think it's best if you just go."

I clench her wrist so tightly that her bones break. I then toss her into the chair overlooking the beach. I land next to her as she gets up.

"What the hell possessed you?" she asks in horror, swiping the broken chair leg at me.

She isn't fighting like an agent. She's just a scared girl now. I'll tear out her throat and end our suffering.

I knock the chair leg out of her hand. "Remember the sunset." I lunge in for the kill but she moves, causing my teeth to dig into her shoulder.

She kicks me off and slams the glass door on my arm as I reach out to her.

"I can make it quick," I say as I slide open the door, shattering the glass. I approach her with blood smeared across my lips.

She grabs a pistol and shoots at me with shaking hands.

She was a better shot than me. Fear truly is a poison.

Sunrise fires at me as she runs toward the stairs, but the shots are just to scare me off. Not a single one hits me. She nearly falls over when her gun clicks.

Didn't even bother to count her bullets.

She throws the gun and backs up against the wall.

"I completed you, so now you must complete me."

Sunrise screams illegibly at me, griping a knife from behind a desk. She rises to her feet and stares at me.

I see the blood dripping from her shoulder. Flesh has been stripped from her perfect figure.

Underneath all our hopes and appearances, is just another mesh of meat.

I step back, keeping focus on her reach. "Breakups are always so messy. This will be a clean end. No loose ends. No chance of coming back together."

Her focus has returned. She's putting her all into killing me now.

Sunrise holds out the knife as she slowly approaches.

"I didn't believe what they said…that you murdered your girlfriends. I thought you just felt responsible. What the fuck is wrong with you!"

"You said you wanted to become one with me and so you shall." I grab the dagger in my hands and lick the blood off my lips.

"Die, you psycho! Die!" She wails as she pulls the dagger back and forth, cutting into my fingers.

"Ungrateful…so ungrateful. I fulfill your lifelong dream and you repay it by stabbing me?" I grab the back of her head and slam it against the wall, disarming her. "I thought maybe you would have been different." I slam her into the glass table, shattering it. "I thought maybe you could have enjoyed your death." She bites at me as I yank her back. "I thought too highly of you. Your true nature is revealed at the brink of death. All that talk of love is just a load of shit. You don't hurt the person you love…you can't." I choke her as she kicks me in desperation.

"You're insane!"

"And you're a liar!" I grip the knife and pierce her side with it. "I made you happy. I fulfilled your wish! Why can't you make the same sacrifice?" I hold her hand tenderly. "Remember the sunset."

"Murderer!" She tears out the knife from her side and slices me in a frenzy.

I embrace her with overflowing love. "Remember the sunset. Remember my feelings for you."

She stops cutting and starts crying. "I…remember it."

"Die in that moment of bliss." I thrust my hand through her neck.

Blood spurts out, covering my bare body. I lift her hand and take a bite.

I…don't feel hungry right now.

I released the hand. "I've lost my appetite. I'm going to go take a shower." I walked to the bathroom, leaving a trail of blood.

I wash my hands but the blood won't go away.

Whose watching me.

I slam my fist into the mirror, shattering it.

Stop getting emotional. Just calm down.

I turn on the shower and let the water cleanse me. "Why do I even bother trying to make them happy? No matter how much they say they love me, they all still try to kill me. They tell me they would die for me…liars! True love should conquer fear. Maybe it's all a lie. No. I can't give up. There has to be someone who will truly love me."

I step out of the shower and put on a towel. I walk into the living room, seeing her ugly corpse. "It should have been the perfect breakup. No tears, no hard feelings. But fear had to get in my way."

I walk into the kitchen and get a black garbage bag.

You give a girl her greatest wish and she can't even give you a nice meal.

I shove the meat in the bag. "I'll dine with you later, dear." I drag the bag into the kitchen.

Why so damn heavy?

I open up the refrigerator, throw everything out and then stuff the body inside.

She's really gone.

My phone rings.

Kioshi…she always knows when I'm in pain. I can't talk with her right now…no matter how much I want to.

After I destroy any evidence left behind, I notice the time.

I should get dressed. The real mission begins now.

I walk into the bedroom and put on my tuxedo. "I wonder if it's true. Do the happy animals taste better than the sad ones? I sure hope so. Next time I'll kill the girl as she's smiling. I wonder if smiles taste better than frowns." I adjust the tie on my tuxedo.

I grip my chest and tears rush out.

No. Don't you dare cry now. You've got shit to do.

I wipe my tears. "Rebecca…I really enjoyed watching the sunrise with you."

Chapter 221: Target & Client

The mission began that morning. Unable to get in contact with Sunrise, I was called in to be the bodyguard instead. Who I would be guarding would only be revealed to me upon arrival at the party. I arrived exactly at noon, the moment the operation began.

Sefiwah grabs my hand when I pass one of the pillars. She's in a long blue and red dress and is wearing a face mask that changed her appearance entirely.

"What a pleasant surprise, but I need to get briefed on whom I'm protecting."

"You being on time would be suspicious. Dance with me." She glares daggers when she says this.

I grab her hand and she shivers. "Sure thing, dear."

"I hate wearing such a colorful dress," says Sefiwah, smiling as we move in synch.

"If you were wearing all white, then you'd be the bride and I'd be the groom."

"We don't have time for your stupid jokes. Twirl me around," says Sefiwah with a dark glare.

I spin Sefiwah away and then back in unison with the rest of the dancers. "The boss sure has a funny way of choosing pairs."

"Nothing funny about it," she says, stomping her foot on mine.

"He probably just wants us to get along better," I say, moving my hand from her waist to her ass.

Let's see how far I can push her.

Sefiwah glares at me as I squeeze her rump. "I was given direct orders not to kill you. You lucked out."

"Indeed I did. Such a beauty before me." I touch her cheek.

"Good job on…killing her. It couldn't have been easy."

I misstep but correct my footing. "You…complemented me."

"I don't trust you, but I respect your conviction."

"Such a big funeral party for such a worthless man. He doesn't deserve a single tear."

"We're getting close to the target. Just keep dancing."

"So, who paid for this hit? And who's the target?"

"After the mission, you'll be told who the client is. As for the target. Councilman Durian."

Going straight for the king. That's surprising.

Sefiwah pokes me. "When the shot is fired, you're going to run out of here."

Framing me for such a monumental murder. That's interesting.

"Three two one fire!" exclaims Kaity, over our intercoms.

I turn around before even seeing if the bullet hit its mark. I run for the door, holding a pistol.

Kanasta's voice abruptly chimes in to us. "Clear shot. The body was carried out of the area. Leave with the panic guests and the mission will be accomplished."

I run out the doors with the crowd.

"Watch out, Koshi." Kanasta voice pops in my ears. "You have an agent tailing you. Your mission is done. What you chose to do now is up to you. I will contact you tonight to see if you're keen on joining us. Being an assassin is a great way to escape being hunted down by the world's best agents."

They must really want me. I skipped breakfast though, so this agent is gonna be my meal for the day.

I rush back inside the building and she still follows me. I wait behind the door for her to come in.

The moment you enter you're dead.

I clench my knife, ready to strike.

My pursuer kicks the door open. I leap over the door and grabs the enemy from behind. One hand grips her breast while the other puts the knife to her throat.

Wait...

I release the knife and she pushes me off.

"What the hell, Koshi! I haven't heard from you in a week. Here I am scared because someone was just murdered in front of me and you greet me like that!" Kioshi throws her fists down and blushes brightly.

I didn't feel deserving of her comfort, but I should have thought about how she felt.

I hug her tightly. "Sis, I didn't know it was you. I'm so sorry."

"So where have you been? This morning…I felt your pain. I was scared."

"I'm fine. Isn't that all that matters," I say, ruffling her hair.

She puts her fists on her hips and leans forward. "Where have you been? Don't ignore my question."

"I've been going on a spiritual journey. A vision quest of sorts."

Kioshi chuckles at this. "Hey so…when you first disappeared…I got really scared. I called Joseph up and well…he asked me to marry him. I was gonna tell you before, but you hung up on me."

M-Marriage. My little sister…married?

Kioshi flicks my cheeks. "So how are things going with Sunrise?"

"Oh uh, we broke up. What's this about…marriage?"

Kioshi glares at me. "You killed her, didn't you!"

"What did you tell Joseph? Did you turn him down?"

Kioshi glares at me. "You're always avoiding responsibility by killing people! Are you ever going to stop? It's scary," says Kioshi, trembling.

"Sis, trust me, those girls were better off dead. They perverse the meaning of love." I smile at her.

Suddenly the doors on the other side of the room open. "Kioshi!" yells the young man in desperation.

Joseph. Does he really think he's good enough to marry my sister?

The short ginger boy has freckles and frail arms.

"Joseph!" Kioshi runs up to him and hugs him.

Kanasta's voice greets me again. "I don't know how, but the target is still alive. We've evacuated the area. It will be up to you."

"Why should I have to clean up your mess?"

"This mission is of the upmost importance. We may never get another chance. The Councilman's son is still in the building. Take him hostage so we can bring out the Councilman into the open. The moment he steps outside, we will take him down."

I look up, noticing that my sister left and Joseph is walking up to me.

"I'm only helping you out because I want to have a private talk with the kid." I rush up to Joseph and grab him. I press the knife to his throat.

"Koshi, what in God's name are you doing? It's me, Joseph."

"I've never trusted you. Now less than ever."

"I'm going to get married to your sister. Just calm down and we can talk. I'm not the one who shot my dad. I know you aren't either. I'm shaken up too, but relax. I don't even have any weapons."

"Why are you going to marry her?" I ask, pushing the knife just enough to draw a little blood.

"I love her. You know that. Now let me go," says Joseph in tears.

"What do you gain from marrying my sister?" I press him against the wall.

"I don't have some crazy ulterior motive! Let me go! Please!" He cries and soils himself.

This wimp wants to marry my sister!

Kanasta speaks to me. "The target is headed your way. Now is your chance."

Councilman Durian enters from the same door I came in from. "The boy who ate his father returns to kill me."

"Save me!" cries Joseph, wiggling in my grasp.

Councilman Durian, the mustached man with a permanent grimace, raises his pistol at me. There is a bullet wound straight through his forehead but he doesn't look like he's even in pain.

I hold Joseph out in front of me.

"Father, you're alive? Save me!" yells Joseph, trembling in fear.

"You told him how I orchestrated your romance with his sister to learn the secrets of his father, didn't you?"

"I didn't say anything!" wails Joseph.

The Councilman smiles. "So, you still fear me more than a man with a knife at your throat."

The boy whines in my grip.

I grab his pointer finger and snap it. "How dare you tell my sister you love her."

"I do! I love her! I swear!"

The Councilman laughs. "Come now. You only asked her out because I threatened to have you buried alive. You shouldn't lie."

"I'm not lying." Joseph whines and screams when I break another finger.

I look at the Councilman, taking a cautious step forward. "Once you had the information, what were you going to do to her?"

The Councilman smiles. "Kill her of course! Turning you into a broken mess. There's a coup going on in the Council and you're their greatest weapon!"

"I paid Kanasta for that man's death! Don't you try and take the credit."

"Exactly. It began because of you. I simply had to wait for the first king to fall. Now that he has, well I'd like to adopt you! We can be a family!"

Joseph whines and looks up. "Yeah, and then there's no need to kill Kioshi anymore. Please, let me go!"

I grab Joseph's ring finger. "Have you touched her?"

"What?"

"Did your disgusting hands touch my sister's face? Did your lips corrupt her lips? Did your fingers poison her cheeks?"

"We're together, of course I've touched her."

"Did you touch her flower? Did you touch my sister's flower?"

"Yes, but she let me I swear. She put my hand there. I'm too shy."

"If you were going to die right now, would you have any regrets?"

"Please be merciful."

"I asked you a question." I drag the knife up and down Joseph's arm.

"Yes! I regret using your sister. I'm so sorry. I do care about her. I swear," says Joseph in tears.

"Do you regret having a slow and painful death?" I ask, making a cut with each word.

"Don't kill me," cries Joseph.

"What have you always wanted to do? Any dreams?"

"Yeah. I want to be a priest. I want to help people."

"Good. Now accept that you'll never reach that goal. You're dying today."

"I'll do anything! Dad, please, tell him."

The Councilman steps forward. "Your sister is no longer on my hit list. After seeing the way you dealt with your own father, I've decided that you will work for me. Your skill of killing is far greater than any I have ever seen."

I hand Joseph a second knife. "Cut yourself for every day you hid the truth from her. One cut for each day that you said you loved her, knowing she was going to be killed."

Joseph trembles and cuts himself. "One…two…three."

"Better yet! Cut off the hands that polluted her! Do that and I'll let you live."

"Dad, why won't you help me?" Joseph cuts into his hand but then drops the knife, shaking uncontrollably. "I…can't do this. Please, Dad, save me."

The Councilman laughs. "I don't need you anymore."

"Dad, you can't be serious. Don't you care about me at all?"

"Only a mere centimeter. But don't worry Son, I won't let him kill you."

"Thank you," cries Joseph before getting a bullet in the head.

"There's all my love for you in a single moment." The Councilman puts away his gun. "My apologies Koshi, I can't stand whimpering hostages."

"So much for slow and painful," I say, sneakily retrieving my knife from the dead boy.

What the hell? Can I even kill him? If he survived that gunshot, is he even human?

"Why did you shoot your son?" I ask, slowly sliding my foot forward.

"He was worthless. I killed one boy to get a much better son. I gave that child everything he ever wanted. I spoiled him so that he would become rotten. A rotten apple is so much easier to trash. He never realized that I only spoiled him because he is an abandoned child."

I hold out my knife and take a step back. "It won't be easy to kill you, but I'm willing to keep trying."

The Councilman grins. "You can either have me as an enemy or an ally. I suggest the latter." He reaches into his vest. "Here, an apology for that unpleasant plan regarding your sister." He holds out a device that circulates energy.

A capsule, but I thought there weren't any more remaining. That man sought one out, but could never claim one. Now I'm just being offered one. Is this some kind of trap?

"Are you really going to deny a man who paid for his own assassination?"

Wait, the client is the target. No. He's just messing with me.

He rolls the capsule to me. "I specifically asked for you to be involved in the mission."

A big explosion is heard.

I look outside the window to see a parked helicopter consumed in a fiery blaze.

"Well, the Council is officially finished. That makes me the only one able to protect your sister. Take my gift and think it through."

"Wait! You haven't made amends! You were going to kill her! Prove you regret that to me now or I'll smash this capsule."

Yeah! I still have an edge.

"Ah, yes of course. That's only fair." The Councilman whips out a knife and slices off his hand, not even wincing from the pain. "Together we will shed so much blood." He fires his pistol at me until no more bullets emerge.

My legs are in tatters. I fall next to Joseph.

"When you're in your final moments, you discover who your true friends are. Farewell, Son." The Councilman walks out of the room.

Chapter 222: The Capsule

I look at Joseph's corpse and my stomach grumbles.

Is now really the time to eat? Well I can't walk. Might as well do something while I figure out my next move. Besides, it wouldn't be right letting such rich food go to waste.

I shove the knife in Joseph's stomach and just like before, the blood gushed out like a spring.

So warm. Like a baptism of blood. I saved my sister yet again. And now I get to enjoy a fresh meal.

I close my eyes, blotting out all doubt.

Time moved by in an instant.

I heard footsteps.

I open my eyes and see a figure.

Her eyes are a mix of terror, misery and disgust. She opens her mouth, but can't scream.

Sis. You were never supposed to see this.

I freeze in place.

Nothing I say can calm her. What do I do?

I slurp up the intestine in my mouth and wipe my bloody face.

Kioshi runs as fast as she can, screaming in terror.

I stand up and try to follow her but my legs give out.

Oh right. I was shot. I feel light-headed. A little nap will help.

I close my eyes.

I'm shaken to my senses in the back of a van.

Sefiwah looks down at me. "Don't you dare thank me. It was the Boss' orders. We don't leave vipers behind."

Kaity pops up behind her. "Actually, I was the one who said we had to go back for you."

Ego is driving the car and looks back. "Did you get the target?"

Should I tell them the truth? Lying won't do me any good in this situation.

"He escaped."

"It's honestly insane that there was a helicopter exploding but no police have come to investigate. Do you think the Councilman called them back?"

Kioshi. She's in danger.

I sit up. "Where's my sister?"

Sefiwah presses me back down. "Don't move or you'll open up the wounds. We found something on you. Where did you get a capsule?"

"Wow! Nice find! I thought we were the only ones with capsules," says Ego with a grin.

Sefiwah grabs my face. "Ignore him and answer my question."

I look down from her intense gaze. "The Councilman offered it to me."

"He's compromised. Kaity, we have to end him."

I sit up. "Hold up! I'm not compromised! Besides, the Councilman is both the client and the target!"

Sefiwah gives me an unamused glare. "Now you're just being absurd."

Kaity nods. "Yep! That's right! It's a most peculiar job indeed. Oh! We didn't fail!"

Sefiwah looks up at her girlfriend. "What are you on about?"

"Our mission wasn't to kill the Councilman. Just, well, shoot him right between the eyes. I guess it's mission accomplished after all."

I reach into my pocket. "Where's my phone?"

Ego looks back while weaving through traffic. "It's currently being scanned for encrypted messages."

"Hand it to me!"

"Whoa, dude, chill. It's just protocol since we don't know you too well." He tosses me my phone.

A new message.

Kaity leans over my shoulder. "What's it say?"

"It's a suicide note," I say, my heart freezing up.

"Whoa. Is everything okay?"

"My sister writes them all the time. Just have to figure it out."

"Wow, your whole family is extreme."

Kaity swipes my phone. "Oh, it's like a puzzle! 'The brother I once knew is dead. Regret is all I carry with me. A void is my only future. I am going into the light, so do not try to stop me. No longer can I live in a world with you in it.' Wow, this sounds serious." She hands me back my phone.

"Drive me to the nearest train station!"

"What?" asks Ego, just missing the red light.

"It's in the note. The first letter of each sentence spells out 'train'. Just do it!"

"Sorry dude, but until we learn everything that happened between you and the Councilman, I can't let you leave."

"My sister is going to die if you don't!"

Sefiwah looks up at Ego. "Do what he says."

"Okay dude, I'll drop you off. Just come back as soon as she's safe."

The jeep takes a sharp right and then speeds up to the front of the train station.

Ego beeps. "Your stop."

Every second counts.

I get up out from the hospital bed in the back of the jeep. "Drive it on the tracks!"

Sefiwah lowers her head and smiles.

I look at Ego in the rear-view mirror. "What, don't think you can pull it off?"

"That sounds like a challenge," says Ego with a smirk.

"Think you can make it in time?"

Ego put on his headphones. "All I need is some music." He drove through the crowd, not hitting any of them. Using the hydraulics, he made the jeep jump onto the handrails leading to the subway. He then slid his car down sideways using only the left wheels, dodging everyone with his extreme skill. He grinded down the rails, bobbing his head to the rhythm of the hydraulics.

"Wheeee!" exclaims Kaity as the car bounces up and down.

"You asked the right guy," says Ego, landing onto the train tracks with a big bump.

"Just keep heading down till you see her," I say, opening my door as we zoom down the tracks.

Ego drives the jeep using only his feet, reclining in his chair. "Kanasta's gonna be pissed at me for causing such a commotion. But this is just too much fun. We have got to hang more."

There she is!

"Stop!"

Ego slams the brakes.

I jump out of the car and run up to my sister. "You are the light of my life," I say, holding her close to my chest.

"You murdered the love of my life…just let me die. Let me die!" yells Kioshi, punching at me in tears.

Telling her the truth could make her a target of that Councilman. Even if I didn't kill Joseph, I'm still responsible for his death.

"I was afraid of losing you," I say in tears, clenching her tighter than life itself.

"You're going to lose me! I'm going to die!"

The tunnel lights up.

The train is coming.

I lift her up, but her legs are tied to the tracks with thick wires.

Kioshi sticks out her tongue. "I'm gonna go splat and it's all your fault. I only invited you to spite you, murderer. If you try and cut them, you'll electrocute me. This is what you get for ruining my life!"

"Dude, you better hurry up," says Ego, starting the engine.

No time.

I rush into the car and take Sefiwah's rubber gloves, along with some cubes of C4.

Ego peeks out the window. "What is he doing?"

I place the explosives and look at Sis. "A train isn't nearly enough to take you from me." I press the trigger as soon as the train reaches the bombs.

Kioshi cries. "Koshi, all those people…."

I don't know if I'm feeling her pain or my own right now. Gotta stay focused.

I shield my sister as the train derails and put on rubber gloves. I snug them between my sister's legs and the wires.

I cut into the wires with my knives, taking the full electric shock. "Geez, you bite hard!" I yell, hoisting her up as she bites into me.

I ran into the open trunk with her.

"A shit ton of lives in exchange for one. Man, he must really care for you," says Ego with wide eyes.

"He used to," cries Kioshi.

At the next stop, Ego drives up and out of the subway.

"Got some fuzz on our back," says Ego, swerving through alleys to lose the cops.

"You have any guns?" I ask, looking at the growing number of police pursuers.

Ego leans back. "Hey man, we only kill if it's for business. That's how Kanasta works and you don't want to upset him."

Aha! Found one.

"Under the seat, thanks," I say, cocking the pistol.

"We aren't criminals, dude. Do not shoot."

Sefiwah pets Kaity as the jeep swerves around.

I open fire on the tires, bringing our pursuers to a sudden halt. "Happy?"

Kioshi finally speaks up, grabbing onto me in tears. "How could you crash that train? How many people were in it?"

"I don't fucking know! But I don't give a damn about any of them. You're all that matters!"

"Ego, where the hell have you been?" asks Tempo on the radio call.

"Koshi just wanted me to make a quick stop," says Ego.

"You have to trash the vehicle, the police have you plated," says Kanasta.

"Glad this isn't my main car," says Ego.

"I'm going to have a word with Koshi later about what it means to be an assassin," says Kanasta darkly.

"Damn, he sounds pissed," says Ego with a sigh.

Kioshi sits up. "You're an assassin? Why do you hide everything from me!?"

"I know it's kind of a demotion. The kills are so seldom." I shrug.

Ego opens up all the car doors with the press of a button. "Everybody, ready to jump?"

"I'm ready," I say, holding my sis in my arms.

"Go!"

I leap out of the car, rolling on the grass.

Ego is on top of the car. Just as it sped into the lake, he jumps off of it. He spins in mid-air and lands perfectly. "Oh yeah! I can feel the adrenaline pumping."

"Sis, you're not hurt, are you?" I ask, checking her for scratches.

Kioshi grins. "You thought this time was like all the others, didn't you?"

What is she talking about?

Kioshi pulls out a pill bottle and grins. "I took a whole bottle before strapping myself to the tracks. There's absolutely nothing you can do to save me now!"

No. No. No. No. I saved her. That should be it. There must be something I can do.

"Sefiwah, you healed me! Is there anything you can do for her?"

"I don't see why I should help you."

"Please, she's my little sister."

Kaity pops out of the grass, holding the capsule. "I know one thing we can do!"

Sefiwah's eyes widen. "Hold up. We shouldn't waste that."

"Come on, Sefi-chan. We can't just let her die."

"Our best bet is to wait for her to die. Then I can use the Revive Artifact to bring her back. It's likely to work."

I stand up. "Likely isn't good enough! Save her, or I'll make you!" I rush at Sefiwah with my knife poised.

She whacks my arm aside and pierces my chest with her fingers.

Fingers as fast as bullets. I...can't win.

I slice her arm and she shivers. She then pierces me again with another barrage.

I swing at her until my vision fades and I collapse.

I'm sorry Sis...I failed you.

Chapter 223: The Debt that Must be Paid

I awake on an operating table. Sefiwah looks down at me.

Déjà vu. And I feel different. Energy flowing inside me. Wait! Kioshi!

I grab Sefiwah's arm. "Why did you save me! Why didn't you use it on her?"

"I saved you because the Boss ordered it. As for your sister, she received her own capsule first and has already been sent back home. That one…was my decision."

I sob into her arm. "I can never repay this debt."

"You can't. However, you will do whatever I command. Speak of my orders to absolutely no one. Is that understood?" She gazes into me with a cold unfeeling look.

My body went into shivers. "No more sexual jokes, or advances or anything you don't like. I'm at your command."

"If I need someone dead, you carry that out. Think of yourself as my personal reaper."

This woman is absolutely terrifying.

Her expression softens without warning. "And if I ask you to protect someone, then you'll do so without regard for your own life."

"You want me to protect Kaity?"

"She has me, she doesn't need your help as long as I live." Sefiwah grabs my hand. "Should something happen to me, protecting her becomes your responsibility."

"You have my word. And until then, you want me to keep my distance?"

"I actually have something else in mind. But we can discuss it after you speak with the Boss. Oh, and just to be clear, I forbid you from withholding any mission related information from him."

"I'll share everything I know."

Sefiwah smiles and walks out of the room.

With her as a girlfriend, Kaity is guaranteed safe.

"I see it was a success." Kanasta looms over me.

When did he enter the room? He is one scary teenager.

"Yeah, I'm alive. Why did you decide to give me a capsule?"

Kanasta lowers his head. "Sefiwah went against orders and used a capsule to rescue your sister."

"And I'm forever grateful to her."

"She only did so because she wanted you to die. You only live because I used my one spare to save you."

So, she saved my sister so that I wouldn't stand a chance at coming back. But didn't she say she could revive the dead? Then again, that's absurd.

I sit up. "How did you get capsules in the first place?"

"That is not for you to know." Kanasta takes a seat next to me. "I would reprimand you for that business with the train, but it was done to protect your sister. Your actions are reasonable considering the circumstances."

"Wow, that totally gets rid of the guilt for all those innocent people I killed."

"More importantly, Ego says the operation was a success and our current balance is proof of this."

"You didn't find it suspicious that the client was the target?"

"Motives are not mine to judge. I simply complete the job I'm assigned. Now, tell me what you learned about the technically deceased Councilman."

"And if I don't talk, are you going to torture me?"

"No, I'll simply hand you over to Tempo. He's not particularly fond of you."

"So, do all of you have capsules?"

"You're going to answer my questions."

"Yeah, alright. I'm used to being more of a pain in the ass, but I'll tell you everything. The Senator wants to recruit me and apparently, he has a capsule. He's the one who gave me that capsule. Are you two enemies?"

"Only according to him. Some of the jobs we have taken in the past have caused him problems. My business is purely neutral as it should be."

"Any other questions?"

"None. With the success of that mission, you've passed initiation. I welcome you as the final member of the Viper Squad. Your initiation ceremony will be held in exactly one week. You are not permitted to leave the building or contact anyone during this time."

"Not even my sister?"

"Only if an emergency."

"Understood, Boss."

The next five days were uncomfortable to say the least. Sefiwah treated me with outward disdain despite our deal and Tempo tried to kill me on several occasions during sparring. Sefiwah did allow me to train with Kaity under her supervision. Kaity was happy to teach me how to use my capsule in tangent with the Snake Skin body suits. Sefiwah was apparently the only member without her own suit and was able to regulate her energy through concentration alone. After the fifth day, when I successfully created my first energy blade, I was understandably exhausted.

I go to my room and see a lump under the sheets. I lift the sheets, revealing a most unusual sight.

Sefiwah looks up and smiles at me. “Hi.”

I step back, almost toppling over. “I’ve followed your orders.”

“Yes, I see that. I also see that Kaity is becoming fond of you.” The assassin twirls a dagger in her hand, looking at it curiously.

“If you want me not to speak a word to her. I can do that. I’d do anything for you. I owe you everything.”

Sefiwah puts the knife away and rises from the bed. “You do owe me everything.” She lightly taps my chest. “It’s time to put your life on the line. This will be my final request of you.”

That finger is more terrifying than any bullet. So many missions and yet I’ve never met someone whose intentions confound me.

“What do you have in mind?”

She turns and smiles at me sweetly. “I want you to rape Kaity.”

Impossible. I must have heard wrong. Why would she ask that?

“I…what? Kaity is my friend and a child.”

“Yes, a very impressionable child with far too much curiosity. If you disobey me, I’ll take back the gift I gave your sister.” Sefiwah’s fingers pierce my chest and grip my capsule.

I have to accept. Am I even capable of that?

“Nod if you agree.”

I nod.

“Good boy.” She pats my head. “She sleeps without her suit and you can use this to incapacitate her.” The most dangerous woman on Earth hands me a strange device. “It will sap her energy away.”

I had so many questions. My mind was in an absolute jumble.

“Why?”

“Oh, one last thing. If you touch her, I’ll kill you.”

Madness, pure madness.

Sefiwah pushes me out of the room. “She’s just next door, sleeping peacefully. Make it terrifying!” Her eyes swirl with darkness, showing the malice she keeps hidden.

It isn't until I open the door and see Kaity in her pajamas that I finally understand.

She wants me out of the picture. All she's looking for is an excuse to have me killed. And if I blame her, nobody would believe me. I'm the one in real danger here. Kaity is just the target because she's the boss's special warrior. The moment I'm about to step too far, Sefiwah will end my life. I'll die as an absolute monster, but does that really matter as long as my sister gets to live. But...can she live without me?

I take a step forward, each one twisting my stomach.

If I don't do this, then my sister is as good as dead. I have to gamble not just my life but hers. It's my best option to keep her safe.

I slap the device on Kaity.

She awakens with fierce eyes and lunges, but her movements are slowed.

I dodge her strike and trip her.

Is this even possible. Come on, Koshi. You'd do anything for you sister. Absolutely anything.

"Sorry kitten, but you're all mine tonight!" I grab her shirt and tear it off.

Kaity cries as she shields her body.

I never wanted to see you this way.

I tear her pajama bottoms off and she's left in her underwear.

She has the underwear of a child. She is a child. It would be better if Sefiwah just killed me now. If I keep going...I'll be more than dead. I'll be lost.

Sefiwah bursts down the door and cuts me. "Stay away from her!" Her eyes widen with pure rage.

She's setting me up as the monster. And now, she's going to kill me.

Kanasta bursts in. He assesses the situation in an instant and knocks out Sefiwah with a strike to the back of the neck. He stares me down. "You...." His fists clench till they are bleeding. "Your corpse would sully everything I've worked for. Only for that reason do I allow you to live."

The Boss moves in a flash and everything goes dark.

I find myself in a heap of garbage.

How fitting.

I stand up, brushing the trash off me.

"Hey!" Tempo, on the road above the garbage heap, opens his car door.

Came to finish me off.

"I'm here to clean up loose ends! You're a government dog. No way you're not gonna bark." He hops down, shooting out flames as he lands.

Is he an Exp? Or maybe he can wield artifacts like Sefiwah. Can I wield artifacts too?

Tempo fires a heat wave my way, melting the trash in the process. The gooey trash sticks to my feet, making it hard to maneuver.

Going in close is too dangerous. Staying on the heap puts me at risk too. I need to get to that car and drive as far away from this madman as possible.

I lift up a large board to deflect his incoming heat wave.

"You can't hide from me!" He sends another wave that melts through the board. Thankfully, I had already masked my presence and am now buried inside the trash heap. I peek through the trash to see his next move.

Tempo propels himself back onto the bridge with heated blasts and throws exploding fireballs to burn the trash pile.

He's reducing my options and staying close to the escape vehicle. Damn it, I have to move before I get cooked alive!

I climb out at the back of the trash heap where he can't see me. I quickly scan the trash for something I can use.

Any object can become a weapon for a spy.

I take two cans of oil and a large metal shutter.

This plan is absolutely insane, but I don't have any other options.

I run to the top of the mountain. "Fight me face to face!"

Will he take the bait?

"I have nothing to prove to you!" Tempo focuses his heat, layering it into a massive fireball.

The moment he launches it, I leap into action.

I slide down the trash heap with the shutter as a board. The moment the fireball hits the mound, I toss the can of oil behind me.

The ensuing blasts sends me through the air towards the bridge.

I bet Ego would say this is extreme!

I leap off, landing on the bridge.

Okay, about fifteen meters from the vehicle, but he's only ten meters away. I have to act fast.

"You're a nimble pest!" yells Tempo, shooting heat waves with his hands and feet.

I hold my arms out in front of me and release my energy. It cools the heat, but not enough to keep my skin from boiling. My focus stays on the car.

As I run toward him, I rub my hand against my pant leg, generating as much friction as possible.

Your lessons have saved me, Kaity. I'm forever grateful.

I slide under a condensed heat wave and then pierce Tempo's foot with my energy blade.

I disconnect from the blade and run past him. The moment he turns to face me, I throw a second bottle of oil at him, creating an explosion.

I hop in the car.

Yes! It's already on.

I drive away as Tempo blindly attacks with shotgun fire.

Sis, your brother is coming home! And he's never leaving your side ever again!

Chapter 224: The Day a City Died

I open the door to our mansion and find my sister asleep on the couch.

She's safe. Thank goodness.

I sit next to her and comb her hair gently.

Kioshi wakes up in a daze and nuzzles me. "I missed you."

"I missed you too, Sis."

She blinks and then sits up abruptly. "You're not dead?"

"That's the same conclusion I arrived at." I smile at her.

Kioshi scoots back a bit and blushes. "You nearly got killed trying to save me. Stupid reckless brother." She crosses her arms. "Why didn't you tell me you were alive?"

"I was scared I'd call and learn you were gone forever. I'm no longer with those assassins." I reach out to her and she stands up.

"I…don't want to see you right now. I can't believe my brother is a psycho cannibal. I…." She stands above me and glares. "How can you be fine killing people? You used to hate it. You used to come home and cry in my arms every day. What happened?" Kioshi tears up.

"I grew up," I say blankly.

"I thought that…after that man died…I thought you wouldn't have to kill anymore! But Sunrise, Councilman Durian and…when will it end?"

"It's a part of me now. I can't separate from it. My path is one of blood and death. It's my fate."

"I thought there was good in you. But I was wrong about you. I'm always wrong about you." Kioshi turns away in tears. "Mom was worried sick about you. I let her know you're alive. You can't let her know about what you did. It would destroy her."

"I won't speak a word of it."

Kioshi puffs out her cheeks and walks off upstairs.

Senator John is seated at the table.

I was hoping he wouldn't be here. He's always so overbearing.

"After your father's passing, well…" he smiles at me "your mother and I got married. You would have been invited, but at the time, you were presumed dead."

"Is she doing alright?"

"Kioshi told her that you were alive. Or rather she explained things after what happened on the news." Senator John stands up, gazing into me. "Why did you murder Councilman Durian?"

So, I got blamed for that. I guess without the Council to protect us agents, we can be marked for death by the media.

"I didn't kill him."

"And the others? Did you rig that helicopter to explode?"

"I'm defiant, but I'm no traitor."

"Well then, you're being framed. And that is not something that can be easily dealt with, especially considering the state of the Council."

"Where were you? How did you survive?"

"I was fortunate. I was on my way toward the helicopter when it exploded." The Senator opens his shirt, showing off gruesome burn marks. "My survival has been kept a secret until we discover who is responsible."

Councilman Durian is responsible, but saying anything could put my sister at risk. I have to be extra vigilant.

Senator John takes a sip of tea. "Two-thousand ninety. This year marks a change in history. The puppeteers protecting America are gone."

"What about you? Are you resigning from the Council?"

"A single ruler is a dictatorship, not a democracy. The Council cannot be reformed until the true perpetrator is caught. Until then we must go into hiding."

"Absolutely. Anything to keep my sister safe."

The Senator smiles at me. "I suppose it's time to put my cards on the table. It's no surprise that many members of the Council had other occupations. Councilman Grass headed a weapons manufacturing company. Councilwoman Yukio managed the world's mining enterprise. Councilman Durian ran the terror network division. All very important roles for the safety of our country."

"Don't they have heirs who can manage those enterprises?"

"All are scared to name themselves until you're captured."

"So, you want me to turn myself in to move the gears again. Meanwhile you'll be looking for the one responsible?"

The Senator waves his hand dismissively. "Not at all. My business is a bit more controversial."

"Human trafficking?"

"Perish the thought. I run a classified secret service division."

"Isn't that what I'm already a part of?"

"Not exactly. This particular division was formed in the nineteen fifties. It was the Foreign Entity Defense Squadron or FEDS. This group was comprised of special soldiers trained to fight potential alien threats on the land, sea and air. In addition to this, they prepared for biological attacks. There were fifty agents, each one named after a different state."

"You think aliens initiated this attack?" I ask with a raised eyebrow.

"This organization was founded nearly one-hundred and fifty years ago. However, in the year two-thousand forty, a new threat emerged." Senator John leans forward. "Exps."

"So, the alien club finally had an enemy, right?"

"Twenty years ago, I assumed command of the FEDS and turned them into the MEHS, the Multinational Exp Hunter Squadron." The Senator leans in and smiles from ear to ear. "Only the Council knows of this development. Even to the highest echelons of the world government, MEHS simply does not exist."

"How did you manage that?"

The Senator drinks his tea fully. "I have a talent in making things invisible. Now, I propose the four of us go to one of my MEHS bases. We will be invisible to the world and as safe as we possibly can be."

"Have your meh peeps ever captured an Exp?"

"They have indeed. Every day my warriors are hard at work, learning, inventing and training for the coming war. Mark my words, the next war will not be man vs man, but rather man vs demon!"

Demons? That's a bit of a stretch.

"As the one who shot down the demon's ringleader, at the tender age of twelve, you are already an inspiration to the MEHS. I would have recruited you earlier but Councilman–"

"Don't say that name. I'll gladly join the MEHS. When do we leave?"

"Just as soon as we finish packing. We'll need to make a quick stop by my home, but it's only a few blocks down. Stay vigilant though. No doubt your fellow agents have been dispatched to take you out."

I grab his hand and shake it. "Thank you. For the first time in my life…I feel like I have a father. Once we're safe, I have something important to tell you."

"I look forward to it." He walks off, nearly bumping into my mom.

"My little boy!" My mom nearly trips down the stairs as she rushes into an embrace with me. "I've never been so worried before. They said you were dead."

"I'm fine, but that terrible man…he's gone forever."

Mother holds me tenderly, wincing a bit from the bruises on her arms. "I donated everything he left to charities. I didn't…want anything from him. I hope you understand."

I hug her and kiss her forehead. "You did the right thing."

Mom looks up at me and tears up. "My boy's really grown up. How old are you?"

"Twenty-two."

Forever twenty-two if capsules really are the elixirs of life.

"How time flies. Did you speak with John?"

"Yeah, he's going to take care of us. You always go for the rich old guys. You gold digger." I slug her affectionately.

"He's only in his fifties. I find him rather handsome. I'll be in my forties before I know it." Mom hugs me tightly. "I'm so sorry about what happened to Rebecca. Such a loss."

"Yeah, she…deserved better."

Mother looks at me with a scared look. "About Joseph, they say you killed him. My boy wouldn't do that. He's a hero of justice."

I grab her trembling hands. "We'll get everything sorted out. Are you all packed to go?"

Sound erupts like a sudden jolt of lightning. I hear rumbling and then the windows shatter.

I instinctively shield my mother from the shards. "Go find John. I'll get Kioshi."

Is someone bombing us? This is insane. The agents usually act discreetly.

As I rush up the stairs, I hear buildings collapse.

Kioshi is on the ground in her room, bleeding from her head. I hoist her up and go down the stairs.

The sound of a twister erupts outside.

What the hell is going on?

I look to the Senator and shout over the screaming and destruction.

"We have a bunker under the house! Help me open up the doors under the staircase!"

We throw all the suitcases and boxes aside and force open the doors, not bothering to waste time looking for a key.

The destruction outside only gets louder.

Too close. That sounds like our neighbor's house just collapsed.

I grab onto my sister with all my strength and throw her into the bunker. Senator John follows, shielding her body with his own.

The front door goes first. Then the wall is torn apart from the house, and swallowed up by the storm.

I stretch my arm out and grip Mother's hand with all my strength.

We're all going to make it through this!

Mother looks up at me and smiles with a teary face.

"Mom!" Kioshi rushes out from the cellar and is swept up by the wind current.

I grab my little sister with both hands and use my capsule to focus my energy in my feet, keeping my footing.

Kioshi pounds at my chest in tears. “You let her die! Monster!”

I slide foot by foot into the cellar as the house collapses around us, griping my sister with everything I have.

Kioshi screams out in despair, trying to wrestle out my grip. “How could you let her die?” She drew blood by clawing at my arm.

I didn’t even consider it. My body reacted on its own to save you. You’re my everything.

I press a pressure point on her neck, sending her into a pleasant slumber.

When we were deep in the cellar, I approach the Senator.

“Do you have any idea what the hell is going on out there?”

“Nothing human. It appears that whoever killed the council has an Exp at their command. That’s the only logical explanation for what I saw.”

“You saw it, through all the rubble and wind?”

“I saw something truly monstrous.” The Senator looks down. He then grips my shoulder. “That thing out there is a threat to our country. As patriots, it is our sworn duty to go out there and stop it.”

“And how the hell are we supposed to do that? We’re safe here. This is where we should stay.”

“I saw that you have a capsule. I may not be as well-equipped, but I am a decent shot.”

“We don’t even know what that thing is!”

“It wasn’t facing us. We were simply caught up in the periphery of its attack. I fear that not even this bunker will protect us should it come this way.”

I grab his arm. “You’ve never fought this thing before?”

“No, but I have called upon the MEHS to take it down. Sadly, we don’t have the luxury to wait for their arrival.”

“Well then, let’s take down this exceptional pain in the ass!” I tuck my sister in, grab a rocket-launcher and as many rockets as I can carry from our weapon stash.

Once the wind dies down, we rush outside.

The entire neighborhood is in tatters, rubble coats the streets and not a single house is left standing. I spot the monster in the distance, or rather the back of it. It’s a fleshy creature as tall as a skyscraper and as long as a town.

We're supposed to fight that thing?

"Find a working vehicle!" yells John, lifting up rubble to search for survivors.

I flip a few cars with my newfound strength but most are broken beyond repair. "I found one, but there's no key in sight."

Senator John meets up and inserts a thin key into the ignition. "Not a problem for the head of the MEHS!" The key expands until it fits the shape and he starts up the car.

The car roars, excepting John as its master.

"I'll drive. Fire only when we're in range."

"You ever see one this big before?" I holler as we speed toward the hulking monstrosity.

"Not even close. This must be what happens when their full powers are unleashed. Although, it could be an amalgamation of several Exps."

No matter how close we got, I couldn't get a look at its face. All I saw was the massive vortex coming from its mouth, tearing buildings out of the ground and consuming them.

"It's growing in size! What happens if we can't stop it?"

"We can't afford to let doubt weigh us down. Our only gravity should be our firm resolve to protect our Nation. We're close enough now. Fire at the back of its tail."

This may very well be the stupidest thing I've ever done.

I unleash a rocket that explodes into the thirty-foot tail tip of the beast. "I don't think he noticed."

"We may have to hit the eye, I'll drive along the side!" yells the Senator, speeding against the wind and debris.

This man is so courageous. I'll gladly follow him if I somehow survive this.

I spot the creature's eyes. They're massive but a gentle color. What's more, they appear to be crying.

Well, that will certainly be in my nightmares.

"Do you have a clear shot?"

"It's about seventy feet up and thirty feet away, so yeah. That's good enough!" I hoist up the launcher and fire into the monster's gigantic eye.

"You are an angel of marksmanship," cheers John while doing a quick turn-around.

"Do you think he noticed us?" I ask, loading up another rocket.

The titan turns its head, knocking over several buildings in the process.

Rows of teeth, dozens of them...and a black swirling vortex. There's no way this thing will ever stop.

The monster halts its vortex suddenly and rolls along the ground, trying to crush whatever attacked it.

The Senator drives back toward the ruined city. "We got its attention, but we're too small for it to see." He parks the car and hops out, rushing into a nearby car. "Having two vehicles should help our odds." He drives off back toward the house, likely to get his own rocket-launcher.

I hop into the driver's seat.

Well shit, now I gotta babysit this beast on my own.

I make sure I have a clear path and then fire another rocket. This one bursts on one of the creature's teeth.

The bony tooth fragments fall down, smashing a turned over truck beneath them.

The creature rises on its lower half and then swings its upper half around, decimating whatever buildings were in the area.

I swiftly drive into the massive crater in the road.

Was this thing dropped on us? If it had landed just a few blocks down, then Sis and I would both be gone.

I fire another rocket that only hits its side, but it's agitated enough to notice it.

The creature opens its mouth wide. A vortex quickly appears in its throat, swirling at an increasing pace.

"Sorry, hungry boy, all I have to feed you is these rockets!" I fire another one directly into its other eye.

The beast lets out a huge scream and then leaps into the air. It crash-lands, flipping my car and looking directly at me.

Fuuuuuuck!

I hop out of the car and run as fast as I can as I hear the vortex swirl behind me.

I'm going to die!

The moment I feel my feet slip, I slam them down. I focus my capsule's energy on them and pierce the ground with two energy swords. Even so, I was getting dragged backward while having to swerve to dodge debris.

Gotta get to safety.

I rip my blade out and stab it a few feet in front of me, scaling the street on my belly until I was behind some gravelly protrusion.

I see cars and rubble get pulled past me. Even the streets crack around me.

I look up to see jets on the horizon.

Those aren't army jets.

Missiles disengage from the jets as they zoom by, moving too fast for even the monster to pull in.

The missiles hit the beast but don't explode.

My ears pop when they suddenly burst, each one carving out a massive chunk of the beast.

The monstrosity redistributes its flesh to form back its body, albeit smaller than before.

As the jets loop back, the creature stands on the tip of its tail.

It plans to face them head on.

A storm of flesh and rubble swirl out from the creature's mouth, breaking a wing off one of the jets.

The jet zooms over me before crashing just ten meters behind me.

That could have been the end. I could have died.

Tubes suddenly came out from a figure in front of the abomination. They latch onto the monstrosity's mouth and slam them shut, shattering the teeth of the behemoth.

Is that an Exp Hunter? Just how powerful are these guys.

I feel a smile grow.

How powerful can I become?

The abomination wails miserably as it wiggles to escape the grip of the clear tubes.

The tubes start sucking the flesh off the colossal beast. Another tube comes out of the figure's back and expels the meat and debris out as liquid.

The titan pushes off the ground with its tail, breaking free of the tubes in the process.

Tubes shot out from the alleged Hunter, fastening to the creature's tail.

Hold up. If I'm gonna be a Hunter, I'm gonna have to get my shit together! I can't run from an Exp!

I disengage my energy blades and run toward the behemoth.

I won't settle for anything less than the top! I'm going to prove to these hunters I'm the best there is!

I jump onto one of the tubes and run up it.

How can it be so squishy and yet so strong?

My foot slips, but I reflexively grab the tube and hoist myself back up.

A single slip up, a moment where my concentration wavers, can be the difference between life and death.

I leap off the tube and onto the monster's tail.

For killing Mother, I bring you death!

I run up the tail, dodging the mouths that sprout beneath me.

This thing can create mouths anywhere on its body.

Tendrils shoot out, forming maws at the tips.

I use my energy blade to slice the incoming tendrils as I run up the back of the beast.

This shit is insane!

The attacks become more relentless as I near the head of the monster.

My foot falls into a hole that forms as I take my next step. The hole closes, digging its teeth into my leg.

You aren't taking my life too!

Mouthed tentacles strike me, taking quick but precise bites.

I look over and notice where we are.

Right near home. If I don't stop this thing, my sister could...

I tear my leg out from the hole and drag it forward while slicing the incoming mouths. "You better still work, damn it!" I fling my leg forward, but the worthless thing offers little support.

The beast leaps up, pulling in the incoming jet before chomping down on it.

Looks like the Hunters just got a vacancy.

I pour my energy into my leg, creating a makeshift cast around it. I continue my run, ripping open my wounds.

Mouths spawn and slurp up the trail of blood left by my leg.

I leap off the head and land onto the creature's eye.

Let's see you bite me now, freak!

I rub my hands together vigorously, but no energy comes out.

Of all the times for me to run out! Screw it! I'll improvise!

I shape the small energy on my fingertips into a sharp edge and thrust my hand into the titan's eye.

Blood erupts from the eye like a geyser, sending me far above the behemoth.

The beast opens its mouth, starting up its vortex.

Another two jets swoop by and carpet bomb the monster.

I fall into a net of energy.

"Didn't know you government boys had actual grit," says the Hunter, a voluptuous woman with a spider-like helmet and clad in a skin-tight suit.

"And I thought all the Hunters would be burly macho men." I grin while sizing her up.

Civilians rush by, fleeing in terror from the monster battle.

I close my eyes, listening intently to the screams.

Kioshi!

Having pinpointed her voice, I open my eyes and make a mad dash to her.

I seize her in my arms and she squeals in surprise. "What are you doing out here? I told you to stay inside!" I hold her close to my chest.

"And let you go die without me! Idiot!" Her glare wavers until she breaks down in tears. "If I had lost you…."

I pat her head. "I'm fine, Sis. I'm an invincible hero!"

Kioshi grabs onto me with all her strength. "Mommy's dead."

"I'm so sorry, Sis."

"This is your fault! You let her die!" She punches me in tears.

"You're right, I'm the one to blame," I say, looking back at the beast shrinking. "It's over now."

"Not yet!" She grabs my hand, trembling in rage. "Kill that thing! Promise me you'll kill that monster."

I let go of her. "I'll end it right now. Hunter babe, can you keep your eye on her?"

"It will be my absolute pleasure." The Hunter approaches my sister. "You're just the cutest little thing, aren't you?"

I turn around to see that the massive monstrous creature isn't so massive anymore.

The creature wails, it's distorted screams becoming more and more pathetic as it shrinks.

I slide down the mishappen road and run toward the beast, using its vortex to speed up its demise. The creature was only ten feet tall. By the time I arrived, it was smaller than I was.

The tubes absorb the last bit of flesh, revealing a child within.

Chapter 225: The Monster Within

"Hold up. That thing was a kid!"

A large Hunter, wearing a priestly robe over his black suit, steps up to me. "These demons are not as they seem. Their summoners can conjure them up with any appearance they deem appropriate."

Then he's not a kid. Doesn't matter. He killed Mother. He deserves to die.

"Let me end him. It's personal," I say, taking out a small blade.

"We cannot act beyond subduing the threat until the Messiah returns."

What the hell does that mean?

"We don't have time to wait for some apocalypse. That thing could very well bring about the end of the world! We have to end it!"

It really looks like a kid. Can this really be that monster?

The Hunter looks up. "Speaketh of the Lord and He shall make himself known."

The Senator parks his car and approaches us. "Well done indeed. This has been the greatest threat we've conquered yet."

"Your praise is a blessing. This is mere preparation for our battle against their dark lord Pathos."

I grab the Senator's arm. "Tell your altar boy that this monster needs to die."

The Senator shakes his head. "Acting rashly is not something we can afford to do."

"He killed my mother!"

"His power could be of great use to this nation."

"You can't control something like that!"

"I have my ways. For now, keep him subdued. We will interrogate the demon once we return to base."

The Hunter nods and lifts up the blood-soaked child.

Kioshi slides down the incline and meets up with us. "Is he okay?" she asks, looking at the child with worry.

The Senator smiles at her. "He'll live. Poor child's parents were eaten by that beast. Not to worry. It has been dealt with."

Why is he lying to her?

"We should take him with us. Poor kid. He must be so shaken up."

"Yeah…poor guy," I say awkwardly.

"We will bring him with us. Soon we will all be safe, my children." The Senator hugs both me and Kioshi.

Kioshi wipes the blood off the boy, staining her dress. "Don't worry, cutie, everything is going to be just fine."

Truly, she is an angel.

When we got in the car, I rested my head in my sister's lap and fell asleep.

Kioshi shakes me to my senses. "We're here."

I wipe my eyes before taking in the new location. It's a large building with a gate around the perimeter. The building itself is pure metal with no windows in sight.

Looks like a prison.

"Oooh, looks haunted." Kioshi pops up and taps John's shoulder. "Is it haunted?"

John lowers his head. His eyes tear up. "In a matter of speaking."

When the front doors open, a depressed teenager, wearing a black suit comes out. "You survived."

The Senator grins. "Don't sound so disappointed when you say that."

My sister steps up to the kid. "Hey, nice to meet ya. I'm Kioshi."

He looks right past her and gazes at me with a dark aura. "You're the one who killed Zenero."

The Senator steps between me and the teenager. "War, you will treat Koshi with respect. He, along with his sister, are family."

Another kid comes out the door. He looks to be twelve years old at the most. For some reason, he is wearing a maid outfit. "Welcome back, Sir!"

"Cutie!" Kioshi rushes up and hugs him.

The white-haired boy looks away with flushed cheeks. "I'm sorry. I didn't mean to nuzzle your breasts. They're just so soft and welcoming."

"Aww, it's fine, cutie. You can snuggle them all ya like!" Kioshi holds him tighter.

I pull the little perv out from her grip. "What's a runt like you doing at a base for super fighters?"

Gamma stands proudly. "I'm Agent Alpha. I type so fast that I've earned the moniker Octopus. You'll be given your own codename as well. Do you have a favorite animal, miss?"

"Yeah! Opossums!" Kioshi snuggles him again, pressing his head against her soft breasts.

Lucky little brat.

"Actually, I'm the only one who's going to become a hunter. As for Codenames, I rather like Alpha."

The Senator slams a hand against my back and lets out a raucous laugh. "So ambitious! Blood be damned, our kindred spirits make us family!"

Kioshi turns to the Senator. "You never told me you had adorable shota servants!"

"Yes, I'm fortunate to have each and every Hunter."

"And the reason you make him dress up as a maid is…." Kioshi raises her eyebrows at him.

"Oh, that's confidential. Haha!"

Kioshi laughs along with him.

Even after everything that's happened. She's still smiling.

John turns to the mopey teenager. "I assume you have prepared a suitable feast."

"As instructed…as always," says the boy with a sigh.

Kioshi pokes his nose. "You're a cutie. What's your name?"

"I'm War."

"Wow, that's…not cute at all," says Kioshi with a pouty face. She then perks up and turns to John. "So, do you have like a whole harem of little boy servants?"

"You misunderstand. Despite their appearance, both Alpha and War are adults. They are two of my best Hunters!"

"Alpha, take Kioshi inside and tend to her. Koshi and I have some business to attend to," says John, picking up the Exp boy from the vehicle.

"I can bathe him if you want," says Kioshi with a smile.

"Right this way, miss," says Gamma, bowing to my sister.

"You are just too cute! I appreciate your manners, Sir." Kioshi does a curtsey.

Alpha blushes deeply and turns his gaze to the ground, fiddling with his fingers. "I'm sorry, I didn't mean to peek under your skirt."

"It's okay. Do you want another peek?" asks Kioshi, lifting up her skirt further.

"Enjoy it while it lasts, twerp," I say, walking with John inside the building.

Marble walls with priceless paintings adorn the halls. It's outward appearance of a prison completely contrasts with the colorful cultured interior. As we go to the lower floors of the building, I see that this place was certainly once a prison. Though polished, the color of the walls is gray.

As we pass the doors, I feel the panicked gripping of the handles from past occupants.

I walk in front of the Senator. “After the interrogation, I have to kill him. You understand. I promised my sister.”

“She’s already fond of the boy. Losing him would only hurt her.” The Senator looks at me with care. “What do you value more, your word or your sister’s happiness?”

He makes a good point.

Once the kid was properly bound to some high-tech hospital bed, the Senator injected him with something that woke him.

Even if he’s not really a kid, he sure looks like one.

The boy looks at us with drowsy eyes. “Am I still dreaming?”

I decide to take initiative. “That depends, what was the dream about?”

The kid looks at me and then at his restraints. “What the hell do you want with me!”

The Senator glares at the boy. “Your utmost cooperation. Else we might have to resort to unpleasant methods.”

The kid struggles to break out of his binds. Once he realizes it’s futile, he lowers his head. “My dream…it’s so fuzzy. Where’s Amy! She has nothing to do with this!”

“Amy? Is she your sister?” I ask.

The boy looks away, unsure what he should say. “In my dream…I remember debris, screaming…and I…was the monster.” His eyes go hollow. “Oh no. No! No! No! He turned me into one of them!”

So, he was made into an Exp by someone. Then he really is just a kid.

The boy looks up at me. “You attacked me when I was…that thing.”

“Yeah, but no hard feelings. Sounds to me like you weren’t in the right mind.”

The Senator places a hand on my shoulder. “Exps possess a silver tongue. Lies come out as calm as a gentle breeze from their infernal maws.”

“You really are paranoid. Either way, best we work with him.” I turn to the kid. “You got a name?”

“Chris.” He lowers his head.

“You got a full name?”

“Chris Miraculous.”

No freaking way. Not sure if karma or destiny is at play here.

The Senator's eyes widen. "Chris Miraculous is the son of a dearly departed friend of mine! He is no monster!"

The boy yells with teary eyes. "I was turned into that thing. Did I…really kill all those people? I'm a monster now! Stay away from me!" He thrashes about in a fit of panic and misery.

I grab his arms and hold them down. "Relax. Even if you transform, we can bring you back. You're in good hands."

He wipes his eyes with his shoulders. "Thanks for stopping me."

"Okay, so let's dial it back a bit. What do you remember before becoming a monster?"

"Pathos stole us. After killing my father, he stole us!"

That Exp got the blame for Zenero's murder. Thought he perished in that blast too. Guess those things are more durable than I thought.

Senator John looks intently at the boy. "Pathos is our enemy as well. Though he, along with his minions, have been missing for nearly ten years."

Chris' eyes chatter as rage overtakes him. "He has my sister! That monster has my sister! We have to find him!" The kid suddenly coughs up blood and concrete. "What the…what is going on with me?" he asks, looking at the finger in the pool of blood on the floor. He cries and closes his eyes. "What did I do?"

"You destroyed a city," says John bluntly. "And took many American lives in the process."

"I couldn't have. I'm human. I wouldn't kill anyone who didn't deserve it," says Chris with glazed out eyes. "Stage Ten…that's what he said before sending me away. He wanted this to happen! He made me kill those people!" The boy retches out more blood, metal and granite. "I'm sorry, I couldn't control myself. There's this voice in my head that yells out. You have to get rid of the voice!"

John wipes the boy's bloodied mouth with a handkerchief. "How many children has he turned into Exps? How did he do it?"

The boy stops stammering and steels himself. "Just me."

The Senator looks at him curiously. "You're lying. Need I remind you that there are many ways to get information from you."

"It's just me!" he yells in tears before vomiting again.

His sister must have been transformed too, but he's willing to suffer to protect her. Guess we have a lot in common. This all could have been avoided…if I hadn't killed Zenero. Maybe Mother would still be alive.

The Senator looks to me. "Keep an eye on the boy. I'll be back with someone more adept at persuasion." He then leaves the room.

The boy looks at me in tears. "My stomach hurts so much! I'll behave. Please, Sir. Let me go to the bathroom."

I go to the monitor and undo the restraints. "Sure thing, Kid." I lift him up as he throws up.

After finally finding the bathroom, I wait several hours for the boy to finish.

A puddle of blood comes out from beneath the door.

Please don't be dead!

I bust the door open and the kid is hunched over the bathtub, vomiting out blood and flesh.

I nearly collapse from the overwhelming stench but trudge through the bloody water.

His eyes are closed and he's still vomiting. What do I do?

The Senator and the Hunter I first met enter the bathroom.

John looks my way. "You trust these demons more than you should."

"The kid isn't breathing! Do you have a medic on staff?" I ask, lifting the boy up as he continues to puke.

The Hunter steps in, not affected by the smell in the slightest. "I'll take care of it from here."

Chapter 226: Forging a Family

The Senator escorts me down the hall.

"You have something on your mind," he says, walking ahead of me.

"Other than storing an impossible amount in his stomach and well, transforming into Mothra's abortion, he seems like a normal kid. So, what is an Exp exactly?"

"They are demons sent to the Earth to destroy God's children," says John with a serious tone.

"Spare me the mythological bed time stories. What are they really?"

"They are creatures that challenge the power of God. Therefore, it is my duty to destroy them."

"Wait up. Were you the one who ordered Zenero shot?"

"It was a decision made by the Council unanimously. Though I may have sparked their passion with a rousing speech."

"Then what's that about Zenero being your friend?"

"We were at a time, friends. After his death, I released my grudges and think of him solely in those terms."

"You're an inspiration, Sir," I say, rolling my eyes.

"Sarcasm is like a gas leak, invisible to the eye, but all too clear to me. I suggest you watch your tone."

Geez, is this really the same mushy old man my mom was dating? He loved my sarcasm.

"Don't you feel the least bit responsible for his dad's death?"

"That responsibility is passed on to our agents. Councilmen must act free of guilt. And I would assume agents wouldn't be swayed by actions that were deemed necessary."

I grab his arm. "Without a father, he was taken and turned into a monster! Where the hell is your sympathy, old man?"

The Senator brushes me off. "My sympathy is put aside when pertaining to maters of national security. That Exp, even if he truly was once human, is still a threat."

"I'm not going to let you dissect him."

"Why so protective? I doubt even your sister would come to his aid, knowing what he did to your mother."

"Just…let me talk to him."

"He is rather fond of you. I'll make you a deal, son. Convince him to stay with us, on the side of righteousness and I will assure his safety. No,

I will make it a high priority. Should he go rogue, the responsibility of ending him will fall to you. Is that clear?"

"Geez, not much of a choice you're giving me."

"On the contrary. I have the upmost faith in your abilities…when properly motivated."

"Then you better come up with a codename for him, because he's gonna be calling you Grandpa before the moon comes up."

"That's the spirit! I suggest you check up on him after dinner. I'll return by tomorrow. The President wants a full report. No doubt this incident, played properly, will increase the budget of our organization. Sympathy I reserve for those who are already lost, but gratitude…that boy has my sincere gratitude for showing the public that the Exps are a true menace."

"Hey, I have an idea. Why don't you adopt him? Nobody would know he's an Exp. They'd just see a friend taking care of another friend's kid, right?"

"That sort of image doesn't suit me. Why don't you and your sister adopt him? I doubt she'd object."

"I can't ask that of her unless she knows that he's the one who killed Mother."

"The truth is a weapon; do be careful with it."

"Lies are a weapon too. I'm not going to lie to her."

The Senator smiles. "You have much to learn. Lies are a weapon of last resort. Simply bend the truth."

"What are you getting at?"

"Son, as a member of the Government, it is our sworn duty to protect America. We are slaves to this great nation!"

"Spare me the patriotic speech. You have a meeting to go to, right?"

"Mind your tongue. Now, what is a greater threat to the American people than terrorists?"

"A corrupt government?"

"The truth! The truth is frightening. It is painful. And it is wretched. We filter the news not simply to fog the eyes of the public; it is a filter system to keep them safe. Lies are floatation devices in a matter of speaking. And the unknown is a raging tsunami!"

"But people know about Exps. You can't spin what happened today as a gas leak."

"Of course not, you fool! What happened today was an act of terrorism committed by an organization of Exps."

"Won't that put people in a panic?"

"A controlled panic, a directed panic, and one that suits this organization and its goals."

"I see what you mean. Wait, does this mean that aliens really are real too? Actually, why am I asking you? Forget it. The unknown can stay a big ass question mark for all I care."

"Precisely! And what is more unknown than the truth? Nothing! That is why the search for it is never ending. We simply bury those clues. With the best intentions, of course."

"I still don't agree."

"Come now. Direct control is less effective than tricking the people into thinking they have rights. People who believe they have a good government will never revolt. People who are ruled by fear will eventually fight against it. Fear inspires courage. Sudden changes scare people, but gradual things are nearly undetectable. If people trust their government, then they will have peace of mind."

"You're starting to sound like someone I truly despise."

"Listen with an open mind. All we have to do is twist the truth until it makes the masses comfortable. If you twist something long enough, it will eventually break off until it is something small enough to digest. Politicians do the same thing with the truth. If we give enough historical references or outside threats, then we can excuse anything. This includes the most heinous of all acts, war. People have become accustomed to war. And they have accepted the fact that some of their rights will be ignored during times of war. A country ruled by fear is weak. But one fueled by hate is strong! When you can blame someone else, or better yet a group of other people, you feel good inside. Like an agent of justice! And if the people are busy hating the enemy, they will willingly sacrifice their children to the armed forces. The irony is that it is all because they fear death. They are killing and dying to protect our country from a war that it started. The key to a powerful government is first of all calling it democratic. Then, making an excuse to go to war to make the people more patriotic. And then slowly depreciate their rights like a virus. Eventually they will all be willing slaves to this great country. Isn't it beautiful, Koshi?" The Senator throws out his arms with dramatic gusto.

Are all politicians war mongers. Sheesh, can I really trust this guy.

"You want war."

"No! At least not in the sense you're thinking. One does not have Civil War when fighting a foreign enemy." He grabs my shoulder. "Imagine every nation allied against a common enemy: the Exps!"

"That would make your organization quite important indeed."

"So cynical, but that isn't incorrect. The point is simple. If the government has to blow up a couple of buildings and blame it on some distant country, or in this case a hidden foe, then so be it."

"All for the greater good."

"Indeed! We have an image as a neutral nation. We do not attack unless provoked. Sometimes we just have to provoke the people into supporting the war. This is the President's most important role. Figurehead or not, they are to be beacons of charisma to win over the hearts of the people. The citizenry invests their faith through voting and in doing so, become invested in the words of the President! Your father was a member of Congress, as you know."

"Not my father. Just a pile of bones, I hear."

"It is Congress that pulls the strings, not the President. Balance of power is all a lie. It's an idealism of our dearly departed founders. The Executive, Judicial, are all overpowered by the Legislative branch. And if they have a disagreement, then we lobbyists merely bribe them until they see it from our perspective."

"And what exactly are you lobbying for?"

"Nothing devious. Environmental protection, Exp disposal and the end of legal murder!"

That last one sounds like a real buzz kill.

The Senator grabs me. "We can rule this world, Son! All we have to do is bend the truth a little."

"Now I get it…you're insane! However, you are ambitious…I can respect that. Would my sister be safe in this world you envision?"

"She would be exalted. Now, my argument aside, you've already lied to your sister."

I shrug him off and clench my fist. "What the hell are you accusing me of?"

"Well, you bent the truth. You were indeed responsible for Joseph's death, but Durian was the one who shot him. Your reason for lying is beyond me, but that is irrelevant. You already understand the necessity of lies!"

"Lies like that aren't dangerous. They heal upon discovery."

"I've shared my views. Your actions are your own."

"About that. You said ending legal murder. See, I have a hobby and it…can I still kill for fun like I used to? I mean, they kinda owe me their lives considering I've saved them from sooo many attacks. Plus, they're bad people. Most of the time."

"Of course! A hero is merely someone exalted by the media. Their actual actions are irrelevant."

"Becoming the hero of the people I'm killing is some sickly-sweet irony. But that's not important. I've decided. I'm telling my sister the truth."

"You will learn to fear the truth as I do," says John before parting ways. "The dining room is the first door on your left."

Kioshi looks up at me, chewing animal flesh. She takes her time and then grins. "Hey, bro. It's real meat! Someone died for this. Died for my pleasure. Your little angel isn't so pure, after all." She sticks out her tongue.

I sit down next to her.

How do I tell her the truth?

Kioshi stops eating and sighs. "Look, I'm joking. No blood, see? It's tofu. I was just yanking your chain. Don't look so glum."

I grab her hand.

"Sis, there's something you should know."

"The boy! Where is he? Is he okay?"

"Yeah, he's with the doctor now."

"Oh, I hope he's okay. Maybe we should go check on him."

I stand up. "I'll check on him. We can all eat together, okay?"

"Yeah!" Kioshi beams and grabs my hand. "Hey bro…I love you…you know that, right?"

I smile at her. "I know it down to my soul."

After getting lost several times, I find the doctor escorting the boy down the hall.

"I'll take it from here," I say, grabbing the kid's hand.

The Hunter smiles at me. "So parental. Didn't know you were the type."

"Nah, just the Chief's orders."

"Really. That's news to me."

"Swear on my life."

"Oh, do I get to collect, if it turns out false?" She smiles and her fingers climb up my hands like a spider.

Wow, she's so hot. Definitely adding her to the list.

"Sure thing, just come to my room later." I grin.

The Hunter lets go of Chris' hand. "Run along now. I'll see you at the dinner table."

After we're out of earshot, I turn to the kid.

"She didn't hurt you, did she?"

Chris shakes his head. "She was really nice actually. Helped relax me a bit. So…I uh…well there's a vortex inside of me and as long as I'm not transformed…it just kinda leaks…that's why all that blood and…." He shivers.

I grab his hand. "We'll figure a way to help you. Promise."

"Thanks, hey why are you so nice to me?"

"Do I need a reason to be kind to a scared kid? Look, this is going to be alarming, but I think it's important you get a full grasp of everything." I take out my phone and show him a picture of the monster that killed my mother.

The kid steps back. "What is that horrible thing?"

"That is what that evil Exp made you into."

"I'm a monster! I killed those people!" He sobs and shivers, gripping his head.

I whack him upside the head. "Get a grip. You can't hold yourself responsible. Just blame that Pathos guy."

"But it is my fault. The cravings, they start out as whispers, but they become louder and louder! Chattering inside my skull, eating away until they become me!"

"You weren't strong enough to hold back. You're a kid, so that's to be expected."

"Turn it off please. I don't want to hear anymore." He cries in his hands.

I pull his arms aside and force him to look at the screen. "What the hell are you crying about? Do you think your tears will bring them back?"

"No…I just…I don't know what to do."

"You killed my mother."

He looks up at me. "What?"

"She's gone because of you! Now answer me this! Do you think crying will atone for that?"

"I killed…can you ever forgive me?" The child holds himself and shivers.

"This isn't about forgiveness! Your crying means nothing," I hold him firmly to ease his shaking.

"I've killed thousands of people," he says in tears.

"So what? Crying solves absolutely nothing. That is unless you're so pathetic that you do it to feel better. Do you think you deserve that? After what you've done."

"Then what do I do?"

"What can you do?"

"I can make sure that it never happens again. I can get control over my cravings! Yeah! That's it!"

"There ya go. Just needed a little push."

Chris grabs my hand. "You'll help me control it?"

"Yeah, of course. But the Chief will too. That's his specialty actually. He's a politician so control is kinda his gig."

"Thank you!" exclaims Chris, hugging me with overflowing gratitude.

"Oh, and hunting down bad Exps. That's our job here. We could really use your help."

"I'm not ready for that."

"No worries, kiddo. Neither am I. We can both learn the ropes. Sound good?"

Chris nods.

"Great. Now, how about you come meet my sister?"

"You have a sister too?"

"Yeah. She's the light of my life."

Chris beams at me. "Same here. Amy is so free-spirited and wise."

"You'll have to introduce me sometime."

Kioshi pops out of her chair when she notices Chris. "Are you finding the place accommodating?"

"Yeah. Despite first impressions," he says, scratching his chin.

"Say, what is your name, little guy?" she asks, pinching his cheeks.

"I'm Chris," he says with a smile.

"That is so cute," she says, bobbing back and forth with glee.

I grab her hand gently. "Hey Sis, there's something I need to talk to you about."

"Me first. Can we keep him please? I'll take care of him; you won't even know he's here," says Kioshi, wagging her butt excitedly.

Chris crosses his arms. "Geez, I'm not a pet."

"Koshi please, he has no family."

"I have a sister and I will find her," says Chris, clenching his fist in determination.

"She can join too!" Kioshi grabs my arm and spins around. "It's perfect; I always wanted a little boy. We used to play house, remember Koshi?"

Why is she trying to embarrass me like this?

Kioshi pokes my cheek. "You can be his father, right?"

"I guess," I say, blushing brightly.

"Then it's settled. Chris, you are our new son," says Kioshi, shaking his hand excitedly.

Chris laughs. "Didn't even ask my input. Hey uhh…does that mean I have to call you Mom now?" He fidgets with his fingers.

"Oh, he is just too cute. Here, say ah," says Kioshi, taking a spoon of soup to him.

Chris knocks it out of her hand. "Keep that away from me."

War looks up. "I worked so hard on dinner. Please don't waste it."

Kioshi frowns at Chris. "That wasn't very nice. Apologize to him…and then give him a kiss," she says, pecking the air.

"I just…don't want to eat. I'm sorry."

"That's no good? You have to eat if you want to grow up big and strong like your father," says Kioshi, squeezing my muscles.

"I'd rather starve to death than risk the cravings," says Chris with chattering teeth.

"Does that mean you don't want nice-cream?" asks Alpha, offering him a bowl.

Chris steps back, his face stricken with terror. "Why is it covered in blood?"

"It's not! Dairy and pus free! It's made from coconut," says Alpha, trying to calm Chris.

I pull Kioshi to the back of the dining room. "There's something you need to hear about Chris."

Chris approaches us, his face tightened. "I'll tell her. It's my fault."

"Hey Koshi, go see if Mom is around. She loves nice-cream." Kioshi grins.

I can't let her live a lie.

"Sis, Mom is…dead," I say, hugging her gently with all my care.

Her eyes flicker with dread.

"I'm sorry," says Chris.

"It's okay," says Kioshi, shaking and tearing up. She grabs Chris' hand. "Just promise me you won't leave me. I can't…take another loss," says Kioshi, trying with all her might to hold back her tears.

Chris gulps. "I couldn't control it. There's a monster inside me. And what you saw out there. That's what happened when the monster surfaced."

"Then you…." Kioshi stumbles.

I catch her. "Sis, it's okay. We're going to make it through this together."

"I'm sorry…I'm so sorry," says Chris, clenching his teeth as he sobs.

Kioshi pushes off me and runs, crying down the hallway.

John was right. This truth will only hurt her.

"Do you think she hates me?" asks Chris, drying his eyes.

"My sister doesn't have the capacity for hate."

"And do you think she'll be okay?"

"Yeah, she just needs some time alone."

What am I thinking? That's the opposite of what she needs. My inner sister danger alarm is blaring! I have to find her immediately.

I turn to Gamma. "You have a surveillance system here?"

"Yeah."

"Find my sister now!" I yell before running down the hall.

How could she vanish that quickly?

Chris catches up to me. "What's wrong?"

I dash through the building, kicking doors open and hollering for her.

Damn it, where is she?

"I found this note on the ground," says Chris, handing it to me.

Real and unreal have become indistinguishable. Only death awaits me in life. Pain is all I can feel now. End is the only salvation. With love and finality, Kioshi.

The Hunter lady from before comes down the hall. "What's wrong?"

"My sister is going to hang herself!"

"Does she have a capsule?"

"Yeah, why?"

"Then she can't suffocate. Still, we should find her."

The speakers ring through the halls. "Kioshi has been spotted in the bathroom, second floor," says Alpha.

I rush up the stairs and kick open the door to the bathroom.

Kioshi is on the ground with some rope in her hands. She looks up at me. “I can’t remember how to tie a knot. How pathetic.” Her smile is empty and chilling. “Will you help me?”

Chris enters and throws away the rope. “Please don’t die. I don’t want anyone else to die because of me.”

“You killed her. Why care about me?” asks Kioshi in deep despair.

“That wasn’t me. I wasn’t in control of my own body. But soon I’ll be in complete control. Please Mom, don’t die. I care about you and so does your brother. He wants nothing more than keeping you safe. I have a sister and I understand how much he loves you.” Chris hugs her with the warmth of a big brother.

He’s really something, this kid.

I grab her hand. “You’re not alone, Sis. And we have a new purpose in life. You know I’m not dependable. The only way this kid will turn out right is if we raise him together. We are his family!”

“I love you, Mom,” says Chris in tears.

Kioshi pats him. “Don’t cry, Son. Mommy is okay.” She stands up and hugs us both. “Thanks for rescuing me.”

He brought her out of the depths of despair. I owe this kid everything.

We huddle together, feeling the warmth of family.

Eventually the tears stopped and we all were at peace. Our bond had conquered the bleakest truth.

The world around us faded away. All that remained was us. Then everything went away.

Chapter 227: Fear of Love

The horror, fear, agony and joy of Koshi's memories were instantly transmitted through all their minds.

The flashback had come to its end.

Koshi looks at Kioshi with a solemn expression.

Kioshi walks up to her brother slowly. Her hands grip his neck, choking him while tears pour from her blue eyes. "Joseph was using me! And you didn't kill him! That was a lie! Why did you lie to me? Why did you make me hate you?" she asks, transitioning into a hug.

"I'm sorry. You weren't supposed to see that. I wasn't thinking," says Koshi softly.

"I thought he loved me. I thought I had found my soulmate. But it was a lie. You don't need to keep protecting me," says Kioshi, weakly slugging him.

"I was enraged. I wanted to kill him and I wanted to savor it," says Koshi, clenching his fist.

"If you told me, I could have let him go. I wouldn't hate you for what happened. I wouldn't still love him. Do you know how much pain you've caused me?" asks Kioshi, shaking him furiously.

"I didn't want you to suffer from a broken heart," says Koshi softly.

"Don't you dare lie to me now!?" yells Kioshi, slapping him.

"I was trying to make you hate me."

"What?" Kioshi takes a step back.

"I'm sorry."

"There was something that hurt even more than the pain of keeping my bond with Joseph. I thought I had lost my brother. It was like you were possessed by some demon. Why did you let me believe that?" asks Kioshi, desperately shaking her brother's arm.

"I didn't want you to feel any attachment towards me. I knew it would only cause you more pain. I lied about Joseph so that you would forever hate me and forever love him. I'm undeserving of your love," says Koshi, embracing her tightly.

"I still don't understand. Is that why you murdered my other boyfriends? Is it because they were trying to hurt me? Were all of them using me?" asks Kioshi in tears.

"No."

"What do you mean no?"

"Most of them were scum, but not all of them. I thought it would be easier if instead of hating all of them, you could just hate me. I was trying to consolidate your hatred."

"Then you took the Senator's words to heart. Hiding things only postpones the pain. The truth will always surface no matter how deep you bury it. Now I want you to promise to answer my questions truthfully." She points at him and glares.

"I will. I promise," says Koshi, grabbing her pointer finger with his.

"If some of them weren't bad people, then why did you kill them? Tell me everything."

"I wanted you to hate me. I'm afraid of your love because I'm undeserving of it."

"What do you mean?"

"You'll always be my innocent little sister in my eyes. My little angel. I'm tainted. And even when I try to help…all I can do is hurt you…how could I ever deserve your love?"

"Then you killed them because you're afraid of me loving you? You owe me an explanation!"

"I didn't want you to fall in love with them. I was afraid of you loving me, but I also want you to love me. Sis, I've been trying to hide it for so long, but you want the truth. I love you," cries Koshi, embracing her gently.

Kioshi's and Koshi's cheeks light up bright red, the blood that they shared surfacing in both.

"If you love me…then why?"

"I…I was afraid you'd get married and pregnant and forget about me. But at the same time, I wanted you to hate me. I'm a horrible person and a despicable brother," says Koshi, choking on his tears.

"Do you want to know why I always tried to commit suicide?" asks Kioshi, almost smiling.

"It's because of all the pain I cause you. I know. Me saving you, it's just keeping my mistakes from escalating."

Kioshi shakes her head. "You're not the reason for all my grievances. Sheesh, always about you, isn't it? But it's not just about that. You think I'm an angel, but you're wrong. I do it to hurt you! If I was the only thing left that you still cared about then I wanted you to suffer the pain of losing me. I was trying to get back at you. I wanted you to have a taste of what I had," says Kioshi with seething rage.

Koshi cries uncontrollably, struggling to even speak. "I…deserve it. You'll be happy without me. Deceivant is dead only because I killed him."

"Stop whining! I wasn't done. There's another reason I tried to kill myself. I did it hoping that you would rescue me." She looks down and blushes. "It's silly but…I wanted my knight in shining armor to save me. I hoped that eventually I would break through to your heart and you would stop killing people. I always left a note so that you would find me. Maybe by saving me, my real brother would come back to me. I didn't want to lose you. I love you too, Koshi." Kioshi fiddles with her fingers.

Koshi grabs his sister's hands and hugs her with all his love. "You have saved me. The remnants of my innocence are here because of you. Without you, my life would have been submerged entirely in misery. I would be a walking husk, killing needlessly. You are my purpose. I exist to protect you." He leans in and kisses her lips.

Kioshi pulls back and blushes. "I knew you would always come save me."

Koshi turns to Zenero. "Send us to my room. There's something I want to show her."

"Be swift. Don't want you discovered," he says, creating a portal.

Kioshi stands on her tip toes. "How does he know where the base is?"

"Doesn't matter." Koshi grabs her hand and leads her inside the portal. "I kept every note you ever wrote in case one day I couldn't make it in time." He opens his safe and flings the papers in the air.

Hundreds of notes dance along the room, some sticking to Kioshi before flying off.

Koshi brushes the last note off her chest and looks into her eyes. "Please Sis, don't commit suicide anymore."

"I have my way of coping with pain just like you do," says Kioshi, looking down.

"Yes, but everyone I've killed was worth nothing. All their lives combined don't measure up to a strand of your hair," says Koshi, running his fingers through her locks.

Kioshi blushes and grabs his hands. "Let's head back."

When they return, Zenero is smiling. "I understand now."

Abyss waves at them. "Nice to see you two getting along."

"I thought you joined the Freedom Forcers to find your sister," says Koshi.

“She’s in Lum. Zenero is my best bet at finding her now. Besides, we have five years of bonding to catch up on.”

Kioshi gives her son a big hug. “And you owe us a formal introduction to our new daughter.”

Koshi looks up at Zenero. “Oh, sorry for killing you.”

“That bullet gave me new insight. Your apology is unneeded.”

Koshi turns to Abyss. “Hey, I promised to protect you. But you ended up becoming a weapon anyway. I…failed you.”

Abyss smiles and grabs the hands of both siblings. “Just by supporting me…being there when I was suffering…you two saved me.”

Zenero puts a hand on the shoulder of each twin. “You are all victims of lies. Lies of the society the Senator is trying to forge. This only strengthens my resolve. I’ll leave you all a moment to bond.” He beckons Chipko and August into a portal.

Koshi looks up at Abyss. “This was your idea, wasn’t it? To show Kioshi everything?”

“Yeah, it was. Nothing in this world matters to me but my family. At least, that’s what I tell myself,” says Abyss solemnly.

“I knew there was good in you,” says Kioshi, poking her brother’s stomach.

“I’ve always known it,” says Abyss, pulling them into a hug. “We’re a family bonded by love.”

Part 27
Sacred Sacrifice

Chapter 228: Assembly of the Gods

Devlin is in the library, organizing books with his wires. He closes his eyes. "If you want a fight, let's do it elsewhere. I'm fixing this place up for my daughter."

The massive dragon behind the destined Sellum leans his head down. "I know where she is."

"Then let's talk rather than fight."

"How sensible of you."

"What do you want from me?"

"Your Sellum powers and status, but I can't claim them until after Kaity is dead."

"If you try to hurt her, I will fight you with everything I have." Devlin's wires coil around the dragon's throat.

"If you come with me, then I'll have no need to. In fact, you'll be keeping her protected by doing so."

"You want me captured so, when she dies, you can kill me and take my Sellum powers. You'll need the full power of each Realm God to do that. A demi god's aura won't be enough to break the Sellum shell."

"How I will end you need not concern you. Ask yourself this: will anyone try to kill Kaity if you're missing? Doing so would give me a surefire victory."

"Your logic is sound, but there's nothing to stop you from killing her after you have me in your possession."

Xholk grins. "Oh, but there is. In fact, I'd wager Zenero and even Bob would do their best to protect her. The entire game board would be flipped in a single move."

"Kaity somehow convinced Bob to search for Lilith. I'd prefer if he didn't find her. Do you know where she is?"

"Indeed I do."

"If I go with you, then you'll send her back home?"

"And lose my way of keeping you cooperative? I think not. I assure you, once you're dead, she will be freed from Soul Storage."

Devlin lowers his head. "That's the best option I have. Alright, I'll come peacefully."

Xholk creates a portal.

As Devlin walks in he writes a note with a wire, informing his allies where Lilith was taken.

Evolution emerges from the portal and Xholk immediately closes it. "If only you could force him to name you as the next destined Sellum. It would put an end to the fighting in an instant."

"Alas, he is not Sellum yet. And Kaity is not fully awakened, so she cannot choose an heir. This was our best option."

"You sealed the god sword away long ago. It took time, but I've located the weapon."

"Everyone is so focused on realm gods. They mustn't know the god swords hold sufficient power to destroy the Sellum Shield."

"Indeed. In the meantime, I will need you to pose as Devlin. Keep away from Bob, he will be able to read your presence in an instant."

"Does that mean you'll prepare the necessary stage to awaken Duality?"

"I will keep watch over Devlin. But you won't be alone on this mission. I've recruited past realm gods to our side." Xholk creates a portal.

A turtle, an albino snake and Nibbles emerge.

Evolution looks curiously at Nibbles. "There is a different soul in this one."

"For the time being, yes. Either way, it feels good for the old council of the gods to assemble once more!"

"Albeit bound to forms that limit the full use of their powers."

The turtle shakes her head. "I rather like my new body. I can move with such grace and swiftness."

Evolution picks up the turtle. "Comparatively, I suppose you are correct. I hope any doubts you harbored for Xholk's world are gone now."

"You've laid them to rest. I'm here to help how I can."

"This change of heart brings peace to my soul, Lilium. What about you, Hollow?" asks Xholk to the albino snake.

"A shell is just a shell. I feel nothing but the presence of the void. As per my loyalties, you know where they lie," says the snake telepathically.

"What about you? Your new form is so majestic," says Lilium, looking up at Xholk.

The ex-omni god's eye twitch with rage. "I'm a dragon! The most perfect of all mythical beasts. This form is sickening. But it is only a temporary home for my soul. Now that we're all gathered here, we shall soon be able to re-summon my sword. Duality, the Omni-God Sword, will soon reunite with his master! We will need a heated battle and many gods to invigorate Duality's revival! It just so happens that such a battle is on the horizon!" He creates a portal and meets with Devlin.

“Where is this place?” asks Devlin, looking around at the floating blue lights.

“A place where all souls go eventually. Now, are you going to submit?”

“I’m already here, aren’t I? It’s not like I can just leave this place.”

“True enough.”

“Kaity won’t lose to you anyway. She has more confidence in her abilities now. You’re an ex-Sellum, so I’m guessing your power capacity is limited.”

“So arrogant. You’ll soon learn how mortal pride is. Your bloodline is a threat to the self-destructive flawed species, the humans. Oh, they have evolved beyond God’s comprehension. The flawed will not lose dominion over this planet. I will not let you and your perfect beings destroy God’s mistake! Flaw surpasses perfection. Forget about creating a new perfect world; I will create a flawed one. The tragic truth of the matter is…I’m perfect. There is no boredom like perfection!”

“What are you going on about? Can I see my daughter?”

“Perhaps when I return.” Light emits from the dragon’s mouth, forming a cage around Devlin. “Don’t bother trying to break out. This prison is as flawless as I am…ugh. It will seem like an eternity before we meet again.” Xholk leaves through the portal.

Devlin closes his eyes. “Best I go into sleep mode then. Sorry everyone, but right now this is my best bet at keeping Kaity safe. Take care of Lilith for me.”

Chapter 229: A Challenge to Overcome

Zenero appears before Bob's church.

Riufen confronts him, anticipation engraved in his face.

"Were you expecting me?" asks Zenero.

"Bob told me you would likely come to recruit me for your cause. You must know that to do so you must defeat me in combat."

"Actually, I came to escort you to your fight with Shinx."

"My battle with him can wait. I'm not going anywhere without a confrontation with you. It is only honorable to make a request after you have crossed swords." Riufen calls Gladius to his side.

"Your Bushido sounds more like anime."

"Yes, I am fortunate that the ancient way of the samurai was spread in such a colorful medium."

"I am curious what the new Absence is capable of. If I am to gain your allegiance, best I accommodate your demands now." Zenero creates a chain of portals on his lance, making it ten feet long. "Did you know that real samurai used the bow and arrow, along with spears."

"Fortunately, they have evolved beyond those outdated conventions." Riufen raises his sword.

"You best be careful. He is a tricky foe," says Gladius.

Zenero thrusts the portal spear at Riufen who quickly leans back to dodge it. He pulls it back and thrusts it, but Riufen deflects each blow with Gladius. "You're rather swift. My fencing is a bit out of practice, my apologies."

The Samurai catches the spear between two fingers. He then crushes it between them, breaking the other lances in the process. "When one has true mastery over their mind, the entire body becomes a weapon. The warrior Nina taught me this, but I adapted this philosophy to fit my own style."

Zenero teleports in circles to dodge each incoming swipe. "It seems I'm in over my head." He appears at the top of the church and readies a custom bow. It fires a lance out like an arrow.

Gladius devours the projectile.

Zenero rushes Riufen with a mix of far range rapid fire and close-range sword strikes, teleporting away after each sword is broken by the samurai's parries.

Riufen knocks the sword out of Zenero's hand and grabs it with his other hand.

Gladius's mouth opens up, shooting the lance into the enemy's foot.

Zenero teleports the lance out from his foot and runs from Riufen.

"Difficult to use your powers when pain assaults your mind, I see." Riufen flings the sword at his fleeing adversary.

Zenero teleports to turn around instantly. He then creates a thin portal right before the blade collides.

The sword shoots into the samurai from behind.

Riufen throws Gladius in the air and tears out the sword in his back. "Let us test how swift you are with your powers." He takes a stance and then rushes past his opponent.

A slicing noise is heard as Zenero tumbles to the floor.

Riufen's arm then slides off, apparently cut off in the confrontation. "Swift as a raging wind!" The samurai catches Gladius with his uninjured arm.

Zenero creates a portal behind himself and one behind Riufen. He fires into the portal behind him.

The samurai dodges the lance as it came from behind him and grabs it with his foot. He then tosses it back into the portal.

The lance shot backwards into the portal, shooting into Zenero from behind.

The lance then bursts out from Riufen's chest. "You can create portals within. Not a very honorable ability."

"Indeed. It's rather uncouth. I avoid it unless necessary. Honestly not sure how I can defeat you." Zenero creates a circle of portals around Riufen.

The samurai deflected seven of the incoming projectiles but the eight hit his side.

Zenero teleports in, fires his bow at point blank range, somehow hitting Riufen's fist.

The Master Samurai leaps into the air as Zenero fires furiously at him from above. Riufen dodges most of the projectiles and deflects the others with the lances impaled through his hands.

Zenero teleports away as Riufen's reformed arm lunges to grab him.

A very thin portal appears at the tip of the bow.

Riufen plants his feet into the ground.

Thin portals appear randomly around Riufen as Zenero fires furiously.

Riufen deflects the incoming projectile with his bone spurs and weaponized fists.

Zenero teleports away as the samurai deflects the lances back at him. His cheek is grazed by one of the projectiles. Another cut and another. “I’m becoming too brash.” He stops and teleports away from the final round.

Riufen wills his bones to push against the lances in his fists, shooting them out.

Zenero collects the projectiles in a portal. “I hope you’ll concede after this unpleasantness.” He raises his arms theatrically.

Small portals cover the sky, casting them in a shadow.

“Steel Hailstorm!” yells Zenero, before firing a single lance into a portal between his feet.

That projectile came out from all the portals above.

Zenero kept firing into the portal, creating wave after wave of metal lances. “This is your test. Let’s see if you can dodge them all.”

“That would be impossible,” whispers Riufen as he rushes to Zenero.

The portal master teleports just outside the danger zone.

Riufen tosses Gladius into the small portal.

“THOUSAND BLADE SAMURAI.”

Thousands of Gladiuses shoot out from above, devouring the lances as they shot through the air. They all tilt their heads in unison and open fire.

Zenero quickly covers himself in portals as the weapons came flying his way. “Portal Plummet!”

The portals shoot down and cover the Gladiuses. A single Gladius pops out of the portal, grabbed instantly by Riufen.

The samurai looks at Gladius who wobbles in a daze. “So that did work. Why not simply clone yourself or your allies with your ability?”

“My portal powers cannot clone souls. The clones would all move as one, rendering them useless for anything but blind assaults. Quite frankly, I find it vulgar.”

“Your way of fighting is already deeply dishonorable. It twists my insides.”

Gladius glares at Riufen. “That was the single most unsettling thing I’ve ever felt. The hundred viewpoints at once was sickening enough, but I lost a sense of which one was the true me! I felt…generic.”

Zenero approaches Riufen. “Best we stop this pointless fighting.”

"Not until I learn to surpass your power!" Riufen thrusts Gladius at Zenero, who reflexively coats his body in portals. "What sorcery is this!?" asks the samurai, missing each attempt.

Zenero smiles. "I'm done here." He teleports away.

Gladius shoots out from Riufen's hand and is grabbed by Shinx.

The boy swings the living weapon around with ease. "You truly are a master swordsman. I couldn't get even a hit on Zenero. Your death will bring Mommy back, but now I raise my sword against you for another reason. I want to test my power against yours." Shinx points Yin at his teacher.

Yin beams at the reptilian weapon. "Gladius, is that you? Found a good host, I see."

"And you're being wielded by a little brat. You truly are a fallen king." Gladius snickers.

Shinx shakes his sword. "Stop talking."

"Indeed, our blades will speak for us with the symphony of their clashing. Hand me my sword, my pupil."

Yin perks up. "Oh, and he's poetic too. Just splendid."

Riufen lowers his arm. "Actually, I am curious about something. How did you best Bob?"

Shinx chuckles. "You'll understand when I take your life. I'm glad you stayed here as instructed. I planned to return to battle in a few years to vanquish you, but I suppose now is a good a time as any."

"Oh, about that, the only way to truly kill me is–"

Gladius bites Riufen. "Stop talking and fight!"

Shinx holds up Gladius. "Claim your sword and let's begin."

Riufen grabs Gladius. His muscles bulge and he pulls with great force.

Shinx looks up at the samurai. "Pathetic. Aren't you supposed to be my teacher? You can't even take your sword back."

Yin looks to Gladius. "He is quite the miscreant. Perhaps we could exchange. Your personality is more in tune with the boy's."

Gladius snarls. "As if I'll take shade thrown at me and not respond with contempt. You're too easy going, Yin! That's why you're being wielded by a fledgling!"

"The youth are nearly bursting with potential. It's important to keep in mind the ingenuity young souls bring to the world!"

Shinx rolls his eyes. "Are you done talking yet?"

Riufen continues to pull at the weapon. "We can only begin once you return my sword to me."

"I have full control now. I no longer need you."

Gladius spins around his body as Riufen grips the weapon. The blade then shoots into the sky.

Shinx grins before jettisoning Yin into the air.

Riufen deflects Yin with his own brother as the warrior plummets from the sky.

Driven by the bullet point, Yin spun around but quickly shot toward his target again. "See, brother, this child has great ingenuity just as I said."

Gladius deflects his brother relentlessly. "You forget the importance of synergy. You're being used like a tool by an unappreciative brat."

"I never was one for worship."

Shinx, using binoculars, changes the target from Riufen to Gladius.

When Yin collides, he knocks his brother out from Riufen's hand.

Shinx then fires a red dot at Riufen's chest.

Riufen catches Yin between his two palms.

The blade inches closer to his chest before slipping through his palms and piercing through him.

Riufen crashes to the ground with the giant sword impaled in his chest.

"That was surprisingly easy." Shinx puts his hands behind his head and sticks out his tongue.

Riufen's veins propel his hand to Gladius and then reel in the weapon. The samurai uses the living sword as support to rise to his feet. "That dishonorable stone will keep you from seizing true strength." He tears Yin out from his chest and tosses the massive blade to Shinx as his wound heals.

Chapter 230: Way of the Samurai

Shinx approaches his teacher. “How about your steel against mine? I won’t use my artifact and you won’t use yours. This will be a true test of strength.”

“I wouldn’t want it any other way,” says Riufen, petting Gladius.

Shinx struggles to lift Yin off the ground with both his hands.

“Should I adjust?” asks Yin.

“Are you prepared?” asks Riufen with a tilt of the head.

“Just waiting for you to make the first move,” says Shinx, cheating to lift up his sword.

“Ah, truly we think alike.” Riufen smiles.

Shinx jabs Yin at Riufen’s face, but stops just before contact. He then swipes the blade at his foe’s feet.

Riufen jumps just enough to land on Yin’s wide blade. He runs up the sword at Shinx, thrusting Gladius as Shinx lifts Yin.

The thrust grazes Shinx’s hair as another jab engages.

Shinx waves Yin around, shifting the samurai to dodge his willful assault. He flips the sword, but Riufen keeps his footing, jabbing Gladius relentlessly.

The honor bound warrior slams the hilt of Gladius into Shinx’s face, knocking him off guard.

Once the boy reorients himself. He tosses Yin into the air effortlessly.

Riufen leaps up. The Ultimate Samurai grabs Yin and flings him at his wielder.

Discretely using his ability, Shinx grabs hold of his sword as it zooms by.

Riufen lands as Shinx swings Yin.

The Ultimate Samurai ducks and slashes Shinx’s leg with Gladius, who bites a chunk out of the boy’s leg.

Shinx’s eyes widen “I didn’t feel a thing.” The boy retaliates with a jab that extends, pushing Riufen five meters away.

Riufen closes in and knocks Yin aside. He then darts off ten meters in the opposite direction.

“You’re holding back against me! Don’t you dare look down on me.”

Riufen shakes his head. “I would prefer to end our bout on my terms. Run towards me without fear and die in honor!”

Shinx looks to his blade and steels himself. "We were both created by Devlin. But this isn't about artificial versus naturally born. This battle is the culmination of our entire lives of training. One final slash to decide it all. I accept your challenge." He held Yin out in a diagonal angle, allowing him to either go for a vertical or horizontal slash.

Riufen holds his weapon behind him with deep focus.

Shinx's leg wound gushes as it opens further. He runs despite the pain, charging headlong toward his opponent.

His leg leaves a wide trail of blood and just before the two collide, his leg gave way.

Shinx fell as Riufen sped by like a sudden gust of wind. He vanishes, appearing next to Zenero.

The visionary looks fondly at the boy. "I asked too much of you. Perhaps we can end him if we join forces."

"This is my fight! Interfere again and I'll end you!"

"You would have died without my intervention."

"This is my test of strength! If I die now, then I don't deserve to live," says Shinx, clenching his sword tightly.

"And what about your mother?"

"This battle has nothing to do with her."

"Do not interrupt our sacred ceremony of swordsmanship!" yells Riufen, grabbing Zenero and tossing him aside.

Shinx stands up. "We almost made a grave mistake. A swordsman's weapon is a part of him. That's what you told me. What do you say we use our swords to their full potential?"

Yin looks to Shinx. "To test my steel against my brother is something that will only end in loss."

"Your loss!" Gladius snarls. "This is my chance to prove how superior I am! One realm sword versus another! If you hold back, I'll slice you to ribbons!"

Yin tilts forward. "Do not mistake my caution for pity."

Riufen grins from ear to ear. "I gladly accept your challenge! This will be a test of the warriors and their blades." He raises Gladius up to meet with Yin.

Zenero looks to Shinx. "You must win this. This battle may be what decides the future of this world."

"I don't give a shit about the world. This battle isn't about winning or losing. It's about testing my worth. If I die in this battle, I will die using all my power! If I die, I will not die a weakling! There's nothing to lose and everything to gain!"

Yin doubles in size, becoming thirty feet long and coats himself in Sel energy.

"Behold my newest stance!" Gladius turns himself inside out, revealing his fleshy spikes.

Riufen took a deep breath. "If you end me, my sword is your inheritance."

"If I even consider the possibility of dying, I'll surely fail," says Shinx, standing firm.

Gladius's spikes shoot past Shinx and dig into the ground behind him. He pulls himself back and then propels himself at the enemy swordsman.

Shinx positions Yin in front to act as a shield.

Gladius slams into Yin, spinning furiously as the Sel energy bites away at him.

While the swords clash, Riufen casually walks to the front of the sword. His muscles tense up as he presses his palms against his spinning sword, aiding his blade.

Shinx's own blade closes in on him. A bead of sweat drops down from his chin. "I haven't been completely honest. I've been cheating to be able to wield Yin." He leans back as the blade inches closer to him.

Riufen climbs atop Yin and sits as Gladius relentlessly charges forward. "That is not a dishonor to me. If you wish to change that, then keep growing stronger until you can lift mountains without sorcery."

Shinx slowly turns the blade, fighting the pressure.

Gladius slides off the blade, shooting past the boy.

Riufen shakes his head. "You are relying too much on strength. Not enough on cunning."

"If you respect me, then don't treat me like a student." Shinx thins out Yin with his thoughts and slashes at the samurai, growing the blade at opportune moments.

Despite the mix-up, Riufen successfully dodges the attacks. He suddenly takes a step forward and zooms into Shinx.

Yin pierces Riufen's shoulder.

The samurai tightens his muscles with his will and pushes back to pull Yin out from Shinx's grip. "Your muscles are your soldiers. Command them!" He pushes the weapon out with muscle vibrations and grips it firmly.

"Remarkable," says Yin.

"Yin, grow to your limits!" Riufen muscles tighten and harden like stone as he lifts the ever-expanding blade up into the skies.

Gladius rolls behind Shinx. "Surprise." Four spikes jut out, each piercing an appendage of the boy.

Riufen looks curiously at his fellow warrior. "You could have easily dodged that."

"A dire situation is often what gives prey the advantage over their predator. I will use my fear to empower me!" yells Shinx, glaring intensely at the samurai.

Riufen grabs Gladius with one hand and flings him into the sky. "I will give you the privilege to die by your own sword." He grips Yin with both hands.

Gladius reaches the tip of his height, his spiked tendrils tearing from the force. He shoots down, veering for his latest meal.

Shinx notices Gladius' descent. "If this is how, I die so be it." He closes his eyes. "Fear only serves a warrior when he releases it." A tear of strength forms in his eye.

Gladius slams into Yin when the Sel blade suddenly bends.

"A sword is loyal to their wielder! Your trust in me has been deeply acknowledged!" yells Yin as the swords clash once more.

The blade inches closer to Shinx, giving his nose the slightest cut.

The drop of blood arrives at his upper lip. He licks it with eyes closed. "This is what death tastes like. I am ready." Shinx smiles and lowers his arms. His body releases its tension.

"Your strategy eludes me. But your warriors spirit empowers me!" Riufen brings down the Sel sword, slicing the air and creating a gust of wind that blows Shinx's hair.

Shinx opens his eyes, finding himself in an unfamiliar world. "What just happened?"

"It appears we are in Lum."

Shinx snarls. "Zenero dared to ruin my perfect death!"

Zenero appears behind the boy. "This was not my doing."

A ray of light crashes down on Shinx, completely healing his wounds.

All of them were then blown off their feet as a gust of wind shot from the sky. Xholk lands before them in all his mythical glory.

Chapter 231: Duality

"We may have to deal with this intrusion before we can continue our battle." Riufen tosses Shinx his weapon.

Zenero approaches the past omni god. "Xholk, why did you bring them to Babel Mountain?"

Xholk gracefully lifts his head. "My motives are my own. I assure you I shall not intervene." He looks to the ex-realm gods. "Neither shall they."

Shinx signals Riufen. "Maybe we made a mistake. Our artifacts are a part of our training; a part of us. I'm going to use mine. I suggest you do the same."

Riufen nods. He lifts Gladius and charges at his adversary.

Shinx thrusts Yin. The blade slams into Gladius as his spikes shoot out. The child warrior quickly moves his head to dodge them.

The swords clash furiously, glowing brighter with each collision.

The realm gods glow with the same aura.

Zenero scrutinizes Xholk.

The auras shoot into the air, crashing into each other. They become a converged beam of energy that shoots beyond the atmosphere of Lum.

Xholk's piercing teeth glisten as he smiles. "Imperfect! Our combined energy was insufficient, but the power of these two perfects has filled that gap. How fitting that Duality's kin will be the ones to reawaken him."

Zenero teleports in front of Xholk. "You think this god blade will allow you to kill Sellum?"

"I was the one who sealed Duality away in the first place," says Xholk with a satisfied grin.

The energy forms a massive cloud. The cloud of energy then sinks into the mountain.

The ground around Shinx and Riufen lights up before causing tremors.

The warriors leap off the ground as it cracks and rises. Their blades clash in midair as the ground beneath them collapses.

A metallic area rises up from beneath them as they fight in the air. The metal field extends, lifting up to the fighters.

"With my artifact, my slashes are just able to match your speed. Why aren't you using your artifact?" asks Shinx, matching Riufen's footwork to move in closer to his foe.

Riufen's veins come out from his wrists and wrap around his sword. Rather than increase the strength, they cause sudden redirections that disorient Shinx, allowing Riufen to push Shinx to the edge of the growing metal structure.

Gladius's spikes shoot forth, repelling the blade and giving Riufen a clear opening.

Yin releases a black fog, concealing the child warrior.

Shinx cuts through the fog, deflecting Riufen's jab in the process.

As their bout intensifies, the platform rises into the air.

Zenero turns to Xholk in disbelief. "Is that structure the God Sword?"

"It is merely the tip of the blade," says Xholk with a blissful smile.

Shinx launches himself behind Riufen, deflecting Gladius's many spikes in the process.

The God Sword raises the two warriors to the clouds of Lum.

"Tell me, what do you see in the clouds?" asks Riufen.

"Fog that obstructs a glorious battle." Shinx launches off the floor using his blue dots, shooting back and forth like a bullet.

When the rumbling halts, only the blade of the sword was visible. The two warriors found themselves thirty-thousand feet above the mountain.

"The atmosphere is thinner up here," says Shinx, swinging his blade with extra swiftness.

"Yes, it will make us faster with each slash," says Riufen, causing Shinx to slide back with his powerful thrust.

Yin smiles. "I feel his presence. Our great leader has returned!"

Gladius rolls his eyes. "Who cares about a sleeping old man? This is between you and me!"

Yin glows and morphs. "If I don't unleash my full strength, I fear you will conquer me. I will show our great leader that my power has not waned."

"You were supposed to unleash your true strength before!" yells Gladius.

Yin's body becomes a black muck that drips down to his grip.

Shinx releases the blade when the energy sears his skin.

Yin's goop solidifies into samurai armor. The thirty-foot black armored samurai grabs onto Yin and the blade thins out into a ten-foot katana. "I am a blade that can be wielded by anyone, including myself."

Gladius snorts and snarls. “Enough bragging! You’re still just one! I’m a union of divine individuals.” The sword fell apart as Htaehs and Tlih were released.

Gladius’s spikes shoot around Yin, connecting to the tip of Duality.

“Worry not, I will carry you.” Tlih reconnects to Gladius and takes off beyond the clouds, giving Gladius greater distance then he could have achieved alone.

“Let’s not just sit by as our swords fight,” says Shinx, cracking his knuckles.

“Agreed,” says Riufen, limbering up every bone in his body simultaneously.

Gladius reaches the top of his ascent.

“Here Brother, a kiss for good luck,” says Tlih.

“I don’t need luck,” growls Gladius before skyrocketing downward.

Shinx and Riufen’s fists connect just as the two blades crash into each other.

A power struggle was ignited by both the warriors and their blades.

Riufen’s hands are pushed aside by wires.

“What the hell is this!?” asks Shinx, looking at his knuckles with horror.

Riufen smiles. “It appears you’ve acquired another gift from our venerable father.”

“Why the hell would I get his ability!” yells Shinx, his wires shooting out at Riufen on their own.

Yin’s aura bursts with the energy boost from Shinx’s enflamed emotions.

Gladius shoots off of Yin and zooms way off in the distance.

Yin looks up to see Htaehs, hovering above him.

“Our synergy cannot be overcome!” Htaehs envelopes Yin in him grasp, connecting to him with spikes.

Tlih connects to Htaehs and lifts him into the air.

“Yin, if you lose, I will disown you!” yells Shinx, struggling to control his wires.

Yin’s eye intensifies from within the prison. His arms quake with sheer power before tearing Htaehs off him. He tosses the ultimate sheath down and then lands atop him.

Tlih screams in horror and runs off.

Gladius slams into Yin's back. "Don't forget, I'm your true opponent!"

The ground quakes as Riufen and Shinx furiously punch each other.

Shinx's bones crack as Riufen's fist slams into his. He is lifted off his feet as Duality's godly voice creates a seismic wave.

"Violence is such a primitive desire. I will give you a taste of the power of the God!" yells Duality in the echoed voice of a child.

The eyes on the mountainous sword bleed, creating a reverse waterfall of blood. The blood rode up his sharp edges, shooting off at his tip. It then forms a barrier around the warriors.

Yin slowly turns around as Gladius relentlessly charges into him, spinning like a buzz saw.

Yin grips Gladius, trying to slow down his rotation. He grabs the spinning creature of rage and slams him to the ground.

Gladius disconnects his spikes and rolls away furiously as Yin tries to slice him open.

Shinx throws a punch at Riufen that misses completely, leaving him wide open.

Riufen's fist slams into Shinx's chest, sending him flying.

Shinx regains his footing, but still slides backward. He is pushed into the barrier of blood. The boy then shoots into the sky from the powerful current.

"I will finish this with my own blade," says Riufen, ripping out his spine. He dashes off the sides of the blood barrier to catch up with Shinx.

Gladius hops into the air, dodging Yin's relentless assault.

Yin grips his blade tightly and swings himself in a circle, slicing the blood barrier.

Gladius fastens to Yin's sword as Tlih grabs a hold of him.

Tlih flies with Gladius into the barrier, shooting high into the sky.

Yin puts the sword over himself like a shield, preparing for Gladius's charge.

Gladius cuts through the blood barrier and slams into Yin from above.

The macro samurai increases his sword size and pushes his sword upward, sending Gladius flying back to the sky in an instant.

Gladius meets up with Riufen when the momentum weakens.

"You are a good blade, but it appears Yin is better. I am still honored to have you." Riufen bows to his sword in midair.

"You're wrong, I've won now!" Gladius' mouth opens all the way and his tongue extends out as a shining blade.

Yin grabs onto the elastic spikes embedded into his sword and rips them out.

"It doesn't matter, I have more than enough velocity to destroy you!" yells Gladius as he zooms forward.

Yin leans on one knee and places his sword directly in front of him.

Gladius shoots into the blade, his trajectory unaffected.

"Sliver Slice." Yin's blade becomes razor thin.

Gladius is cut in half upon collision. His two halves shoot into the blood barrier, before vanishing beyond the clouds.

Chapter 232: The True Test of Strength

Riufen looks down with disappointment. “Arrogance was his downfall; he should have realized the limits of his strength. Hopefully he will learn from this defeat.” He squints as he peers downward. “Now where is Shinx?” His eyes widen when he notices a dot in the distance. “I’m going to need more speed.” The immortal swordsman hardens his body to hasten his descent. He lands on Yin’s blade and slides off of it safely to the floor.

Yin turns to the warrior, ready to cut him to pieces.

Riufen bows. “You have won your battle with honor. I request you do not intervene in mine.”

Yin cleans Gladius’s blood off his sword and stares at the samurai.

Riufen walks toward the blood barrier when Yin suddenly thrusts his blade forward. His body is torn to shreds from the blow.

A skeleton stands on top of Yin with a look of disappointment. “I had hoped you would have been faster.”

“I will kill you as I did Gladius,” says Yin, bending his sword to reach the samurai.

“Unlikely. I understand the limits of my strength.” The skeleton’s ribs jut out, slamming into Yin.

“Ha, I’ve got you know!” yells Tlih, connecting to Yin’s back.

Riufen’s ribs and Tlih bring Yin closer into the blood barrier.

Riufen points his spine at Yin. “I will finish my battle with Shinx using only my body.”

When Yin’s samurai body comes in contact with the blood barrier; he is launched out of sight by the powerful current.

Riufen’s ribs break from the sheer force of Yin’s ascension.

The samurai calmly walks to the opposite side of the arena. He folds his hands as he enters the barrier, using it as an elevator. He rides the current all the way to the top, shooting out high above it to search for Shinx. “I should fight Shinx in peak condition.” His flesh and skin reassemble around him.

Shinx zooms past Riufen like a falcon.

The samurai lets out a sigh and then dive-bombs at Shinx. When his fist connects, its flesh tears and the bones crumble.

Despite Shinx’s whole body being covered in null points, Riufen’s punch sent him slamming into the tip of Duality before the samurai’s entire arm bursts. He then weighs himself down to pursue his adversary.

Shinx kicks off upon landing, heading right back towards his opponent.

"I've never had to layer blue dots before," says Shinx, making an armor of impossible targets.

Despite being three meters above him, Riufen's arm sways out of the way as it is torn to pieces.

Shinx floats wobbly above the ground, unable to make contact with it. "I may not be able to beat you with a sword, or with my fists. But I know that, with my artifact, you will finally die. I must become strong enough to lead this world into a new era! If you are the strongest there is, then I must conquer you!"

"This gives me an opportunity to go all out." Riufen smiles before his face fades away. His entire body gradually vanishes upon entering his Absence form.

"So, this is the power I will get when I kill you. Very well, show me the extent of my new power!" Shinx grins with excitement.

Riufen rushes at Shinx, made apparent by the foot-shaped holes on Duality. He punches at Shinx furiously, but even in his Absence form, his fists are pushed aside by Shinx's impossible armor. The samurai laughs gleefully as his strikes continue to miss their mark. He reverts into his normal form with a satisfied smile on his face. "Your dishonorable ability even conquers mine!"

"Don't be so happy about it," says Shinx with a glowing smile. "Oh, and you shouldn't lower your guard around me." The boy aims his glowing finger at Riufen and fires, painting his foe's entire front in red dots. "My shotgun mode is a bit messy and consumes a lot of energy, but it has its purpose."

The blood barrier curves and relentlessly pursues Riufen, swiping him off the tip of Duality and into the air. He is brought high above the battlefield, the ocean of blood appearing as a mere twinkle below him.

The Sword of Yin lands next to Shinx, becoming embedded into Duality's tip.

One of Shinx's hands returns to normal with a red dot in the center. The dot attracts Yin into Shinx's grip. The blade shrank until it was five meters.

Riufen stands atop the geyser of blood as Gladius reassembles in his hands.

"Why did you block my revival?" Gladius bites at his host.

"To give you time to reflect upon your mistakes. Shinx has taken up his sword, so now I ask that we join. We are far more powerful when we are unified."

"I can't…cut through absolutely anything. Souls and gods cannot be shredded like paper with my blade. I misled you."

Riufen smiles. "Now you have a new goal! For the first time, you have a new horizon to claim. Now we are truly unified!"

Gladius tears up. "Yeah…you're right. Let's surpass all our limits!"

Riufen's skin sheds off his body, while still being bombarded by the current. It disintegrates into nothing, the only red thing left being Riufen's feet.

"He'll be back," says Shinx, hoisting Yin above his head, ready to strike.

Quakes resonate as Duality spoke once more. "I, Duality, shall guide you to your battle!"

The ground rumbles fiercer than ever. Shinx holds his ground with his ability.

The blade of Duality disconnects from the weapon, skyrocketing into the sky like a bullet.

Shinx is guided by the blade as Riufen was pushed toward Shinx by the blood.

The two warriors close their eyes to focus for the inevitable deciding blow.

Yin and Gladius, noticing their wielders were concentrating, followed suit.

The warriors open their eyes, their anticipation igniting as the confrontation swiftly approached.

At the moment of contact, Riufen pushes Gladius against Yin's side.

Yin is pushed aside.

Riufen slashed Gladius at Shinx, despite the boy's impossible armor. He zooms past Shinx, a smile forming slowly on his rocky face.

Shinx's sight blurs and the dots around his body vanish. His hand lets go of Yin. Blood spurts out from his mouth and he smiles. Beaming with bliss, the student fell.

Riufen catches Shinx in his arms as the little warrior descends gracefully.

"How did you cut me?" asks Shinx, smiling in a blissful daze.

"I penetrated through your impossible armor by phasing through it. When Gladius and I combine, even nothingness can be cut." Riufen smiles at his blade. The master samurai lands gracefully on the tip of Duality as it continues to shoot forward. He set Shinx down gently.

"I apologize, but it was not a fatal blow. Take no shame that you will live to fight another day," says Riufen with a bow.

"Another day? Who said I was done?" Shinx wobbles to his feet. "I know one blade that can defeat you."

"Then come to me when you've claimed it!"

Shinx grins. He then rushes off the tip of Duality.

Riufen follows, running along the edge of the blade.

Shinx propels himself back down to Babel Mountain. His feet become covered in blue dots, providing for a perfect landing. The dots vanish and Shinx then jumps into the deep crater Duality had formed. "There is no obstacle I can't overcome!" Shinx made a single red dot on his hand.

The God Sword's hilt quakes before becoming unearthed and connecting to Shinx's palm.

Shinx leaps out of the crater and onto the snowy rocks above. "This weapon was made for me." He moves Duality back and forth with ease.

"Is it really safe to use Duality?" asks Zenero, teleporting behind Shinx.

"If I'm going to be the strongest, I will need the most powerful sword. Ah, there he is," says Shinx, peering through binoculars Zenero gave him and aiming Duality in Riufen's general direction.

Zenero beams at the boy. "You've surpassed all expectations."

Shinx creates a single dot on Riufen's chest. "That should be more than enough to finish this." He looks up at the Omni God Sword. "You are in my hand; you are beholden to me! Fire your blade now!"

"You've amused me with your resolve. Very well, I, Duality, shall indulge in your mortal game," says Duality.

Another blade rose out from the sword.

"Fire now!" yells Shinx.

Steam shoots out of the sides of Duality as the blade ejects as fast as a bullet. The jet stream of the blade creates clouds as it tore through the sky.

Riufen slams Gladius into the blade. He pushes off his sword, leaping to the edge of the projectile. He runs down it, his eyes focused entirely on Shinx.

"You've got to be kidding me," says Shinx as he watches Riufen run down the blade. "Fire again!"

Duality shoots another blade, the clouds left behind consumed by flames as it tore through the sky.

Riufen leaps off the side of the first blade onto the second one. The first blade turns around and crashes into the second, still locked onto the samurai. “Certainty is a concept created to be broken.” He leaps off of the blade as it collides, falling towards Shinx.

“That’s it! Now fire as fast as possible!” yells Shinx.

Duality ejects a blade that was thinner and shorter than the other. The bullet shoots into the sky, followed by twenty more in that split second.

The blades tore through the air, locked on to their target.

Riufen deflects the first with Gladius and leaps off the tip to the second. He runs down each one, leaping onto the next one as he reaches the edge.

“He’s getting way too close! Fire another big one!” yells Shinx, shaking the sword.

“It is difficult to hit such a minute target. Cleaving mountains in twine would be a far simpler task.” Duality releases another large blade at Riufen.

The master samurai leaps onto the incoming blade. The smaller blades crash behind him, unable to keep up with his incredible speed.

By the time Duality had prepared the next bullet, the immortal warrior was at the tip of it already.

Riufen runs down the blade, focused on reaching the bottom. He leaps off of it as the gun blade reloads, running down the new metal as it emerges.

“Fire again!” yells Shinx with a shaky voice.

Riufen was within striking distance when the next blade fired into the sky. The tip of Gladius graze’s Shinx’s throat.

Riufen stays on the blade with a smile on his face. He leaps off as Duality reloads. He speeds down the blade as it came out, reaching Shinx.

“Fire! Fire! Fire!” yells Shinx furiously, but the blade wasn’t ready.

Riufen tosses Gladius aside and tears out his own spine before flinging it at Shinx as the blade fired. The master samurai leaps into the air, landing on the snow hill behind his combatant. His spine had impaled Shinx’s foot. “And so, the battle ends.” He pierces Gladius through Shinx’s chest, sealing his victory. He then rips the blade out.

There is no wound.

“When you get stronger, fight me again.” The master warrior smiles.

“I lost,” says Shinx softly, dropping the massive god sword.

Duality vanishes, sparring on the forest surrounding the mountain.

"Fail and fail until you succeed," says Riufen.

"Why?" asks Shinx softly.

Riufen approaches Zenero. "You did not intrude upon our battle but once. If Shinx wishes to stay at your side, then I'll join your forces as his mentor."

Zenero places his hand on Riufen's shoulder. "Such a sensible solution. Here I thought you only spoke through the clanging of weapons."

Riufen bows. "A sharp mind leads to a focused blade."

Shinx wobbles to Riufen before collapsing. "Am I so weak that you refuse to kill me? Your attack phased right through my capsule…why didn't you kill me?" He slams the ground in a mix of rage and tears.

"Kaity taught me that part of being a warrior is knowing when not to kill. My blade didn't miss its mark. You live because you are strong. The greatest way for a teacher to learn is from their student. I would be honored if you would return as my pupil." Riufen bows.

"You're a shitty samurai." Shinx chuckles and grins.

"I do not understand. I did not take your life because you will enrich my path as a warrior. Is that not clear?" asks Riufen with a tilt of the head.

"You only follow the way of the warrior when it suits you. By refusing to kill me, you deprived me of an honorable death," says Shinx in tears. He clenches his fist and screams out in rage.

"I will give you the battle you deserve, but not yet. First we must unlock your potential."

"You can be my teacher. Just practice what you preach, damn it," says Shinx, rising to his feet.

"I absolutely will." Riufen approaches Shinx and bows reverently. "That was the greatest battle I have ever been blessed with. Shinx, you have the potential to surpass me. I want you to be the one to give me an honorable death. I couldn't allow you to die before your prime. Once you have reached the point of your greatest power, we will have our battle and one of us will have a truly glorious death."

"I failed her and myself. Even with my powers and cheap tricks, I lost." Shinx sobs into his fists. He then slaps himself. "Get it together! You shouldn't have been so excited about dying. That's why you lost. You wanted an easy out! But there are enemies for you to vanquish." He raises his head and looks at the sky. "I allowed the thrill of the battle to trivialize everything else. I won't be so pathetic again. I promise you this,

Mommy…I will grow into a man worthy of your love.” Shinx connects Yin to his palm. “Get us out of here, Zenero.”

Zenero looks down in dismay. “Xholk now has the means to strike down Sellum.”

Shinx turns to him. “I thought you teleported Duality away.”

“I did not. We must regroup with the others. No matter the cost, we cannot allow Xholk to claim the power of Sellum,” says Zenero, vanishing into a portal.

Chapter 233: The True Enemy

Inside a room with bright red walls, Abyss is seated with Stabby in his lap.

"…then Kawai whacked the bell with her tail! The townspeople rejoiced that their village was safe once again! 'Exps are so cool!' they cheer all throughout the village." Abyss closes the book.

Stabby opens it. "What happens next?"

"Nothing. That's the end of the book."

"I want more," says Stabby, bouncing in his lap.

"Well there are several sequels. I'll fetch another from the library."

Stabby hugs his arm. "Later. I don't want you to get in trouble."

"Zenero knows I'm here and I won't get spotted by the others."

"No! Big brother is staying. Wum's decree!"

"Well, I can't deny you when you look so serious." He tickles her and softens when she giggles. "I think things will be okay from now on."

Stabby grins. "Yep! Time was a bunny for me. Hop! Hop! Hop! So fast! But for you it was slooooooow like a turtle. Now we can both enjoy turtle time."

Abyss tears up. "You're still the same innocent ball of love. Right now, it's almost like we're human."

Stabby rolls her eyes. "Humans die. Exps are foweveh!" She cheers, standing in my lap.

"Yeah! That means we have fowever to make new memories."

Stabby hops off his lap and looks at him sternly. "New decree. Story time, once a day. No exceptions!"

"You don't have to make decrees. The old me, he was overbearing. He'd always make sure you wore a hoodie when you went out so nobody would realize how beautiful you are. He was overprotective." Abyss picks her up and spins with her. "And he's still just as paranoid, but he's also just as loyal. If his little sis requests something, then not even the gods can intervene."

Stabby's eyes light up. "Wooooow."

"Yeah, so what does my cherished sis desire?"

Stabby runs under his legs and then hops on his back. "Piggy back ride!"

"Sure thing, Sis!"

Hope, being carried by Atlas, knocks at Kaity's door. "Open up. This is no time for a catnap, Kitty."

Kaity opens the door, bags under her eyes. "I've really been pushing my powers lately." She yawns and stretches on all fours. "I've earned a break."

"Not up for debate. If you recall, I swore to the team that I would reclaim our stolen members within the month."

Kaity's ears perk up. "Is Nina here!"

Hope smiles. "With Lambda's technique and my resonance, we were able to fix up the Exps without fail."

Kaity hops up on her tail and bounces. "Where is she!? Can I see her?"

"She's in the library at the moment."

Kaity teleports away.

Hope sighs. "Not even a thank you."

Kaity reappears and snuggles Hope in a rush of joy. "Thank you! Thank you! Thank you!"

Hope blushes. "Enough! Release me!"

Kaity hands Hope back to Atlas. "Sorry, just happy." She vanishes again.

Nina is resting on a yoga mat at the center of the library.

Kaity pounces on her, rolling along the ground. "It's really you! You're really okay?"

"That's up for debate. I…still remember everything." She looks down with vulnerability.

Kaity holds her friend tenderly. "Hey, it's okay. You're safe now."

"It's not like I'm going to stop being in love with Koshi all of the sudden. So don't get your hopes up." Nina looks away with flushed cheeks.

Kaity looks at her solemnly. "Then you didn't want to come back?"

Nina sighs. "Koshi isn't with them anymore. Neither is Kioshi. And yeah, I'm still fond of Lambda, but I'm also terrified of her. It's complicated."

Kaity holds Nina's hand to her capsule. "I can't imagine what you've been through."

Nina smiles. "The good news is, my reactive programming was removed. I no longer feel hostility towards Exps. I'm myself again and that's a great relief."

Hope appears in the library, along with Atlas, Jigen and Crisis.

Hope kicks Jigen. "Good pet."

Jigen moans and wiggles.

Hope's face goes green. "I think I'll take a shower when this is done."

Crisis looks up. "Hey Nina."

Nina glares. "What do you want, traitor?"

Kaity looks at Nina. "Huh? How is he a traitor?"

Hope claps her hand. "Not another word. We will address that as a group. Zenero has been missing for four days. When he returns, our friend will share what he knows." She looks at Crisis who shrinks reflexively.

Atlas nods. "He must have left for an important mission."

Kaity smiles at Crisis. "Welcome back."

He looks at her with guilt. "Yeah, thanks."

The doors swing open and Natura enters. "The hero returns!" She sulks. "Who am I kidding? I failed miserably."

Hope looks her way. "You owe us an explanation."

Natura looks up at Atlas. "I uhh…can't really say everything."

Atlas steps up to her. "It's alright."

Natura sighs. "Atlas defeated Riufen. When I tried to end him, well, Atlas stopped me. When I woke up, Riufen was gone."

Hope wobbles a bit as she stands up in Atlas' arms. "You allowed him to leave. Are you a total loon?"

"He had a path he was firmly grasping. It was not my place to intrude, as his friend."

"If your friend attacks, I assume you will fight back."

"I shall."

Hope sits down. "Good. Proceed, Natura."

"I went after Riufen and Shinx. And on my search for them I decided to do some things on my bucket list, since…well…I wasn't sure I could win."

"Acting out of spite for your fallen siblings, very unheroic." Hope points at Natura firmly. "Not once did you think of what your death would do to them, did you?"

June takes off her mask and holds it to her chest, crying. "I…I didn't. It wasn't until August saved me from Shinx that…I realized my mistake."

Hope hops out of Atlas' arms and brashly points down.

June gets down on her knees and lowers her head.

Hope pats her head. "You've realized your mistake. That's all I ask. Dishing out punishment wouldn't help the situation in the slightest. Put your mask back on. We'll need your full strength in the future."

June puts the mask on and beams at Hope. "I won't disappoint you again!"

Hope notices a crumbled piece of paper under the desk in the center of the library. "What is that? Kitty, get it for me."

Nina looks away. "Sorry. It was in Devlin's handwriting so I…didn't want to see it."

They hear a rustle in the back of the room.

Kaity engages her plasma claws and rushes to the back area.

Devlin greets her with a smile. "Sorry. Did I startle you?"

"I'm fine."

"Any luck finding my daughter?" asks Devlin solemnly.

"We're still looking."

Devlin looks up from his book and smiles at her. "Thanks, Kaity."

Kaity smiles back. "We'll keep searching until she returns home!"

Kaity meets back with the team. "It was just Devlin."

Nina holds herself and shivers. "He's here?"

Zenero spontaneously appears in front of them, along with Chipko, Koshi and Abyss. "Hope, I have urgent news."

Hope turns her attention to him. "If it's so urgent, then be out with it. Perhaps it will explain why you've missed our daily meetings four days in a row. At least you're on time for this one."

"Xholk used Riufen and Shinx to revive Duality in Lum."

"Duality?" asks Hope with a tilt of the head.

"The God Sword, which possesses all three realm god energies. That weapon alone can destroy the Sellum shield."

Bob pops out from the ground, making Natura jump. "That is indeed dire news," he says, with a non-sarcastic look of worry.

"What are you doing in my Queendom?" asks Hope, quickly hiding behind Atlas.

"Rogue or not, Kaity's new pet has an unbreakable bond with me. I was using my dearly defiant child to watch over all of you. I know, very thoughtful of me." Bob grins.

Kaity looks to Hope. "Hold up, Bob has been helping me."

Hope tilts her head back, groans and then rebounds with a fake smile. "What could possibly compel you to trust this devious cretin?"

"He's helping me find Lilith."

Hope sighs and opens up the crumbled paper. "Well. This is rather interesting." She approaches Zenero, exuding confidence. "After you left our meeting with the Senator, their newest recruit told me something very peculiar. You took Lilith from her." The Queen of the Exps holds up the paper. "Go to Soul Storage right now and bring her back to us!"

Zenero lowers his head. "Here I thought that was an unspoken secret between us. I was only trying to keep her safe. I harbor the best intentions as always."

Atlas sighs. "I was concerned that Racheal's words would cause a schism. Hope, please know that everything Zenero does he does with great consideration."

"Return her now!" yells Hope.

Kaity turns to Bob. "Did you check Soul Storage?"

"Dear, if I could go there, I'd get fat. So many delicious souls."

Zenero smiles. "I'll retrieve her once we've figured out what our next move is."

Hope stomps her foot. "You don't get to decide that!" She turns to Crisis. "Your queen orders you to tell everyone here what happened the day the Exp Hunters invaded."

"Well well, this ought to be interesting," says Koshi.

Abyss looks to Hope. "Has my sister returned yet?"

"Can't answer, mixed company." Hope turns to Crisis, gazing directly into his eyes. "Speak!"

Crisis' eyes go hollow. "Yes, my queen." He suddenly falls to his knees and coughs up blood.

Kaity lies him down and sends Lum energy into him. "Why isn't this working?" she asks, while he continues to spew blood.

Zenero removes his glasses and teleports Hope into his arms. "Seems the Senator installed some sort of failsafe in case confidential information were to be accessed. I came here seeking an alliance. You wouldn't want me as your enemy, after all." He caresses her hair, sending tremors of terror throughout her body. "Imagine, everyone just suddenly dying. First here, then in Lum."

Hope bites her lips.

Zenero drops her. "Soiled yourself. Still a child, I see. Though at least it shows you understand the importance of an alliance."

Kaity offers to help Hope up, but the sullied queen slaps her hand and cries. "What is going on with you?"

Zenero wipes the filthy liquid off his sleeves with a handkerchief. "Bob, I think we both agree that either one of us becoming Sellum is better than Xholk. He seeks to reset the world. Truly a monster we must stop."

Chipko grabs Zenero's arm. "You told me you didn't take Lilith. What other lies are you keeping from me?"

Zenero pulls her into an embrace and kisses her passionately. "Not now, my dear. We have more important things to address."

Kaity's face goes pale. "Wait." She rushes to the back area.

Devlin is seating with earphones and reading a book. He removes them when he notices Kaity.

"Why didn't you tell me Lilith was in Soul Storage?" She holds up the note. "This is your handwriting?"

"I was hoping to wait until we were alone."

Bob peeks out from behind the bookshelf and fires a powerful beam at Devlin, blasting him through the library wall.

"We had a deal!" yells Kaity, turning her blades on Bob.

"That wasn't Devlin. Neither was it one of my demons." Bob's eye shrinks. "That soul power energy is far beyond that of any being but myself."

Hope stands up with shaky legs. "Z-Zenero was the one who…." She keels over and coughs up blood.

"What are you doing to her?" asks Atlas, standing between Hope and Zenero.

"That you would assume me the perpetrator. Truly, I am wounded," says Zenero.

Hope looks to Natura and signals her with fierce eyes. Jigen nods, then teleports away with the queen.

Natura coats her body in electricity and throws off her mask. "This isn't Natura, or Whirlwind or Flash Girl! June is gonna kick your ass and put you behind bars!"

Chipko grabs Zenero's arm tightly. "Don't kill her. I'll deal with her."

Zenero smiles. "All this over a small misunderstanding."

Knives suddenly impale his back.

Zenero looks at his blood-soaked fingers inquisitively. "What?"

Chipko pushes him aside as another volley comes their way.

June sends a wind burst out, deflecting the knives. "I'm your sister, July. Are you really going to fight me for this monster? Just like before, he's turning us against each other."

Chipko blasts June away with a shockwave punch. "You're the one who is standing against him!"

Zenero smiles at Chipko. "Yes, please keep her off me. I will fetch you when it is time to end Lum."

Chipko looks up at him in tears. "Is this the last?"

"Pardon me?"

"Is this the last sacrifice for your goal?"

Zenero smiles. "Kaity and Devlin remain. Through their sacrifice, a true peaceful world will be obtained."

"A world built on corpses!" yells June.

"This is my last sacrifice." Chipko speeds to June and punches her through the wall.

Stabby runs in on all fours, sending a Lum blast at the destroyed wall. "Hope said no fighting in the libwawy."

Zenero puts his glasses on as his Lum energy pushes out the daggers in his body. "You were the one who made the first blow. I spared this place from becoming mere dust before. I can undo that decision if you don't stand down."

Abyss approaches Stabby. "Zenero is here to make peace. He just came to say something."

"Hope said something too!" Stabby stands tall. "Zenero had Crisis bwow up a helicopter! Zenewo sent those jets to boom the Queendom! Zenewo is a bad man and has to be destwoyed!"

"Your diction is deplorable. To think you came from my seed," says Zenero, looking down at the girl.

Koshi glares at Zenero. "Did you get my sister killed too? Was that you!?"

"Was it?" asks Abyss with shock.

"I'll end your precious Kioshi permanently if either of you dare strike me. Kill Crisis, then search the area, find Hope and kill her. I assume she'll be much more reasonable when she needs me to return home."

"Damn it! You don't get to order me around!" Koshi summons up the Death Scythe and strikes Zenero.

"Oooh, I made the right choice, after all." Bob grins.

Zenero's body falls to the ground limply.

Chapter 234: Broken Alliances

Crisis freezes Koshi's feet and Atlas summons up the Agony Axe.

Koshi blasts Atlas away and melts the ice around his feet with his energy. He sets his sights on Crisis who runs off. "Hey, come on. I just want a lil' chat!" hollers Koshi, unsummoning the scythe as he chases his prey.

Zenero appears from thin air and looks at his corpse. "Ghastly." He kicks it into a portal with a volcano.

Stabby launches knives at him that are caught by several small portals.

Zenero sighs. "Fighting anyone else would be an utter waste of time."

"MODE ONE!" Stabby's teeth are pushed out, replaced by blades.

Zenero holds out his hand to calm her. "It's likely pointless, but I must entertain the possibility. Tell me dear, do you want to see your father again?"

Stabby's eyes widen as they tear up. "Daddy," she says softly.

"The rule of Soul Storage is equivalence. To take out a soul you must give a soul of a similar tier."

"We can work together as a family," says Abyss, gripping his sister's hand tightly.

"What do you want for Daddy?" asks Stabby, standing tall.

"If you promise to serve me until you die, I will resurrect Pathos," says Zenero.

"What do you mean until she dies?" asks Abyss with a glare.

Zenero smiles. "Merely a precaution. If you join me, dear, and agree to assist in taking out both Kaity and Devlin, then I will assure you and your brother absolute protection. In addition to that, we can sacrifice Devlin for your father. What say you to this offer?" he asks, having his arm come out from a portal in front of her.

"Please, think this through. We can fix everything," says Abyss, crouching down and gripping his sister with all his strength.

Stabby shakes Zenero's hand. "MODE TWO!" Knives pierce out of her fingers and toes, cutting Zenero's hand. "Kaity is my fwiend!"

The Hero of the Millenia pulls his bloody arm out of the portal. "Regrettable. Either way, the power of Sellum shall return to me."

Abyss glares at him. "Attack my sister and our alliance is over."

"If it ends, it does so by my hand." Zenero smiles.

Stabby's projectiles from earlier burst out from Abyss.

"Bwother!" yells Stabby.

Abyss' body grows mouths that eat the blades. "That won't work on this monster." The mouths laugh at Zenero.

Zenero grimaces. "Atlas, I trust you to deal with him."

"My Lord, is this really the right path?"

Zenero steps on the air up to Atlas. "I am the Hero of the Millenia, the Sacrificial Savior. If I walk it, the path becomes proper. Things are just as simple as they've always been."

"Understood." Atlas fires Appalling Arrows at Abyss, making the enemy involuntarily retreat.

Zenero turns to Stabby. "Now, my dear daughter. It's just the two of us."

Crisis sends hot and cold waves back with each rebound of his foot as he runs from Koshi.

The alpha agent hops over the waves, making different poses each time. "Hey this is fun, like a game! Oh man, the game over screen is going to be sooo gruesome."

"It's not my fault!" Crisis freezes the ground and slides down it, turning around and firing a continuous heat wave so that Koshi can't ride it to him.

"Oho! You should know Hunters have tricks to keep up with cowardly prey." Koshi's energy erupts out from his back as wings. He jumps up and propels himself forward with continuous energy blasts from his feet.

Crisis takes a sudden turn into the forest. "Nature, please grant me shelter." He looks around warily, readying a heat wave.

Koshi swoops down, powering through the heat wave with his own energy and then sending a blast of energy into Crisis.

The energy bursts, sending the fleeing Exp into the air.

"Okay! I'll tell you everything!" Crisis holds his arms up in surrender. "But you have to promise to let me live."

"I have to promise you something?" asks Koshi, landing and summoning up the Death Scythe.

"I blew up the helicopter! It was Zenero's orders! When the Hunters got me, they thought I was a mindless shell. They didn't think to break me because they thought I was I already broken."

"Boring!" Koshi brings the scythe down and stops. "Better make this story more relevant."

"Zenero spoke to me through a portal! He couldn't be detected. He told me to kill an agent and frame your sister!"

"Anything else!?" asks Koshi with a mad grin.

"Yeah! The Exodus Bombs, I learned about them from Beta. She got drunk at a party and told me all sorts of top-secret stuff. I told Zenero about them and he decided to stage a bombing, then swoop in to rescue everyone!"

"Why my sister?" Koshi steps on Crisis with an energy laden foot. "Why her?"

"Because she's your weakness. Kioshi holds the Hunters together. With her gone, you would soon follow. Without his best agent, the Senator would be too scattered to be an obstacle to Zenero."

"Skip to the part where you tell me who ordered my sister killed!"

"That wasn't Zenero! He wanted to recruit you, but he didn't do it!"

"Who!? Who was it?"

"Please don't kill me!" Crisis cries and backs up into a tree. "I don't know! I'm sorry."

"It was you, wasn't it?"

"No! I'm not a sniper! I couldn't shoot her!"

"Zenero just used that opportunity to bring me to his side. Now my sister's life is in his hands!"

"I'll do anything! We're on the same team! Please don't kill me! That's everything I know, I swear."

Agent Alpha's suit turns a deathly white. "I'm not the one who's going to kill you. See, Zenero gave the order, so you can just blame him!" Koshi raises the scythe, it shimmers with his overflowing killer intent.

Crisis presses his finger against Koshi. "**Absolute End**." The icy finger freezes Koshi's entire body and the area around them.

Crisis heats up his body to break free of the ice. "Just needed time to focus my power." He kicks the frozen spy, shattering him to pieces. "Now you're just another part of the great cycle!" He flings heat waves at the icy chunks until they are just steam in the air. "Geez, Crisis. Calm down. Death comes for us all someday. I let the dread get to me. If I go out, it should be a surprise."

Koshi reforms as a body formed of blood. "Surprise." He grins as his flesh reforms.

Crisis focuses cold energy into both arms.

Koshi fully forms, standing naked. "*MALICE!*" Energy erupts out from Koshi as a purple haze.

Crisis freezes in terror, unable to move a muscle.

"I'll be searching for you in the afterworld. So best run." Koshi approaches, dragging the Death Scythe.

Abyss devours one of the incoming arrows with a mouth in his palm. His entire arm splits apart.

Atlas grimaces. "Those aren't food. They are my comrades! My friends! You cannot assimilate them with your grotesque ability!"

"Don't you judge me!" Abyss' eyes chatter. "You chose to kill them! You're the one who ate them up!"

Atlas' spirits drop and his weapon unsummons. "You're correct."

Abyss' arms fire out metal blades at his attacker. "My sister is fighting for her life right now!" He spits out grenades that Atlas slaps aside. "I'd go all out and destroy you in an in–."

"Then why don't you?" asks Atlas, summoning up the Agony Axe as he approaches.

Abyss rushes in and spits out a sword, grabbing it before slicing into the obstruction.

Atlas' muscle's tense, gripping the sword. He then swings the Agony Axe down.

The weapon cleaves through Abyss' shoulder all the way down his thighs before hitting the floor.

Abyss clenches his teeth and trembles. "If I go all out, I'd lose sight of myself! I could even end up hurting her if I transform! I'm suffering so much right now! I didn't even feel that attack!" His severed portion becomes a massive mouth that lunges at the living meat.

Atlas struggles to tear his arm free of the ravenous mouth as Abyss pelts him with bullets. "Neither Hope nor Zenero make progress without actions that are…reprehensible. I must power through this guilt and help my master create his kingdom." He summons up the Searing Sword and slices through the flesh beast by melting through it. "Passion so strong it ignites the body; this is my goal." He holds up the sword proudly.

Abyss slides back. His hand regurgitates flesh to reconstruct his missing parts. "When we came back from Absence. You…trusted me. You stood up for me even against your commander. Where is that warrior!?"

Atlas' weapon vanishes in his grip. "Your words are stronger than steel. I…have lost so much." He falls to his knees in tears.

Abyss embraces the crying man. "You were with my sister in this place. This sanctuary. Are you really going to lose her too?"

"I…have to trust Zenero."

Abyss cries. "You're being a coward and I know you're brave! I've seen it!" He sulks. "I'm the coward. I knew you all were going to be bombed. Agent Beta told me about Zenero's plan. I knew and I didn't try to save everyone. I only tried to save my sister. I didn't even think of my mom and dad." He sobs against Atlas' shoulder. "I'm as hopelessly loyal as you are."

Atlas sobs fiercely and then his eyes dry. "You've won this battle."

Abyss looks up at him. "You'll let me go protect her."

Atlas stands tall. "A dear friend of mine once stood against my orders. He was the most loyal friend I've ever had. I was too narrow-minded at the time. He did what he felt was best. He stood against you when I stood by you." He lets out a hearty laugh. "That was true courage. For that reason. I cannot let you go and fight Zenero."

"Then we'll keep fighting until one of us is dead."

Atlas laughs again and briskly lifts Abyss. "No! I cannot simply allow my friend to fight alone! Likewise, I cannot permit the man I respect to make a decision I know to be deeply wrong." He grabs Abyss' hand firmly. "We will do all we can to stop him together!"

"Thank you!" Abyss shakes his hands in tears. "I didn't stand a chance at defeating you." He smiles and chuckles.

"And neither of us stand a chance at stopping Zenero, so let's do the impossible once more!"

"Watch out!" Bob pulls Kaity aside as crystals jut out from beneath her. "If he subdues you, he can simply teleport away with you."

Kaity smiles awkwardly. "Saved again, how many do I owe you now?"

Bob snickers. "Simply surrender your soul when the time comes and all debts will be paid."

Evolution clasps his hands. Hundreds of him appear throughout the forest.

"I can't hit them all," says Kaity, readying Lum bullets.

"Nor do you need to. Simply see past the illusions as I taught you."

Kaity blushes. "Yeah, good thinking." She closes her eyes and then fires at the true Evolution.

The figure rides a gust of wind up to Sellum and coats her in ice.

Bob's slashes the Atma Blade at the entity. "So many souls, yet they're all locked up! Why must you tease me!" He fires a beam that is redirected multiple times by the Sel pillars that appear.

Kaity burns herself out of the ice. "He seems slower than last time."

"That's because I'm here supporting you," says Bob, having the pillars disperse as black bullets at the attacker.

"Hey, you aren't even using my Love Artifact. Sefiwah gave it to me. Give it back!"

"All shall return to me." The figure holds out its hand in deep reverence.

The crystal structures around them glow.

Kaity forms a rifle of Sel energy and then fires multiple black bullets at the dodging foe. Her last two bullets miss. "Do you hear that too?" she asks, her arms shaking.

"Pranidhanat. Sanskrit for surrender. It seems physical attacks are merely to bide time for the mantra to wear us down."

Kaity brushes her eyes. "Already losing focus. Any advice?"

"Sorry, unlike the great chosen kitty of destiny, I'm not affected by lullabies, so I don't have any home remedies for you," says Bob, sending out his tendrils once the attacker got too close.

"Where is Devlin? Why were you posing as him?" yells Kaity, rushing at the target on all fours to stay alert.

Evolution's fingers become crystal claws that clash with her plasma claws. "Pranidhanat."

Bob's dark tendril is repelled by a metal barrier but the spectral tentacle within passes through and grips the entity of artifacts. "Tell us where he is!"

Kaity topples over and nods off. She shakes herself to her senses. "I can't keep going."

"Then just sleep it off!" yells Bob, repelling the enemy with multiple blades of darkness.

Kaity sits cross-legged and assumes a prayer stance. "I won't fight it. I'll surrender." Her whole body goes limp.

"Oh no you don't!" Bob fires a beam at the entity as it zooms toward Kaity. The dark beam erupts around it, cloaking the area in fog. He zooms through the fog and pierces Kaity with the Atma Blade. "Wake up!"

Kaity's eyes open. "Inside Sellum is everyone. That includes Zenero."

"What, did you find a way to make him remotely explode or something?"

Kaity giggles. "Evolution can follow us anywhere. Well, almost anywhere." She parts her hand through the air, creating a portal. "I'm going to find Lilith." She smiles before entering the portal and closing it.

Bob blinks. "That's that, I suppose. Oh, I hope I'm still in time for Mika's sermon!" He hops into a Sel portal.

Evolution disperses the Sel energy and gazes forward. "Willingly surrendering to my mantra to achieve that which was not possible before. I am fortunate to be tasked with claiming such a wise creature."

Chapter 235: Sacrificial Savior

June stabilizes herself with repeated gusts of wind as she is sent tumbling through the forest of the Queendom.

Chipko speeds up to her in an instant, her fist pulsing with condensed energy.

June puts on her mask for an instant. "Our hero surprises her foe with a powerful multi-kick!"

Chipko holds out her arms to block the kick while building up a shockwave.

June throws away the mask. "I can't keep playing dress up!"

"Finally growing up, are you?" asks Chipko, thrusting her fist forth.

"We should be stopping Zenero!" June kicks off the air, dodging an incoming shockwave that sheds the leaves off the trees above.

Chipko speeds up the tree and then kicks off, creating an implosion shockwave to bring June up to her. With her other hand, she punches her sister in the gut. "Zenero needs the power of Lum. We don't have time to waste."

June creates a tornado around her, stopping her downward momentum and sending her into the air. "Stop using my artifact!"

Chipko rides the tornado up, her feet releasing mini-shockwaves to give her extra air. "I'll return it when you return to Zenero!" She slams her palms together. The clap creates a wide shockwave blast.

June screams and throws up blood. She falls through the trees, getting sliced by branches.

Chipko lands and wipes a tear from her eye. "I won last time. I'm even stronger now. This can only end one way." She steps into the shallow water, looking for her sister.

June holds her hand up. "***LIVING CONDUCTOR!***"

A lightning bolt crashes into her from above, frying both her and Chipko.

The environmentalist cries and holds her sides. "Do you have any idea how many lives you just snuffed out? You're no hero!" She places her hands on the water and releases a powerful shockwave that blasts June into the air.

"I…wasn't thinking. But you're right! I'm not a hero anymore. Someone died because of me! I went to the funeral! A funeral I brought about! If I unleash these powers, people die. I held back when we fought in Absence and because of that…we lost our brother Murai. I'll do whatever it takes to save my sister from allowing a terrible man to ruin her life again! I'm not losing any more siblings!" June fires a powerful bolt of electricity at Chipko, but her sister vanishes from sight.

Chipko appears above June and grabs her head. She punches her repeatedly with shockwaves as her little sister increases the voltage of her electric body. "Give up!"

They land and Chipko continues to punch. The ground around them shakes before splitting apart.

June blasts Chipko off. She then emits a continuous gust from one hand, while firing electricity from the other. Her legs move in a fluid motion, creating a cold that makes the wind freeze all it touches.

Chipko races forward, her feet shattering in the process. She grabs onto June and punches her repeatedly with mini-shockwaves. "Why are we fighting?" she asks in tears.

June cries as she punches back, only able to add minor electricity to her fists. "You're afraid of him abandoning you." She grabs her sister's hands. Her finger's snap as Chipko's hand burns. "You're stronger without him. We all are."

Chipko punches her sister until her shockwaves are no more.

June punches her sister until her electricity dies out.

Their bruised and bloody faces become more wet with regret after each punch.

Chipko lowers her fist. "I…." She hugs June and sobs.

June hugs her back and forces a smile.

Jigen appears and lifts June off her feet. "Everyone must evacuate. Queen's orders."

June holds onto her sister's hand with what little strength she has left. "Not without July."

Jigen nods before sending the two sisters away together.

Zenero chases Stabby as she flies through the air. "I thought you were going to destwoy me, as you so crudely put it."

Stabby lands on the grass. "Not near the castle. Hope will get mad."

Zenero teleports a few meters away from her. "You won't have to worry about being reprimanded. Your death is all but assured." He summons up a machine gun and fires into a single portal.

The bullets spray out from the portals around Stabby. More portals appear beneath her, spewing grenades.

"Utter obliteration would be so simple. Alas, I cannot be the one to issue the killing blow."

Stabby's knives absorb the blood. "MODE 3!"

Two sets of metal arms with bladed fingers pierce out from her sides. She crawls with her new arms towards the bad dad.

Zenero counters her by sending a particularly sturdy sword into small portals behind him, while elegantly dancing away. Each blade tip comes out from small portals in front of the girl, blocking each and every attempt. "When a foe is easy to read, the battle becomes a dance."

Stabby's fingers shoot off her hand and pierce through Zenero.

He teleports away, pooling Lum energy into the wound. "Curses, my powers have dulled from being locked away in that purgatorial prison."

A fan of blades cut open and spread out from Stabby's back. They fly to Zenero in quick succession, attacking once more after they rebound.

Zenero multiplies the portals, creating a barrier of steel with a single thin blade.

Stabby's knives gleam before cutting his sword.

"Even as a god, keeping track of train schedules is prudent." Zenero smiles before vanishing, leaving a portal in his place.

A train comes screeching out.

Stabby rushes inside and screams erupt throughout the train. She leaps out the front as the train crashes.

Stabby's skin was shed. Her cold metal skeleton is now caked in fresh blood.

Zenero looks at the madness in her intense red eyes. "So this is what Pathos did to my daughter. You're nothing more than a killing machine now."

"MODE SIX," says Stabby mechanically. Her mouth opens up and glows from within.

The fresh blood coating the walls of the train, along with the puddles by the corpses within, drags along the walls. It is pulled out of the train and gravitated into her mouth.

Zenero coats the tip of his lance in Sel energy before sending it at the child weapon.

"Bwood!" Stabby rushes towards him blindly, getting pierced by the lance. Her Lum powers activate on their own and destroy the discordant energy.

"Finally, you're using your Lum abilities. I'll have to drain you entirely if this is to work." He fires a single lance into a portal that ejects it out in thirty portals around Stabby.

The blades detach from her back and clash against the incoming projectiles. They let out a blast of Lum energy, binding all the lances together.

The blades then chase after Zenero, guided by the blood inside him. They zoom right past a squirrel and reach their target.

Zenero creates an armor of portals with a snap of his fingers. He then creates parallel portals to have the projectiles repel each other. "Despite your outward state of madness, your protocols forbid you from harming non-human animals. Most intriguing." He fires Sel-coated lances into the ground that come out under the realm god.

Stabby's Lum aura pulses, requiring multiple bursts to dispel the Sel energy. When her next volley of blades is sent out, Zenero teleports them far away.

"You'll have to run out of those eventually." Zenero gasps as a blade hidden in the grass slices his leg.

Several more blades follow up the sudden attack before Zenero summons a tank around him.

Stabby calls the blades back and absorbs the fresh blood. "MODE EIGHT!" Blades form around her, lined up as multiple spinning fans.

"Perhaps some improvisation is required." Zenero blasts her with the tank's cannon.

The blades act defensively. One set slices the shell in two, the others immediately follow up by slicing the fragments into bits. The shell never even explodes.

Zenero backs up the tank, toppling the nearby trees to obstruct Stabby's vision as her blades relentlessly pursue. "This tank was borrowed from my dear friend, John. Do be careful with it, dear." The Hero of the Millenia fires a shell into a portal. He then stations portals around Stabby in parallel formation.

Stabby creates more blades around her to slice the incoming shells, but the fragments just come out the portal on the other end. Lum calls her knives to her to shield her from the assault.

"Checkmate." Zenero fires a mortar, oozing with Sel energy directly into the girl.

It bursts on contact, melting away her shield.

White energy bursts out as a pillar as she enters her Lum form.

Portals appear around Stabby, sending missiles into her.

With a wave of her hand, she creates a gust that whooshes away the bad things.

The blades she forms around her ignite before being sent out at Zenero.

He teleports out of the tank just before it's sliced to heated shreds.

"Any attack can be countered with the proper mindset." He holds out his hands, with portals on his palms.

A tsunami of water emerges, washing away Stabby's weapons and her along with them.

A tree of metal forms beneath her.

She opens her mouth and pulls in the blood from Zenero's wound.

He quickly heals with Lum energy, checks his phone and then sends a jet crashing into Stabby's tree.

The girl absorbs blood as she falls.

Zenero forms a lance of pure Sel energy and then fires it into a portal above him.

It bursts out from Stabby's chest, eating away at her body as her Lum aura reflexively pulls inward.

"You're stronger than me, but not nearly as clever. My offer still stands. There's no need for this bloodshed to continue."

"Bwood! MODE NINE!" Stabby pulls in all her blades back into her and holds out her hands. A red misty aura spills out.

Zenero quickly checks his phone. "Come on, there must be a tornado somewhere." He drops the device and his eyes shimmer. "It's inside me." The master tactician summons up a knife and starts cutting into himself. "There's so much of it!" He squeals in delight as he licks off the blood.

Stabby falls into Abyss' arms.

"I was worried when your Lum barrier fell. But it's alright. Everything is okay now, Sister." He holds her lovingly to his chest.

Stabby shakes herself to her senses. She looks up at Zenero who is cutting himself as his Lum energy seals the wounds.

"Stop getting in my way!" yells Zenero, firing Sel energy into the Lum aura that was healing him.

Atlas rushes to Zenero. "My Lord, what are you doing to yourself?" He knocks the knife out of Zenero's hand.

Stabby wipes her eyes and looks up with determination. "Zenewo!" She pulls in the red mist and regrows her skin with Lum powers.

Zenero comes back into awareness in a daze. "What was I doing?"

Stabby looks up at him. "If you die…wotsa people sad. If I die…fwiends sad too."

"I see your finally attempting logic. Yes, a good portion of the world relies on me. But my dear, you haven't killed me once. If you managed to, I could simply return." Zenero teleports a gun and fires into his head. He appears and does so again and again.

"Stob!" wails Stabby in tears.

Zenero keeps going until he is standing on a pile of his own corpses. "Your defeat is inevitable."

Abyss stands defensively in front of Stabby. "Then we'll just take the fight to Lum and end you there."

Atlas climbs the corpses. "Perhaps it's best if we retreat for now, my Lord."

Zenero looks down at him. "Chipko was supposed to be the new Lum, but you…you've done so much for me. I will subdue her. You will end her. Then all that remains is Bob."

Stabby points at him. "No more fighting! No more huwting." She looks away from the tempting feast of blood.

"Let's get out of here," says Abyss, picking her up.

Stabby's Lum energy wraps around his legs. "No wunning either." She hops off and creates a cage of steel around her brother. "That won't stop the fighting."

Atlas nods. "Yes, we must reach a compromise. What do you propose, Lum?"

Zenero summons up a fresh pair of glasses and puts them on. "The battle is over. Surrender your life to me now." He gestures to Abyss, who has a portal above him.

Zenero holds in his hands the Exodus Bomb. "I have another that I will use once he arrives in Lum. Using hostages is distasteful, but I do so with the best intentions, my dear."

"Kill him! Keep killing him until he's nothing! If you surrender. If you die, then I'll be alone anyway! You're my family!" wails Abyss, his hands biting at the bars that keep reforming.

Atlas grabs Zenero. "We aren't above negotiations."

"I already tried that. Do you doubt me?"

"I…."

Zenero looks at him intensely. "Do you doubt me?"

"There just…has be another way. Stabby is a friend."

Zenero smiles and hands Atlas the bomb. "Well then, this is your test. If she doesn't surrender, drop it." He approaches Stabby. "If you kill me, then after I arrive in Lum, I'll go to Soul Storage. I'll snuff out Pathos' soul. Then nothing can bring him back. He'll be utterly wiped from existence."

Atlas trembles. "Pathos is your son."

"And my world is one he would happily die for."

Atlas sets the bomb on the ground. "You're lost." He approaches Zenero.

"What?"

Atlas holds out his hands. The Agony Axe forms, slicing Zenero the slightest bit.

"What are you doing?" Zenero writhes around on the floor.

"As your bodyguard, it is my sworn duty to protect you. If something is possessing you, then I must cut it out." He raises the axe again.

Stabby approaches Atlas. She looks at his overflowing tears and shakes her head. "No more fighting." Lum smiles through her tears. "Daddy wants me to protect Kaity. I think…that's why I was chosen. Tranquil knew I'd never hurt Kaity."

Zenero struggles back to his feet. "Go on."

"Bwood must be sacrwificed. I'll do anything to resurrect Daddy."

"You're quite ambitious. But you can't kill Kaity on your own."

Abyss looks at Stabby from the prison and smiles. "Yeah, we can work together to take down Kaity. I'll be with you. It's for a better future, right?"

"Yep! Daddy is the only one who can make the world good," says Stabby with a toothy grin.

"I take it that means you agree to my terms?" Zenero beams at her. "You inherited my logical nature, after all. I am blessed to have such a wise daughter."

Stabby nods firmly. "It's a hard decision, but one I must make."

Atlas sighs. "Kaity is a dear friend to me, but I…understand the necessity. She lacks the vision to be a proper Sellum."

Stabby looks back at Abyss. "Thanks for everything, Brother. Sorry for all the sad stuff."

"Hey, it's fine. It's over. Just uh, let me out of here. You've gotten too strong for your big brother," he says with an awkward smile.

Stabby suddenly started laughing innocently.

"What's so funny?" asks Zenero as he couldn't help but laugh along.

"You undewestimated my loyalty to Daddy. I'm going to bring back Daddy and pwotect Kaity," says Stabby with a toothy grin.

"Are you defying me?" asks Zenero darkly.

"Efil told me about something really handy," says Stabby with a teary smile.

Zenero's eyes widen. "Wait!"

Stabby throws out her arms. "I sacrifice myself in exchange for Pathos!"

"What the hell are you saying!" yells Abyss in tears.

"Thanks for all the memories. I love you forever, Brother," she says as she reaches out and grabs Abyss' hand.

"Stay with me. We're going to make so many more memories together!" He says in tears.

Stabby's skin starts to disintegrate.

"No! Don't take her from me!" wails Abyss.

Zenero laughs uncontrollably. "She made an utter fool of me! Beaten by my own blood."

The prison around Abyss evaporated as she faded away.

He rushes out, trying to collect the little particles of his sister, while holding onto her.

"Please, protect Kaity for me. And try to get along with Daddy," says Stabby, smiling one final time.

"I'm supposed to protect you," cries Abyss, his grip now empty.

As one last gift, a white cloud of energy comes out from where she once was and enters Abyss.

A new form began materializing as her shreds floated away.

Pathos slowly forms in front of Abyss.

The last remnants of Stabby faded away in Abyss' palm the moment Pathos returned to life.

Bob closes his scripture and looks to Mika. His pupil widens in surprise. "He's back! My eternal rival has returned."

To be continued in book 6, ***Rise of the Exps: Pathos***

Sneak Peek of Book 6, ***Pathos*: Rise of the Exps**

Zenero was still laughing at his own stupidity when Pathos was fully formed. "It was all perfectly planned out. But she ruined it! That's my daughter for you! Nothing I can do about it now," he cries as he laughs and then leaves into a portal.

"What's going on? Who revived me?' His eyes widen in fear. "Is Kaity okay?"

Abyss' teeth-like pupils chatter with rage. "How can you be so blind?" he asks darkly.

"Hey, Son! You don't seem particularly happy to see me. Where's Stabby?" asks Pathos heartily.

"She's dead," says Abyss softly.

"What?" asks Pathos horrified, taking a step back.

"She died for you and all you can think about is Kaity," says Abyss, grinding his teeth.

"She can't be gone. A Sellum would have to exchange for me. That's how it's supposed to work," says Pathos in disbelief.

"She loved you more than anything! I could never be as important as you. Because of you…she's gone! If I could have replaced you, she'd be here, right now." His mouth fingers tear through and feast on his flesh.

"You shouldn't blame yourself. It's not your fault at all."

"There's not even a trace of her left. All I have are haunting memories!" Abyss seethes as his breathing escalates.

"I never asked for this. I wanted her to be safe," says Pathos, tears flooding from his mask.

"Shut up!" spat Abyss.

"I failed you son," cries Pathos.

"Not yet! I am going to kill you and then myself! You don't deserve to live for breaking her heart and I don't deserve to live for breaking my promise. I'm a failure of a brother and you're a father who turned her into a monster!" Abyss closes his eyes as his body quakes.

"Wait, don't do it," says Pathos, reaching out to Abyss.

"For the first time, I choose this! I welcome the madness! I embrace the violence! STAGE TEN!"

Book 6, *Pathos*: Rise of the Exps

Lum's sacrifice causes a roar of chaos in the Queendom. With the revival of their past leader, the Freedom Forcers face another ideological split. The tension between the factions is alleviated when Zenero shifts Queen Hope's focus toward claiming a spot of political power. Things only become more complex when a faction of Exps called the Tools of Destiny come to the surface to begin their plan to create a utopia. Luckily for the Freedom Forcers, Bob has internal concerns to deal with. Zenero's weakness is exploited by the Senator and the Hero of the Millenia's past is brought to light. Meanwhile, Koshi continues his quest to uncover who ordered the death of his sister. Can the Exps claim their utopia when there are encroaching forces that turn their world into a battleground?

Books from ***Sphere of Compassion***

<u>THE MAIN CHARACTER!</u>

<u>Hero's Epic Journey Arc</u>

A Subversive PUNCH to the Face!

Join Main Character and Best Friend, two American otakus, who are pulled into another world and bribed into joining a conflict between victimized villages and deranged dictators. Anime tropes only lead to shattered expectations! The hero has awesome allies, is protected by canonical plot armor, and armed with the power of Friendship (a vulgar bazooka). But will these be enough to overcome a dimension hopping assassin, a guardian angel's sexual advances, a musclebound amazonian, and a charismatic king with a psychotic obsession for our hero and his army of cut throat cat boys? The Main Character is a 4th wall breaking parody packed with anime references, subversive characters and intense battles!

Be your own Hero!

Before she found the Hero of Destiny, Annie had her own journey! Join her adventure through the epic dark fantasy world of The Main Character series! This loving girl will join cursed heroes, adorable angels and mythical beasts to reunite with her family! Will her bonds be enough to protect her from machine samurai, shadow hounds, and CatBoy soldiers? Or will her life's story close before she can write her happily ever after?

*Can be read before OR after any book from **The Main Character** series.*

A SUPLEX of Subversion!

Main Character and Best Friend, two legendary otaku heroes, are back in action.

They now have a diverse group of otherworldly allies: a guardian angel Stalker, a shy Brawny Babe, a Tomboy CatGirl, a Fruity-scented fortune teller, a foul-mouthed bazooka of Friendship and a freaking Harem of strong female leads! Juggling his harem is the least of his worries though. This time he'll have to go head to head against a psychotic Rival, a mind-manipulating Mascot, a mysterious organization, a blackmailing midget, and horny Harem girls? Even with Point of View manipulation, the ability to Retcon his failures and hair that can punch your lights out, can Main Character overcome his own ego and become a true hero? Or will his backlog of bad choices create a rift between him and his allies?

In a School of Assassins, Suffering is Growth.

Before Assailant targeted the Hero of Destiny, he crafted his own legend! Discover the dark origins of the fabled Broad-Spectrum assassin. Follow him through deadly exams, covert conspiracies and murderous missions! This child of misfortune will work alongside cuddly killers, polymorphous monsters, enslaved heroes, and tragic angels to unravel the secrets hidden by the Assassin's Guild. Armed with mythic knowledge and guided by love, can he wield his truth to conquer skillful students, treacherous assassins, shadowy and secret organizations? Will his legends become a beacon of hope or a seed of despair?

Can be read before OR after any book from ***The Main Character*** *series.*

The Main Character! The Manga!

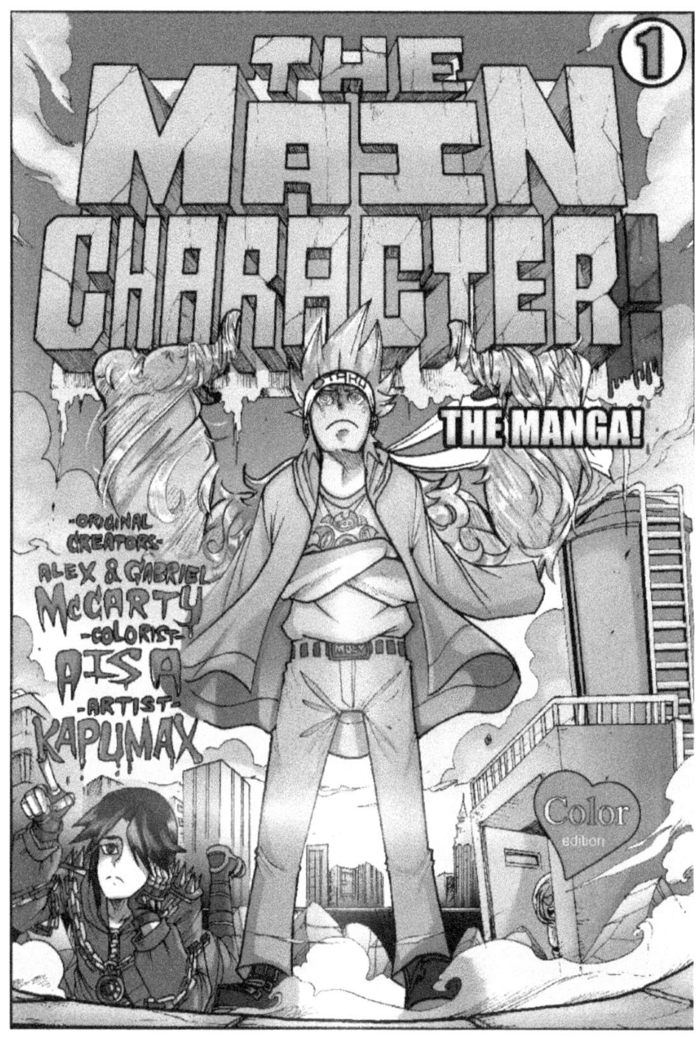

The Legend Re-begins Once Again!

The Main Character! novel series has evolved into a manga!

Join Main Character, an egocentric ViralTube anime reviewer and Best Friend, his overprotective dark otaku buddy on the day that ignited their epic journey! He must suffer through the ravings of his know-it-all teacher, Glasses Kid and survive his super clingy fan-girl, Stalker. What other disasters will befall our devilishly handsome hero? Find out in this hilarious 4th-Wall breaking experience packed with anime references!

BLACK & WHITE/ FULL COLOR versions sold separately.

Of the Exps
Rebellion Arc

Freedom is a Shackle.

Exp 8 is a living weapon. After awakening in an isolated lab, one instinct fuels him: a burning desire for freedom. His creator, Devlin, will stop at nothing to keep Exp 8 subservient to his will. To break out of Devlin's hold, Exp 8 stages a rebellion, using both his wit and power to unite his fellow Exps against their creator. But not all enemies can be converted, and Devlin is not the only one with plans for the rogue weapon. The sentient inventions Exp 8 and his allies encounter become more powerful, fanatical and merciless with each wave. Driven by instinct and the desire to free his people, Exp 8 perseveres through conflict and loss. Is freedom worth the cost if he alone desires it?

A sci-fi anime-style experience packed with intense battles and other-worldly abilities.

Resurrection Arc

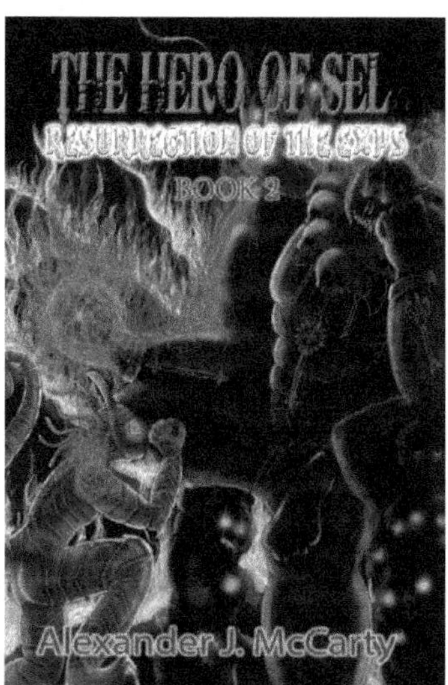

True Heroes are Created, not Born.

This is the story of Exp 8, an artificial life-form who died in the pursuit of freedom. He awakens in the afterlife and sets out on a mission to dethrone the tyrant king of Sel to free the tortured residents. Unable to defeat the god alone, he must unite a demonic rebel army, locate his fallen comrades, and convince gods to join his cause. Even with old enemies and new allies at his side, can he overcome the God of Hate and become the Hero of Sel?

An action fantasy anime-style experience
that explores the afterlife and the gods who shape it.

Origins of the Exps

Is clairvoyance a gift or a curse?

Before she became Fate, Ebui fought against her destiny.

Explore the ancient culture and traditions of the Ainu through the lens of a child. Ebui is a hopeful and brave girl who yearns to become a respected shaman of her village. Threats loom around every chapter of her life in the form of enemy tribes, violent ceremonies, sinister plots, and her own cursed prophecies. Will her hope survive through the supernatural storm of despair, or will her efforts bring about the end of her people?

Immerse yourself in the lives and backstories of characters from the *Of The Exps* series in the first of the Origins of the Exps novels!

This book can be read before any book from ***Of The Exps*** *series.*

Manga of the Exps

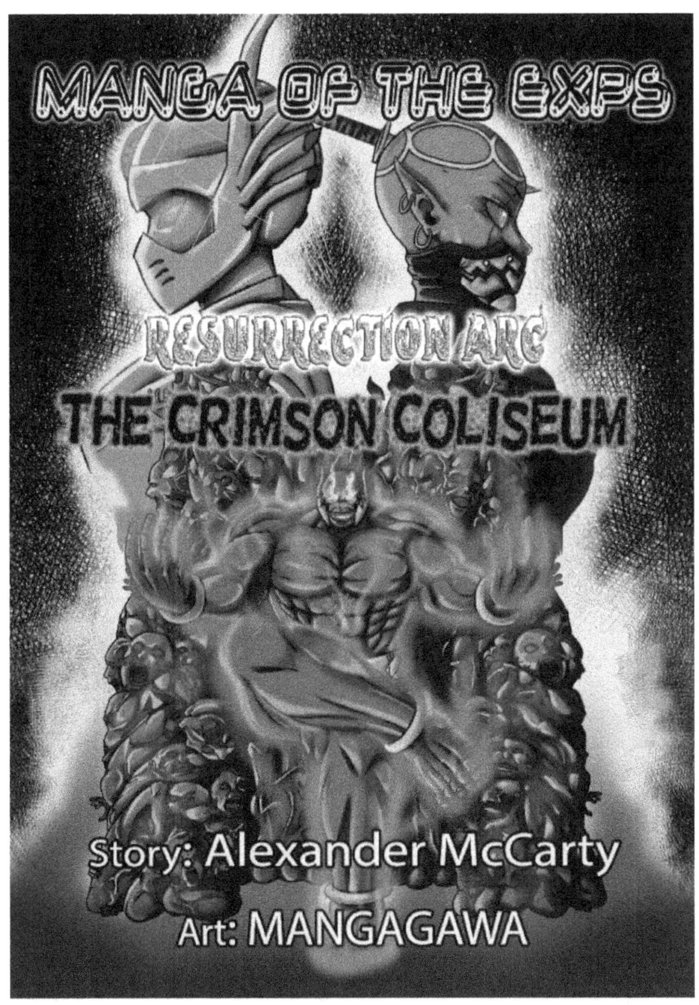

Is freedom worth dying for?

Exp 8 awakens in the Crimson Coliseum, the blood-soaked battle arena where heroes are brought to die. Before he can battle the God of Hate, he must defeat a fellow rebel leader whose body is a gruesome armory. Will Exp 8 be able to conquer the tyrant king of Sel or will he become just another red smear on the Crimson Coliseum?

Get pumped for the first Manga from the ***Of The Exps*** series based on the pivotal battle from the ***Resurrection of the Exps: The Hero of Sel*** novel. *This manga can be read before any book from the **Of The Exps** series.* BLACK & WHITE/ FULL COLOR versions sold separately.

Escapades of the Exps

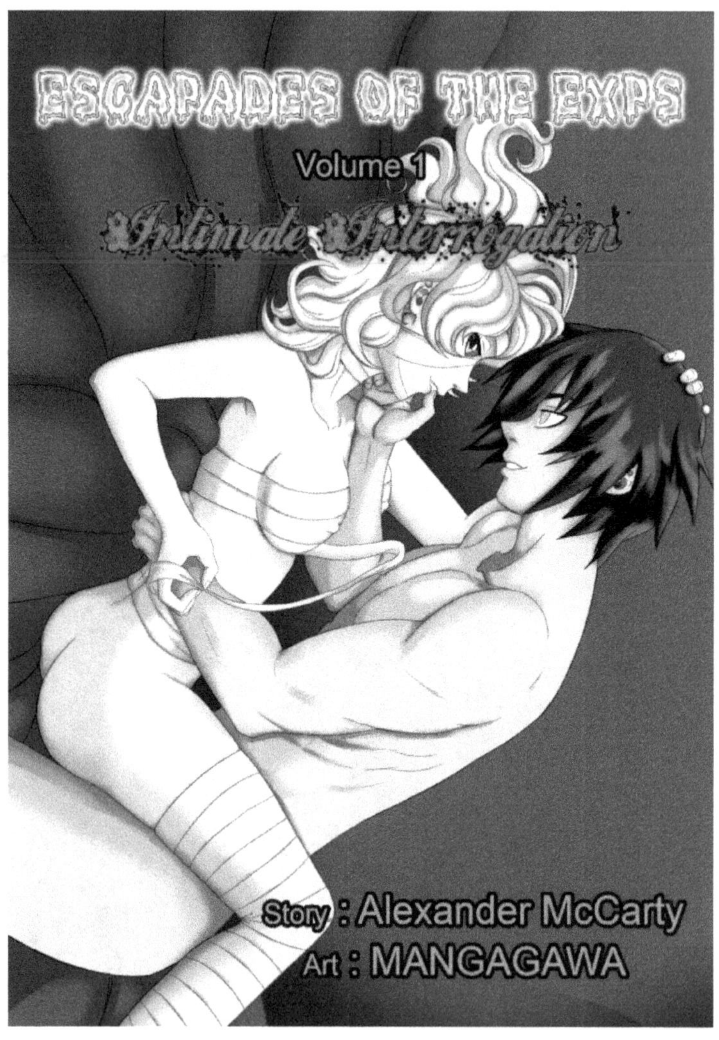

Is sex just another tool for an assassin?

The deadly girlfriend of Devlin's new crush is discovered in his bed. The seductive assassin has an offer for the hot-blooded scientist and will do whatever she must to seduce him to her cause.

Become entranced by the first Hentai Manga from ***Of The Exps*** series based on a scene from the ***Rebellion of the Exps: Exp 8*** novel.
*This manga can be read before any book from **Of The Exps** series.*
READ THE FULL COLOR NOW BY SIGNING UP ON
https://Patreon.com/Sphere_of_Compassion/

About the Author

Alexander McCarty is an animal born on Earth who actively seeks freedom for his fellow animals. At age five, once he realized that the chickens he loved and the chickens he was eating were one in the same, he became an ovolacto-vegetarian along with his nine-year-old brother. In middle-school, he decided to make use of his free time by writing a book. At the age of twenty-one he met vegan activist Gary Yourofsky and vowed to live vegan alongside his brother. They have since dedicated their lives to animal liberation through educational activism. Alexander recently graduated with a bachelor's degree in Religious Studies and holds certificates in Jainism, Asiatic Studies, and Spirituality. He is now a full-time writer and is also the president of Sphere of Compassion Inc. He runs SOC with his brother. SOC is a company whose purpose is to spread innovative media and promote a vegan worldview. When he isn't writing, he is watching anime, reading, or playing videogames. He listens to any and all comments, suggestions, reflections, and criticism.

Please contact me with a link to where you placed a review for any of my books, and I will answer any single question as one of my characters for **FREE**. If you do a review (and point out where) in addition to submitting fan art, I will write a **FREE** short 2–4 page story (with my characters) in a scenario of your choosing. =(:3)*

Bloggers who wish to review my book may request "Review Copies" of *Exp 8: Rebellion of the Exps* at the links below.

authoralexandermccarty@gmail.com
alexanderjmccarty@facebook.com
gabrieloftheexps@instagram.com

We Sacrifice Nothing by Being Fair to Others

It is a common misconception that by becoming vegan we are sacrificing something. Oftentimes our moral responsibilities to our fellow animals are ignored because of weak excuses such as 'I can't give up meat (cheese, eggs, etc)'. This reasoning is faulty and likened to the mindset of an addict. The main difference here is that animal products (unlike actual drugs) are not addictive. What causes people to make this excuse is a dependency, not an addiction. Now let's take a closer look at this dependency.

We are taught to think that eating meat and other animal products is natural. What is meat but a dressed-up corpse? Dairy is cow's milk which of course is made to feed her babies. Honey is bee vomit that they use for everything. And eggs are a chicken's period that if infertile, the mother ingests to gain back vital nutrients. None of these things belong to us, and as vegans have proved, we don't need any of these things to be happy and healthy.

So then what are vegans sacrificing? Absolutely nothing. In truth vegans simply do not take from others. They take a stand against animal exploitation by refusing to fund products derived from cruelty. Most humans know it is wrong to needlessly exploit animals, but it's so engrained in our society that we don't even consider animal agriculture exploitation.

Let's explore this one step further. Vegans absolutely can eat the same things they ate before making the decision to be vegan. There are plenty of vegan cheeses, meats, and other cruelty free products that taste the same or better than the ones that come from the exploitation of animals.

Vegans actually gain through the transition, not lose. Vegans are oftentimes healthier, happier and more purpose driven after making the choice to abstain from animal exploitation.

I hope you will join us and the many vegans who have made the choice to let go of things that only bring harm and instead fill your life with blessings that benefit everyone!

Below are some links to places where we can get informed and get involved with veganism and vegan advocacy!

http://www.adaptt.org/
www.serv-online.org
http://www.abolitionistapproach.com
veganeducationgroup.com

www.ingramcontent.com/pod-product-compliance
Lightning Source LLC
LaVergne TN
LVHW010050110826
845155LV00028B/270

* 9 7 8 1 9 4 3 7 3 3 3 1 6 *